Gregory Nor

Gregory Norminton was born in 1976. He read English at Oxford and trained as an actor. His first novel, *The Ship of Fools*, was published by Sceptre in 2002, and in 2003 he won an Arts Council Writers' Award for *Arts and Wonders*.

Also by Gregory Norminton

The Ship of Fools

Gregory Norminton

Arts and Wonders

SCEPTRE

First published in Great Britain in 2004 by Hodder and Stoughton
A division of Hodder Headline

A Sceptre Paperback

3 5 7 9 10 8 6 4 2

A CIP catalogue record for this title
is available from the British Library

ISBN 0 340 82103 5

Typeset in Sabon by Palimpsest Book Production Limited,
Polmont, Stirlingshire
Printed and bound in Great Britain by
Mackays of Chatham Ltd, Chatham, Kent

Hodder Headline's policy is to use papers that are natural, renewable and
recyclable products and made from wood grown in sustainable forests.
The logging and manufacturing processes are expected to conform to the
environmental regulations of the country of origin.

Hodder and Stoughton
A division of Hodder Headline
338 Euston Road
London NW1 3BH

To Christian, Benjamin and Xavier

Contents

I BOX MY EARS TO NO GREAT PURPOSE. I poke the holes with a finger and rummage about inside as though to dislodge water. But I cannot silence the voices. Their mutterings trouble me. Do you never, in the crouched silence of the night, hear the whisper of fluid in your ears? Low murmurs, as though every sound stored within since the womb continues, muted, behind a cave wall? That reservoir of noises fills inexorably; the fuller it gets, the louder. What fearful rumours, what pressure on the brain! The clamour – my lifetime crashing against forgetfulness – threatens to overwhelm me.

I sit, hunched and aching, on my straw cot. Taking stock of my bones. My innards yawn and grumble; gases escape me with a sigh or sadly trumpeting. I imagine the sleep draining out of me, spilling down towards my feet and leaking into the floorboards, until the feet turn from blue to grey to chalk-white, which is all I have left of pink. Of course the noise in my head, that subterranean rumour, continues. But I hear cicadas outside winding up their clockwork. Swifts whistle and I fancy them flickering like cast lines above the fields, skimming the cream off the dawn. Then comes the expected, longed-for knock: tentative as ever, lest it disturb my corpse (I am after all quite ancient). The door opens with its familiar creak. Teresa's dark eyes find mine. I am grateful for her smile, and surprised by it – as I am every day at late mercies. Teresa brings me milk still warm from the goat, and tufts of buckwheat bread which I soak to pap in the bowl. Enquiring after her boy, I learn of a night made restless by belly-gripe. I promise my usual remedy (pure placebo, learned from a swindler in Prague) and Teresa withdraws.

It goes without saying that I have no more money to repay her kindness. She and the widow will keep me to my end, or as near to it as they can stomach, if I read them correctly.

After eating, after stool, I wash at the bowl those parts of myself which I can reach. Dressing, even simply into rustic rags, consumes an inordinate amount of time. No wonder old men ruminate. What else can the mind do with so much leisure – flitting back and forth through time, lumbered with this insupportable slow animal? Rhhahh! Damn these twisting, unresponsive stockings. I cannot bend my knees sufficiently – nor for that matter my back – to touch the tips of my toes. I, a man that has lived closer to his feet than most. Disgusted, I fling the stockings across the bedstead and shuffle barefoot into the day.

The animals have beaten me to it. Teresa's humble menagerie, infused with sap and low life. I – that have heard the Emperor's lion roar and numbered the feathers in a dodo's wing – take in their scrabbling. Nunzio's rabbits gnaw at their hutch. A coterie of chickens puck and scratch. The nanny goat, chained to an olive tree, crops her circle of grass, grazing that circumference as keenly as any compass.

Emerging from shadow, I find the sun still gentle, warming to its task. The country lies stretched before me, undulating and green-mantled, the willows trimmed, the dark cypresses like untorched candles. There are fathoms of vines, fruitful avenues doused in soft light and, beyond them, impressively clustered, the familiar contours of Fiesole. I have travelled, in fifty-one years, by an elaborate route back whence I started. I was born not far from here, you see, in the shadow of the Duomo, whose bells, drifting across the landscape to my chamber, grant the old man hours much shorter than his infant self enjoyed.

Advancing (to use the word loosely) through dew-wet grass, I approach my seat. I am weighted by a book, by parchments and ink, with an ominous leather strap on my wrist and a goose quill lodged behind my ear: a parody, I dare say, of my industrious past.

The murmuring is constant, a pressure in my head.

Sighing, I lower myself on to my seat (the bench hewn from an oak's trunk by Teresa's husband) and arrange my implements. Resting the Thesaurus hieroglyphicorum *on my lap and the inkwell beside me, I open the great blank of my commonplace book and, daunted beyond endurance, gaze back at the cottage. Teresa and the widow are working in the vegetable plot, resurrecting carrots. They shake them by the hair and pluck dirty tendrils from the roots. Then they fling the carrots on to the verge, glancing from the arc of thrown vegetables at Teresa's son, little Nunzio, scrawling in the dust with a stick. How I wish I could join them! To labour honestly, as Adam did, with the good soil packed beneath one's nails, instead of this squinting, scratching work that awaits me. Confined to this sad flesh, with dimming eyes – old despite myself – I must account for my life. I must retrace my journey, for futurity, lest all the voices in my head sink into the earth with me. And I thank God for granting me my own death, when I might have had it stolen from me. For I have seen men burned and trimmed by steel, flung unreadied into the black lake. Do they watch me from its depths, those lost souls? In my Life I must speak for them all. It is no easy task: from dreams to reincarnate ghosts, from tatters to fashion garments. My pen quivers at the task, as though it would take flight.*

For the sake of all that is past, lector future *Tommaso Grilli begs your present sympathy.*

I

Monstrorum Artifex

I

A Changeling

Now I shall tell the Truth of it.

When I was born (so my father claimed, my mother dying on my birthday) the midwife shrieked '*Mostro! Mostro!*' and slipped in amniotic fluid. Striking her head on a bucket's lip, that impressionable woman lost consciousness. So it fell to my mother – still gushing like a fountain – to smack my bum and set me bawling. She plucked me, marbled grey like tripe, from the linen; whereupon she caught sight of my face and for an instant hesitated to strike.

'Think yourself lucky,' my father would say when he showed me my reflection, 'that a mother's love is blind.'

The blow came. I duly cried and turned from grey to pink. There was commotion and great bustle of relatives in the bedchamber. I was passed from hand to hand, held upside down like Achilles in the Styx, until my father turned my head to the heavens. There were calls for water and towels and a priest. My father kissed my mother's soaking brow and held her vague fingers. Some wise relation whisked me from the scene: where my mother, interceding for me to the last, expired of aesthetic shock.

The loss, to my father, was terrible. I must have heard (for all the amnios in my ears) from that other room, where my aunt gripped me at arm's length, his gulps and groans. Nobody could console him: least of all his guilty, grotesque child. 'Keep him out of here!' my father shrieked. 'Keep that killer away!'

Thus, before I could speak or even sketch a noose, I was a murderer: guilty of subtle matricide.

For several months – long after the baptism and burial – I was entrusted to a wet nurse, one Smeraldina, who must have loved me in some fashion since she allowed me near her breasts. Smeraldina and I occupied the upstairs of my father's house, far from the clutter of his studio with its drills and chisels and busts of alabaster. My father, for his part, remained below, chained to his work as Ulysses to his mast, for fear of frenzy. There was a contest between us to see who could howl the loudest. I dare say my father won. It was not until Christmas that I was allowed into his presence; and even then Smeraldina had to hold me, while my aunts and uncles (my father's in-laws) presided over the encounter in case things turned ugly.

'He has the full complement of limbs,' my uncle Umberto ventured, 'and seems properly equipped downstairs. The face is . . . rather shocking . . . but then much of it may die down as he grows older.'

Anonimo Grilli brandished the sketches he had made, in her lifetime, of my mother. Her rare beauty, her near perfection of figure, were plain for all to see – had they *forgotten*? From handsome boughs bad fruit cannot grow. So it followed that I was a changeling, or a demon, smuggled into the lamented womb. Smeraldina, a pious woman, lifted her hands to block her ears. Then, with a smirk of apology, she picked me up where I had fallen and offered me to the paternal gaze.

I was not, by virtue of my deformity, an ingratiating child. Perhaps Smeraldina had trained me to smile at the blur of my father's face. For I did smile, yes, and gurgled too. The pink fist of my left hand, upon which my fortunes would one day depend, escaped the blanket. And my father, to the held breaths of all assembled, offered his clay-caked finger to my grasp.

'Some bonds can never be broken,' my father told me

whenever, drunk, he referred to this moment. 'I could not reject you, Tommaso. And indeed, have I ever? Have I ever, in spite of everything, neglected your upbringing?'

The in-laws sighed at a tender scene of reconciliation. Smeraldina, seeing my father's eyes swim at contact with his son, cautiously eased me on to his lap. There I sat, as best I could, still gripping my father's finger, and ogled the implements on his table. Anonimo Grilli (for want of a better idea) fumbled for a spatula and held it close to my eyes. I must have squinted.

'He will be an artist,' said Smeraldina. 'Just like his father.'

If, in my earliest years, I found any place in my father's life, it was on the edge of his fretful existence.

Anonimo Grilli was a sculptor. Born and bred in Florence, of solid mercantile stock, he had displayed from early childhood a most unprofitable talent. He could make things with his hands, beautiful things. At the age of eight he crafted his own toys out of wood: small bestiaries of lions and horses and bears. By the time he was twelve, with black down sprouting on his upper lip, he was casting nymphs out of mud from the banks of the Arno. His own father, Jacopo Grillo, lamented with voluble fists the boy's artistic leanings.

'I was a badge of shame to him,' Anonimo would tell me. 'I fouled my clothes and left my hair uncombed. My hands were always caked in clay.'

My grandfather, Jacopo Grillo, knew of sculptors only through the Florentine guilds. These were hired to decorate villas; they peddled coats of arms; they were no model for his only son. 'No dispute, no debate,' he used to warn, raising his index finger. 'You're going into silk, my boy, make no mistake.'

9

Three years later the sculptor Jean Boulogne, better known throughout the world as Giambologna, added Anonimo to his corps of assistants. (Jacopo Grillo, though grievously hurt by his son's disobedience, could not refuse him the honour of serving, indirectly, the Grand Duke himself. Yet he turned his back on the boy, and would keep it turned, until death sundered them for ever.) Hoping to assist his Flemish master, my father was confined instead to casting work. Under the watchful eye of Antonio Susini, he helped produce small bronze copies of Giambologna's art, which sold, to the sculptor's fame, throughout Europe. It was sweaty, frustrating work. But Anonimo persevered, learning his craft on the sly for three long years, until one day Susini put in a good word for him and he assumed his full apprenticeship.

Giambologna, a genius modeller of clay, refrained from actually making his statues. That secondary task – the labour of fashioning stone, with its ignoble stain of physical effort – fell to his assistants. Thus my father perfected, in those early years, the pert breasts of *Florence Triumphant over Pisa* for the Palazzo Vecchio; he tousled the hair of Samson with a drill, and fixed his jawbone in the eternal apex of its murderous flight.

It was in Bologna (where his master was based) that my father met my mother, Beatrice. She was the daughter of one Antonio Raimondi, a Genoese marble merchant, who would eventually relinquish her with a most handsome dowry. Anonimo's future seemed assured; all the more so when, in April 1574, Cosimo de' Medici – that great patron and tyrant – died. Anonimo heard news of the death in a state of rapture. An effigy was required, you see, for the lying-in-state. My father was to assist Giambologna in modelling the Grand Duke's face and hands.

Cosimo's corpse reposed in the Palace of the Signoria.

Recently embalmed, it reeked of resin and talcum and cinnabar pigment. I imagine my father scoring the hairs with a wooden knife into the moulded wax. How nervously attentive he must have been, watched over by impassive guards, scrutinising the famous beard, and with half an eye on the corpse lest its eyes should open. And how lifelike was the outcome. The Grand Duke's clay, that pallid dough, repeated in wax. With its implicit meaning: 'The Medicis Never Die.'

Soon my father was trailing the ceremonious procession as it made its way through the streets towards San Lorenzo. A great number of painters and carpenters (many of whom Borghini had assembled for Michelangelo's funeral) had decorated the church with skulls and skeletons. Anonimo admired those grinning mementoes. Standing at the back of the nave – almost outside in the piazza – he glimpsed above pious heads the decorated effigy of the putrefying duke. And ambition consumed him. It burned in his chest, like the urge to fill a deep well with one's voice. He knew that his apprenticeship was over. Would he settle now for a life of quiet excellence, the craftsman's lot? Wherever he looked in the church, the gaudy pomp of life's continuance – the rich costumes and florid pendants, the embroidered cloth of the baldaquin, all the bequests of the dead to the living – disarmed the comical skeletons. Just as Francesco de' Medici consoled himself for his own mortality with allusions to his father's triumphs (triumphs which, by virtue of heredity, he would surely emulate), so Anonimo Grilli, in claiming his artistic freedom, laid the path to his own destiny.

With a selection of models, made of wax from Giambologna's studio, my father earned a place at the Accademia del Disegno. He found himself for three years among painters, sculptors and architects, under the patronage of the Grand Duke. Anonimo and Beatrice were married; and soon his clay reliefs, of dimpled putti with faunish legs, were to be complemented by a creation of their flesh. For Beatrice was expectant, and with her dowry Anonimo bought our first house on the Via dell'Oriulo, where they might craft to perfection their first-born child.

Six months after my birth and its shattering consequence, Anonimo Grilli was summoned by the six consuls of the Academy. Mired in grief, he had failed to meet a commission. Rough sketches, scrawled an hour previously, of Diana at her bath could not save him from expulsion. Unsatisfied with having murdered my mother, I had ousted my father from his vocation.

Throughout my childhood – until, that is, my own precocity became manifest – Anonimo struggled to find work within the guilds, which despised him for his former status. He was, in spite of his drunkenly vaunted genius, reduced to the status of a hireling. More often than not, he would have to leave me to the care of relatives in order to undertake a commission out in the country.

'Plastering some bloody chapel in Vallombrosa. They might as well pack me off to Sicily, with a bag of bird shit for stucco!'

To work as a plasterer was demeaning for so proud an artist. How he resented the luminaries of the Academy, where in his imagination a nebulous chair awaited him, stark for his absence. But it was not social ambition, merely, which gnawed at his innards. My father's talent had been hard done by: soiled, denigrated. He longed to rescue it from ignominy.

Thus the two of us existed, separate within the same walls, tortured by mutual longing – my father for success, myself for my father.

The absence of something – a vital ingredient for life – was apparent to me from my first suck. My insatiable hunger dragged Smeraldina and her successors dry. Hot as a furnace, red faced and toothless, I would not be calmed by the perfunctory harassed gestures of my nurses (who had, after all, other mouths to feed); nor by the cooing of relatives, on their ever less frequent visits to the Grilli household. I sought my birth mother, that mouldering womb. Failing which, I could have settled for my father's love.

Alas, between conflicting emotions of joy at my existence and grief at my mother's death, my father chose grief; or rather it chose him, as a stray dog adopts a charitable stranger.

The years passed, and I learned, unbidden, the usual tricks of childhood. Scuttling crab, tightrope-walker, clown – I was all of these things, over time. Burbling rhetorician. Greek tragedian with a grazed knee. So many guises and disguises. Yet none entitled me to my father's affection. An only child, I suffered his grief like the presence of a shadowy, superior brother. I might leap and hoot and clown about, the prize my father's gaze; but his smile would fade on me and his eyes grow dull again with sadness.

'Why don't you play outside?' my latest nurse would huff. 'The garden's full of crickets – try to catch one.' (It took me years to wise up to *that* trick.) 'Your daddy's busy. He mustn't be disturbed.'

Is it any wonder that I grew so badly? My face, I'll grant you, was a disaster from the outset; but my limbs, at birth, must have seemed promising enough. Alas, deprived of affection, like a plant of water, I put forth unlovely shoots. That is to say that nothing grew in proportion. My anatomy is a hotchpotch, a fusion of parts from unequal models. Thus my legs, which are plump and hairy like a faun's, hunker down to narrow martyred feet. My upper torso is fully developed, with a ribcage that juts pompously forward, giving me the appearance of being trapped for ever at the summit of a sigh; yet my hips are narrow, balanced on chunky thighs, and my buttocks are childishly pert. (In some places I am better endowed. My manhood, for what it's worth, is short but uncommonly thick, and I have big hands that look like paddles on the ends of short, dimpled arms.) But how can you assemble this jumble of parts into a unified whole? As for my face, will not a list of features (a lush's nose, a weak chin, a tongue too big for its cave) merely confuse your mental picture and set lumbering through this book a gruesome composite, the impossible invention of a fevered brain?

My physical ugliness suffused me with shame. The fact of it was driven home by my father, who would cry out in dismay whenever I wiped my grotty nose on his lap or clung with muddy fingers to his apron. A lifelong hater of spiders, I used to maintain within my reach a tankard and papers with which to remove unwelcome visitors. My father, whenever I penetrated his inner sanctum, would steer me back to my nurse's arms with the same tight revulsion.

What could I do to atone for my monstrosity? The children in the street played willingly with me at first; yet within a few years I was cast out of their company. Jeered at, pelted with grit and sometimes stones, I had to slink away, molten-eyed with impotent rage. Nor could I race home bawling, with my face blemished, in expectation of solace. For the plump breast of my nurse (how constant that part of the anatomy was, while the faces above it came and went) averted itself quickly from my hideous grief. Affection, from those mercenary successors of Smeraldina, came at a premium which my father could not afford.

Lest I labour this account of my misfortune, however, I ought to record its uses. Rejected by my fellows, I wandered the streets of the city in a watchful daze, my head bowed to avoid the attention of curious strangers. In this penitential attitude (which seemed most successfully to render me invisible) my eyes settled on life's minutiae. I observed the tireless commerce of ants: how they carried, after a murderous hailstorm, the wings of butterflies like sails above their heads. Weevils that shone like gems sat unjudgingly on my thumbnail. I remember once how I rescued, with a straw, a mantis twitching in the glue of a puddle. Clinging to that trembling stalk, the insect ruminated on its predicament. I carried it carefully into the sun, where it basked to dry itself, stroking the moisture from its body. I could not say how long I sat there, in the hot dust with traffic all about me, watching the mantis's ablutions. Finally the quizzical head, with its fearful black eyes, tilted in my favour. I fancied that the mandibles quivered in inaudible thanks. I glimpsed two yellow wings, with indigo eyes at their centre – and the mantis fluttered, to my startled gasp, into the cloudless sky.

Umberto Raimondi (my uncle and inheritor of the Genoese marble business) was a dark, florid gentleman who filled his wealthy leisure with books and could never shake off a sense of obligation to his dead sister. He stumbled upon me one morning as I entertained a beetle in the Piazza della Signoria and brought the toe of his boot within inches of my rump before recognition stopped him.

'You!' he exclaimed. 'Why are you sitting in the dust? I took you for an urchin.'

The beetle fell from my thumb on to its back. Its legs flickered uselessly. I tried to right it.

'Don't ignore me, boy,' said my uncle. 'Look up – how impertinent.'

I obeyed and blinked at his sun-shadowed face. Neptune from his fountain gazed askew at my discovery.

'Does that father of yours know where you are?' (My

nurse had nodded off into the many folds of her chin. I had escaped, pursued only by her snorts.) 'Get up, Tommaso. Has the cat got your tongue?'

So many questions to answer: where should I begin?

With startled expressions of consternation, Uncle Umberto marched me to his house on the Via dei Calzaiuoli. His voice, and our footsteps, glanced sonorously off Apuan marble. Servants bobbed and curtsied; I felt their eyes trailing in my wake. My uncle directed me up a wide staircase and thence, through dark windowless corridors, into his study.

Never before had I seen his library. Panels in the walls were painted with artefacts: books and paintings, medallions hung on nails, scrolled papers enribboned with red lace. The image of objects preceded their actual counterparts, for behind the panels sat all the wonders of Learning; not the ancient books only but new works also – on cosmology and geometry and the New World, Vasari's *Lives of the Artists* and the *Life of Michelangelo*, books on botany and exotic beasts, with for good measure some enchanting romances.

Uncle Umberto perched on his chair. He rested his hairy, jewel-carbuncled fists on the broad plain of a cherrywood table and scrutinised my face.

'What were you doing?' he asked as I sidled past his hounds. (Brutus and Achilles paid me no more attention than a shadow; at full height, their jaws came level with my throat.) 'Tommaso, I was shocked. I thought you were begging.'

'Oh no, Uncle.'

'You were staring at something. What were you staring at? You're not a simpleton, are you?'

'It was . . .'

'You understand my question?'

16

'I was looking at a . . .'

'We can't have you traipsing about the city like a cretin.'

Sensing my fearfulness, yet disinclined to soften his tone, Umberto gestured for me to sit. I straddled a polished stool and cowered at the edge of his desk. The hounds behind me panted, their wet tongues lolling.

'I want you to read these words, Tommaso. Tell me what you see.'

With a plumed quill, my uncle scratched on a corner of parchment. Then he held up several words for me to read. I had no idea what they were.

'*Figlio*, Tommaso.'

'*Figlio?*'

'And this?'

I stared at the second doodle. It looked like a profile of jagged teeth.

'You really don't know?' my uncle marvelled, sitting back.

'Neither word?'

'I know what "son" means.'

'But you cannot *read?*'

'If you read it I know what it means.'

Thus my illiteracy was discovered – a common enough condition. Yet I was of literate stock, I could not inhabit the same mental slums as hoi polloi. Umberto, with a sharp pluck at his beard, decided on a remedy. 'My responsibility towards your late mother obliges me to act,' he said. I was, in spite of everything, his late sister's offspring. My value resided in that: like a bad painting made in his dotage by a great master. 'You will come here every morning. Not to my *studiolo* but downstairs – in the kitchen. There is a table set aside, in an alcove. You've plenty of light there from the window. I shall pay for your tuition. Tell your father, when you see him.'

But my father was not keen to hear. He raged at the

17

meddling old windbag, my benefactor, and nursed for several days a brooding silence most eloquent of his injured pride. I was, however, allowed to attend my lessons.

I sat with swinging feet on a high chair, breathed on by my tutor – a sallow young scholar called Piombino, who reeked of stale sweat and bad teeth and so accepted my own flaws without complaint. He applied himself with great patience to a mind no longer malleable. I had difficulties learning by rote; for instance, I had to imagine letters as living things before I could master them. A was an eye peering into an abyss – the small-case b was a snail climbing a branch – C was the shape a cat makes when it rolls itself in the dust. Similar methods worked for numerals. The gliding swan 2 was pursued by her mate, flying 3. Nostalgic 7, staring back at his past, never noticed hourglass 8 squatting at his back. I was especially proud of squatting-man 4, for which I was roundly scolded.

'Can't you take things as they *are*?' my tutor complained. 'Must everything remind you of something else?'

Yet I was permitted to make use of my strange mnemonics, and within a year was roaming my uncle's bookshelves. The more intellectual fare I left to one side. I crammed my head with romances and tales of chivalry, devouring *Morgante* and Doni's fantasies with an avidity to rival the (as yet unborn) man from La Mancha. Infused with these stories, Florence became my playground. I directed my garish knights in mounted charges down the Via del Corso, chased distressed damsels across the Ponte Vecchio and lodged a dragon beneath the cathedral's great cupola.

It was in the elaboration of these fantasies that I began to draw monsters. They peeped from the margins of my copybook into the calligraphic foliage: monkeys with the manes of lions, hares perched on cicadas' legs, wild men sporting tusks like Turkish moustaches. Sketching became

18

a compulsion, the fruit of seeds sown in my early wanderings. Whereas before I had admired insects for their
own sakes – passively like a mirror – now I meant to
record my observations. Reality, with all its maddening
and unpossessable detail, began to make my inventions look
bland and improbable. With deft strokes I recorded my tutor
resting his chin on his fist, his glossy nether lip protruding as
he corrected my sums. I studied closely his large ears, which
thrust forward eagerly, as though in competition with his
eyes to observe the world. Such particulars intrigued me
more, I confess, than the whole (for the uniqueness of which
they were, after all, responsible), and soon my copybook was
a butcher's slab of disembodied parts – ears, a nose, severed
hands and floating eyes.

One morning, a week after my (uncelebrated) tenth
birthday, my secret pleasure was discovered. Late in an
algebra lesson of uncommon tedium, my tutor caught me
sketching the unusual grip (a white-nailed, three-fingered
clamp) which he exercised on his pen and snatched the
offending cartoon from my lap.

'So this is what you get up to, instead of working.'

To my mortification, he scrutinised my drawing, holding
it up to the light, level with his eyes. His scolding expression
softened to gawking silence. I squirmed on my chair as my
tutor looked at me. Then he flipped back, slowly, through
the defaced pages of my copybook.

'Did you . . . ? Tommaso, be honest now.'

'Yes, sir.'

'Did you do all of these drawings?'

'Yes, sir. Sorry, sir.'

'I mean, uh, your father didn't help you?'

It was a baffling notion; my mouth became a trough
for flies.

'Tommaso,' my tutor resolved, 'I am confiscating your

copybook.' I was instructed to return home. I was to wait in my room for a summons. None of my hot tears could save me. 'Hurry along now, boy. And don't dawdle, because I'll *know* about it.'

With leaden feet, wailing like a bloodhound at the moon, I made my way to the kitchen steps. But my tutor could not wait for me to complete my mournful exit. With great smelly excitement he brushed past me in the stairwell, the copybook's pages fluttering like a bird in his grasp. 'Shoo! On you go! Your uncle and I shall follow.'

Ah, how I chewed my fingers on that terrible journey westwards. I considered entering the Duomo and praying for divine help. But like the sinners on Hell's forecourt, I was doomed beyond hope of mercy.

In my father's house all was silent. Dreading the coming storm, I hid myself in my bedroom, where my complacent toys (wooden horses and soldiers, gifts from the Raimondis when I was born) offered me no sympathy. I must have slept, exhausted from sobbing, for I was startled by a knock at the door, and beheld on the wall a dusty grey blot of evening sky. My latest nurse summoned me, with all the authority of her many chins, downstairs to my father's studio.

They stood incongruously together, those three figures from different compartments of my life, in a line against the wall. My tutor (that cruel snitch) held my copybook before his groin. My father, a little unsteady on his feet after hours of quiet labour, wore an unfamiliar expression.

'Come forward,' said my uncle. 'Be seated.'

There was a table with a stool beneath it. A sheet of paper was weighted by three sticks of charcoal on the table's surface.

'Pick up a charcoal.'

My tutor placed an alabaster bust of Homer on the edge of the table. My father, less confidently, arranged a bowl

20

of fruit – grapes, peaches, furry apricots – beside the bust. His eyes did not even flicker at mine as he straightened and retreated.

'Now then, my boy,' said Umberto. 'We want you to draw, as faithfully as you can, the objects placed before you.'

I gripped the thinnest charcoal. I did as I was told. Blind Homer in his paper window sniffed at a bowl of fruit. He could not see, as I had seen, the deep scar in one of the grapes, with its sticky exudate, nor the mouldering bruise on a wound-dark peach. Having mastered these things, I was wholly absorbed by the bowl's variegated patterning when my father emitted a hoarse cry. A black spider blotted my drawing as it was snatched from the table.

'It's some kind of witchcraft,' said Anonimo, brandishing the picture and pacing the floor before my desk. I felt the draught swept up by his loose shirt and sleeves.

'Or rather – a sign of heredity?' With a wink (which was shocking enough in itself), my uncle Umberto flicked me a coin. I flinched as it clattered off my desk on to the brick floor. It was my first payment.

'Give him something else to draw,' thrilled my tutor, clapping the tips of his fingers like an excited girl.

'Like what? The Sistine chapel?'

'His father's portrait.'

Anonimo shook his head. He backed away from gestures of entreaty as from serpents. Umberto, however, was able to persuade him, steering him with a friendly pinch to a chair set out by my tutor.

'Don't worry, *papà*,' I said, cross-legged for fear of peeing. 'I'll make you handsome.'

'Just make it quick.'

I turned over my sullied paper to the clean reverse. This was a face I could draw from memory, with its strong chin and potent expressive nose, and the greasy black hair that curled stubbornly above either ear. Uncle Umberto came behind me and gripped the back of my chair. He would not leave off breathing above my head (the air escaping with a whistle through his nose) until my fingers ached from the effort and I had worn away the charcoal to a stump. It was a good likeness, I felt, although the breezy smile – of a man benignly at ease with the world – was a preposterous liberty, unrelated to the model. Finally, as the house itself seemed poised for an outcome, my hand was stopped by my father's hand. His palm was hot and clammy. I looked along the outstretched arm, not quite believing that it would be attached to anything.

My father's voice quavered: 'He has done enough.' I glimpsed the tip of his tongue wet his parched, mottled lips. 'He has proved his worth.'

2

Midget Pie

Curious, how we can amble for years along a well-defined path, drearily comfortable in its certainties, until a chance encounter, a first step into the heather verges, alters our course for ever. I had known some contentment in my pre-literate existence. Nobody notices the deformities of a vagrant child; stooped with insignificance, he is not worth the effort of an insult. Try to imagine then, what might have been, had Uncle Umberto sidestepped me in the Piazza – had I never learned to hold a pen – had not my tutor snatched the sketch from my lap. Could I have survived to decrepit old age on alms and garbage? As it was, as actually came to pass, Fortune did not leave me alone. When I sketched my father's features, she sat up and took notice. She cocked a bevelled eyebrow at my unsuspected talent. She *interfered*.

'There shall be no more lessons at your uncle's house,' my father declared. 'I will make you famous. We will fix our name in history.'

How swiftly, how astonishingly, my status improved. Anonimo smiled at me in the morning. Tunelessly whistling through his teeth, he ruffled my hair and coaxed me into his studio, where I was made to sit, like a lion couchant on a tombstone, at his feet. He opened his well-thumbed copy of Cennini (*Il Libro dell'Arte*, that indispensable compendium of sound advice and unspeakable rhetoric) and read to me of the artist's lofty spirit. ' "Begin," ' my father began, ' "by decking yourself with this attire: Enthusiasm, Reverence, Obedience, and Constancy." ' First principles, it appeared, were moral principles. I was to abjure the company of women, which made an artist's hand flutter like a leaf in the wind. I should bind myself with respect to the authority of a master.

So began my training. I learned to fix lines with ink, how to shade folds with washes and to erase errors using the soft of bread rubbed between finger and thumb. Then there were parchments to be prepared, and the monotonous tinting of paper with terre verte and white lead, with beans of vermilion and bone dust.

On a cool day of low, dilute cloud, my father and I left the city in search of willow sticks. We walked side by side deep into the country. The lank green boughs of the willow trees caressed our heads, nodding assent to our plunder. My father broke the willow sticks and sharpened them at each end like spindles. As we ambled along a shaded bank, I insinuated my hand into his. My father's fingers were plump to the touch and cold, like uncooked sausage. I received a sharp squeeze (too sharp) and relinquished my claim.

'Now,' my father said when we had regained the city, 'take these to the baker's. Tell him to roast them well – you'll fetch the charcoals in the morning.'

So I ran to Giuseppe's on the Via Torta, the casserole swinging like a censer on my arm. The fat baker had fun, as usual, at my expense. 'Why don't *you* squeeze into the casserole? See if the job's well done.' Wiping his brow with a rag and picking flecks of dough from his apron, Giuseppe rolled me into imaginary pastries. 'Little dwarf cakes,' he warbled. 'Midget pie. Ooh *haw*. Ooh *haw*.' As he bent to relieve me of my burden, I saw the pores of his nose all clogged with flour. His pale mushy skin looked in need of a pummelling. 'Come back in the morning, my little cream puff. I'll bake a gingerbread man the size of my thumb. You'll get indigestion.'

The following day, our sticks were burned black in the

depth of their tomb. I tested them, as my father had shown me, on a portable piece of gessoed panel. Neither brittle nor unyielding, they were perfect. The alchemy was good.

'Well, if it isn't my little freak.' The baker's shop was crowded: Giuseppe stooped beneath a forest of upheld loaves. His assistants (pale, interchangeable starvelings with blistered hands) struggled to relieve the customers of their dough, which needed baking *pronto! pronto!* 'Remember,' the baker yelled against the din. 'You *draw* with them. You don't *eat* them.' A scuffle broke out at the rear of the crowd. Unbaked loaves became projectiles – I witnessed the ascension of their floury ghosts. 'Eh! Eh!' protested Giuseppe, thrusting forth his great belly and presenting his palms to the ceiling, like an overweight, invisibly burdened Atlas. Bending low, I burrowed between customers' legs until I reached the door. With a squeeze I burst free, into the softly shadowed morning.

Back home, I found my father in his studio preparing a clay Hercules for my imitation. The demigod gloated, pressing with his foot the head of an expiring (mouse-sized) lion. My father, with a rose thorn, was adding bristles to Hercules' thigh.

Unbidden, I assumed my place at my work stool. From having tiptoed past my father's studio, I was now its focal point, the axis upon which all things revolved. It did not occur to me to find such a transformation in my fortunes suspect. I drew the objects set out for me with the bravado of happiness. My pen swept like a bird in flight, soaring on warm currents of joy. The ink not yet dry and the parchment swollen (with bumps like the scabs on my knee), my father squeezed me into his chest. I inhaled his acrid masculine smell and felt the intimate rasp of his chin on my forehead.

'You're my little gold mine,' he whispered.

* * *

25

Cennino d'Andrea Cennini, in his *Libro dell'Arte*, recommends a year's exercise at drawing before an artist can put pen directly to paper.

My father waited two months.

By early autumn he had collected, from my labours, a portfolio of two dozen drawings (on kid parchment, on tinted cotton paper) which he wedged into a pasteboard pouch and carried to his former colleagues at the Academy. On that chilly, overcast morning, when uncommon fog softened the city's clamour and one could imagine, though far from grassland, the lush blades wet beneath one's feet, I was aware of nothing, sleepily innocent of my father's ambitions. It never occurred to me that I might seek *fame* from my drawings. They were executed for my father's pleasure; they made me acceptable to him.

My nurse podged and kneaded me from slumber. 'He can stuff his orders,' she muttered. 'Make food, Bianca. Pour drinks, Bianca. Bend over, Bianca. It's not honest. I've got enough on my plate. Turning up with a lot of strangers and not a word of warning. Get *up*, you lazy runt. They're waiting for you downstairs.'

I flung (if you'll pardon the hyperbole) my bare legs from my blanket and levered myself to a sitting position. Bianca pulled a shirt over my head. She slapped at my pillow-shocked hair to tame it and spat into a hem of her apron to gouge the sleep from my eyes. 'You look a sight,' she complained. 'When did you last drag a comb through that thicket? Ugh, don't yawn in my face! I've known cats with nicer breath. No, you *can't* have breakfast. Go down. *Hurry.*'

Blearily, on a marionette's legs, I descended the staircase. From my father's study I heard male voices, a bass grumbling such as courtiers make before a play.

'Ah, the prodigy,' a spectacled gentleman with a very pink mouth declared. A dozen heads turned in my direction, checked themselves in empty space, then looked down. 'Well, come in, boy, come in.'

My father relaxed visibly at my entrance, as though someone had cut a taut wire in his spine. 'Tommaso,' he said, 'these gentlemen are from the Accademia del Disegno. They've come to meet you.'

I saw that our visitors had been passing round my drawings.

'Well, Anonimo,' said one of them. 'You've brought us here for a demonstration. Let us have it.'

'Or is it a case of like father like son?' said another. 'Promising much and delivering little.'

'Let him copy this drawing,' said a third man of elephantine amplitude, waving my Madonna-of-the-fields.

'No, this one.'

'No, *this*.'

I was steered by a powerful hand on my shoulder. Somebody moved my stool; a pencil was placed in my hand. I shall not trouble you with the particulars of my performance. The audience gathered about me, blotting out my light. I felt as though I were at the bottom of the ocean, watched by clouds of octopus. Only the frantic knitting and unknitting of my father's brow egged me on, until a passable twin of my ink-and-chalk Madonna coalesced on the easel.

'Mm, not bad. For one so young.'

'Of course, the original composition—'

'Quite—'

'I mean, is that a crossbill or a parrot?'

'It's clearly neither.'

'And that cricket, in the second drawing, is much too fat.'

'It's too fat for a cricket.'

27

'Oh, it's nothing *like* the original.'

Grudgingly, with many cavils to reveal their discrimination, the academicians discussed the quality of my work. My father bristled at old grievances, a deep carmine blush about his jowls. He seized my wrists.

'Is not this enough in itself?' he demanded, making my fingers shake. 'Look at these stumps. How can they master a style without trembling? Look at his *face*. Gentlemen, my son is remarkable. Not just another artist. Like a talking ape, he is a herald of wondrous Nature.'

The academicians drifted away, laughing and sniffing the air at the threshold. Only Sandro Bondanella – that pious and affluent painter – stayed behind, shifting his weight from leg to leg and absently tugging at the slack of his throat. He and my father tossed silence like a ball between them until the guests had gone. Then they whispered together, as close as spies. I sat on the stairs trying to hear the conversation.

'He'll need a costume, of course,' said Sandro Bondanella.

'He will?'

'You cannot present him in a loose shirt and breeches.'

'But I'm not sure that I can afford—'

'Tush, my friend! To gather wheat, first you must sow the corn.'

In the week that followed, my father sold off much of his collection (including a bronze inkstand shaped like a crab, in whose clappers I had delighted to trap my fingers) to pay for my tailor. I found myself stranded on a table-top in the Oltrarno as a meagre old man, who smelled strongly of leaf mould, conveyed my proportions, through pin-cushion lips, to his eager apprentice. In other circumstances this would have been humiliating – to have one's shortcomings so blandly remarked upon. But the tailor was mirthlessly punctilious and I was thrilled when, poking me by accident in the perineum, he addressed me as *'signor'*. Over several fittings my costume took shape. Blue, amorphous patches (I was forbidden, during the operations, to look at things closely) were grafted to my chest and limbs. The tailor would stand back, clucking – his cheek approached the cheek of his apprentice – then he returned once more, tugging a sleeve or tucking a hem until his instincts were satisfied. Meanwhile, at home, I was instructed in courtly manners. My father taught me the reverence, and how to flutter my hand as though wafting perfume towards my nose.

'*Papà*,' I said. 'What am I learning these things *for*?'

The question, so often repeated, irritated my father. 'You'll not be asked to do anything you cannot do already,' was his only reply. Perhaps this intractability, this refusal to enlighten me about things to come, was a sign of paternal solicitude? Possibly he meant to spare me unnecessary anxiety before the event. If so, the policy failed. I learned, for the first time, what it is to live in fear. Apprehension and uncertainty (those itch-mite companions) burrowed under the skin of my sleep, and bruises ripened under my eyes. 'Stop looking so miserable,' my father would complain. 'Think of the sacrifices I'm making for you – ungrateful child.'

But I felt helpless. My throat seized up whenever Sandro Bondanella called to visit. With his white locks and rich clothes and restless, opportunistic eyes, he seemed an emissary from a foreign world, a place of patronage and power, whose dust I imagined puffing up from his cloak when he draped it across a chair. Sandro Bondanella disregarded me; every word he spoke in my presence was obliquely encoded. There was talk of 'projects' and 'buyers'. Then, one day, all mystery ended. Enthroned in my father's best chair, the painter said:

'The Count and his family are looking forward to your visit. Is *he* prepared?'

My father, who was poised uncomfortably on my stool, wetted his lips. Puffing out his cheeks, he nodded; a tiny muscle flexed in his jaw.

My time had come.

Clearly there has never been a shortage of artists in Florence; yet gifted dwarfs are thin on the ground. So the banker Gossaert declared himself *tickled* to meet me. A few days later his competitor, Ercole Marsupini, resplendent to the point of vulgarity in crushed velvet and gold braid, tossed me a florin. 'To think that such a thing—' he marvelled, shaking his head at my ink-and-wash likeness of his daughter. 'The god Apollo has a sense of humour.'

I became a performing curiosity: the Freak with the Hand of God. Small crowds gathered on street corners to see me in my blue harlequin's costume. I suppose they enjoyed a perceived paradox – that a being so badly drawn, foreshortened by a myopic and with proportions lamentably botched, should yet possess an eye for beauty.

'Signor Marsupini was satisfied,' Sandro Bondanella smiled at his fingers' ends. 'The unique contrast of – shall we say – Form and Function has proved every bit the success we had hoped.'

Over the winter months, I was summoned to palazzos throughout the city, where I entertained wealthy patrons by immortalising, on peach-tinted paper, their fidgety brutes. During these performances my father, who fawningly officiated as master of ceremonies, sometimes patted my cheek and ruffled my woolly hair. It was my only remuneration: to enjoy (on stage if nowhere else) my father's affection. The audience meant nothing to me: I could think only of that caressing thumb, of the indulgent palm on my shoulder, and glimpse, when I dared look up from the sitter, my father's dilating nostrils, his creased and mirthless eyes.

How could I have understood at that time the wry symmetry of human love? For while I strove to please Anonimo, he was redeeming himself to his dead father. Jacopo Grillo had thought him a fool – incapable of turning a profit – but now he was proving otherwise. The mercantile instinct had resurfaced in him; as it would, many years later, in his diminutive son.

With money coming in from our association with grand families, my father might have been expected to adopt a swagger. He had shown resourcefulness and resilience. Yet members of the Academy simpered at our passing; they sullied our heels with insolent glances and guffawed as soon as we turned a corner. How could we not hear the gossip which prized my skill above his; which declared me (in debt to Dante) 'il miglior fabbro' – the superior craftsman? Stung to action, my father began work on some new sculptures. These were to be farmyard animals, feathered or hackled with lumps of clay, in a style perfected by his former master. I peeped at them in progress beneath their cowls. The goat was bloated, with buckling hind legs that needed an intrusive bronze support. A mallard languished, half-made, encased in mud from the depths of its lake. As for the turkey – a poor blighted cousin to Giambologna's wattled and ruffled beast – its beak was blunted, the eyes about as bright as a cooked trout's, and the wings crumbled in a terminal moult. It pained me that I could make such judgements: that aesthetic sense should eclipse filial duty. With tremulous, compensatory enthusiasm I helped my father set out his stall outside our house. He sat there with his arms crossed, as though daring people to visit. A few brave souls, conscious of our house's famous resident, inspected the wares on offer.

'Fancy that,' one man remarked. 'The little chap's a *sculptor* as well.'

My father's prices fell throughout the spring, until we could not *give* the sculptures away. At the same time, to rub salt in Anonimo's wounds, my own fame spread throughout Tuscany. Sandro Bondanella presented us with summons as far away as Pisa and Volterra. One fine May morning, as our funds were running low, my father and I set off, with a burdened mule between us, for the Castello della Quèrcia.

Our journey, along the road to Bologna, lasted two days, and although it was a strain on my legs (I was forbidden to encumber our ancient mule), I was glad to leave behind the city, with its rumours and intrusions. We stopped briefly, at Pratolino, to admire the mountain god Appennino, recently carved in all his wild enormity by Giovanni Bologna. My father fought hard to conceal his amazement at that straining giant; I gawked with abandon.

'You know he's alive,' I said.

'Who is?'

'Appennino. The great god of the mountain.'

'He doesn't *look* alive.'

'That's because he lives longer than us. He lives at the speed of mountains.'

'What nonsense.'

'And he speaks too. Only you can't hear him. His voice is too deep, it's much too low. And he says one word, a single word, every century.'

We plodded on through the midday heat, stopping only once to eat olives and salami beneath a spreading pine. Though few words were exchanged between us, I felt certain that my father shared my joy at our surroundings; for the dense bright forest throbbed with birdsong and the murmurous industry of bees; squirrels leaped and scampered overhead; a green woodpecker fled at our footsteps and I watched its undulating flight along the broad, dappled avenue. When we found the roadside freshly rucked up by tusking boar, my father sat cross-legged beside the mule while I searched for fur and hoof marks. Finally, as dusk approached, the swelling hills rewarded us with a view of the Mugello, that incomparable valley.

By nightfall we had reached the inn at S. Piero a Sieve, a few miles from the Castello, where a room awaited us courtesy of our patron. The inn was surprisingly full; it stank of goat shit and sweat; the inhabitants eyed me suspiciously as though I carried a shrinking disease. Chilled by this reception and dismayed at the prospect of having to share a bed with my father, I managed to drink some of his wine at supper. All the other guests steered clear of our table, where we sat feeding the mosquitoes and listening to dogs as they barked at the moon.

At that rustic table, over the course of a tasteless meal, my father drank himself into a fury. I had to endure his jeremiads against God, the Academy and Mankind, only too aware of the attention we were attracting. 'Shut up, you drunk!' someone yelled from a clapping window. 'Quiet! People are trying to sleep!'

By much placatory effort (the burly innkeeper, in spite of orders from the Castello, had rolled up his sleeves to chuck us out), I succeeded in lowering my father's voice. He did not growl or grow mawkish; a malicious eye gleamed at me through the shadows.

'I never told you about your *mother*, did I? I mean the particulars – the exact particulars of that accursed day?'

'Please, *papà*.'

'No, no. You're old enough, it's time you knew.'

'Don't, please.'

'When you were born the midwife . . . an ugly bitch, I forget her name . . . the midwife screamed: "Monster, it's a monster . . . !"'

33

So I heard – not for the first time – the story of my birth as recalled by my father.

A few minutes later, having paid two brutes to drag my father upstairs, I pinched back the filthy sheet and lay down beside him. His slumber was brutish and heavy; there was some danger he might lash out and knock me senseless. I lay wide awake in the swimming darkness and contemplated my mortal shame.

'My lord and ladies, where there is misfortune God brings comfort. In His Mercy He has blessed my son with Divine talent . . .'

No applause greeted my father's pronouncement. There were polite inclinations of feminine heads. Servants, standing like sentinels at the doors to the hall, stared in mental vacancy. 'Go on, boy,' my father whispered as he retreated crabwise to the back of the stage. I stood in my tight ruff and constraining waistcoat, my toes snuffling, like blind moles, in oversize satin slippers, and blinked at my audience. It consisted of the Signora Isabella Ripellino, her several daughters and half a dozen ladies-in-waiting. Elegantly dressed in brocade and silks, they perched upon chairs and flapped their embroidered fans. I took three steps towards the blank canvas and felt a gentle flutter of revulsion in their midst. A daughter laughed. The Signora's fan snapped shut and performed a delicate ellipse towards the daughter's knuckles. That chastened gasp encouraged me a little. 'Humbly,' I said, 'I request' – groping for my midget's stool – 'a volunteer for my . . . for my, um . . .'

I had spotted her in the audience. Fresh faced, with lips slightly parted, she waited politely for me to finish.

'. . . I need a volunteer,' I said limply, and sensed at once who that would be. Bobbing up gaily (as much as the wide train of her dress permitted), the Signora's youngest daughter volunteered. There was some indulgent applause as she swept on to the stage. Covering with dainty fingertips her laughing mouth, the young girl composed herself for her portrait. Although scarcely taller than myself, she seemed to gaze at me from a dizzying height. I felt my face on fire; my ears seemed to curl up like roasted petals.

*

But I can sense you frowning, kind reader, and ruffling through those pages already conquered (already laid to rest) in search of a lost connection. What was the cause of my humiliation? Ah, to know that we must reverse the clock – just a little, by a handful of hours.

We had reached the estate of Carlo Ripellino late in the morning, hot and weary from our exertions. My father, who remained taciturn after his nocturnal excesses, managed with great effort to brighten for the major-domo who greeted us at the gatehouse. We were led along a broad avenue of sweet chestnuts (I could hear the crepitant awakening of fresh green leaves) until we reached the outbuildings, where servants were ordered to feed and refresh us.

It was on the cold stone of the kitchen floor, beside a gaping empty hearth, that I dressed into my costume. (It was crumpled after two days' journey and smelled distinctly of mule.) Looking up from a stubborn button, I saw my father slumped at the table with his eyes closed: no doubt summoning his energy. I understood, from the major-domo, that we would not be called for until after the Signora's luncheon. Therefore, taking advantage of my father's rest, I stole outside to explore.

I had not strayed far from the outbuildings when she appeared. Skipping like a dryad, some nymph of the olive groves, she stopped with a start. Her pale, delicate feet were naked and freckled with grass seed. A coquettish breeze, relishing her chestnut hair, sifted it for sheer delight. She stared at me with dark swollen eyes.

'What's *your* name?'

I felt my soul quiver. I was in the presence of an elemental power – some force of Nature heretofore unknown to me. 'Tom . . .' I said. 'Tommaso, if you please.'

'Good morning, Tom Tommaso.'

A cabbage white butterfly, fluttering clumsily between our eye-beams, severed their connection. The young girl bent at the waist and, with hands crossed behind her back and her legs angled out for balance, leaned against the bough of an olive tree. I felt myself floating towards her, yet my feet did not move.

'Aren't you the little painter?' she asked eventually. 'Is it you? Is it today?'

I performed a neat impersonation of a gasping fish, which made the young girl quake with laughter. She rocked back and forth against the olive tree – held her breath – then hopped sideways, with a doe's lightness, into the singing grasses.

'Catch me,' she cried, 'if you can!'

Enchanted, bewildered, I pursued her through groves and copses and meadows. I had no thought of what I might do if I succeeded in reaching her. My heart and lungs felt on fire, as though they might shatter through my ribs and ascend to Heaven.

For an hour, perhaps, I chased my quarry – following bright laughter in an oak wood, then careering off in the opposite direction after a glimpsed heel or flutter of pale blue skirts. 'Where are you?' I cried, maddened at her ability to duplicate herself and appear in two places at the same time. 'Stop running so I can find you.'

'But I'm here,' came the reply, and I spun round to find her beneath a parasol pine. To my astonishment, she stretched out imploringly her pale, delicately downy arms.

'You can kiss me if you like.'

'What?'

'You can kiss me if you wish. But I want you to hop. On one leg. Otherwise no kiss.'

The exchange seemed fair – I knew nothing of trading in these matters. So I hopped, panting like an eager puppy.

'Now stand on your head.'

'Sorry?'

'You heard.'

'I don't know how to.'

'Stand on your head!'

'Oh, but . . . no, but—'

Frantic not to spoil my luck, I grunted and puffed. I curled up like a dormouse, with my skull to the ground, and managed to perform a clumsy forward roll, collapsing in a heap at her feet. There was tittering, not of birds, from a neighbouring hedgerow.

'Get up,' my tormentor said impatiently. 'No, not yet. Get *off*. First I want you . . . I command you to walk like a duck.'

Yes, I nodded, yes, a duck, of course, *anything*.

'Waddle for me. Come on. And start quacking.'

'Wak wak,' I screamed. 'Kwek kwek.'

It was then, while my fists were tucked under my armpits and my buttocks jutted out for a tail, that out from behind the hedgerow spilled laughing, staggering spectators. I never saw them clearly – not in the haze of my embarrassment. They were three brunettes like their sister, and identically dressed: her accomplice doubles, stooges to my humiliation. The hilarity continued for quite some time, until a bell resounded through the trees and the girls scampered, in a flurry of skirts, back to the Castello.

*

And now my enchantress, the cruel nymph in all her finery, was sitting for her portrait. To my left, amid the blur of spectators, the Signora was struggling to silence her tittering daughters. They were all in on the farce. Together they had divested me of mystery, of any shred that I might have possessed of dignity. Perniciously simpered at (how dumb and insensible can adults be not to pick up on these things?), I did a stupid thing: a very unwise, dangerous and satisfying thing. My father was first to see what I was drawing. He fidgeted and bit his lips at the narrow squinting eyes – at the coarse eyebrows that joined hands above a pinched snub nose – at the bloated lips that drooled over a pimpled chin. There was a stirring of scandalised dissent from the assembled worthies. I heard the Signora huff loudly; chairs cried out as their occupants rose in protest. Oh yes, I wiped the smile off their faces.

Two weeks later, my disgraced father and I left our home in Florence and set out, under false names, northwards to Milan.

3
Arcimboldo

In the capital city of the Imperial Province of Milan, our lives were changed utterly. Instead of notoriety (mine), we had obscurity (ours). Instead of declining wealth (the vestiges of my mother's dowry), we had jobbing poverty. And here was a climate to reckon with – those close humid summers which, at their worst, induce a universal torpor, the bladder-pinching winters, when snow creaks underfoot and everyone's mouth is haunted. Why, you may wonder, did my Tuscan father choose that northern city, from whose rooftops one can see, on a clear day, the snow-capped peaks of the Alps? Because it was a place where he could be true to his name: anonymous, like a sardine in its shoal. Because in its babel of tradesmen and travellers one might drown out one's darker thoughts. Because, in short, Milan was far from Florence and *far removed* from Florence.

Our first lodgings, in a single, foul-smelling room behind the Naviglio Grande canal, were replaced within two months by a garret on the Piazza Santo Stefano. In case this sounds like affluence regained (we were a stone's throw from the San Bernadino chapel), I should add that our two rooms were on the fourth floor, with a lonely window between them, that I never had a bed to speak of – only a mattress slung across the boards – and that we owned no privy save the street.

'It's not so bad,' my father growled as we moved in. 'Blow the cobwebs off, put down some floorboards and we'll be bloody cosy.'

There was no room now for Anonimo to sculpt. But it did not matter: he had renounced personal ambition.

Instead, to earn a crust, he cut stone on worksites along the Corso di Porta Romana, while his twelve-year-old son offered people their portraits on the Piazza del Duomo. The tedium of waiting for someone sufficiently curious or vain to sit for me was intense; or would have been, if intensity were not boredom's opposite. Sometimes, when pickings were slim, I moved my wares (a dwarf-sized easel, paper, a couple of stools) to the Piazza Mercanti, hoping to catch some customer drifting beneath the arches. On other occasions, to stretch my legs and knock some life back into my eyes, I wandered up the Corsia dei Servi, or entered the mighty Duomo to implore – with paganish fervour – the Tabernacle of the Nail of the Cross for a solution to my misery. Behind the altar, the wooden choir was still in progress. It grew as slowly as a forest and I used to inspect it for signs of change. I also came to admire a statue of St Bartholomew – that unfortunate missionary whom the early Armenians flayed for his faith. I was appalled and enthralled by that decorticated saint, who wore his skin like a loose gown and held it over his privy parts (had they too been stripped?) while he contemplated his Salvation. How artfully the sculptor represented every muscle and sinew of the standing cadaver, so impossibly alive in its double death (of martyrdom, of marble). I wondered whether taxidermists were up to the task of mounting humans and, imagining my own pelt, lamented how little space it would take up on some ogreish Armenian's floor.

'Perhaps this was taken from life?'

I turned, startled. An aged gentleman behind me contemplated the statue. His steep patrician's nose flared: I peered up cavernous and bristly nostrils. 'Do you think the sculptor had a sly word with the hangman? Hm? On the Piazza della Vetra?' Swaying gently on his feet, with his hands clasped behind his back, the old man looked at me closely. His eyes were dark and deeply pitted; they reminded me of the rings of grain in a tree. The face was long and faintly equine, balanced between a green skullcap and a soft ruff. I was dimly conscious of rich and elegant garments but failed to look the rest of him over.

'What do you mean, sir?'

'I merely wonder. How does anyone know what a flayed skin looks like? I'm told Michelangelo endowed *his* Bartholomew, in the Sistine Chapel, with his own features. Have you heard of Michelangelo?'

'Yes,' I said. 'Of course.'

'Of course you have,' he nodded, and a smile formed beneath the curl of his moustache. 'It's no use these days just imagining the human body. We must get our detail from the flesh.' A priest, rolling on the benighted globe of his belly, eyed us with suspicion. 'I knew a man who crucified his servant – not fatally, you understand – to see what effect it had on the human body. Perhaps our sculptor used the skin of a murderer? Or a thief? There's a kind of immortality for you.'

'*I* wouldn't want it.'

The old man seemed to consider my reply. 'No,' he agreed. 'Me neither.' With a dip of his melancholy head, he drifted away. I watched the black cloak and skullcap recede down the nave. Then I smirked ingratiatingly at the loitering priest (hoping for a good word) and left the Duomo to resume my vigil on the piazza.

At the day's end, as weary hawkers dismantled their stalls and conjurors garrotted their bags of tricks, I traipsed home to a supper of lentils and gruel. These were typically cheerless affairs, conducted in grim, masticating silence. We laughed rarely, my father and I. Yet I recall one occasion, when I brought my father lunch at his work site on the Corso di Porta Romana (it was his usual slab of bread and

41

ham, with a raw onion which he devoured as one might an apple, meaning to keep strangers at bay), there was a sudden commotion, like a clap of thunder, behind my shoulder. Workmen dropped their tools and rushed to the side of the road.

'What is it?' I cried. 'I can't *see*.'

Sun-baked backs marred my view. I heard grunting and braying and thin, mousy shrieks. My father reached beneath my arms. To my delight, and not a little pain (for I carried a good deal of weight on my toddler's legs), he hoisted me on to his shoulders, whence I could see to the centre of those bobbing, dusty heads.

Had I *heard* such a tale, I should not have believed it. A Cistercian monk, making his way by ass to the Abbey of Chiaravalle, found himself crushed between his mount and a powerfully aroused stallion. The ravished ass protested. Pressed between stud and receptacle, the monk did likewise. But no screams or invocations could deter the horse as it strained, pop-eyed with passion, towards its goal. 'Whore!' cried the ass. 'Help!' squealed the monk. And the crowd exhaled. Men laughed like bad actors, flinging their arms into the air and slapping one another's thighs; women, falling over their bosoms, clutched and retched. It was like some Bacchic frenzy, and I was not excluded. Never in all my childhood did I laugh so heartily – or so heartlessly. The old Cistercian's back was broken. It took three days for him to die.

On Sundays, after Mass, my father wanted only to sleep, weighted down by brute animal tiredness and sighing with relief the instant his head touched the pillow. Abandoned, I would sneak into the Giardino della Guastalla where newly-weds strolled, ostentatiously in love, and the chaperoned daughters of aristocrats studied their copybooks. Alas, I could not revive the serene watchfulness of my younger self: that intense scrutiny which I had applied for hours to simple animal life. What was this yearning which distracted me, this hunger which mountains of cheap bread could not assuage? My eyes grew restless: they floated up whenever young girls passed. Black or fair, I scrutinised whatever each possessed of femininity. I became a collector of long-lashed glances, mentally sketching the grace of a careless gesture, the conversational tilt of a head – all that voluntary and incidental witchcraft. It was a passive occupation, however. My only physical proximity to the fairer sex occurred at the washing-troughs beside the canal. The washerwomen rocked on their knees, like damp Mahometans, their pendulous breasts lolling. I admired their strong manly arms and the toughness of their fingers embroiled in the limbs of wet linen. When I knelt among them, they greeted me as a quaint and pitiable child.

'How's our little dwarf?'

'Where's your mammy, *bambino*?'

'Have you washed behind your ears?'

It seems inconceivable, I agree, that I should have found an admirer beneath those echoing rafters. And yet there she was, unquestionably watching me down the line. I felt her grave and enquiring stare: it was a magnetic force of which all my lesser senses were conscious before my eyes. The usual, beggarly ruses for escaping attention failed me. I coughed and scratched my head; I wiped my brow and applied myself to the annihilation of stubborn and imaginary stains. 'So let her look,' I told myself. 'She's probably just curious. Another gawper with a soft spot for midgets.' But every Friday, when I went to wash our clothes, she had moved one place closer to where I worked. She was quite old, at least thirty, and bewilderingly knowing. Her eyes were dark and voracious, her mouth was . . . in fact I have no idea what she looked like, I was terrified, must I describe *everything*?

At last the day came when she was washing at my side. Whether by accident or design, her black curls fell across her cheek, concealing from the others our mute and exhilarating glances. There was a tempest in my belly: booming hills, groaning rocks, trees exploding. Outwardly, my left knee nodded its imbecile head. I understood, from the animation of her eyebrows, that I was to follow her behind the crumbling wall of a canal-side privy. She picked herself up and left before me; halting briefly to scratch at her heel and assure herself of my courage. None of the others seemed to suspect this earth-shattering conspiracy, and I scampered as fast as I could to our place of assignation. There we stood, face to navel. I had to balance atop a pile of bricks to reach her ample and suddenly naked breast. I must have made, at that sudden unveiling, a retreating gesture, for she clasped my ears in her wet hands and pulled me to her.

Broad-minded reader, she suckled me. Nothing in the world of art had prepared me for the astounding expanse of her aureola; it reminded me of the false eye emblazoned on the wings of certain butterflies. I was afraid of the plump blue veins that fed her breast. A coarse hair stuck between my teeth. I remember the angry nipple, as hard as a knuckle, and the shock of my erection, like a bud nudging towards the light. Eventually, she pulled away and murmured: 'That's enough, my pumpkin. You've had your lot.' Now the breast – that glorious white moon – was gone; in its place, a black widow's shirt and strong fingers tying strings. 'Take that home and work on it,' she commented, with a downward glance, as she left.

It took me a long while (humming, yawning, drumming with my fingers on my hips) to settle. Then I returned, with turmoil in my heart, to the company of washerwomen.

'Bravo, piggy!'

'Copped an eyeful, did we?'

'Ah, leave him alone, the poor terror.'

Several women, in on the dare, winked at my seductress and nudged their neighbours. But mockery could not hurt me. I had glimpsed an unimagined future where my oddness – the curse of my childish stature – might work in my favour, to the fulfilment of female perversity and my own insalubrious gain.

Later, at home, I discovered that solitary diversion so despised of Old Testament prophets and practised it with the zeal of a recent convert. I fanned the flames of my lust with lewd and anatomically improbable drawings. Sometimes I towered above my conquests, who shivered with delight in my priapic shadow. Alternately, I was a grinning homunculus, tiny as a mouse, diving into the fragrant and uniform foreshadowing of cunt. You may smile to note that these lascivious imaginings would prove my most original work. For I was unfamiliar with any precedents. Primaticcio's mutilating nymphs, the lubricious black masses of Hans Baldung Grien (with their fiery wombs and goaty fornications) were unknown to me. Nor had I developed – despite my humiliation at Castello della Quèrcia – that high-minded hatred of the Weaker Sex which insists upon its poisonous properties and laments to see Aristotle, that lofty intellect, ridden on all fours by a pot-bellied Phyllis. I was enflamed, certainly; but I did not blame the object of my desire. Besides, my father also suffered. I could sense the frustration build up within him. I heard his stamping foot at supper and tried not to notice his restive eyes. At last he would jump up, snatch some coins from his money box (the key to which he kept on a chain about his neck) and, without so much as a farewell, escape the building. Crouching at the window, I would watch the top of his head (so baldly innocent) as he marched his appetites to the Brera quarter. Poor man: I was the thorn in his side – a pint-sized chaperone forbidding him erotic pleasure. Late at night he would return, kicking each step on the stairs as though testing for woodworm. He clattered about with his key in the door before penetrating, with a grunt, our stuffy chamber. At last he would discompose himself for bed, sighing like a sick old dog and trying noisily not to wake me, while I pretended to sleep on my uncomfortable couch.

It was after such a brittle night that I met Arcimboldo. Or rather, met him again. He stumbled across me in the piazza – quite literally, since he was admiring the cathedral at the time. Profusely apologising, the aged gentleman offered me a paint-pimpled hand.

'Well, well,' he exclaimed as I righted my easel. 'So our conversation was between experts. Is this your self-portrait?' It was a clumsy dawdle, executed out of boredom and without the use of a mirror. Arcimboldo glanced from the life to its image. 'Did you teach yourself?'

'Yes, sir.'

'*Really*?'

'Completely self-taught.'

I had no idea who he was, and cast about in my mind for a polite way of enquiring.

'Permit me to introduce myself. Count Giuseppe Arcimboldo, court painter to his Imperial Majesty and your humble servant.'

If he was a madman, there could be no harm in tempering him. So I bowed as my father had taught me. Arcimboldo flung back his left leg and reverenced, with his palms exposed like Christ before his disciples. 'It is an honour to meet one so able, so young. Did you ... I say, that day in the transept, did you notice the stained glass window depicting St Catherine of Alexandria? Did you like it?'

'Um . . .'

'Did you *see* it?'

'Yes,' I lied. 'Very nice.'

'What did you think?'

'Very nice.'

Like a ruminant horse, Count Arcimboldo chewed the overdroop of his moustache. 'People rarely pay attention to windows. Because they serve a function, they think the art of secondary value.'

'Did you make it, sir?'

'Lord, no. Konrad of Mochis was the master glazier. I designed it. My father, Biagio Arcimboldo, was a painter too. Have you a father?' The short hairs on my neck bristled. 'He must be very proud.'

'It's my mother who encourages me. My brothers and sisters – none of *them* can draw – tend to get jealous.'

'Yes, it is a consequence one may suffer.'

'But then I give them cartoons and that makes them happy.'

Lying in this fashion to a man of reputation, I felt no shame. He listened so politely that I almost believed my own falsehoods. 'I am going to be apprenticed to a baker,' I said. 'My father says there is no livelihood in painting. I must forget it and learn a proper trade.'

At this last, brazen invention, the Count clucked and shook his head. 'But I have not asked your name. How can I be of use to you if I do not know your name?'

'Tommaso Grilli, if it please you.'

'Grilli? Did you say *Grilli*?'

My throat tightened. I could only nod, fearing discovery; but Arcimboldo had never heard of my father.

47

'I myself am a creator of *grilli*,' he said. 'If by that we can agree that we mean fantastical creatures.'

'Fantastrical . . . ?'

'Did you not know the word?'

'But it's me.'

'So I understand.'

That my family name (having lately shed the blooming -o for -i's barren stem) signified anything so apt was depressing news. Count Giuseppe Arcimboldo, on the other hand, quivered with almost boyish enthusiasm. He invited me to his house, where I would receive such assistance as might serve my unjustly endangered vocation. He seemed kind, for all his strangeness: so I packed up my equipment and followed him.

The guardian of his palazzo greeted us with a silent scream. His beard was a tangle of briars, his hair a coarse thatch braided with corn. He was a forest god – ancient already at the foundation of Rome. His lifeless eyes stared at the leafless stones, at the garish human scene. Horrified by deracination. Count Arcimboldo performed an elaborate knock on the portico's teeth. Almost at once the grille snapped open, and a young man, trapped inside the divinity's throat, peeped out. 'Christ Almighty,' he said, blinking.

'Mind your language.'

'Sorry, sir.'

'That's no way to greet your master.'

'It's this bloody darkness. I'm turning into a mole.'

'You are not.'

'Burrowing about like I was underground.'

'Fernando, open the door. Can you not see we have a guest?'

No surprise or disgust registered on the servant's face at the sight of me. Having unlatched and opened the door, he

48

stepped back as he might to let pass his master's hound. Then the front door crashed behind us and we were plunged into gloom. My hands fluttered out at my sides; I snatched them back when, accidentally, I touched Fernando's knee. 'Might our *guest*, sir, not be glad of a torch to light his way?' Unheeding, Arcimboldo wafted past the blackly looming staircase. 'He keeps all the shutters closed,' Fernando muttered into my scalp. 'Blooming madness, if you ask me. A *fortune* wasted on candles.' I distinguished the pallor of the servant's hand and followed the direction of its pointing index. Arcimboldo passed noiselessly through a doorway. I pursued the eddies that floated from his gown and found myself inside a high-ceilinged chamber. I knew this from the hush – that way a space holds its breath when people enter. Heavy curtains were draped across the windows. There was a buzzing of flies, and I glimpsed in the rare spots of daylight decaying fruit, a yawning lily, roses on the turn. It was difficult to see where I placed my feet. Grapes burst between my toes. I crushed an apricot and nearly skidded. My host picked his way more carefully through the obscurity. I heard him murmur and fiddle a key in a lock. 'Ah,' he gasped, finding whatever it was he sought. There was a bristly noise, then a hiss, and a blinding light.

'Mind your eyes.'

When I had blinked away my tears, and with an ignis fatuus still flashing on my brain, I saw Arcimboldo lighting candles. There must have been a dozen stands, each hung with spilled wax like a frozen spring. Arcimboldo carried a taper from one to the other, guarding the flame with his hand as a mother shields her child's eyes from ghouls at a fair.

'Here he is. The god Vertumnus.'

Arcimboldo lit the lips of an oil-lamp and took it up. There was no tremble in his arm: the long yellow flame barely flickered. Obediently, I stepped through dusty pools of light to stand beside the Count. The long shadow cast by his nose across his cheek denatured his face. He looked like a wax effigy, a depiction of the magus; but his eyes shone with childlike ardour.

'Very nearly finished,' he said. 'Just the nose and the chin. The chestnuts are no good. Half rotten. I'll improve them from memory.'

Alas, you that know nothing of a neglected painter will have no conception of that wondrous being, Vertumnus, the Etruscan god of bounty. He stared at me with blackcurrant eyes: animate, mythical and faintly malevolent. His cheeks were peaches and his lips red cherries. Marrows, aubergines and a radish constituted his throat and chest, to which a gown of flowers was pinned by an onion clasp. But my words are blind: a feast for the eye cannot be matched by ten volumes of prose. Crowned with fruits of the harvest, with hazelnut husks for a moustache, it was a dazzling conceit and somehow familiar, in the way of masterpieces.

Watching my amazement, Arcimboldo grinned. 'You cannot disassemble him, can you?'

True enough. The effigy, constructed of disparate flowers and fruits, cohered as one majestic being. Each grape and marrow and ear of corn was carefully rendered as itself; yet each part belonged to the unified whole.

'Vertumnus was also the god of Metamorphosis. He could assume any form he chose. Be careful where you *sit*, my boy.'

This was sound advice, as the studio was littered with discandying matter. It was as though Vertumnus himself, having sat for his portrait, had discarded parts of his anatomy on departure. I picked up a spray of cranberries and compared it to its image on the canvas. The copy was perfect, right down to the twin leaves and the number of berries.

'For the fabulous image to convince the viewer,' said

Arcimboldo, 'let its parts be copied faithfully from Nature. It is *detail* which gives life to an object. If you wander too far from Nature, nothing you paint will please. Even monsters are made of flesh.'

As though to prove his point, Arcimboldo fetched from the walls a number of small paintings – copies no doubt of larger originals. These 'Four Seasons' represented the ages of Man. A rosy-cheeked youth, composed entirely of Spring flowers, faced his counterpart and destiny in Winter, a gnarled tree with roots for bristles and ugly fungus lips. Summer was Man at full power, a laughing composite of fruit. He stared unfazed at Autumn, whose beard of wheat and Dionysian crown were ripe for harvest and harvest's only end.

'Mankind, my boy, is not apart from Nature. And Nature is a part of Man. Do you not replenish your body with fruits? So are you not *made up* of them?' Arcimboldo sank his teeth sonorously into an apple. 'Motif fur humus,' he said, and swallowed. 'Notice the humours. *Siccus, calidus, humida, frigidia*. Unite all four in one figure and what have you? The Universal Man.'

The painter continued in this philosophical vein while I gorged myself on his paintings. I interrupted him, foolishly, to ask why he worked with curtains closed. It should have been apparent that Arcimboldo's paintings were executed by artificial light: it gave them their hermetic mystery, that dark and dream-like charm.

'Why the darkness? Because I prefer it. It sharpens my focus.' Arcimboldo sat chewing his apple, pleased to watch me as I studied his inventions. As for myself, I felt like a man who, having wandered too long in a desert, is suddenly dropped at sea. Craving what surrounded me, I was unable to possess it. 'The painting is also a portrait of my patron – provider of bounty to his subjects as Vertumnus to Mankind. You have *no* idea what I'm talking about, have you? Forgive me. I am old, I forget the world is not my invention. Let me tell you about the Emperor . . .'

Thus I learned of the Habsburg Rudolf, in a soliloquy, distilled no doubt over many years, rich with ornate figures of speech. Arcimboldo described how the pious youth, already possessed of that famous chin, had brought Spanish manners to the Viennese court. The new monarch was blessed with a fancy of uncommon fecundity. Memories buzzed about his crown of the riches he had seen in the Escorial: all the arts and wonders assembled by Felipe of Spain as a haven from the tempests of office. Some kings hunger for temporal power, demanding vast tributes of blood and soil. The Emperor Rudolf's ambitions were gentler. He would assemble the greatest treasure-house in Christendom. To this purpose he surrounded himself with astrologers, artists and craftsmen, great talents of the likes of— (I forgot the names, they meant nothing to me). Arcimboldo had been a favourite of the late Emperor Maximilian; now he travelled with his successor Rudolf to the new seat of power in Prague. With eyes rolling as he pictured its spires and towers, Arcimboldo described the splendour of the city on the Moldau – the solemnity of a stone bridge, the imposing castle, and what apartments and cabinets were built there by the new Bohemian king. 'He has a lion, you know. It roars at daybreak. Some say the Emperor's reign is harnessed to the royal beast's fortunes.' Did Arcimboldo believe it? He could believe anything of an emperor who possessed a statue of Daphne made of red coral, who boasted a unicorn's tusk and a mandrake shaped like the crucified Christ – the simulacrum precise right down to the agony on His tiny face. 'I entertained both emperors in turn with the sweet harvest of my labours. Masques, pageants. Studies of animals painted by hand. In gratitude Rudolf confirmed the nobility of my name. I was made a gift, on my return to Milan, of fifteen hundred and fifty florins.' Arcimboldo caught his breath long enough to be sure of my admiration.

'Why,' I asked him, 'did you leave Prague?'

'Why does a salmon return to the stream where it was spawned? I am Milanese, like you. I want to die in the city of my birth. And complete the circle of my life.' The old man leaned forward off his stool. He found on the table a colour study, on plain parchment, of a blushing pear. Watching him scrutinise it in the light from his lamp, I sensed that *Vertumnus* would be his last creation.

Over the subsequent months and years, I would relieve my father of my company to visit the painter in his benighted palazzo. A bond of affection grew between us. It was one of those delicate friendships which can flower, at either end of a life, between a child of uncommon maturity and an elder still charged with youthful enthusiasm. When the Emperor received his painting in Prague, he rewarded Arcimboldo with the title 'Comus Palatinus'. The old man seemed to rise on his pins. His nostrils flared at fragrances that wafted about the summits of his ennoblement; he caressed, with bony fingers, a new silk ruff, and paid rheumy-eyed tribute to his patron. I wonder now, had I decided already to try my luck in that far and magical Bohemia? Was the notion mooted, whisperingly, in some dark antechamber of my soul and allowed to ferment there, in the way of rebellions, until the day of action? Arcimboldo weaved tales of the emperors that fired my imagination. Gripped as I was by growths and queasy pulsions, I ached for life to deliver its rumoured blessings. How was it possible to exist, day after day, bound to the wheel like a beast of burden, when Arcimboldo described the drolleries he had invented for his masters? Hungry for kinship, I dared not venture that I too had been a *buffo aristocratico* – in a fashion. Instead, I maintained the illusion of a lonely and preternatural talent, which Arcimboldo felt duty-bound to nurture.

One bright morning, as sunlight, tinctured by the curtains, gave the study a glaucous and pond-like atmosphere, the old Count sat me purposefully on my stool. I watched as he lifted the lid of a long wooden chest. Supporting himself with one hand on a precariously bended knee, he rooted about with the other and unearthed a squarish object wrapped in green velvet. Having straightened (with a gasp and an audible click of cartilage), he stroked back the corners of the cloth to reveal an elegant leather pouch. Arcimboldo unfastened the string that bound the boards and reverently removed a wad of old parchment. Each sheet was covered in writing, sometimes legible, often in mirror hand. There were diagrams of fortifications viewed from the heavens, crablike siege engines and grotesque heads bloodlessly disembodied. I saw floating pyramids; awful revelations of flood and storm; the flowering petals of an unbuilt cathedral. I gawked at a sphere which – opened like a fruit by some anatomist's knife – revealed a crouching fetus. My soul quaked at this God's-eye view of hidden things, and I pitied the bald infant still sheltering in its defiled and studied shell.

'The notebooks of Leonardo da Vinci,' Arcimboldo whispered. He explained how his father had known Leonardo's pupil, the painter Bernardino Luini; how Luini's son had lent Arcimboldo the notebooks, which he then copied, propped on his elbow beside a mirror. 'Leonardo's mind was almost divinely capacious. The works of Man awaited him in the world of Forms. He had only to reach into its shadows to grasp them.'

So began my induction into the mysteries of Art. Arcimboldo

weighted heavily his moral concerns. 'Do not seek knowledge for the wrong reasons. Neither compulsion – if it lack restraint – nor the vanity of display can ever come to good. Books are useless in the hands of a fool, and misunderstood they may prove a *hindrance* to reason.' The old man echoed Leonardo when he praised experience. 'No matter his authority, do not believe what a teacher tells you if your *senses* tell you otherwise.' Never again, after Arcimboldo, would I apply myself so keenly to the exercises set by a tutor. Puffing out my cheeks with effort, I came to grips with perspective and copied Leonardo's anatomical studies. I learned to refine my shading, both in paint and charcoal, until shadows and light blended together like smoke, without strokes or borders. Arcimboldo, sitting beside me and nursing most days a wheezy cough that ascended, with a loose rattle, the rusty flues of his throat, reached over my shoulder to correct an outline or blend my cross-hatching with a blurred, rasping finger.

'Very good,' he murmured. 'You are coming along.'

As soon as I had absorbed a lesson, however, I became distracted and wrinkled my nose at the faintly urinous odours that emanated from the old man. Perhaps he sensed my restlessness (once or twice my swinging heels may have struck his shins instead of the legs of my stool). Then Arcimboldo – ever the gentle master, who rewarded talent before he chastised sloth – adjourned proceedings to his unkempt garden. I was encouraged to find shapes in the most inauspicious places: staring at a stucco wall whose damp stains slowly revealed faces, exotic beasts, chimerae. Each pattern, which the mind engendered, I fixed on paper, while Arcimboldo jauntily located the original stain. Try it for yourself, fledgling artist: it loosens splendidly the eye and limbers the fancy for taking flight. Studying the random blots made on a page by a flicked quill, you may discover most ingenious forms, because (and here I quote the great Da Vinci) 'by indistinct things the mind is stimulated to new inventions'. Yet do not underestimate the rigours of this training. It is one thing, for pleasure, to find shapes on walls and in clouds – quite another to endow imagined beings with a semblance of life. Studying my master's work, I understood what pains he had taken over it. (You cannot take the pain out of painting.) For Arcimboldo was neither capricious nor fantastical. 'Madness is not creative,' he said. 'One needs a steady hand, a clear eye. Necessary distance. To dream on paper you must spend your life awake.' Gentle skimmer, you that mistake feigned ecstasy for actual madness, he possessed in uncommon abundance that wit which sees – and enables others, less sighted, to see – the hidden resemblances between things.

In the summer of my sixteenth year, a day came when I failed to wake the sentinel. I knocked at Arcimboldo's door until my knuckles ached but the forest god's mouth would not open. I sat on the step beneath the lintel and experimented with various postures, seeking the least uncomfortable, until I settled with elbows on my knees and my chin in my hands. A drifting cloud cast its frown across the street. In the distance vendors sang, tradesmen haggled, children shrilled and hollered. A plump widow eased her breasts on to the wall of her house and emptied a pail of slops into the street. Then there was nothing: no performance to jolt me from my stupor, only a cat mewing somewhere, invisible.

Just as I was preparing to leave, a pebble hopped and struck my shin. Somebody whistled tunelessly. It was Fernando. He fairly skipped towards me, winking with a sideways grin at the silver sky. 'You don't look yourself when you're sitting down,' he said. 'I thought you were a man kneeling on his legs.' He produced a chain from beneath his shirt to which a key was attached. 'Come to pay your respects, have you?'

'Um . . . as always.'

Fernando froze with his key in the lock. 'Has nobody told you?'

'Told me?'

'Have you not heard?'

'Heard what?'

'The Count is dead.'

Fernando chafed his throat with quick fingers, as a dog scratches at fleas. Now he was assaulting the front door with his knee. The lock must have been rusty because he had to use his shoulder against it.

'Well, come on. I won't bite.'

My feet had corpsed: I dragged them unwillingly beneath me. Once inside the hallway, the syllables uttered by Fernando in the street assumed their full weight and proportion. The Count was dead. Somebody had opened all his shutters. Furnishings that until now had lurked in darkness were starkly exposed; reflective tables, convex mirrors, the gleaming peaks of the dark polished staircase – everything solid, tangible and particular.

'He left something for you,' said Fernando.

A second door yielded without resistance. I was dimly aware that I ought to be grieving; yet my eyes were deserts and, except for a vague flutter in the bowels, I cannot pretend that I suffered. Fernando, without once knocking, entered Arcimboldo's study. Here, too, the shadows had been banished. They hid in nooks and corners, squeezing themselves behind books and paintings. The heavy green curtains had been removed, leaving the windows exposed like mouths without teeth.

'Do I have to hold your hand?' demanded Fernando.

The studio had been swept clean. No trace remained of

professional clutter, of the old man's leavings. Every lustrous surface – the cold blue walls and gaping chairs – awaited a new occupant.

'There's a package for you. And a letter.'

In the centre of the table, my exercise sketches had been gathered into an irregular wafer and bound together with a green ribbon. Fernando hoisted me onto a stool so that I might see, beneath the ribbon's knot and sealed with red wax, a letter addressed to His Most Imperial Majesty. Sanguinary fire rushed to my face – I fancy the stool beneath me quivered. Was this some sort of *joke*?

'It's a letter of introduction,' said Fernando, 'for you to show to the Emperor. It's written there, look. He said you mustn't open it.'

Wax had formed small dark rubies on the parchment. I felt with my finger the initialled stamp of Arcimboldo's ring. Then, briefly, I found my voice.

'Where are Leonardo's notes?'

'Whose?'

'The notebooks of Leonardo. He kept them in that chest over there. His copies of the originals.'

Fernando pouted and shrugged. He knew nothing of his late master's affairs. I noticed a burnished silver ring on one of his fingers; his silk hose and taffeta jerkin were surprisingly handsome.

I climbed down from the stool, embracing my worthless papers. I cannot recount my short journey back through the transfigured hallway; nor with what pious platitudes Fernando expelled me from the palazzo into the suddenly populous street. My papers fluttered in the breeze. The letter slipped and fell to the ground – where I very nearly left it. I felt like a shadow player who, having spoken his lines, lingers in the wings to watch more memorable actors sweep his memory from the stage.

4

Gian Bonconvento

'Mufon. Pujof.'

A sharp-snouted leather boot nudged my thigh. I wiped my face and nose with my sleeve before looking up. 'I'm just watching,' I said.

'No, no.'

'I was his pupil.'

The Spaniard stooped to show me the wiry black hairs on the back of his hand. 'Mufalon,' he said, 'Jew – *pujof.*' Flicking his fingers, he attempted to drive me from the church, lest I encumber the faithful with pleas for charity.

'I'm no beggar,' I protested. '*Yo no soy* beggar, you oaf.'

'Hof?'

'*Amigo del muerto, estoy.*'

Woozily the soldier menaced me with the flat of his sword. Even inebriated – even Spanish – a man cannot readily bring himself to strike a dwarf. Nonetheless I feigned a retreat. Leaning against a plane tree's mottled trunk, above the reek of cat's urine, I bit my lower lip to quell emotion. The sky brimmed, trapped in a glass of brine.

They were burying Arcimboldo in S. Pietro della Vigna. (Friend, if you should pass that church on business, seek out its chill shade. Cross yourself before the altar, spread your hand on the cold tombstone and speak his epitaph. Sound Arcimboldo's name amid the plaster saints.) The funeral was richly attended. Wealthy patrons had swept into the church with pages and consorts in tow; artists, wearing as many shades of black as the jackdaw, eyed one another with lofty disdain; even ambassadors were in attendance, their faces sombre with politic duty. What had these strangers to do with Arcimboldo? Yet they, admitted, blandly observed the obsequies while I had to hide behind a tree, some latrine for every mog in Milan, forbidden to mourn him. The patrolling soldier did not wander off but collapsed, with a clank of Toledo steel, on the church steps.

Walking home with the singing of psalms in my ears, I felt that my life was finished. I had lost my only tutor, and with him any hope of advancement. His letter addressed to the Holy Roman Emperor could not buy transport across the Alps; nor had I acquired, in our brief years together, an expertise sufficient to find employment.

My father met me outside our building. He was dressed in borrowed finery (that frilled shirt was too clean ever to have drowned at *my* hands) and his face was flushed with anger. 'Tommaso, where have you been? Have you forgotten our appointment?'

No, I had not forgotten. For days he had been telling me of a 'meeting' which would secure my 'future'. Even the loss of Arcimboldo had not dislodged the prospect from my mind. It had coloured my sleep with dreams of enslavement: a butcher's gruesome arsenal – tinctured vials of an apothecary – blank tombstones in a mason's yard.

'Come along, we mustn't keep the man waiting. What's that smell?'

'What man, *papà*?'

'The man who's waiting to meet you.'

'Why is he waiting to meet me?'

'Because we're running late. Did you rub against something?'

How I hated keeping up with my father when he was in a hurry! I felt like a puppy trotting at his feet. Soon the sweat was stinging my eyes and my ribs threatened to splinter; so we stopped on the Corsia dei Servi while I gasped and reached for air. My father glared at the curious tradesmen until he could contain himself longer. 'Let me carry you, for the love of *God*.'

'I'll be – wait – almost there . . .'

These manifestations of discomfort became, I confess, something of a performance. I could find no other way of stalling. Surely, I thought, I was about to be bartered – apprenticed to some base profession? If my father would not tell me our destination, I would try my hardest not to get there.

'Climb on my back, lad.'

'Don't worry – oof – I'll make it.'

'Climb on my back, damn you!'

Miraculously recovering, I skipped a few paces. But my father was too quick for me and I spent the rest of our journey clinging to him like a fieldmouse to its dam.

We jogged north towards the Porta Orientale – the old city gate, to whose pickpockets the weary traveller may relieve himself of his worldly burden. Fat whores leaning at open casements followed, with languid eyes, our two-headed monster. A couple, mistaking me for a little child, smiled at our imagined play. I could feel the strain in my father's shoulders and longed to tighten my rein on his throat – to delay the inevitable by a few choking minutes. Instead, with my jaw knocking on his skull, I brooded on adversity. Not until my return, many years hence, ragged and bruised, to Lombardy, would I glimpse the perverse concern which Fate has always shown for my survival. Good fortune need not present itself in glittering robes: it may dress like a beggar, a mad old tumbler in the rain whom we spurn to our cost. How many times have I slandered my luck, calling it misfortune? Ignorant of His plans for me, I have cursed God with the fury of an ant for a kindly averted foot.

'Get down now – haw – you walk – what *state* are we in?'

The load had been too great. Even without me on it, my father's back retained the memory of my weight. He stood misshapen, like a damp prop of clay. I suffered pangs of guilt – that bitter juice of Duty – and longed to exorcise his phantom burden. Instead we progressed in silence: myself shuffling and recalcitrant, my father righting himself by small, wincing inches. He said, 'I suppose you think I want to punish you. I know how you resent me.'

'No, *papà*.'

'Am I such a lamentable father?'

'Not at all.'

'What kind of tyrant carries his victim on his back?'

The city dwindled about us, the stink of humanity abating among fields of thyme and nodding lavender. We walked among bright orchards of apricot and peach; through kitchen gardens checkered by vegetable plots with brightly baubled tomato plants. A lone scarecrow – crucified on a cabbage Golgotha – twitched a hand of flyaway straw. My sorrow extended even to him: fodder stuffed in a tattered cloak.

Turning east, we faced the warm brick church of San Babila. I saw my father's open hand swaying and wondered with dread if I was meant to take it. I exhaled with relief as we circumvented San Babila's stork-thatched campanile: I would not be abandoned to that refuge for changelings.

Leaving the dusty road, we waded through a sea of high singing grasses. Crickets sprayed about us like spindrift. Above the broad gusting waves of grass a villa rose, a promontory behind dark cliffs of cypress. The ears of meadow grass tickled my nose, subjecting me to a most gratifying sneezing fit, from which I emerged only when a small bank brought us ashore. Still wheezing and trying to rub out my face, I followed my father across an empty terrace. The villa's creamy walls were stubbled by suckers of dead ivy;

its slanting roof was flecked with guano and dry moss – the red and white and black of peppered salami. Behind the villa's shuttered façade, and separated from it by a cherry orchard, stood an ancient, shrugging barn, with crumbling walls tufted by weeds and a subsiding lintel like a snaggle tooth in a gaping mouth. A second, smaller outbuilding (perhaps a stable for a mule) sat farther off, its door bolted from the outside.

In the absence of any welcome, I scurried behind a hedge of privet and watered the dry roots with my fear. (The hedge died a few months later.) My father huffed as I buttoned my flap. He took my hand – my wrist, rather – with a grip like a manacle.

'We've made him wait too long already. Best behaviour now, Tommaso. Remember the mess you made at the Castello.'

He marched me, with dismaying force, to the open door of the barn. I could smell animal glue, linseed oil, fresh shavings of poplar. And my father relaxed his grip on my wrist, because it was no longer necessary.

'Where is the Maestro?'

Four pale, undernourished boys hovered about their chores, transfixed by our entrance. My father nervously cleared his throat and repeated the question. 'He is expecting us, I hope? We're a little late.'

The boys' eyes drifted forlornly to their toes. The two farthest from us were grounding a panel with gypsum; a third was tracing a grid on a stretched canvas. The most senior-looking youth, who had been crushing linseed with a pestle, hugged the mortar in the crux of his arm.

'This is my son, Tommaso Grilli.'

The apprentices peered at me with expressionless faces. I must have looked a proper halfwit: staring at inanimate brushes and palettes, at the sepulchral heap of nails on a bench beside me.

The linseed boy hummed softly, as though refreshing his throat, before speaking. 'Gian Bonconvento is at church,' he said. His face was narrow and shrewish, unhappily complexioned with thickly gathered freckles and a nest of ginger hair. The long nose, bent in remembrance of a fracture, shone with grease, its blackheads like seeds in a strawberry. 'He'll be back soon. You can wait for him here, if you like.'

'But *we* are late,' said my father.

Nobody had any use to make of this statement: it dropped between us like an exhausted bird. The panel-grounders tentatively dipped their clotted brushes; the grid-tracer eased his rule up the canvas slyly, as a spy might hide a letter in his enemy's presence. Only the ginger youth summoned the courtesy to clear a pair of workshop stools for us. Backing away with my father's thanks, he clipped me with slyly insolent eyes – a groundless look of contempt which he carried with him to his desk and transferred to the battered contents of his mortar.

Thankfully I had not long to wait, sitting with my back to the door as wetness gathered in my armpits. A sonorous yawp in the orchard might have been a yawn or a battle cry. I watched the brows of our insolent hosts tighten. Immediately they redoubled their efforts, pounding and chafing with theatrical zeal. Then I heard, outside the workshop, a falsetto mangling of the Mass for the Dead.

'. . . *dona eis, Domine, kyrie eleison* . . .'

I looked over to my father, who hovered inches from his stool, poised for obsequious greeting. His eyes were trained intently on the entrance.

'. . . *liber scriptus proferetur* . . .' (Now baritone.) '. . . *in quo totum continetur* . . .' (An abrupt, listening silence. I was stiff with fear at the presence behind me.) 'Well now, good day, my little fellow.' A blessing hand patted my crown and then, on second thoughts, transferred itself to my shoulder.

'Maestro—' said the ginger boy.

'Silence, Giovanni.'

'But this gentleman—'

'Signor Grilli, I most humbly crave your forgiveness.' The mellifluous newcomer coasted like a planet into my vision. Decorated in black doublet and gold-filigree hose, he shook my father's hand with such vigour that his own massive flesh shook: the fat belly canted over tremulous thighs, the neck bulging like a grub from its collar. 'Funerals are such consuming affairs. They remind us how little time we have by robbing us of it.'

My father assembled a suitable expression of concern. 'None of your family, I hope?'

'A painter – a second-rate painter. I barely knew the man.' (My father gasped politely, betraying his ignorance.) 'He was a buffoon. Il Conte dei Capricci. I should say he matters more to worms underground than to Mankind above it.'

Reader: I have never so despised a man without having seen his face. I suppressed a desire to smash something valuable.

'Signor Bonconvento, you do me great honour.' My father coughed and deposited his timidity like a cherry pip into his fist. 'I know what an undertaking it is to train an artist, having been there myself. Allow me to introduce my son.'

'Please,' said the Maestro. He turned heavily on the spot, like a bull in a pen, and searched the empty space around me. 'But where is he, exactly?'

'He is there, signor.'

'Where?'

'Standing in front of you.'

Bonconvento's eyes threatened to light on my flattened hair. 'This is his brother?'

'I'm sorry – whose brother?'

'Your son's brother.'

'Tommaso?'

'They're *both* called Tommaso?'

'This *is* Tommaso.'

Bonconvento's loose-jowled head ticked forward. He restrained, with a constipated wince, his disposition to mockery. Our eyes locked horns – then disengaged.

'You never told me that your son was mute.'

'He is not mute, Maestro. Simply overawed by the occasion.'

'Does he move?'

My father's voice tightened. 'Usually.'

'Well, he knows how to handle a brush – if that was his work you showed me. I should never have guessed he was so . . . *quiet*.' Bulging forward, the Maestro doused me in his meaty breath. 'Now then, Tommaso, shall we introduce you to the family?' Biting his tongue in a smile, Gian Bonconvento closed his fingers about my arm. I was dimly conscious of my father's presence as we steered between the benches.

The apprentice named Giovanni, who earlier had given me the evil eye, beamed with affection at his master. There was something too bright in that smile: it was hard to confront, like the sun reflected in a shard of silver.

'Giovanni is our oldest pupil. A fine painter and a wit. Mind his tongue, young Master Grilli.'

'It can lash,' said Giovanni.

'And it is forked like the serpent's.'

Anonimo Grilli – out of his depth like his son but less able to conceal it – found this exchange hilarious, too hilarious.

'Now these industrious little monkeys are brothers: Piero and Mosca.'

'Mosca?' piped my comical father. 'That's a strange name for a boy.'

'He likes his food,' Bonconvento complained. 'Like most growing lads, it's all he thinks about.'

I found this hard to believe, looking at Mosca's pigeon chest. The pair could not have been much over twelve: the kind of bland, moon-faced boys whom, years later, one never quite remembers, with the same sad, staring ears, pink as intimate flesh, and blue veins visible beneath opalescent skin. I bade them good afternoon, pityingly. 'Ah,' cried the Maestro, 'the prodigy speaks. Keep your brushes up, boys. Mind the lumps: a grounding should be smooth as cream . . .'

The brothers nodded and resumed work.

'Finally we come to Vittorio. My finest pupil.' (Gian Bonconvento glanced across his shoulder at my distracted father.) 'He has modelled for me, you know. How like an angel he looks.'

A strong, Grecian profile pearled with sweat and licked by damp curls; full feminine lips barely troubled by embryonic down, a hint of shadow at their creases. A soul was no more visible within that characterful mould than in a marble bust. Vittorio's large, hazel eyes coasted free of all volition; they snagged instantly on my face, then drifted loose. He was Bonconvento's favourite.

The tour completed, we were whisked away to a corner of the workshop. Huddled with the painter and my father behind a screen of unfinished paintings, among lopped plaster limbs and severed heads, I felt suddenly alone: powerless; acted upon.

'Appreciate, young man, the sacrifice your father has made for you. You shall belong to the workshop of Gian

Bonconvento – Milan's greatest painter. I have adorned altars and palaces. I have moved the sighted to tears before our Lord's Passion and our Lady's Sorrow.'

'I have saved up for this,' my father said. 'All my life, I've saved.'

'We are a community of priests, Tommaso. Our task is sacred. To translate the mysteries of God to Man.'

'I have worked, I have slaved, only for you.'

'To bring your talent to fruition.'

'To bring your talent to fruition.'

And so, against expectations, I resumed my formal training. When or where my father had come into contact with Gian Bonconvento, I would never learn. Beside the debt of gratitude owed by a son to his father, I was now more than ever his creature: caged and fed at his expense, enslaved by his ambitious love. Throughout the visit, Gian Bonconvento played the role of kindly patriarch. I had to understand that I was entering a strict creative order. The pursuit of all Great Truths demands abstention from life's shallow pleasures. So, for my talent to flourish, I had to renounce my former life. Contact with family would be restricted, lest the recollection of home life softened my resolve.

'You must abstract yourself from the commonage. It is impossible to serve two masters: God and the World.' The massive, grub-like head descended, eclipsing the rest of Creation. 'Are you prepared to make your pledge?'

'He is prepared.'

'I must ask the boy.'

'Tell him "yes", Tommaso.'

A mouse was scratching at my brain, trying to gnaw its way in. Pressed between allied wills, I burst out: 'Yes! I am prepared!'

A whistling gust of air struck the nape of my neck; it was my father exhaling. Gian Bonconvento, a bloated Atlas

68

righting himself, presented me with his sequined groin. 'Tomorrow,' he said, 'you will begin.'

Our last evening together we spent at the Fenice tavern near San Fedele. I was dazed by events, a year's worth of shocks undergone in a single day. My father also seemed distracted, his eyes restive within a mask of celebration. We had no means of scaling the wall between us and sighed with relief when steaming bowls of *casoeûla* floated through torchlight on to our table. I attacked my portion hungrily. Pork and cabbage and *luganega* sausage dulled my apprehension of the morrow. Bonconvento's dimpled fingers, the cruel glance of Giovanni and Vittorio's vacuous beauty, became benign ciphers in a dissolving dream. I was conscious only of hope reviving, and patted Arcimboldo's letter beneath my shirt as though it were a living thing in need of reassurance.

My father did not seem to share my appetite. Entranced by the steam rising from his bowl, he ruminated on some inner pressure until he could contain it no longer.

'I was apprenticed to a master once. I sweated and bled to get there. No help from *my* father, old Jacopo. *You're going into silk, my boy, make no mistake.* But I got round him. I found a way.'

Stuffing my cheeks with pigskin and noisily sucking wine, I heard for the last time the legend of my father's youth: all the details of his rise and fall, his admittance to and expulsion from the Accademia del Disegno. He had expected, with reason, great joy of his powers. Widowed, a melancholy madness had undone him. Now I, that despite my deformity had inherited his talent, would make amends for my murderous birth.

'No gift is unconditional, boy. God can take it away if you prove unworthy of it.'

By the time I had demolished my meal and scraped from

69

the bowl every trace of cabbage juice, my father's piled helping was beginning to congeal.

'These coincidences.' He sighed, heavy lidded. 'My skills embedded in you. This afternoon I saw Mercury, Giambologna's Mercury, cast in bronze. It might have been my work – perhaps I cast it. Don't you see? These recurring patterns are *intended*. They're God's way of showing us plans . . . that God has plans for us.' The buxom *padrona* caught my father's eye and he belched, with all the gusto of a stage drunk, for more wine.

After emptying his third flagon (peering into its orifice to dislodge a final drop), my father boasted about his accomplishments. 'I trimmed the Grand Duke's beard. I made his hair like God made Adam. Who can say as much? You? Can you? Little pipsqueak.' Intoxicated, he began to quarrel with the shade of his father. He summoned him up in the chair between us; he patted his back with bitter sarcasm and pleaded with him for a little understanding. The wraith of wine (Dionysus's spy, who lives like a jinn in bottles and tugs the hearts of drunkards) moved my father to tearful remorse. 'I went against his will, Tommaso. I was that hungry for fame I tore myself from his grasp . . .' There was an irresistible affinity, a sinking urge, between my father's chin and his arms folded on the table. 'He died before I made peace with him. Ah, if only I could sit him down and tell him. I'd tell him, sit down, Pa – drink with me – all that doesn't matter now . . .' When, with fumbling affection, I tried to ease his grief, he snatched his hand from mine. Something awoke in him, an oracular glare. 'Don't insult me, Tommaso. Never cross me as I crossed my father. The cost to you will be terrible.'

Through tears I tried to speak, to assure him of my devotion. But Anonimo staggered gaseously to his feet. He slapped coins on to the table to pay for our half-consumed meal and – possessed by a defunct gesture – bisected my nose with his raised index finger.

'No dispute,' he said. 'No debate.'

When I walk, loyal reader, I give the impression of a man treading grapes. Seeing me hobble, Gian Bonconvento baptised me '*il Zoppo*' – the cripple. The insult stuck. The other apprentices, angling for favour, took to repeating it in the Maestro's presence. Only timorous Mosca used my proper name, whisperingly. I hated him for it, refusing the offer of his miserable alliance.

One night early in my apprenticeship, sardonic, ginger-freckled Giovanni rustled towards me. We were confined as usual to the outhouse, a mouldering barn without cushions or bedding. 'Do you want to know why they call him Mosca – the fly?' Giovanni's lips were crepitant in the latticed moonlight. I drew close to his stubbled chin, into the ambit of his musical voice.

'Because,' I ventured, 'he's small like a fly?'

'What would that make you – a gnat?'

'I'm bigger than Mosca.'

'You're *older* than Mosca.' I envied Giovanni his sharp tongue. Words gave him an aura of power. 'Have you noticed how they talk between themselves, without moving their mouths?'

The prone brothers stirred and, sighing, resettled. Their limbs were intimately tangled – an octopus dragged across a beach.

'Is it because he doesn't mind what he eats?'

Giovanni spluttered. 'Go on, listen to him sleeping.'

Anxious to please, I crawled through drifts of straw towards the brothers. It was vital to keep my curiosity alive, to stave off despair. For you must know that we could never venture out of Bonconvento's reach. He locked his apprentices inside the barn. We washed ourselves at a drinking-trough that was furred with green scum, we bedded down on greasy straw and gaped in oblivion until daybreak. Only Vittorio was lodged in the villa, as a reward – Giovanni leered – for excellent work.

A bluebottle was buzzing about in the rafters. I searched with useless eyes for the sound's provenance. It was Mosca gibbering in his sleep.

Giovanni sat up when I returned. 'Well?'

'He needs mothering,' I said. 'Can't they be allowed home? Just sometimes? They're so young.'

Giovanni hunched closer: I could smell his hungry, leathery breath. 'Listen, Zoppo. They're dogsbodies. Fundamentally untrainable, the runts of a litter. Ma and Pa were glad to be rid of them.'

'But surely someone's paying for their training?'

'Don't you believe it. We're all slaves here.' I felt the heat of a malicious grin, inches from my lips. 'Try to understand, Zoppo – there's nowhere else for us to go.'

The cultured turner of these pages may well admire Gian Bonconvento: if by that name we mean his works. Fed by the engraver Roelant Schepsel, demand persists for *Samson Blinded* and *Salome's Dance*, while his sweeping crucifixions, cast against tumultuous skies, are greatly prized by the Church. Yet though his art be Christian, his heart was not. A battalion of wrestlers could not have squeezed, from all that mass of blubber, a mite's fart of love. The Maestro, you see, was powered by hatred. I could hear him expectorating at his window in the morning, hawking up great lumps of bile. He shouted at his cook Maria for his breakfast, which was always served late and burned and cold. Stooping on the grass while Vittorio washed him with a sponge, he trumpeted angrily, his slack hairy belly incontinently dribbling. There was a strange security (I would not say comfort) in the constancy of his abuse. We knew, as the bolt across our door shifted, that he would spit and draw a lazy foot across the froth. Then he would cuff each of us about the ear and begin his dawn tirade. He had inspected our efforts of the previous day – were we lepers, with stumps for fingers, to work so badly? Piero and Mosca had dried the oils to cakes in their bowls – perhaps they wanted to eat them for breakfast? And why was I *smirking*? Perhaps I'd prefer to live in the gutter, out on the Corso with tumblers and cripples, since I was evidently of their party? We weathered these storms, looking down at our grass-tigered feet lest our gazes provoked him. Ultimately, we knew, Bonconvento's antipathy towards us could never exceed the loathing he felt for his rivals. 'Fraudsters, the pile of them. Utterly devoid of merit.' Even more hateful were the illustrious dead. It was as though he envied them the completion of their work. They were excused the crusted brush, the goat glue, the daunting contemplation of a virgin panel – and all for what? A vanishing trick. At Leonardo da Vinci, whose *Last Supper* we were permitted to see in the rectory of Santa Maria delle Grazie, Bonconvento could only scoff.

'Painted in tempera. No wonder it's such a blotch. In a century there'll be nothing left to look at.'

Indeed, that poignant scene had badly deteriorated. A resigned and melancholy Christ had only just predicted his betrayal, yet already the frantic denials of his disciples were receding into a sickly mist. Only the food on the white tablecloth retained its freshly baked lustre. The apprentices stared at those insubstantial loaves (whose invisible crumbs fell to my level) and licked their chops.

'Observe, my boys, how genius fails with poor materials. If nothing you paint can last, why bother painting at all?'

Bonconvento shook his head at Our faded Saviour. 'Still, what can you expect, from a *Florentine*?'

The allusion was not lost on the others; they looked at me and mimicked their master's ugly squint. It was worth a second turnip each at supper that evening.

The Maestro, you see, controlled us by a capricious system of punishment and reward. If we pleased him he gave us extra rations, blankets, even dispensations to flash our tongues at the seminarists at Arcivescovile. Our apprentice work was central to this system. Each allotted task was a sign of favour or disgrace – from the manufacture of glue by powdering bone, to the completion of a painting by one's own tremulous hand. Vittorio (with whom, in three years, I cannot have exchanged more than a handful of platitudes) was the workshop spy, reporting on sloth, malice or – to keep us sweet – occasional signs of application. Then Bonconvento would erupt into the workshop with a rod to dispense justice. This took many forms. Beatings left angry welts in the back of one's thighs. Demotion to menial tasks caused simmering resentment. But by far the most dreaded punishment was to be summoned, by a curling dimpled finger, to Bonconvento's villa. Mosca and Piero, trembling bow-legged above a shattered cup, would sob as sentence was pronounced and had to be dragged by Vittorio to their unspeakable appointment. Only my utter lack of physical beauty spared me from a similar fate; while Giovanni, smearing himself with grease from the membrane of pig's bladder used to cover oil paints, cultivated protective boils about his grippable neck.

In spite of this intimidation, my craft made excellent progress. I discovered that I was a natural mimic, capable of handling paint in a fashion indistinguishable from Bonconvento. It was a simple trick – like putting on another man's voice – but it gained me the Maestro's wary attention.

Perhaps he saw in me the dreamed-of shadow self: one who could lift from his bullock's shoulders the terrible burden of work. So he kept me in the workshop long after my peers had been packed off to Maria and a cheerless supper. He acquainted me with various cheats of the painter's craft. I learned how to transfer a drawing to a panel by placing a sheet of paper coated in black chalk between the two and tracing the outlines with a stylus. For the study of drapery, he taught me how to soak cloth in clay slip so that, in hardening, it might preserve the happy accidents of the folds. (The heavy drowned cloth was thrown over an articulated figure. Art's scarecrow, it caused me to start whenever I entered the workshop.) I understood that I should keep these sessions with Bonconvento a secret. In the daytime I worked, like the others, as an assistant. When the Maestro (with my unacknowledged help) completed a painting on parchment, it was our onerous task to mount the work. The dread of making a mistake gnawed at our innards: you can imagine how, going at six weeks' work with a flat iron, the hands feel huge and loath. There was a danger, as we dried the adhesive paste, of scorching the parchment, and I recall one incident, when a papilla of flesh tone smouldered on the Maddalèna's breast, how Mosca (who was not even responsible) fainted into his brother's arms. We stood for inspection about the mounted work, braced for disaster. But Gian Bonconvento never noticed a thing. Boredom and the complacency of natural talent saw to that. If a problem vexed him, he fell back on figures of conventional taste. Strict study from Nature wearied him. He refused to use female models for female figures, obliging his favourite to pose instead. Thus, beneath her virginal blue, the blessed Mary bought by the Borromeo family is really Vittorio Monza grinning at a sack of hay; as for Lucrezia, transfixed on her honour-salving

75

blade, she began as a naked boy clutching a straw to his chest.

The significance of these gender transformations was clear. Bonconvento had the power of a god over our lives.

It was an instruction disguised as permission – coercion with an implacable smile. Bonconvento one morning, with cherried breath (coquettishly pulling and popping his fingers), made it clear he would not object to my bedding down in the workshop, far from my nocturnal straw. This would keep me at my devotions: it would cut the rind from the meat of my day. So I curled up beneath a blanket in the empty space and averted my eyes from its poised shadows. Every sound was a heart-stopper, a thawed portrait creaking to life. I imagined the Maestro lying in bed: his belly swollen to spherical, his buttocks bruised like a peach, a fly scaling a bristled thigh, a flaccid penis basking. Relieved of his responsibilities, he sauntered late into the orchard and released the boys to void their pent-up bladders. Then he rolled into the workshop, where (alerted by his elephantine tread) I had resumed my work.

'No, *no*. The light strikes from behind. Paris's armour is too dun.' Selecting an ermine brush, he gathered his manifold chins in his hand. A callous dab of white lead, huffily smudged; an appraising backward step, balletically mimicked by his apprentice. 'The Trojan seems unfazed by his judgement, do you not think? Let us see a little dread. And a touch of vermilion, I think, on Venus's cheek . . .'

Reasonably, given my efforts to please, I might have expected to meet with universal favour. Yet Bonconvento was troubled by my too easy imitation of his grandiose style, while the apprentices hated the increase in his affections. Only Giovanni showed me some kindness. He continued, despite my entreaties, to call me Zoppo; yet there was a new regard for me in his eyes, a hint of wariness in the folds of his mirth, etched by the fact of my talent. He with his wit and I with my brush fancied ourselves immune to our condition. One afternoon we sat with our backs to a weeping resinous cherry and agreed that our stay at Bonconvento's villa was entirely voluntary: an accord that we might toss aside whenever it pleased us.

Months passed and Giovanni became my friend – the first, of my own age, I had ever had – though I only considered him as such after he spoke the word of *me*. 'Zoppo,' he whispered, 'I must take a dump. Come and squat with me.' I blushed at such peasant manners; but Giovanni scoffed at my discomfort. 'Oh now, come on. If friends can't shit together, what's the use of them?'

Leaning with our backs against the workshop wall, we engaged in privy conversation. (I strained without success, cupping my hands about my bashful member, while Giovanni sighed and admired the distant Duomo spires.) Bare buttocked, we ambled down paths of yearning conjecture, conjuring sylphs with soft hands and pink mouths who, following months in a manless desert, fastened themselves like limpets to our desire. Giovanni, being older than me and more seemly, made great play of his alleged conquests. I kept to myself my own encounter with a blue-veined breast. Like flotsam to a man at sea, the intimate secret kept my spirits afloat.

I was working on the Maestro's Last Judgement when Giovanni finally confessed to envying my facility. I nearly fell from my stool at this most disarming of compliments. It was his idea – fluttering like a moth from his mind to mine – for me to paint myself among the Damned, a tiny crouching figure with the tools of his trade rammed between his buttocks. Henceforth as I tucked and nipped, a demonic tailor, the sinful flesh of my inventions, Giovanni urged me to conspire with him in a scheme to gull our master.

'Do you know, Tommaso, what work he's undertaking next?'

'I don't want to know.'

'The Annunciation.'

'Please, Giovanni. Whatever you're brewing, don't tell me. I've no desire to be your accomplice.'

'But Zoppo, where's the danger? You know the fat ass would kill to keep you.'

I refused to listen, shaking my head and scowling. For all his imperfections (my cautious angel told me), Gian Bonconvento was an instrument of my destiny. With no better life to escape to, it pleased me to imagine my (unattributed) Last Judgement hanging in a church at Bergamo: my secret and fabulous portrait, hidden amid the tumult of wretched souls, goading the worshippers to their knees.

'I know what the trouble is.' Giovanni smirked. 'You believe the Maestro will give you credit for your work. In the end, for this drudgery, there'll be a reward in Heaven.'

'He cannot deny my part in his paintings.'

'Because he's such an honest bugger?'

I fought against these provocations; but Giovanni was resourceful in persuasion. He smuggled from the villa a list of Bonconvento's paintings, which I studied with febrile fingers.

price in florins		_size in feet_
400 fl.	Leda and the Swan. Original by my hand.	4 x 3
500 fl.	The ecstasy of St Teresa, life size,	7 x 4

estimated one of my finest paintings.

| 900 fl. | Mary Magdalene bare chested and repentant, painted by me, after an original by my own hand in the possession of Fedrico Borromeo Archbishop of Milan. | 7 x 9 |

| 600 fl. | Venus, naked, with Adonis, begun by one of my pupils after a picture painted by me for the Palazzo Durini, completed by myself. | 6 x 8 |

| 800 fl. | A Judgement of Paris, very elegant with many beautiful girls, painted by one of my pupils but entirely retouched by my hand. | 8 x 12 |

| 900 fl. | The Torment of the Damned, with many piteous naked sinners, original by my hand. | 7 x 14 |

Having read – and reread – the Maestro's half-truths and untruths and outright lies, I let the scroll curl up and fall to the floor. Giovanni knew how to rouse an artist.

'Are you proposing, by any chance,' I said, 'that we cut off his balls?'

The crate contained a wax corpse. We picked the straw from its bronzed limbs; we dressed it in sumptuous cerecloth and tried to right it on its feet. 'No, no, no! Don't stand him up. He's the Archangel.' The Maestro conjured with reverential fingers two swannish wings projecting from the shoulder blades. He showed us the cartoon with which he had instructed the model's sculptor (my heart skipped and then sank at the meaningless name). It depicted Gabriel descending from Heaven to announce the Virgin Birth – his seraphic fingers indicating the highly favoured womb. In the manner of Tintoretto (whose Jove and cherubs converge, through starless space, upon a spurting breast) Bonconvento planned to suspend the model from the rafters, so that the forms, transposed to canvas, might delight the eye. Giovanni asked:

'And who will represent Mary?'

Vittorio shuddered and stepped with tremulous toes into his old costume. His Madonna's cell consisted of a cherrywood lectern, unglued from cobwebs in San Babila's crypt; an accounts ledger masquerading as devotional reading; a neat and narrow bed with a Persian rug oversheet and plump embroidered cushions; a kneeling-cushion for prayer; and the requisite vase of white-throated lilies. For backdrop we had only the stone wall itself, upon which Bonconvento had scuffed the outline of a window, whence the Holy Spirit, in a dove-transpiercing shaft, would strike the Virgin's brow. At last, with Vittorio in place, it was time to suspend the model. (Being made of frangible wax it was not life size. But then who is to dictate angelic proportions?) Mosca and Piero atop a ladder threaded rope through the cross-beams, while Giovanni, gaping below, captured the dancing ends. It was a business fraught with strain: to find the correct angle of elevation. The model's feet had to be twenty degrees higher than the head, so we strung one rope across its thorax, another to its waist (the figure was held together by a spine of lead piping), and two more about the ankles. It was a cumbersome archangel that ended the day swaying gently from the rafters, its counterweight three terracotta pots filled with orchard soil.

'Well done, my boys.' The Maestro levered himself off his

seat. 'Vittorio, you may undress now. I shall start to paint tomorrow.'

In the genial aftermath of our labours, while Piero and Mosca sat panting and the Maestro, pretending to tamper with props, ogled the nakedness of his darling, Giovanni crouched low beside the counterweights. I caught his sly glance as he clawed, from the pot, a handful of earth and allowed the dark threads to spill through his fingers.

Weeks passed in (not unhappy) industry. Bonconvento sketched and painted, smothering with amorphous flesh his seat of voluted marble. He concentrated on the figures and their clothes, while I attended to the cell and the alpine view beyond. Giovanni and the brothers slaved to produce our materials, grinding pigments on a porphyry slab, while Vittorio as the Virgin nodded to sleep, lulled by the soft industry of brushes, by the smell of linseed and walnut oils and by the Archangel Gabriel creaking on his rafters.

Your brave conspirators toyed at first with the idea of cutting the ropes: slicing tendon from tendon until the lot snapped. But this was too dangerous. Arriving after the disaster, Bonconvento would guess our guilt immediately. 'We need it to seem like an accident,' whispered Giovanni. 'I have an idea.' We drilled a hole in one of the counterweight pots, trying to make it look natural. How we snorted and giggled, Giovanni drilling while I kept watch at the workshop door. The earth in the pots had dried to powder: it seeped slowly, so that Bonconvento on his return (supported by Vittorio and the brothers) suspected nothing.

The painting by now was progressing well, its underdrawn participants patched with bright colours. The dove of the Holy Spirit which, stuffed and suspended, was beginning to moult, looked bright and divine by my intercession. Trembling with trepidation, I was adding filigree to the Madonna's dress when

I felt Giovanni's fingers on my shoulder. Was he restraining me, or fighting to keep his own resolve?

An hour passed, then a second. A scudding fly patrolled the dusty rafters. Gian Bonconvento was squinting at a crust of paint on his thumb when the Archangel stirred. It was barely perceptible at first: a gentle rocking. The outstretched fingers indicated Vittorio's belly, then his groin – his groin, then his lap – his lap, then his knees. Piero, witnessing a miracle, cried out in wonder and Giovanni, moving to stop his mouth, nearly kicked over a stool.

'What *is* going on?' Bonconvento demanded. 'Can't you brats be still for an instant?'

'But mice . . . but mice . . .'

'Piero, you must master your bladder. Be patient while I finish.'

At that instant the Archangel fell. The legs jerked, still attached. The head and arm struck the stone floor. Vittorio, snorting horribly awake, kicked the lectern and sent the ledger flying.

Giovanni said: 'Jesus.'

The model's face, which the sculptor had not troubled to finish, was crushed, its nose an imprint of a nose, its forehead savagely cracked. As for the arm, it lay severed from the torso, its lead bone gruesomely exposed and the fingers bent at an obscene angle.

Bonconvento arose unaided, his fury constricted by surprise. The pot floated above the ground, trailing ballast like ashes from its base. I watched as Bonconvento cupped his hand and caught the soil. 'Who?' he whispered. Boiled eggs simmered in his head; he glowed as red as a beet. 'Who did this?' No fool, he scanned his workshop for the culprit.

Giovanni gave himself away. It began as a tremor deep in his guts; it travelled down his arm and into his hand, which rested on my shoulder. I tried to slide away from that incriminating touch. Giovanni's laughter burst like a stop from a bottle, a riotous cachinnation. I told myself that this was the end, the annulment of my senseless life, while Mosca peered at the puddle slowly gathering at his feet.

'Giovanni *malvagio*!' (The Maestro ran the words together, as though 'wicked' were a family name.) 'You will meet me in my quarters.'

Giovanni wiped the corners of his eyes. 'I will not.'

'I beg your pardon? What did you say?'

'I will not meet you in your filthy quarters.'

'You will do as you are told.'

'I will not.'

Gian Bonconvento's flesh gathered into a quivering rage. Seizing a pestle (the very pestle Giovanni had wielded when first I met him), he smacked it hard into his palm. 'If you value your life, you will obey me.'

'You'll pound me, will you?'

'I'll pound you.'

'With your little pestle?'

The Virgin Mary advised gravely: 'Giovanni, do as he says.'

'Yes,' begged Piero and Mosca. 'Please don't upset him!'

Bonconvento advanced implacably with the pestle raised. Cowering in shadow, I understood that deep scars were being opened between the Maestro and his apprentice. I was a trespasser in a private feud, ignorant until too late of its ancient pedigree.

'I despise you,' said Giovanni, holding his ground. 'I've *always* despised you.'

'What? From the instant they dumped you at my door?'

'You're a monster.'

'Hark, the prodigal bastard! You don't know how lucky you are. I should have drowned you like a runt in a sack. I rescued you from poverty.'

'I'm twice the artist you'll ever be.'

A scream of warning presaged the assault. (Bruising custom had taught Vittorio the reflexes of his master's violence.) Gian Bonconvento's arm blurred and Giovanni crumpled. I thought he was struck in the chest from the way he folded.

Everything froze, like Creation at the instant of its Fall. Then Bonconvento staggered, deflating like a bladder. The pestle hatched from his fist and fell to the ground. 'Look what you've done,' he murmured. 'What have you done?' Listing as though drunk, he drifted towards the door. Vittorio and the brothers followed, running, to placate him – leaving me alone with the injured Giovanni.

Rocking slowly on the floor, he huffed and groaned, a tendril of drool expanding from his lower lip. 'I won't tell on you,' he said. 'I won't tell him about you, if that's what you're afraid of.'

'I'm not afraid.'

Giovanni moaned. I thought of the noise Mosca made when sleeping.

'What did he hit?'

'Me.'

'Are you bleeding?'

'I don't know.'

'What is it? A rib, is it? Has he bruised a rib?'

Giovanni snorted and shook his head. Gently rocking, he slowly lifted his right hand – his painting hand.

'What?' I said. '*Three* ribs?'

Only then did I see that his fingers were broken.

*

It was the end of Giovanni's life as an artist. Clutching his shattered hand, he left Bonconvento's workshop the following morning. A few florins were slipped by a shameful

84

Maestro into his pockets; Giovanni seemed unaware of the gift. All the while I hid behind Vittorio and the brothers.

And so I lost my only friend. I had not dared to plead on his behalf, or joined him in defiance by admitting my part in the prank. I told myself, as he walked away, that I was innocent of betrayal. Surely Giovanni had hated the life laid out for him. Was it not a welcome release, the desired end of his rebellion? I was barely involved in what had taken place – a spectator only.

I was only ever looking on.

My first escape was a fleeting affair.

I awoke on the morning after Giovanni's departure unable to make sense of my surroundings. I could not remember why I was in this place, sweating to enhance a stranger's reputation. Was I not born a free man, with a man's freedom to walk wherever he pleases?

Easing open the workshop door, I slipped into the dawn. The world felt unpeopled and renewed. A soft mist smelling of mushrooms clung to the orchard grass; the villa's terrace glistened with snail-dew. I crept beneath Bonconvento's shuttered window, intending to return before breakfast. Why, I berated myself, did I feel almost happy as I greeted the storks keeping watch on San Babila? Slipping on to the Corso di Porta Orientale, where already local farmers were unloading their crops, I expected the prone snoring lumps in doorways to jolt awake and toss their daggers at me. But the beggars clung needily to their dreams and I returned to Milan barely noticed. Winding my way, with a floating head, through familiar streets, I knew that I was attempting the impossible – trying to re-enter my past, to climb back into the womb of it.

On the Piazza Santo Stefano, my father's building was catching on its yellow face the first rays of the rising sun.

I tried the communal entrance and found the door locked; so calmly I retreated to the wall of the chapel and waited for the city to waken.

During that short wait, I rehearsed a plea to my father. I pictured him unaltered after three years, as though I had been gone a few hours only, down by the canal docks, say, or skulking about the abandoned Hunting Gardens. He smiled at me and opened his arms and sat me down to eat his breakfast, an egg hard boiled. He asked me what I had learned from Gian Bonconvento, and was I grateful for his foresight in sending me to him? I nodded my head while stuffing it with egg and watered wine. Could I be released, *papà*? Now that I was a man – in all but stature – and trained in the art of painting, could I be released from all those duties that prevented me from *being*?

The instant the door of our building opened, I recognised her. She was our neighbour's wife, a compact little woman with breasts tucked high like a portable shelf, whose scolding voice we used to hear on the landing. I ran with slapping sandals to meet her. 'Signora, signora, please, let me into the building.'

Overcoming her startlement – and then a compensatory urge to pat my head – she wrinkled her nose in recognition. 'Don't I know you?'

'Tommaso Grilli. I'm your neighbour.'

'Ah?'

'I've come back.'

'So I see.'

'To spend my fortune.'

'Oh, but not *here*, signorino? We've got rats. (Well you remember the cockroaches.) I found one on the stairs. Oh, it was horrible. Tail like a snake. Are you *sure* you want to move back in?'

'My . . . my father's expecting me.'

86

'Oh, is he with you?'

'I'm sorry?'

'Because he seemed so sick of Milan. When you shut up shop my husband went over and wished him luck.'

'Wished him luck? Where?'

'On the landing.'

'No, I mean . . . luck for what?'

'Well my dear, didn't you just say—?'

'He's *gone*?' (I think, to keep myself from falling, I must have gripped her skirt.) '*When*, signora – when did this happen?'

'I thought you said he was with you?'

'Tell me where he went!'

Panic, like yawning, catches on the air. The signora's voice rose in harmony with mine. 'I don't know, I don't know anything,' she cried.

'Please, please – before I *explode* – where did my father say he was going?'

Thin lipped and blanching, the signora was backing away towards the door. 'I, I . . . I don't know . . .' The key glinted in her hand; she fumbled it home. 'I'd better ask my husband. He's upstairs, I'll find him.'

I knotted my fingers in my hair – I slapped my brow.

'Please,' said the signora. 'We don't want any trouble.' Deftly she hopped the chasm between step and open doorway. 'I don't know where your father went. He just took his equipment and left.'

The door swung shut and a bolt slid before I could leap to catch it. In response to my pounding of her door, the signora faintly apologised. Then she must have slipped away into the cool grotto of the house. I repeated my question to a shimmering flock of doves.

Where had my father gone?

* * *

87

If I had not escaped Milan a stowaway, I might have learned the answer from Bonconvento. But you, swift reader, would gladly cast Anonimo Grilli aside. It is *my* story that sweeps you along. Therefore let me tell you how I escaped from bondage.

Three months after the breaking of Giovanni's fingers, the Annunciation was finished and gold paint drying on the Virgin's gloriole. One bright September morning, the apprentices (none of whom addressed me since 'the accident') began hurriedly to tidy the workshop. Bonconvento puffed and sighed with excitement. 'Zoppo,' he said. 'Zoppo, we have a visitor coming.'

'A customer, Maestro?'

'A buyer. Straight from Bohemia.'

I blurted stupidly: 'The Emperor's coming here?'

'His *agent*, you cretin. I permit you to stay, if you keep your deformity out of sight. I want you to see the range of my connections.'

The brothers and Vittorio (whose beauty, with the turn of summer, was beginning to coarsen) fled at the rumble of wheels and horses outside. I rushed to my folded mattress and slipped Arcimboldo's letter beneath my shirt; then hid behind the Judgement of Paris just moments before the agent entered. He was short and stout, quizzically eyebrowed, with a fashionable beard and a black, disorderly nest of hair. His sharp eyes appraised the workshop swiftly, and twice I feared he glimpsed me behind the canvas.

'Signor Bonconvento, it is an honour to make your acquaintance.' The agent's Milanese was flawless. Thrusting forth a cross-gartered leg, he bowed low, trailing an ostrich-feathered cap.

'The honour is mine, Signor Merrick . . .' (The agent sniffed.) '. . . to serve in my humble capacity his Imperial Majesty your master.'

'His Majesty honours Signor Bonconvento and instructs me to express his admiration for the Maestro's considerable artistry . . .'

Reader, assume a continuation in this vein. I guessed that the list of paintings which Giovanni had shown me months ago had been written for this Merrick. 'So this is the completed work,' the agent said. Muttering obscurely, he chewed a knuckle and gestured with his other hand at details that pleased him. Lumpen beside his customer, obsequious Bonconvento wheezed. I crept unnoticed behind their backs and escaped into the orchard.

The Bohemian agent was travelling in a carriage laden with sacks and boxes. Horses rested beneath the cherry trees, crunching grass and shedding quantities of dung. Erotic reveries must have drifted through one blinkered head, causing a phallus to stretch like a mollusc from its shell. Farther off, a small guard of soldiers dressed in Habsburg livery sat playing cards, their pikes and standards resting on their laps. Nauseated by hope, I hauled myself into the carriage, crawled beneath its canvas and hid among the luggage. It was hot inside, with leather and oilcloth giving off a stuffy odour and barely a crack to breathe through.

Dulled by the heat, I must have dozed off.

I awoke with an inward fall to find the carriage moving. My body felt the gradient; I could hear the tramp of horses' hoofs. With movements covered by the noise, I managed to dislodge a crate and peep through the canvas flap. I looked without success for a trace of Milan in that unstable crack. I thought I heard Bonconvento calling me but it might have been anything – a croaking wheel, or cattle lowing.

By nightfall we had reached the foothills of the Alps. The cool air gripped me by the throat. I needed sorely to pee.

My difficulties were solved when a soldier's blind hand found me instead of his supper. I was dragged out of hiding, my feet bumping behind me, and interrogated in a strange language punctuated with slaps until Merrick the agent intervened. There was an exchange, incomprehensible to my buzzing ears, between the art collector and the captain of the guard. Then rough hands relinquished me and Merrick spoke.

'Why were you hiding in the carriage? Were you thieving?'

'I must go with you to Bohemia,' I said.

'We don't take runaways. Where are your parents?'

'I am a grown man, sir, of nineteen years.' Somebody scoffed. 'I'm an artist. The Emperor wants to meet me.'

'Does he indeed?'

'I know he will.' The captain of the guard – a grim bluff of armour – was itching to boot me off the mountainside. He pleaded for permission but my interrogator hesitated. He eyed me as he had the Annunciation, with wary interest. 'I was trained by Count Arcimboldo,' I said. 'He wrote me a letter to present to the Emperor.'

'This crumpled piece of trash?'

'It's his, I swear.'

He turned the letter over, nearly lifting it to his nose for a sniff. He begged a soldier for the use of his lantern and scrutinised the seal.

'The gentleman does not lie,' he said, adding a magic formula that set the guards at ease. 'I don't know where you've sprung from – and I ought to send you packing. But I do know this seal and the hand is unmistakable.' He crouched peasant-fashion on velveted knees. 'My name is Jaroslav Vavřinec Meyrink. I collect art for the Emperor Rudolf. What, young sir, does the world call *you*?'

5

The Flayed Man

The Emperor Rudolf sat on a chair with his ear to the brim of the Singing Fountain. The musical thrumming of water on the basin delighted him, and he required of his courtiers that they bow reverently to listen. When all had concurred for a hundredth time at the marvel of the thing, the Emperor arose – flapping his fingers at necessary assistance – and set off to patrol his gardens.

I saw little of Vertumnus in that great-jawed, puggish figure. Servants, courtiers and guardsmen surrounded him: a scurrying affirmation of the solitude of State. Try as I might, I could not penetrate that obsequious throng. It crossed a path and entered the flower garden, where elegant ladies sank in a surf of lilies, lowering their eyes at the imperial presence. Rudolf was heading for his Lion House: former stables which housed not only the pacing, flame-headed lion but also a bear and two arthritic leopards. Parrots, gaudy as tumblers and almost as agile, were tethered by golden chains to cherry trees. I walked beneath them, ingesting the dust of their feathers in an ecstasy of sneezing. When I recovered, I found myself alone in the flower garden, watching with stupid streaming eyes the two halberdiers standing guard at the gate. A hand settled on my shoulder. It made me gasp with fright. But when I saw the hand – so hairy that it seemed to be gloved – and connected it to its owner, my shock subsided. 'My God,' I said. 'Creeping up on me like that. Are you trying to *kill* me?'

The werewolf frowned: he was not given to figurative speech. 'Quite the contrary,' he said.

I had left him outside the Ball Game Hall, frustrated at my lack of progress towards the Emperor. A keen horticulturist, he had been admiring a plant whose name, either in German or Italian or Spanish, was unknown to him, when the royal party had appeared. 'Everyone must wait his turn to see the Emperor,' he said. 'Ambassadors, gentlemen of the Estates. The rules that apply to them apply also to you.'

'But it's been almost a *year*.'

'Simply to stand in his presence is an honour.'

'What's the use, if I can't talk to him?'

'One never talks *to* the Emperor.'

A gust of sycophantic laughter swept the courtyard. It bounded off the aviary where forlorn dodos scrabbled, it glanced off the house where the ape they called the Orange Man sprawled, languid as a starfish. The Emperor was tossing titbits to his lion.

'Do not fret,' the werewolf said. 'We're getting closer. At this rate, you may meet his Chamberlain before the century ends.'

In its cell, the lion disconsolately roared. I forced a hollow laugh. The werewolf, you see, was not joking.

*

Nine months earlier I had entered Prague under cover of darkness: the double darkness of night and sleep. The carriage, of which I occupied a damp corner, shuddered to a halt, and I opened my eyes on Jaroslav Meyrink shaking my knee. I should explain that I was rambling in a feverish fog, the consequence of drenching thunderstorms endured between Pilsen (where our wheels got stuck in mud) and Karlstein. Soldiers whispered in tremulous torchlight. A voice like my own said:

'Giovanni?'

'No, you're dreaming. Wake up, you must get down.'

With an automaton's obedience I clambered from the carriage. We stood in dung and wet straw. Meyrink beckoned me through puddles into a muddy courtyard. Coins were dropped into a calloused palm and I was led up a creaking staircase into a low-ceilinged attic. Looking for Meyrink in the penumbra, I heard his voice muffled as though coming from behind a door. I was to wait here for instructions, it said. In time a messenger would come to collect me. I swooned in a bed pelleted with dust and asked wisps of cobweb the questions that I should have put to Meyrink.

In the morning, bells and lowing woke me. A harvestman crawled out from under my sheets on angular threads. I fled barefoot to the window and, balancing on a wobbly stool, pushed back the shutter. Instead of towers and palaces, I saw only drab, ramshackle houses in a mist. The square below was a cattle market: the country come to town. Already it was bustling with stock, with peasants wearing their caps awry and buyers prodding the flanks of cattle. From near by wafted the abominable stink of herring, so high and salty that no head-cold could protect me from it.

The fat innkeeper with a wen on his scalp brought me a skin of broth in a bowl. To my dumbshow enquiries he replied that his inn was called U Kachna – 'At the Duck'. I was to spend ten days here, a prisoner to expectation. How I ached and groaned to explore the city, even briefly, to put stony flesh on its notional skeleton. Yet I dared not leave the inn for fear of missing the messenger. Occasionally, when the rain eased off, I ventured as far as the narrow courtyard where, dusty lunged, I gulped the pungent air. Once, finding the courage to tempt impish Chance, I paced a few yards alongside dusky houses and glimpsed the New Town Hall with a skyline of grey and golden towers beyond. I tried to imagine Meyrink working my cause at the Castle but my faith was gone. Finally, impelled by the evaporation of my benefactor's funds, I made my own way into Prague, equipped with Arcimboldo's commendation.

The bell tower of St Vitus cathedral would be my beacon. I tried not to scurry, concerned for my dignity, through the market's competing smells. On a wide thoroughfare (whose purpose was to sweep away the stench of herring) a few youths were kicking the life out of an inflated bladder. I fled from malicious jeers when the ball was booted into my path and I ridiculed myself attempting to return it.

Hurrying on, I emerged from houses on to the bank of a swollen river, and hearing Milanese spoken beneath a portico I asked for directions. A bald, almost identical pair of merchants with warts on opposite sides of their multiple chins thought my question very stupid. I feared for a wild second that they recognised me from my performing past; but I was no more real to them than they to me, and they pointed me glumly northwards.

The Stone Bridge which spans the Moldau is sentinelled by two towers. Citizens bustled me under the archway of the sombre original on to the great sweep of the bridge, where they crossed themselves in passing before a lonely crucifix. Seeing the Castle on its gardened seat above Kleinseite, the Little Quarter, I swallowed the fizzing juice of apprehension. Sheets of bleached linen danced on apple boughs on Kampa Island. I heard the chatter of mill wheels in the mill race. Soldiers at the Customs House waved people by, keeping in suspense a ragged and moustached man whose battered casket, opened upon a table, revealed rows of coloured phials. On Bridge Street I saw finches cramped in wickerwork cages, knives displayed like gathered shells in hawkers' laps, cakes and sweetmeats and plaited bread, carp plopping in barrels, hand-carved madonnas, Calvinist pamphlets curling from trays, tallow candles with tapers to light them, a purblind urchin gnawing at a jew's harp, young girls with smudged

94

faces selling wild flowers whose roots, still spilling earth, curled from their fists, a busker beating time with a tabor while a pug at his heel wheezed into a flute, an apothecary proclaiming the miraculous properties of currant-coloured water to a sparse and sceptical audience. Through a gap in the houses I glimpsed royal trees changing to rust and ochre, and antique ramparts defending the structures that dwarfed them. I felt a gentle incline, as though the Castle had foundations which rucked up the earth. Short of breath near the summit, with a chemical burn in my chest, I admired a grand palace decorated to resemble a Florentine palazzo, and stumbled to a halt a few yards from the gatehouse.

To my dismay the Castle Square was awash with vagrants. They gathered about the gates with their hands cupped as though testing for rain. I was to experience intimately the proximity of wealth to poverty in this, the political hub of the Empire: *Pragus capit regni*. Brandishing my letter of commendation, I was unable to express my purpose, the sentries speaking only German and scatological Czech.

'*Pittoro sum,*' I said. 'Endorsement *hic, Rudolfus rex.*'

The two soldiers took the trouble (an artistic flourish, this) of pretending to make an effort to understand me; they nodded and stroked their beards and wheeled me about to face the Archbishop's Palace. No doubt I was not looking my best, caked in clothes so old they must have seemed a mangy skin. A brutal kick in my seat (they dared where once a Spaniard wilted) sent Arcimboldo's letter shooting from my fingers. It glanced off a cobble-stone on a previously battered edge.

The seal was broken like a scab.

Beneath the shedding boughs of a chestnut tree, I waited for night to fall. Finally the watch was changed and I tried my luck with a fresh sentry.

'*Ich bin amigo* Meyrink,' I said. The sentry fixed me in the prong of his squint. 'Jaroslav Vavřinec Meyrink? Oh, *bitte*, you bastard.'

The autumn air chilled – it grew its frosty crystals beneath my skin. Murmuring in German, the cross-eyed sentry waved me away. So I spent the night in the open, eking out the laggardly minutes, snarled at by suspicious beggars.

Before dawn the heavens opened, shaking out their slops. Pressing against the chestnut's trunk, I watched as vagrants grumbled from their sleep. In the grey hatching of the rain they looked like animated mushrooms. I watched, in despair of rescue, as carts of provisions lumbered through the Castle gates with horses nodding and peasants clutching at their cloaks. I rubbed my streaming eyes and looked again at the two figures detaching themselves from the vaporous shards. In the fore was the squinting sentry, with a familiar gentleman behind him.

'Signor Grilli?'

'*Yes*.'

'Signor Grilli, come out of the rain.'

'All right.'

Jaroslav Vavřinec Meyrink flourished his sodden panache. 'You have this fellow to thank for your rescue,' he said. The sentry blinked, puffing droplets off the tip of his nose, and to my surprise he swept a blanket about my shoulders. Now, with Meyrink in the lead, we pattered towards shelter. I was indebted to the heavy rain for disguising my grateful tears.

Crossing the drawbridge of the Castle, we entered the front courtyard, where the sentry peeled away to reassume his duties. As a guest who, ushered towards a gleaming feast, is vexingly pulled aside to a frugal broth, I was presented with handsome palaces only to end up in the royal stables. There I dripped in a murky storeroom – a sort of mausoleum for correspondences. Damp logs spat and fizzled in the fireplace; glumly we exposed ourselves to their feeble heat.

'You must be hungry,' said Meyrink. Without meeting my eye he delivered a loaf of rye bread from its cloth and deposited a cold hunk of mutton in my hands. To compensate for our silence, I grunted contentedly.

We had not forged a close friendship in our month's travels. Across the Alps, through Bavaria and Nuremberg into Bohemia, Jaroslav Meyrink had slept at roadside inns while I crouched in his carriage among the shuttered paintings. He worried, I think, that he had robbed Bonconvento of his assistant. Yet Meyrink of the Castle was even less jovial than his travelling predecessor.

'I have brought you as far as Prague,' he said, 'where you desired to come. But I cannot take responsibility for you – do you understand? The world is a harsh place. You must consider the lilies of the valley . . .'

'Yes?'

'Horses eat them.'

I digested this information as best I could. 'Have you organised a meeting for me with the Emperor?'

Meyrink wheezed sarcastically. He scrutinised his feet, placing them heel to toe. 'I *have* secured you brief employment. Now don't get excited, for Heaven's sake. Yes, yes. Your hand is greasy.'

Having advised me to wipe the corners of my mouth, he escorted me through unanticipated corridors to meet the Court Painter, Bartholomeus Spranger.

'*Ein Augenblick!*'

A gentleman stood with his back to us, facing an open casement. He shook himself while we averted our eyes and was a long time fastening the flap of his breeches. Then he turned and strode forward with arms outstretched as though to embrace me. I found myself palpated, tousled by powerful hands, studied in the mouth.

Bartholomeus Spranger, although aged, remained a potent figure. I was impressed by the deep furrows etched by concentration into his brow. White curls of hair peeped from a red velvet cap pushed high on his head; yet the beard, despite its wearer's age, remained sparse, a peppery fluff about sensuous lips whence emanated a reek of almonds. 'Very good. Yes, yes, Herr Meyrink – he will do perfectly.' (This much German I could understand.) I asked Meyrink whether he wished to see a demonstration of my skills; but already the painter was upturning papers and coughing and extracting shards of charcoal from his waistcoat.

'When he's finished,' whispered Meyrink above my ear, 'make sure that he pays you.'

'What am I supposed to be doing?'

Bartholomeus Spranger beckoned me deeper into the room. Jaroslav Meyrink, unacknowledged by his colleague, bade us good day and withdrew. I was alone with the maniac.

'Lie down please,' Spranger said in my own tongue, 'next to the skull.'

'Whatever for?'

'Sprawl across it – like so. Try not to kick the plaque.'

'This board?'

'It is a plaque.'

'What does it say?'

'Cabbages, two halers a pound. But in the *painting* it will say: today me, tomorrow you. What . . . what are you doing?'

'I'm . . . I'm lying on the skull.'

'But you are *dressed*. Take off your clothes.'

Reader, I would have paid you not to laugh. Reluctantly peeling off my damp garments – which exhaled in the rending a mortifying stink – I folded them as best I could across the back of a chair. Bartholomeus Spranger, preparing a small study canvas, plucked pins like spare teeth from his mouth and looked up every few seconds at my humiliation. Suppressing shivers, in gooseflesh, with my nether regions shrinking, I reassured myself that there was neither malice nor perversion in those glances. Spranger's expression was familiar to me from having worn it often myself. It had about it the bland observance of a mirror.

The small painting for which I served as model was to be a *vanitas* – a meditation on mutability. Your humbled narrator, doubling as a corpulent boy, leans across a chop-fallen skull and indicates an hourglass with his sinister hand. To the viewer's right, where the literate eye must, by force of habit, founder, a plaque spells out the allegory: *Hodie Mihi Cras Tibi.*

In this fashion my likeness was fixed for a posterity which poets please to call eternal. The resemblance was only partial. The face, for instance, leered in a manner not yet native; the scalp, shorn of my Semitic fuzz, was topped with the golden locks of a cherub. My manhood, let it be noted, is more substantial than that impish pipette.

Bartholomeus Spranger, as he worked, was in the habit of eating almonds which he kept in a pewter bowl at his elbow. This involved no vacuous suck but rather a steady process of attrition, provoking sonorous cracks from his hard-set jaw like the implacable tightening of a bolt. It set my own teeth aching. But Spranger was oblivious to my discomfiture. Only when we stopped for lunch did I regain my autonomy, escaping the inanimation of a studied object.

'Tell me,' he said, 'where are you making your stay in Prague?'

'I have nowhere to stay.'

'Then you must stay here. Yes, yes – until I have finished.'

We assembled a mattress from sooty cushions. Bartholomeus Spranger would bring me meals of bread and cheese and apples. Forbidden to explore my surroundings (indeed, the door was locked at night), I would pass the time in Spranger's workshop admiring his sketches for the forthcoming painting. Whatever became of the end product in Bohemia's subsequent catastrophes, I cannot say. Perhaps it was sold off by Rudolf's successors to finance their dishonourable reigns, or by the Winter King to pay for his defeat at the Battle of White Mountain? It could be that the painting was destroyed; or else it languishes in a conqueror's vault, glimmered at by passing candles, unworthy of a victor's attention. Prague in my time had no Cassandra to foretell its disasters. Thunderous rumours were faint amid the splendours of Rudolf's city, and none could have guessed what cankered tubers would pierce the new century's soil.

'All about us are the Emperor's museum. Yes, yes. His *kunst und wundern*, his collections, are in royal palace and passage beyond.' (My face flushed at this information.) 'The royal stables will be converting – it is planned – for statues. It is why I must lock you up. You understand? No thievery permitted. On pain of capitation.'

'I wouldn't want to steal anything.'

'You might,' said Spranger, 'if you saw it.'

To occupy the sluggish hours, I imagined the wondrous objects gathered in the Castle; not only the sculptures and paintings but also Rudolf's basilisk, his unicorn cup and bezoar stones deposited in the intestines of ibexes. Sometimes Bartholomeus Spranger would lay aside his charcoal to describe, with lambent eyes, the Emperor's *indianisch* paintings on paper and silk, a cup hollowed out of a rhinoceros horn, homunculi in alcohol, nails salvaged from Noah's ark, a phial of dust from the Hebron Valley out of which God fashioned Adam, eerily lifelike automatons, musical clocks and hummingbird feathers. My head spinning at these marvels, I forgot the shame of my nakedness and the gelid suction of the floor on my hams. Spranger's descriptions swam and sidled into my brain. I dreamed at night that Vertumnus was exploring the workshop. With fingers made of roots and twine, he pulled back my flimsy coverlet and deposited me on velvet cushions, as though I were one of Rudolf's alrauns – those mandragoras shaped in the earth like little men. Awaking, I peed as Spranger had taught me, in a golden arc, out of the window into the moat. There was a wooden covered bridge to the right of me, which the Emperor had built to conceal himself from his subjects. It was at Bartholomeus Spranger's casement that I first heard the imperial lion roar. Sounds of the menagerie enthralled me. I posed for the painter's swift and dispassionate scrutiny to the cries of peacocks and the lusty eructation of rutting stags.

'You must be having new clothings,' Spranger declared at the end of our third session. 'My son is *zehn*, ten, years of old. He shoot up – *fwooish* – out of his clothings. No, no, little sir, tomorrow I bring for you.'

Thus on the fourth day, with new clothes awaiting me, I found the courage to pilot our conversation. I expressed, with the relief of an unburdening, my dismay at Meyrink's coldness towards me since my arrival in Prague. Bartholomeus Spranger explained that the art collector had troubles of his own. 'The Emperor was not pleased with him.'

'Why, what did he do?'

'Did not do. Paintings by Dürer, Pieter Bruegel, Parmigianino – these Rudolf likes. But Meyrink did not find in one year. Instead he shows, how is it said, *initiative*.'

'What,' I muttered, 'did the Emperor make of Gian Bonconvento's painting?'

'Gian who?'

Spranger's fleeting hand whispered on the paper until its edge was black and glossy. 'Herr Meyrink is fallen in the Kaiser's estimate,' he said. 'Demoted to sub-curator, he will have answers to the Šacmistr – the treasure?'

'Treasurer.'

'Is Ottavio Strada. He plays well his cards, that fellow. Yes, yes. His sister Catherina is, um, mistress on top of Rudolf. So do not be troubled by Meyrink his behaviour. It is difficult life in the Court.'

Herr Spranger explained the elaborate, arcane rituals of Castle life. I learned how courtiers revolved about the throne as angels in the crystalline heaven radiate from the Primum Mobile. Rudolf the Spanish-mannered – 'Rudolf of Few Words' – resided behind a series of thresholds. Any citizen, once admitted to the Palace, could access Vladislav Hall, that vaulting public market at its centre. Beyond that one had to petition Octavius Spinola, the Stall-Master, for admission to the Vestibule; thence to the Green Chamber, where noblemen and artists, alchemists and ambassadors, fulminated against one another in formal silence. Finally the Emperor's Chamberlain, Wolfgang Rumpf, summoned the lucky few into the Imperial Presence in the Privy Chamber. Had Spranger ever got so far? Once, upon his investiture. What works of art had he discovered there? A table, since I asked, and a fetching silver inkstand. Who were these household officers who dispensed the Emperor's favour? The sons of Great Families, of course.

'Then surely,' I mused, 'he that controls access to the King controls the kingdom? By deciding what the King sees of it?'

To this question Spranger preferred to play deaf, crushing a nut between his molars and attacking with gusto a misapplied stroke on the paper.

'And what about the collections?' I asked. What of the

paintings and sculptures, the art objects and cabinets stocked with natural wonders? Ah – here lay Rudolf's demonstrable power. He conferred status or revoked it by granting access to his galleries. As an onion peels away to its eye-watering core, so one progressed through layers of value. Whoever attained the innermost chamber glimpsed the *arcana imperii* and glowed ever after with aulic knowledge.

Shortly before luncheon, my host announced that my services were no longer needed. Now was the time for me to act. Scrabbling into young Master Spranger's breeches, I suckled for spit and cleared my throat. 'Herr Spranger,' I said. 'I have carried this letter for years. Please – the seal is already broken.'

The Court Painter knotted his brow at the dog-eared, mangled paper flipped into his hand. When he had read its contents, he stared at me as though I had fallen from the moon. From being a shadow player on the stage of his fancy, I became, by Arcimboldo's posthumous intervention, a living persona.

'Maestro,' I said (how corrupt the word felt on my memorious tongue), 'grant me one more night in your workshop. All I ask is a number of candles and the free use of your instruments.'

Spranger nodded, mumbled, shook his head in confusion.

'For me to show you,' I explained, 'what I am capable of.'

I felt a boiling in my belly – the urge to *create*, to snatch a sheet of paper and populate its wastes.

'Very good,' Spranger agreed. 'I will get you, as you ask, some candles. And food.' He turned, wet lipped, in the doorway. 'To see what you are capable.'

Three hours sufficed for me to complete the drawing. I had made good use of my nights, admiring in the glow of the moon the milky eroticism of Spranger's art. It was easy to imitate his lithe nudes. My Danaë was languorous like his Omphale and I crouched, doubled up, avidly engendering the swell of her mons Veneris. Once the charcoal outline was finished, I confirmed it with black ink and white chalk highlights, lingering on the folds of Danaë's flimsy gown and the golden shower that seduced her.

In a warm stupor of satisfaction, I slept beneath my pastiche. When the Court Painter returned in the morning, there was no groggy haul on to the shore of waking. I sat up at once to enjoy his stupefaction.

'Yes. Yes, a considerable skill.' I was not wholly satisfied by his chill smile. 'But it would not do,' he said, 'always to be repeating others.'

Bartholomeus Spranger continued to study my Danaë (crushing a sugared almond in the vice of his jaws) while I ate my breakfast of apple and cheese and gawked noisily into a cup of beer. I was instructed, quite forcefully, not to stir from my place.

'I must see,' Spranger said, 'to the matter of your employment.'

My hunger sated, and quivering with new hope, I pretended to myself to doze, curled up like a cat in the ropes of my blanket, until stomach cramps drove me for air to the window.

In the yard of the Lion House two gentlemen were strolling. I scrunched up my face to distinguish them more clearly – and with a sharp inward shock realised that the russet figure on the left was *not human*. Its arms were of an impossible length, as though they had been stretched upon a rack, and it wrapped them about the waist of its companion. The monster's brown belly dragged over crippled bow legs. As for the face – my *God* – it was a grotesque mask, a savage travesty of Man.

I emitted a puppyish yelp when Spranger stuck his head

about the door. 'Herr Grilli,' he said, and like me he was short of breath. 'I have a gentleman here. He is wanting an artist, while I find a place for your, ah, skills in Court.'

A day that had begun so promisingly took a second lurch to nightmare; for the apparition that filled the doorway was covered from neck to crown in dense brown fur. It smiled through that savage wool, a childhood ghoul incarnate. 'Your servant,' it said. 'I would be most honoured if you might consent, in the English manner, to shake me by the hand . . .'

A polyglot like many in Prague, Petrus Gonsalvus spoke Dutch with his wife, Italian with his children and German to his pupils at the school of Týn. Once, when he stubbed a toe, I heard him curse in florid French; but when he prayed he prayed in Spanish, for Spanish was his mother tongue.

He was born on the island of Tenerife, already half concealed beneath a haze of brown hair; yet the midwife, upon his delivery, sighed with relief not horror, and while his mother guided the hairy face to her breast, his father received many boisterous slaps at the inducible proof of his paternity.

'People in my family have been like this for generations,' Gonsalvus said as we walked through Kleinseite. 'You have nothing to fear – we are only men.'

No craven appetite devoured the baby Pedro; his toothless gums could not have torn flesh. As for the moon, it shone full upon his crib, devoid of metamorphic powers. Yet he suffered from the midday sun and with every season his coat grew thicker, so that his earliest memory was of choking like a cat from the fur balls on his pillow.

The young child lacked for nothing in affection. His mother and father adored him; children of the village tied ribbons in his beard and made him the focus of their play.

Poverty soon curtailed these humble joys. Sobbing at the doorway of their house, his parents entrusted him to a gentleman of France – a 'Doctor Medicus' who promised a dignified life of learning for their son.

So Pedro Gonzales came as a child to Paris, where, under the amused aegis of the second King Henry, he received a courtier's education. Scholars, once they had seen past his strangeness, marvelled at the sharpness of his mind. He became Pierre Gonzale, a numerate beast. Algebra and geometry consoled him for his loneliness: they offered order and stability, the artistry of patterns, and only the necessity of juggling numbers to entertain the *dames galantes* soured his pleasure.

Following the King's death and in accordance with his wishes, the regent Queen Catherine kept Pierre at the Louvre. Philanthropy had no part in the equation. He was offered as a plaything to the royal siblings, who despised him, however, for his precious manners and the sebaceous grease which plastered the hairs to his face. When the young Prince Henry tried to shave him using a silver dagger, Pierre was lucky to escape with only a scar on his throat.

Despite such misadventures, the *loup garou* endured into manhood, a dependant of the Crown. When another French harvest failed, however, there were fiscal grumblings at court. So Pierre Gonzale was sent as a gift to the Regent of the Spanish Netherlands: Margaret of Austria, Duchess of Parma. At the court in Namur he met his future wife, Marie. Of their courtship I know nothing; nor do I care to imagine her guardians' aversion to this fearful-looking suitor, regardless of his education. It would seem that Margaret of Austria gave the union her blessing. Four children were born: two sons, then a daughter and a third boy, all afflicted like their father. Thanks were offered to God for each one.

Faced with mounting debts, Pierre Gonzale Latinized his name and, with royal permission, offered public demonstrations of his talents. Although the money was greatly needed, he longed to believe that his audience of Spanish officials and merchants from the Weighhouse attended out of mathematical rather than freakish curiosity.

Then it was time to move again – to the native city of his patroness.

The family, as it travelled through the Empire, sustained itself by submitting to medical curiosity. Their condition needed a name if medicine were to possess the fact of it. One doctor ventured *Hirsutia Lycaonus*, but Gonsalvus rejected its allusion to the murderous Arcadian king. The famous Basle doctor Felix Plater (who tried to extract, from samples of their body hair, a cure for baldness) preferred the term *Hypertrichosis*, and seemed satisfied that he had done great service to his patients with the diagnosis. In Parma, finally, they were examined by the Bolognese Ulisse Aldrovandi, who intended with his detailed notes to preserve the marvel for future generations.

'Our fame expands beyond us, like ripples in a pool,' said Gonsalvus as we made our way past the Old Town Hall. 'My family will not hide away, as though we were creatures of the night.' It was, he said, for his two youngest children that he had come to find me. 'Carlo and Caterina are blessed – yes, sir, blessed – with unique distinction. I mean to teach them the value of their natures.' He looked at me askance. 'I trust you will find no hindrance, in their condition, to the love which their innocence is owed?'

'Of course not,' I replied, noticing the wide berth which citizens accorded our progress through the town. What gossip, what whispers clung to our coat-tails? Who would not boast, to their spouse or neighbour, of having seen a werewolf consorting with a dwarf?

'No, of course,' echoed Gonsalvus. Then he patted me kindly on the shoulder. 'You have my confidence entirely.'

The family lived on the Old Town Square, in a whitewashed building beneath the dark spires of Our Lady before Týn. Frau Gonsalvus welcomed us at the door. She was a handsome woman, with hair still golden and a matronly figure. Her soft curtsy prompted my own bashful bow, and my voice was cracked: '*Wie geht es Ihnen?*'

'*Gut, danke* . . .' With a glance of enquiry at her husband, Frau Gonsalvus continued in accented Italian. 'You must forgive our humble dwelling. We share the building with other schoolmasters, and very few of them have children.'

They had more space, however, than I was accustomed to. Their low-beamed quarters smelled of cabbage and cinnamon, of musty books and, well, wet dog. I was taken at once to their dining room and offered a chair.

'How good it is to hear a native speaker,' said Frau Gonsalvus. 'You must speak to me at length, signor.'

'Our sons . . .' said Gonsalvus.

'. . . our eldest boys . . .'

'. . . are left behind in Parma making their own fortunes. So you see, it is sweet sorrow to hear Italian well spoken.'

'We are such a muddle of cultures,' said Frau Gonsalvus, absently sweeping her husband's shoulder. 'I could not tell you what language I dream in.'

Instantly obvious, even to me, was the couple's tranquil intimacy. Petrus Gonsalvus followed with soft admiring eyes the common gestures of his wife. She moved easefully in the ambit of his gaze, at home with his horrible body. United in attention, with their arms crossed upon the table, they asked me about my life and travels. Many of my replies were honest; yet in order to gain their goodwill, I felt compelled to withhold certain details.

'Signor Bonconvento must be pleased,' said Frau Gonsalvus, 'to have so charming an apprentice for his ambassador.' I smiled and felt my throat creak. To my boundless relief, no testimonials were required of me.

When his wife had left us to fetch cakes, Petrus Gonsalvus prised from his extensive library (at least a hundred volumes thick) a leather-bound casket. Setting it on the table, he caressed its brass clasp with the naked ball of his thumb. 'Herr Meyrink told me about you days ago,' he said. 'I hope that you, of all men, shall understand.'

The casket lid snapped open. Gonsalvus reached inside and withdrew a curled scroll. 'This is a copy of the front plate of Joris Hoefnagel's natural history – *Animalia rationalia et insecta*.' He began, with infuriating slowness, to unfurl the parchment. 'Hoefnagel was in Amsterdam when he received the Emperor's commission. Four volumes of natural history, hand painted, for the Imperial Library. Help me here.' The parchment longed to curl up: we pinned its reticent edges to the table with our palms. 'You will recognise, I think, this specimen.'

Hoefnagel had painted a portrait of Gonsalvus in ruff and cobalt-blue gown, with peaceful Marie resting a hand on her miraculous husband's shoulder. Together they occupied an oval of brown ink, where they appeared to sprout from a barren mound of earth. Marie's gaze, settled on a distant object, was beyond the viewer's grasp; but Petrus Gonsalvus boldly met one's eye. His living elder (for the work was more than a decade old) reached across my shoulder to point at the inscription. '*Homo natus de Muliere*.' Man born of woman, despite foolish assumptions.

At that instant, I understood what was expected of me. Having posed for Hoefnagel all those years ago, Gonsalvus had been gratified by the lucid dignity of his likeness. For his children to enjoy the same assurance, their father would commission me to paint their portraits.

Frau Gonsalvus returned, wafting her children into the room. Eight-year-old Carlo, who was carrying food on a tray, precociously bowed and the tip of his nose as he bent entered the honey cakes. Caterina, a proud girl of twelve whose beauty, inherited from her mother, was obscured by thick fur, stared at me with dark and shameless eyes. Imagine the mutuality of our stupefaction! Never before had I seen children of so outlandish an aspect; while they, for their part, had to absorb the seeming childishness of this adult-mannered stranger. We sat at the burnished oak table and broke cake together. (Gingerly burrowing into the pile, I excavated a pristine slice.) The children slouched and swung their heels and looked in hope of relief at the window's grey face. Both were dressed for the occasion. Carlo wore a salmon-pink coat and a hat into which his almost russet hair had been combed. Caterina beside him wore a grey dress. Ruffed like Carlo, she had a delicate coronet high on her head; it tickled her scalp perhaps, for she kept trying to scratch beneath it.

'Children,' said Gonsalvus, as Carlo manoeuvred an ambitious slice of cake into his mouth. 'Signor Grilli is a painter. He is going to paint our portrait.' A glance, seeking and receiving confirmation, was exchanged between the parents. 'He will stay here as our guest. I expect you to treat him as you would a brother . . .'

Frau Gonsalvus lightly touched her husband's wrist. 'As an uncle, husband.'

'Ah, yes. Of course. As an *uncle*.'

He looked at me sheepishly, if you please. But I was not offended when Frau Gonsalvus laughed. The hovering risk of insult had landed, and no harm was done.

* * *

There followed in my life a rare period of happy industry. I was given a room to myself and a soft bed all my own, whose comfort, after years spent on various floors, I could scarcely tolerate. My back ached from kindness and my feet itched, disturbed by the absence of dust. At dawn a school servant – a mournful, sloping-eyed widow called Marta – confronted me with my breakfast on a clattering tray, which she dropped almost accusingly at the foot of my bed. I ate hungrily the strudel and pancakes before rinsing my face, with a gasp, at the icy bowl.

The mornings were mine to spend as I pleased. I read a good deal from Gonsalvus's library and worked hard, with the assistance of Frau Gonsalvus and her children, to nurture my fledgling German. (I cherished, covertly, the shapely figure of my hostess and the fragrances that bloomed in her wake. Yet she was absent from the lubricious pageants of my dreams, where other females were pressed into service. To parade her, in her stays, in that frictionless void would have been an abomination.) After luncheon, which the family ate together, I would follow the children to the parlour, which served my purpose on account of its west-facing windows. The light was best in the afternoons, leaving us little time in which to work. Carlo and Caterina had to hold very still, mastering the normal fidget of their youth, if we were to make any progress.

The more I studied my young subjects, and sought the finest paintbrushes (on loan to me from Spranger's studio) with which to paint their facial hair, the less troubled I was by their affliction. Carlo, who was uncommonly sharp for his age, made me laugh with his impersonations of the teachers at Týn, while Caterina quietly maintained a pose as dignified as any lady.

Come the evening, when candles were lit, animating the walls with amber pools and fluid shadows, the pupils at the school were set free. They rumbled and shouted in the cloisters below us. Shortly thereafter, Petrus Gonsalvus would return to greet his wife and rollicking children. Carlo tugged at his father's arm, sitting on empty air. Gonsalvus stroked himself free and joined me in the parlour, still wearing his scholar's gown. Alas, I had only candlelight for painting his portrait, and told myself to memorise his natural colours for the final touches. Gonsalvus posed with remarkable composure – a far better model than Spranger's recent, fidgety putto.

'Paint me, I pray you, as I am. Neither flatter nor cajole but record God's work faithfully.' Posing with his right hand on the strut of a chair (which would metamorphose later into a limestone bluff), Gonsalvus asked only that I give him pristine hands. 'For the hand by its dexterity has enabled Mankind to count and create. It is the tool of civilisation – Adam's abacus. Endow us, therefore, with ordinary hands, that the viewer may recognise affliction as mere surface.'

Consider, good reader, how the world is glutted with deformity. The sick, the lame, the goitrous poor surround us; and we could so readily join their ranks, cankered by a wound or devoured by the pox. Even those fortunate enough to have avoided the parasites that twist us from our spiritual shapes have cared for parents distorted by sickness and age. Surrounded by such norms of imperfection, who will despise a man merely on account of his resemblance to a dog?

And so I painted, capably denying to myself that my *own* work – work, that is, divorced from another artist's influence – was mediocre. I had a sharp eye for a painter's mannerisms, for his ruses and illusions. But alone I could make only a journeyman's effort, a passable likeness of reality.

Haunted by this intimation, I told Gonsalvus of my youth

spent in other artists' shadows. I told him of my brittle father; how the Academy was to him as Eden must have been for Adam – the purple hills to which he turned his face in sorrow and recrimination. Though he claimed to despise his former colleagues, my father had continued to hold their assumptions. Many decades of precedent had been pressed into his service: whenever he had felt a need to diminish me, Cennini and Vasari and Michelangelo lined up behind him, sagely nodding their ghostly heads. Petrus Gonsalvus sympathised. When I told him about the kindness of Arcimboldo, he assured me that he had seen copies of his paintings. He seemed to savour the irony that Arcimboldo's disciple – an impressionable lad nourished on capricci – should now, by his commission, faithfully and without artifice be recording supposedly fabulous beings.

'But every man that departs from the norm is not defective,' he said. 'On the contrary, Tommaso. The flawless beauty has yet to escape the ideal of her form, she *lacks* distinctive features.' (I knew – and did not wish to know – that Gonsalvus was embracing me in his conceit.) 'The rarer one's appearance, the more unique. We are proof, my friend, of God's infinite imagination.'

In my hours of idleness it became my practice to roam the city, allowing the spectacle, or its mist-veiled absence, to permeate my senses. I recall the leaden wash of damp pavings; a stone bell carved into the wall of a palace; the brassy tang of impending snow, which fell at last in mute flurries, like feathers of ash against the clouds. On Childermas, Prague's windows were blinded by cataracts of frost. I felt invisible, like a beetle in a box, as I scuttled down the narrow arteries that feed the Old Town's heart and stood before the astronomical clock waiting for it to strike.

It was Carlo who explained the clock to me: how it

measured lunar and astral migrations, enclosing all Creation within the bounds of Time. I learned from my precocious companion (whom passers-by with animated elbows mistook for my brother) to interpret the calendar's mysterious symbols. Into my idle drawings I smuggled Cancer's clapperclaws, the slurred chapel windows of ♍, a bug in the bed of ♎ and sunlit ripples on the pond of ♒. The clock, though wondrous enough in its complexity, had yet to house the clockwork Apostles which, along with the Turk and tolling Death, so charm today's visitor to that sad city.

'There's a dark story in that clock,' said Carlo, huffing for warmth into his hairy fist. 'Long ago, about a hundred years ago, it was broken. So they got this master clockmaker to fix it . . .'

'What was his name?'

'Hanuš.'

'*Gezundheit.*'

Carlo frowned, raising comical hairs on his brow. 'Uncle Tommaso, *listen.*'

'Sorry.'

'This master clockmaker fixed the clock. He was so good and it worked so well that the councillors got jealous. They didn't want anyone else getting a clock like it. So d'you know what happened? Do you to know how they stopped him sharing its secrets?'

'Tell me.'

'They flipped out his eyes.'

'No.'

'Yes.'

'They *blinded* him?'

'But Hanuš got his revenge. When his wounds were healed he stole into the clock tower. His apprentice helped him up. And there, because his life was finished, he plunged his hands into the works . . . and stopped Time in its tracks.'

Carlo, his story accomplished, puffed up his chest. The clock clucked and ticked its finger at human vanity.

'Really?' I asked. 'Is that really true?'

Carlo shrugged. 'Don't you wish it was?'

Oh, reader, I wished for many things. I wished for word from my supposed champions at the Castle. I wished, with sultry nocturnal fervour, for the favours of an unfussy girl, and for the rekindling of creative fires long choked in me by frustration. Dreams of failure gnawed at my sleep – marathons through glue, shying apple cores, fervid whores with padlocked fannies. As the family portrait neared its completion, I cursed Meyrink and Spranger, damning their proverbial eyes and regretting bitterly having surrendered my naked likeness to the derision of shadowy courtiers. Prague, so dense with stories, seemed to exclude me from its mystery, every turn inside its labyrinth leading only to a closed door. My exclusion from the Castle, and the snowbound darkness of January days, caused a melancholy to pulse deep within my veins.

Petrus Gonsalvus, noting my maudlin disposition, took me to buy fish on Charles Square. He meant to lift my spirits; but ever the pedagogue, he could not resist indicating the windows of the New Town Hall whence councillors had been thrown to their deaths, marking the onset of the Hussite wars. My pessimism was contagious: grimly he described (and grimly I listened) how Kleinseite had been sacked and Vyšehrad destroyed in the fighting. When I expressed surprise that a Spaniard loyal to Rome should be teaching in a Hussite stronghold, Petrus Gonsalvus responded with rare impatience.

'Do you think Euclid or Pythagoras are subject to theological dispute? Mathematics, signor, is immutable, like the God these infants fight over.'

* * *

As some men, even honest ones, find themselves drawn to the Church, so Petrus Gonsalvus had a vocation for teaching. It was beyond his powers to suppress, for the sake of proud sensibilities, his compulsion to impart knowledge – to make green the deserts of the mind. Therefore he disciplined my promiscuous reading, choosing those books which would plug most effectively the gaps in my education. He tested my Latin and Greek; produced arrangements of numbers that looked to me like occult invocations; lectured me on the joys of Learning. Although he possessed several Bibles, and was given to perusing a broken-spined edition of the *City of God*, Gonsalvus emphasised for me the works of the Ancients. I meditated on Marcus Aurelius, learned my duties from Cicero, discovered the universe with Lucretius and the dignity of Mirandola's Man within it. Best of all, I remember the sensation of opening Vesalius's *De humani corporis fabrica*. Upon each plate of that anatomist's bible the models posed, stripped layer by layer of flesh. It reminded me of the statue of St Bartholomew in Milan and I peered warily at my own skin, almost sceptical that it could be composed in like manner. I spent many hours poring over that rare book, threading the letters, which clung like mites to the anatomies, with the Latin glossary. How strange, I felt, how sad, the animation of these flayed beings. They posed with artistic grace, shorn of defining features and incapable of blinking. On the plate which depicted the primary muscles, a butterfly's wing of lettered flesh sprouted from the monster's arm. Skin hung in strips, like molten wax, from his fingers; it drooped across his sinewed foot like withered leaves. What could he be looking at, this animated corpse? Emasculated, with testicles draped like tassels on his thighs, what shrub or eglantine could possibly hold his attention beyond the bounds of the plate? I have an idea, reader, that my undertaking in writing this book is mirrored in that picture. Is not this confession a kind of dissection, an unpeeling of myself? Pray do not wrinkle your nose at this flayed man, at the peeling lips of his sinful flesh. I would show you the organs that propelled me, the valved pump that beats, a living fabric beneath the skin . . .

The Gonsalvus portrait was completed in February. I had invented a backdrop for the figures: the mouth of a cave, such as wild bears might favour. This was to show, by contrast with their clothes and manners, how refined my subjects were from beasts.

We gathered in the dining room for the grand unveiling. There was a smattering of applause. Caterina stood with hands on her hips, defying her likeness to meet her eye; Carlo studied the painting as though it were his own reflection.

When Bartholomeus Spranger joined us briefly, good form alone prevented me from assailing him with questions. He quaffed two cups of hot spiced wine as though it were water, directed his boys to collect the brushes and paints and apologised for his speedy departure. 'The Emperor has read the Arcimboldo letter,' he told me as he shrugged into his coat at the door. 'He says he recollects with love the Milanese Count. Until this day he admires, um, the ingenious faces.'

'So do I have a meeting? Will the Emperor meet me?'

Bartholomeus Spranger patted the air with his fingers. 'Patience, my friend. You have many competitors for His Majesty's favour.'

'But the letter says—'

'He wants to see more samples of your work.'

The family gathered about us in the hallway. Carlo and Caterina reached between their parents' legs in a silent battle of pinches. Perhaps Spranger sensed my disappointment, for he softened his tone. 'It is considered, in view of your, how is it said, aptness?'

'Aptitude,' said Gonsalvus.

'*Ja*, that you be, er, concentrate on natural history. Snails and moths and so forth.'

The next day, to restore my courage, Petrus Gonsalvus brought me his rarest possession. It was an album of nature studies by Cornelis Stamper – sixteen plates, in luminous watercolour, depicting hawk moths and fritillaries, damselflies with tender-laced wings, rose chafers in a spume of petals, a woodpecker laid out on a table, its dead eye gleaming like a drop of oil. Consequently I had a model to work from. As a tick feeds upon its host, I fastened to my Dutch predecessor. Spring flung out its blossom at the world. I wandered with the children in the countryside, gathering snails, beetles and the powdered ossuaries of owl pellets, which I painted in borrowed watercolours in unlikely conjunctions, keeping one eye on Stamper's methods. Profusion of forms was my goal. Amid curlicues of honeysuckle and yellow pimpernel, I concealed a jay's feather, spiralling snail shells, two houseflies on a deformed tomato, a plump and mercifully defunct maybug, and the almost perfect sphere of a tawny owl's egg. For want of a quizzical mantis, I studied a grasshopper beneath a glass lid. When, later, I pinned it to a strip of card, Caterina scowled and denounced me as a murderer.

Writing these words – a stale old man, my art fallen from my fingers – I long to claim that I took pleasure in my work. Alas, I made of it a joyless chore, a mechanical pandering to expectations. I dared not venture from the safe coves of emulation. My only skill was in mingling borrowed conceits to disguise my thieving nature.

In May, when the studies were finished, I returned to Prague Castle. My bladder felt bloated by hallucinatory pressure; my back was a swamp of perspiration. I handed my portfolio to a sentry at the gate and departed, empty handed, to wait for my summons.

It came the next day – delivered without ceremony by a liveried servant. Frau Gonsalvus and the clamouring children watched me break the imperial seal. I was to attend upon His Majesty in the Royal Gardens, on the occasion of his Sunday constitutional.

*

The retinue, with ostrich plumes and handkerchiefs, flurried about the Emperor like fish about a promontory. Rudolf was returning to the Palace, feeling perhaps, like the spider's dam, devoured by his ravenous dependants. We stood in the settling dust outside the Lion House, watching the crowd recede. Some peasants began forking new straw over the enclosure walls. Petrus Gonsalvus sought words to console me.

'Do you want to see the Orange Man? The ape, you know, that you saw from the Castle window?' My silence was like crawling lice to him: he persevered with his lame babble. 'Come along, Tommaso. I'm told there's an aperture in the wall. Oh yes. He's *extraordinary*. You really should see for yourself . . .'

Even on tiptoe, I could not have hoped to reach the peephole.

'I understand he was brought back from the Indies. Dutch traders. The dodos came in the same consignment. He does look rather wretched, I must say, crouched up so. I presume it *is* a he? Oh yes, look.'

Through gritted teeth, capped by black clouds of ire, I commented that I could not look, that I would not look if I could. My only desire was to leave these accursed grounds. After almost a year, one wasted year of hope and expectation, the Emperor had failed to look my way.

'He's very sympathetic, you know,' said Gonsalvus, attempting to compensate for my blindness. 'He's scratching his chin like a true philosopher. Such leathery hands. Lord, I think he sees me! Now he's trying to pick himself up. Do you know, if it wasn't blasphemous, I would almost say that he looks – how would one say – *human.*'

At that instant, my surprise was split in two.

To my right, Bartholomeus Spranger came bounding through dappled light, pressing his cap to his head, with Jaroslav Meyrink behind him flourishing a sheet of paper. Above me and to my left, Petrus Gonsalvus the peeping mathematician was flung backwards by a perfectly calibrated volley of shit.

6
Swindlers

There was nothing to keep me now in the Old Town. Despite the pleading of Carlo and Caterina, despite their mother's pregnant silence when Spranger read aloud the terms of my commission, I was resolved to seize my chance. In truth, it was not much of an opening. The Emperor Rudolf had neglected to sign the document which Spranger had drawn up for his rheumy eyes. Instead, it was a minor clerk in the Bohemian Chancery who had scrawled his imprimatur – a crimson wormcast on sandy parchment – granting me a modest annuity in return for 'Documentary Illustrations of His Caesarean Majesty's Natural History Collection'.

Frau Gonsalvus rested a hand on her husband's shoulder – that gesture preserved for ever in Joris Hoefnagel's portrait. 'Where will Tommaso live?' she asked. The children chanted: 'With us! With us!'

I longed to escape, however. When Spranger brought me to the Royal Palace to arrange my accommodation, I accepted with delight the offer of lodgings in the Hradschin: the Castle district.

The musty clerk was bald like a rabbit skinned for the pot. He picked at the tips of his inky fingers. 'You understand, Herr Grilli, that we cannot accommodate *every* newcomer to our—' He balanced his head on his spine, casting about for the right word. '—to the pullulating *ranks* of Court artists. It is beyond Bohemia's means to furnish you with superfluous luxury.'

'What he's saying is—' said Spranger. I thanked my friend: I understood German well enough to understand.

'Therefore,' said the clerk, 'you shall reside at the Golden Ram on Neu Welt. One room only. It is a holding place for *worthy cases* while we bleed ourselves to find better lodgings in the Castle.'

Would I – could I – expect one day to be lodged in the Castle? The clerk's head snapped up from his papers. 'Don't hold your breath,' he said.

Bartholomeus Spranger smilingly took the proffered key and we left the New Land Rolls, accompanied by the cicada song of clerical quills. I was guided through the Castle, past the sentries who, one year previously, had kicked my backside and now seemed not to recognise me. '*Not* advisable.' Spranger grinned, staying my injurious gesture.

Beggars were cursing fate with their stumps, or pressing their foreheads into the mud of Castle Square, as we made our way east to the old city walls. Neu Welt was a quiet lane of humble cottages inhabited by Castle servants. Several of these cramped dwellings were dignified by aureate names. There was a Golden Pear, a Golden Foot and my own, the Golden Ram, which I would share with the painter Fučik (whose noisy copulations were the only proof of his residence) and the clockmaker František Schwaiger.

My own room was at the top of the cottage; that is to say, on the first floor, reached by a spiralling, cob-webbed stairwell, with a single window overlooking the lane. Anticipating my dismay at signs of recent occupancy (the previous resident, a glover promoted to a small house in Kleinseite, had left behind, in the manner of territorial dogs, a mouldy reminder of his passage), Bartholomeus Spranger assured me that men of such distinction as Johannes Kepler and Tycho Brahe (whose metal nose so delighted the horripilated ladies) had themselves spent time on Neu Welt.

'It's quite all right,' I said, gathering on the ball of my

finger a miniature cap of dust. 'This is a room of my own. You could not dishearten me if it were infested with cockroaches.'

Reader, it was.

Initial delight at my promotion subsided to gentle melancholy. Perhaps it was the quiet of my lodgings, or the view from my window of a garden wall beneath trembling aspen, whispering ash. Neither of my housemates engaged me in conversation. Fučik was absent during the day, while the clockmaker directly beneath my room was timid as a mouse, fleeing in the stairwell the moment I met his eyes, which were the colour of sperm oil and owlishly magnified by glasses. As for Spranger, being engaged on three paintings at once he had little time for me. I waited and waited for my first commission, exhausting my small allowance in a tavern on Spornergasse, eating peas and cabbage with pig's knuckle. I acquired a liking for Bohemian beer and found to my surprise that the tavern was breathing, its low ceiling distending and retracting like the soft of a belly.

Twice in that month I visited the family at Týn, only to find Petrus teaching and the children with their tutor. Frau Gonsalvus sat with me, exchanging platitudes about the weather, while I fought a mad desire to blot out the world by plunging my face into her breasts. She implored me to stay until her husband's return; yet my fear of weeping before his great, shaggy kindness compelled me to make my excuses. Happiness is experienced only with hindsight – as one fails to behold the pattern of a curtain when one's eyes are up against it. I had enjoyed, in the Gonsalvus family, a respite from my desolate wanderings: a dappled bower bright with the clarion of children's laughter. Yet I fled, like Ulysses from the lotus slopes, to sequester myself in Neu Welt for the sake of my ambition.

*   *   *

When finally work came, it took the form of a small boy knocking at my door. He tipped a clutch of whorled shells into my palm: little spiralling hats, miniature samples of the sea when you fitted them to your ear, they made when clutched together a noise like broken eggs. The delivery boy (whose name was Eduard or Ewald) returned an hour later, staggering beneath the weight of a wooden casket. I sent him away without a haler, unable to afford even token munificence.

Inside the casket I found a note from Jaroslav Meyrink instructing me to copy faithfully, with ink and coloured paint, the shells in my possession. The casket yawned open for my attention. It contained utensils and papers necessary for small-scale artistic work, including an oak-lidded tray of watercolours. Evidently I had mimicked too well the illustrations of Cornelis Stamper; for I was given to study only the loose change from the Emperor's collection. I might have hoped for the arcane, mysterious objects which he was reputed to possess and of which both Arcimboldo and Spranger had spoken. But neither holy relic nor natural wonder was permitted to leave the safe seclusion of its cabinet. I had to make do with trinkets: leathery monkey paws, the boiled skull of a paradise bird, stuffed civets that fixed me with (literally) beady eyes, a mongoose pelt and beetles impaled, like empty plate armour, in small wooden caskets. Hope of preferment and financial need ensured my diligence in copying these objects; but I took no pleasure in my task.

A scorching summer burned itself out. Winter brought deep snows that nearly immobilised me. On the River Moldau everyone was a Messiah, walking on water. The traffic at the ice fairs stained the ice brown, as certain mosses leave a patina on window glass.

One morning the painter Fučik left the Golden Ram never

to return. I saw only his back as he balanced on the frosted cobbles, a canvas bag slung across his shoulder. To this day, when I imagine him, his face is obscured by a cloud like pictures of Mahomet. Jaroslav Meyrink, calling to see that I had not frozen to death in my room, implied that Fučik had been dismissed from service for idleness. Meyrink, on the other hand, had redeemed his faults and regained Collector's status.

'Take me to the Court,' I begged him. 'Introduce me to lords and ladies, to other artists. Get me out of this *hole*.'

Shivering on my stool and wrapped in blankets from my bed, I told him that I heard the Moldau creaking; how, when I dropped my head on my pillow, I could make out the faint tinkling of crystals in my blood. Meyrink clammed up at this show of emotion until, in my frustration, I knocked over a black phial. 'Good Lord,' he exclaimed, 'your ink is frozen.' He was relieved to have found a resolvable problem. 'This won't do. One cannot *work* in such conditions.' In a swoop, he had crushed the door-latch and leaped into the stairwell. 'I will get firewood sent to you at once,' he called out; adding at last, from the safety of the street:

'Never fear, Tommaso. I shall not let you down.'

Sure enough, a fur rug arrived from the Castle (not a new one, you understand), ensuring, along with regular deliveries of dry logs, that I would not die of cold that winter. The social thaw took a little longer to begin; and its warming winds came from unexpected quarters.

Prague, under a ruler who prized his books above his subjects, was carrion to the meat flies of Europe. Swindlers, forgers, confidence tricksters – men gifted in all the subtle arts – swarmed here in hope of nourishment. A few were dreamers of sorts, conjuring rabbits from secret-chambered boxes, levitating with the help of discreet ledges, or selling panaceas whose miraculous properties were limited only by the salesman's eloquence. Might these parasites not have served a purpose, brightening mental darkness with a little wonderment? Still today – over thirty years later, having seen enough of God's Paragon to believe he may be the Devil's work – I do not like to admit to myself that our meeting was intended. No shadowy mastermind, surely, could have set that threesome spilling towards me when, by taking another street, I might so easily have thwarted his design?

It was darkling, a clouded twilight of early spring, when I laboured up Spornergasse sunk in dreams. The drunken revellers above me were midway through a trawl of Kleinseite taverns. (I will tell you their names before we meet them.) The leader, Luboš Hrabal, bounded ahead of Jaroslav and Botuslav, the Mušek twins, who were as thin as Hrabal was fat. I paid them little attention in the moments before they lost their anonymity. Hrabal turned in his corpulence to share a joke, thus obscuring the brothers' view of obstacles below. They came fast through the gloom. At the last instant a patch of ice thwarted my attempt at evasion. The fat man belched: '*Kristus*!' Rebounding off Hrabal's belly, I fell on my backside into the slush. Hrabal, for his part, staggered as the impact travelled through his fathoms of fat. Jaroslav and Botuslav bowed beneath his wavering arms, attempting, like scrawny Atlantes, to prop him up. But Luboš Hrabal could not be rescued. The vast edifice shook. Guffawing with incredulity at his earthbound bulk, he crumbled, dragging down his twin pillars.

Owing to the gradient of the street and to the spill of meltwaters beneath him, the fat man began to slide, descending several feet on his rotundity. 'Help me!' Hrabal spluttered. 'I'm heading for the river!'

Jaroslav and Botuslav hooted with laughter. Scrabbling to catch the flailing arms of their companion, they slipped with him down the slope. '*Pomoc!*' one of them gasped, seeing me above them. '*Zastavte!*' But the cause of their trouble seemed to enjoy his slide, gaily asking passers-by for directions: '*Jak se dostanu k Mostecká?*'

Seeing my incomprehension, one of the brothers pleaded in German. 'Help us! Grab a hold of my brother. Between us we may just stop him.'

Concerned as ever for my dignity, I was tempted to leave those drunkards to their slippage. Yet my blood was heated: I had encountered so little hilarity in my life that my body longed to be racked with it. Therefore I took the plunge – throwing my shirt front into the wet sludge – and dug my fingers beneath Botuslav's belt.

'*Guten abend*,' said Luboš Hrabal, as one might greet a fellow traveller. 'Soon I will start charging passengers.'

Perhaps my added mass, small as it was, proved the braking counterweight; for with a gritty rumble we ground to a halt. Hrabal sighed, almost with regret, and waited with his piggy eyes closed for someone to haul him back to his feet. Naturally, I joined the salvage effort . . . and for my contribution was pressed into the drinkers' company.

'Come,' said Hrabal, 'get shit-faced with us. I buy first round – it cannot cost much to fill your little belly.'

So I was pummelled and caroused into the Golden Dumpling on Bridge Street. Luboš Hrabal quickly proved the most voluble of our company. He sat, a monarch of spit and sawdust, holding forth on all manner of obscenity, while the Mušek twins laughed and drank like troopers. At first sight there was little to tell between them. Both men sported a pointy beard; both had woolly, flyaway hair which they tugged every so often, with tapering fingers, behind their ears. Botuslav, I would learn, hardly ever spoke, while

Jaroslav could reach impressive heights of garrulity so long as Hrabal was silent. I noticed, when they smiled, that Jaroslav had four teeth in his upper gums while Botuslav had only three.

'We are all crook,' Hrabal said, quaking with laughter. '*Ja, ja*. I have been, for twenty year, *ein Gross Lump* . . .'

'Oh no,' I said. 'I wouldn't say that.'

'He means a scoundrel,' shouted Jaroslav above the chatter; my German was not yet perfect.

'*Ano*, a big *Schwindler*, a, how you say, go-lucky fellow. We all three live on our wits – and heartily, you ask my friend here.' (He patted his belly.) 'Botuslav and Jaroslav, myself Luboš Hrabal of Český Krumlov, with native cunning can empty fool's pocket! Charm the ring off lady's finger!'

Swaying at the table's edge, I drank from a magic flagon which seemed, for every gulp, constantly to replenish itself. Botuslav and Jaroslav sat a young barmaid on their knees, sharing her backside between them. I was conscious of sweet perfume, a shallow cleavage, Czech innuendo. I nearly observed to my fellow drinkers the miraculous properties of my flagon, when the landlady topped it up from two massive jugs. Hrabal leered in admiration at the woman's powerful arms, at the magnificent breasts straining against the dam of her corset.

'What strength, *ne*? Imagine stamina of such woman. You could die happy between her legs.'

'A terrible picture,' said Jaroslav, with a sour face. 'Luboš and Zdenka going at it like bears.'

'Two mountains,' said Hrabal, 'crashing together.'

'A great underpass, one tiny traveller.'

The twins cackled and rocked the barmaid on their knees. I half expected Hrabal to throw a punch for this insult; but he too bawled and wept with laughter, giving Botuslav a slap on the cheek as though to swat a mosquito. The barmaid perching on the brothers' knees tried to share their hilarity, though she had, so far as I could tell, no German. She was blonde, pretty enough no doubt in daylight but the very essence of beauty in that nocturnal tavern. Fascinatingly, her mouth opened a fraction of a second before she laughed. I stared intently at that pink aperture, at the curling tongue and pearlish teeth. Stirred by drink like a boat at sea (though my body was stationary), I struggled to believe the intimacy of her returned gaze.

'Not yet fourteen,' Hrabal whispered with a warm blast in my ear. 'Milk and honey. She likes you – look.'

Leaning forward on molten legs, I asked for her name. There were starry points of derision in the Mušek brothers' eyes. The girl's face was painted, a base of white powder with rouged cheeks and blue smudges about the eyes. Again I tried some courtesy. '*Těši mě*,' I said, and caught myself staring at her breasts. The beer was a millstone about my neck: I could not pull up for decency's sake.

Jaroslav squeezed the barmaid's chin with his fingers to lower her head. He whispered a suggestion in Czech. There was dissent; the girl flushed beneath her powder and her lips parted hotly. '*Ano*,' insisted Jaroslav. Shaking her flaxen tresses, the girl tried to get up; but the twins clung on to her wide flannel skirt. They made soothing noises, they smiled reassuringly and dragged her back, with a bump, on to their knees. Botuslav or Jaroslav (I no longer knew which) placed a coin, a gold ducat no less, on the table within the girl's reach. Her eyes widened; they became piercing blue spheres of need.

Luboš Hrabal gathered up the vastness of his thigh to permit the escape of a thunderous fart. 'Watch this,' he said.

We all studied the barmaid's face as she considered the ducat. She began to rise and fall on the brothers' knees as they nudged her from buttock to buttock. The tobacco fog of that murmurous tavern filled with a low moan. The sound grew and broadened; it became a tormenting and monotonous jeer. Jaroslav and Botuslav bounced the girl between them. Her tresses shook, the small breasts beneath her bodice raised their eyebrows, as rhythmically she rose and fell. I could not be sure whether she was smiling or scowling.

'Wooaah!' cried the brothers, and Hrabal added his gravelly bass. 'Woooaah!'

With the speed of a frog catching a fly (a pink flurry of arm, a hand shutting about the coin), the barmaid snatched her payment. The Mušek twins seemed pleased to part with their ducat. I too laughed, I too applauded – missing contact between my hands and snapping my little finger.

'When you are finished,' said Luboš Hrabal, 'we will be here for you. Don't forget. And don't forget to *find us*.'

The girl took my hand; her palm was moist and cool, with a hint of coarseness about the fingers. Dizzily I suffered her to guide me between raucous tables, until we penetrated a hot and hellishly flamed kitchen. A cat on a table lapped milk from a saucer. A red-bearded man, stripped to the waist, was busy roasting a piglet on a spit. I felt sick, like a condemned man on his way, through unfamiliar rooms, to the scaffold.

At two identical doors the girl stopped, bringing my tumescence against her rump. I sensed hesitation in the curling of her fingers. The pig-turner shouted at us across the glowing pewter. '*Do leva!*' His voice was rasping, scorched by brimstone. '*Pět minuty*, Růžena.' She pulled me petulantly towards the wrong door. '*Tamten!*' screamed the cook. '*Tamten – do leva*!' The girl was exasperated: she flung open the left-hand door and tugged me violently inside.

I saw, in a shrinking seam of light, wooden steps, a scurf of carpet and Růžěna clapping the ducat into her mouth.

Then she closed the door. I breathed heavily, hotly, like a dog near a furnace, as unseen fingers grappled with my breeches. Růžena pushed me up several steps and I felt her breath on my belly. As she gathered up her skirts I fell against her and she tutted with impatience. Our intimacy was conducted in wordless darkness: two bodies glued together like slugs in a cellar. I was lost, pressed between wet pillows, the weight of her body crushing me on the tattered steps. Guiding my hands to her breasts, which were tugged awkwardly from her corset, Růžena huffed and grunted. More bewildered than intoxicated, and aching in my groin from the need to pee, I tugged on a cold button of flesh. Twice Růžena arched violently and had to scrabble me back in place, while I apologised and sobbed and sought her gold-sealed mouth with mine. '*Nein!*' Růžena protested, and forced my face to the pallid dough of her breasts. Paroxysms raked my back. Her fingers sank their fangs into my neck. The walls of the world collapsed about me as Růžena pulled me clear to spend on her skirts.

When it was finished, she scolded me in her own tongue. Then she stamped away, up the staircase, disgorging the coin into her palm. I gathered up my shame, a clammy mollusc, and returned with tingling limbs to my new-found friends.

Luboš Hrabal and the Mušek twins drank a toast to my lost cherry.

'Stick with us,' Hrabal said, 'and you be a man, my son.'

Effortlessly as a stone through water, I sank into sin. My work demanded little of my time and none of my creative effort, so that I squandered whole days and nights in the company of my new friends, laughing at Luboš Hrabal's tall stories and gaping in obsequious amazement at the Mušek brothers' magic tricks. In their prime, Hrabal explained,

Jaroslav and Botuslav had posed as alchemists. They had excelled in the exploitation of human need.

'We promised children to barren couples,' said Jaroslav. 'The fertilisations of alchemy would bless them, we said. Both of us were more beautiful then, and plenty of husbands got mostly what they prayed for.'

Hrabal rocked in his gallons of fat and, laughing, slapped my knee a dozen times. He claimed that the brothers could transform a live trout into gold and then back again; that with a little red powder they had secured themselves lodgings, good meats and fine wines over several years. In pork grease, later, at the Golden Eel, Botuslav sketched for me the secret compartment of his alchemical pot which, opening in the heat of the furnace, appeared to 'kill' the base metal and release its primary soul. Voluble twin to his practical brother, Jaroslav bamboozled me with talk of fixation and rubedo, of sapientia and peacock's tail and the philosophical child. He showed me, as we huddled like conspirators about the table, a stirring wand made of wax which melted in the crucible, releasing the nuggets of gold inside. Considering their claims of success, I ought to have found suspect the poverty of the brothers' clothes, which were threadbare and bleached by sunlight and smelled of constant use.

It was Hrabal who anticipated my suspicions. 'The boys got tired of easy money,' he said. 'You know how it goes, Tomáš. Artists need fresh challenges.'

Today, instead of alchemy, the Mušek brothers dealt in potions. They made syrups for toothache and some acrid bolus for belly-gripe, since folk most readily trust a physic when it is distasteful, nauseating and an agony to swallow. Mute Botuslav would play the apothecary on Charles Square, while Jaroslav with his dog Latin praised his *aurum potabile*, elixir of life', which consisted of honey, verbena and camomile. Sometimes I would help them flog thimbles of a sticky glue, which Jaroslav called the juice of the sundew. 'A peerless cure for warts, madam. Guaranteed to excite copulation in cattle.' Shamelessly, to ageing and unaided farmers, the Mušeks sold the twisted roots of white bryony, pretending that these were mandrake roots for bringing to foison their wives' barren wombs.

As for Luboš Hrabal, he earned a crust posing as a surgeon.

'Venus and phlebotomy! We fear both, gentlemen and ladies, yet who can live without?'

As weeks passed without a sighting of my scornful Růžena, I was invited deeper into the tricksters' confidence. Hrabal showed me the black lacquered hardwood case where he kept his surgical tools. Teeth-pulling was his speciality; he had travelled for several years throughout Bohemia performing to crowds at country fairs. As for cutting, he had watched a barber once slice open a man for the stone, and considered that training enough to perform the task himself.

'You should surgeon sheep,' said Jaroslav. 'Honest. You could dock a ram without even meaning to.'

Hrabal exposed a fat yellow tongue.

'Tomáš, if you ever want a mole removed, tell Luboš you've a bellyache. If you bleed from the head, ask him to sew up your knee. The farther you start from the wound, the better the chance he might treat it by mistake.'

Hrabal took this badly – in the one telling occasion when his humour failed. It required Botuslav and mighty Zdenka to haul him off Jaroslav's neck; then two rounds of beer to soothe his rage. It transpired, when later he had gone for a piss, that Hrabal had fled to Prague from Mělník after performing a near-fatal bleeding. Clumsy with drink in a patron's house, he had sliced through the daughter's tendon and most probably crippled her for life. 'But hush about this,' said Jaroslav, upon whose throat an angry weal was blooming. 'Nobody in Kleinseite must know about the balls-up. It would not be good for custom.'

Teeth-pulling and potions cannot have sufficed to pay for the epic quantities of beer and pork which the friends consumed in the Golden Dumpling, or the Black Sun, or in the yard of the Golden Pear opposite my lodgings. Sometimes, tiring perhaps of my company and the smiling it demanded of them, the Mušek twins would mutter between themselves in Czech. Arriving early for lunch one day, I caught them slavering into a lady's silk purse, which either Jaroslav or Botuslav dashed into his lap the moment he saw me.

Why, you may wonder, did I not part company with these villains? Was I not God's creature, imbued with Christian teachings? Even allowing for my vague and frustrated desire to see Růžena again – that is to say, allowing for my lechery – I ought to have considered how ill fortune clings to a swindler like shit to a shoe. Prague, after all, was awash with tricksters whose luck had abandoned them.

It was on Týn Street that one such mountebank accosted me, clapping his hands inside a black cloak and making improbable incantations. I recognised him as the salesman of quack medicines whom I had seen detained long ago outside the Customs House. He was in a sorry state, his face decayed and cratered, his once flamboyant moustache now ragged as a wet stoat's tail. He had taken up residence with his open case on the Old Town Square, where he twirled with soiled fingers the shreds of his glory and glowered at the indifferent crowd. The few teeth still loyal to his mouth he appeared to prop up with his tongue.

'My countryman!' he exclaimed after I swore at him in Italian. Blocking my attempts to pass, he forced me into a grotesque dance. 'My name,' he said, agitating his cloak in a manner that seemed to anticipate thunderbolts, 'is

Geronimo Scotta. *Your* name begins with a . . .' (He twisted about a prognosticating finger.) '. . . ffnnggttsszzaadd – *em*.'

'Gee.'

The trickster did not blink. 'I was born in Parma. *You* were born in . . .'

'Verona.'

'Verona, yes! I have made miracles in Verona. I am Scotta the distiller, Scotta the alchemist. Do you wish to know your future? Will-you-be-rich? Will-you-be-loved?' He aligned a finger to his nose and made a prophetic squint. 'You are familiar with the science of metoposcopy? I propose, for a contemptible fee, to predict your future, signor, from the contours and irregularities of your cranium.' His hands fluttered like moths about my head. 'Mmm . . . yes . . . I see it all. Gold and women. A great heap of treasures. Here, in the hollows of your temples . . .' He shrank back, pulling in his hands as though stung by nettles. 'But no! I cannot!'

'What's the matter? What have you seen?'

'It is nothing.'

'Is it some kind of calamity?'

Geronimo Scotta rolled across his folded arms, as though gripped in the belly. 'The metoposcoper's art is painful to the practitioner. For a little contribution, by way of incentive . . . one greshki, say . . . I will force myself to the task.'

I was just about to reach for my purse, enchanted by the possibility, the faintest risk, that Truth might speak through quackery, when Petrus Gonsalvus bore down upon us. He must have seen us from the arcades of Týn school. His face, naturally so placid, was savagely distorted. Even I expected the snarling teeth to bite.

'Leave the boy alone, you *swindler*.'

Geronimo Scotta, faced with Nature's miracle, looked a

theatrical drab. 'Pepper, gong,' he gasped, and ravelled up his cloak beneath his chin. 'Petrus Gonsalvus . . .'

'Don't pay this vagrant for his deceptions, Tommaso.'

'He wasn't trying anything,' I protested.

'Right. That's right, Herr Gonsalvus. We're just passing the time of day.'

Gonsalvus, however, was fierce. 'What does *my* face tell you, Scotta?'

'*Your* face?'

'Yes, this face of mine. What does it augur for my future?'

'I don't know . . . Upholstery?'

'Did your handsome mug, when you raced into Prague in your velvet carriages with your forty horses – did it predict what a vagrant scab you would become? The future is not determined, Tommaso. We are masters of our own fates. Those who would tell you your fortune are trying to make their own.'

Geronimo Scotta gathered up his shredded dignity and sauntered away without pretending to defend himself. As for me, I trembled with humiliation. Gonsalvus, by his intervention, had drawn eyes from all across the square.

When his own passion had subsided (which it did rapidly, like a kraken barnacled from inaction sinking back under tranquil waters), Gonsalvus proposed that I accompany him to his home. I was painfully aware how freakish we looked in each other's company.

'Please forgive any embarrassment I've caused you. You must have a bite of something to eat. It is such a long time, Tommaso, since the family had the pleasure of your company.'

Ungrateful worm, I squirmed and shook my head. Shouting improbable excuses of overwork across my shoulder, I ran back towards the river, crossed the bridge, and regained my lonely Hradschin cave.

All night long I lamented that I had made the wrong decision.

I resolved, with the freshly washed dawn, to apply myself more closely to my work for the Castle. Blackbirds opened their throats for gladness; a daisy nodded sagely on my window sill. I had only just dipped my quill in ink, however, when Luboš Hrabal shouted my name in the street. Cursing under my breath (and cursing myself for cursing, since it soiled my pledge of virtue), I stamped downstairs – sending Schwaiger the clockmaker scuttling back to his room.

'I am trying to *work*,' I said at the door.

Hrabal had brought me a visitor. He was a courtier of modest wealth, sporting a velvet doublet, with his belt slung at the Spanish Habsburg angle. 'I understand you are a painter,' he said, barely acknowledging, with a flicker of his darkly pitted eyes, the rusty flourish of my bow. Luboš Hrabal, behind the stranger's shoulder, made dumbshow gestures of encouragement.

'Yes, sir – your servant.'

'Can you copy?'

'Copy?'

'Yes, perfect reproductions of ex*tant*' (he fairly wrenched off, with sharp infantile teeth, the last syllable) 'I say ex*tant* works of art?'

'Unquestionably. I mean, for the purpose of study . . .'

'Then paint this.' The gentleman plucked a medallion portrait, a lurid watercolour, from the silken folds of his sleeve. 'You have two days. My employer will pay you six talers if the copy satisfies him. Naturally, this transaction will be of no interest to your acquaintances . . .'

'He has none,' Hrabal intruded, 'save myself and the twins.'

The munificent gentleman seemed not to hear. 'My

name,' he said, 'for our purpose is Matthäus Friedrich Moosbrugger. Apply yourself to the matter, you will find my employer a most generous patron.'

When the apparition had vanished, Hrabal floated, grinning, before my eyes. 'What did I tell you? What did I say about stick to your friends? Now you sod your court pittance. Six talers is three ducats. For a lick of paint? *Three*.'

Three ducats, I replied in a daze. Three tumbles with Růžena in the dark.

Forgeries for money: base materials turned to gold. How I swaggered, a glorified copyist, in my plush new clothes, with my hands compressed inside white gloves and my nostrils bristling at fragrant pomanders. Sometimes Moosbrugger, sometimes Hrabal came to the Golden Ram to remunerate me or deliver my latest commission. Hrabal amused himself tormenting František Schwaiger, twisting the arms of his clocks and spitting in their vitals.

'Please, sir, *please*!' the clockmaker squealed, nerved throughout his body for a catastrophe. 'This is an outrage – against an Imperial servant!'

I ought, once Hrabal had gone, to have apologised to Schwaiger, to make peace with a man whose grievances would surely drive him to the Castle. But I hated the clockmaker for his meanness, for his pusillanimous twitching. All day long I could feel him working in his burrow. When Hrabal called, I thrilled at the sound of excited voices that briefly thawed our frigid lodgings.

My shadowy patron's agent, Moosbrugger, was closely acquainted with my trickster friends. Once I saw him at their table when, thirsty after a day's forgery, I went to find them in a Kleinseite tavern. Moosbrugger at my approach bade the others good evening. I felt the gelid beams of his eyes; then, with a mutual tipping of hats, the gentleman was gone. As though he had cast a cloud upon them, Hrabal and the Mušek twins sat up from a slump, their expressions brightened, and we dazzled the night with our carousing.

'Do not take offence at these expressions of amicable concern,' wrote Petrus Gonsalvus in the first of several unanswered letters. 'It is common knowledge that you have befriended an unregenerate class of gentlemen, rogues that live by trickery and deceit. A man's name must be cultivated, my friend, like a vine. Among weeds and rank grasses it cannot ripen . . .' I growled at these paternal intrusions and set my teeth against pious counsel. 'The too trusting effusion of young blood hardens you against sound advice. Herr Meyrink will no longer vouch for you; nor does your strongest ally in Court, our mutual friend Bartholomeus, look kindly on the company that you keep.'

These words clenched, blackened and expired in my hearth. Upon receiving and refusing to read a final letter from Gonsalvus, I took myself to Jan Fux's shop beside the bridge, where I bought a broad hat of rabbit fur with an ostrich feather upon it, allowing me to rival for plumage those Hradschin popinjays who sauntered about the city with perfumed handkerchiefs pressed to their noses. Thus I was grandly over-dressed (my waistcoat Argus-eyed with sequins, my points concealed in leather boots) when I came late to our appointed meeting, firmly resolved, after six timid months, to buy a second turn on the stairs with Růžena.

She was nowhere to be seen when I entered the Golden Dumpling. Zdenka and a new girl (skinny, with a brown haze above her lip) looked down at my panache. Zdenka mimicked my duckling's gait.

'*Kachna! Dobrý večer, malá kachna!*' The new girl snorted and caught a string of mucus on her sleeve.

I found my companions hugging their table in a gloomy, sausage-hung corner. There was a fifth member to our party. Although he was out of uniform, I recognised at once the squinting Castle sentry who had saved me long ago from the blasting storm. He was squeezed between Hrabal and Jaroslav Mušek, his ungracious features rigid from grinning.

'Tomáš!' Hrabal cheered. 'Meet our new friend – Herman Bumm.'

'I'm sorry?' I said, not hearing.

'It's not your fault,' said Bumm. From the intensity with which he surveyed the dying head on his beer, I could tell that he remembered me. (Jaroslav, catching my questioning eye, made the explanatory sign of empty pockets; then he spread his fingers like a fan and inspected spectral playing cards.) I had heard how Rudolf's guardsmen supplemented their paltry salaries with goldsmithery. No doubt Herman Bumm lacked the talent. Living like his comrades in a narrow lane between the White Tower and Dalibor – struggling to provide for his wife and child – he had tried his gambler's luck, only to discover that he had none. Now, sitting without his armour in this iniquitous holt, he looked more out of place than a crab in a carp barrel.

'You are man for taking risks, eh, Tomáš?' Hrabal nudged Bumm with his naked, whitely crusted elbow. 'We have little wager going, Bumm and Luboš. A gentleman's dare.'

'Moosbrugger has placed money on the table,' said Jaroslav in a low voice. 'His employer likes to play games, moving pieces from afar.'

'Like a chess player,' said Botuslav; and I was so surprised to hear him break silence that I missed the beginning of what followed.

'. . . and take a look *around*,' said Hrabal. I gazed from man to man, as though the words I had missed might be floating between them like down from a flight-struck bird.

'Herman Bumm will help us get our snouts inside. No harm doing, remember. It's just a wager.'

'You won't . . . er . . .' Bumm swallowed and flicked a nail at his tankard. 'You won't *upset* anything? Because the Emperor will see, and if not him then Strada will see, if anything is . . . out of place.'

Hrabal pressed a knuckle into the guardsman's arm, chortling at his worries.

'Aren't you excited?' Jaroslav asked me.

Excited? Reader, I was barely attending to the matter. I was colicky with desire, casting about the Golden Dumpling for a glimpse of my sullen darling. She was absent – as she had been for weeks – from our drunken concourse. When finally I succeeded in plucking Zdenka's sleeve, I asked, perhaps a dozen times, where Růžena might be this evening.

'Hřbitov,' she said at last.

'Sorry, where?'

Zdenka was keen to move on. The heavy jugs of beer spewed in her hands.

'*Prosím vás – nerozumím.*' I did not understand. '*Kde je Hřbitov?*' Was it in the country?

There were curses and shouts for beer. Zdenka shook her head angrily. '*Tot,*' she said.

'What?'

'In see crowned.' Then, spitting at my feet, she departed, pert with a sense of her own virtue.

I took in very little of what followed at the table. My system had suffered a cruel shock. Above all I felt cheated. Death had nullified my only conquest, depriving my manhood of its witness. To drown my sorrow, I drank myself stupid; so that I entirely missed the details of my involvement in Moosbrugger's scheme and wandered like a sleepwalker to that dismal September night when Hrabal, the Mušek twins and myself, assisted by poor Herman Bumm, broke into the Emperor's galleries.

Night had fallen when the Mušek twins came to fetch me. I had been drinking much of the afternoon alone in my room and now, with a trail of plum brandy still corroding my gullet, I followed the twins up the empty alley of Neu Welt. On Castle Square the chestnut trees whispered to us to be quiet. We stepped over mounds of human trash, trying to avoid the slug-like excrement that littered the rain-greased stones. Fifty yards north of the Castle gates Jaroslav stopped and, cupping his hands together, gave an owlish hoot. Luboš Hrabal clambered out of the moat. He looked grossly swollen about the waist, as though he had been gorging himself without pause for several days. Winking at me, he pretended to rest on the top of my head. I was overpowered by the smell from his armpits – a mixture, particular to Prague, of cheese, sausage and river water.

'Let's get to it,' Jaroslav said.

True to his word, Herman Bumm awaited us at the gatehouse. Moosbrugger, he informed us, had distracted his comrades with the anonymous gift of a laxative pot roast. We were free to sweep, unchallenged, across the drawbridge into the open courtyard.

'Quickly, boy,' hissed Bumm when I froze to admire the steeple's shadow. 'Come *along*.'

'I'm not a boy.'

We were scurrying now towards a building that adjoined the Royal Palace. Somewhere within its cold dark flanks the collection awaited our profane gaze. 'Don't get caught,' whispered Herman Bumm. 'I have a family, remember.' He crossed himself vigorously, flinched at the knee as though he might sit down, then doubled back to his post.

'The Wide Passage,' said Hrabal, who was trying, quite

improbably, to flatten himself against its outer wall. 'This is where *you* come in, Tomáš.' He indicated a single window, high up in the wall, which stood ajar. Only a child could have clambered through – to encounter who knew what drop on the other side. I understood with horror what was expected of me.

'Oh no,' I said. 'No, *no*.'

'Damn you, *yes*. Because you don't chicken now and get home alive – understand?'

Jaroslav rested a gloved hand on my shoulder. 'The boy understands,' he said. 'Climb up on Hrabal's shoulder. We'll push you through the window. Once inside, run to that door over there – see it? Now there's a bolt across it. All you have to do is unlock the door for us.'

Without daring to protest, I found myself squeezing through the infantile aperture. I pinched my balls excruciatingly on the window's ledge and skinned several knuckles on the long way down.

My heart felt bruised by its own pounding. I was in a corridor, a tunnel almost, by its silence, and darker than the moonless courtyard. By touch alone I located the door and opened it to the others. Hrabal, Jaroslav and Botuslav pushed me back inside. They whispered rapidly in Czech. A flame snapped awake on the snout of a flintlock. Two hand-cupped tapers floated northward, gradually confirming the hint of a door at the far end of the corridor.

Up until now, I had fooled myself into believing my companions' pretence of a wager; for I longed to see the wonders of which Arcimboldo and Spranger had spoken. When Hrabal shook three sacks from beneath his shirt and handed one to each of his partners, I could deceive myself no longer. Moosbrugger had paid them (had paid *me*, with my forgeries, for my loyalty) to steal from the Emperor's collection! I felt panic flood my senses. I thought of trying to dissuade them. But my voice had gone, flown like a bird from out of my chest. I cursed myself for having burned Gonsalvus's letters and for the wantonness of my criminal life.

'Stay there,' ordered Jaroslav, while his brother picked the lock. 'We need a man on the lookout.'

'Lookout for what?' I quailed. 'How will I alert you?'

The lock clicked and Hrabal eased open the door. 'We'll know from your screaming,' he grinned.

Then they slipped away, like eels into the depths.

Twice, in the slowly oozing minutes that followed, I started at the sound of my own breathing, convinced of a stalker in the darkness. How lost I felt, deprived of bearings by darkness and brandy, with my legs vague beneath me. It occurred to me that I had fallen prey to a trick, a practical joke engineered by those laughable rogues. What fun they were having at my expense – fat Luboš, who cherished his belly like an expectant mother, the newtish Mušek brothers, who plainly took none of my dwarfish pretensions seriously. No doubt Moosbrugger was watching me at this very instant, with Herman Bumm scrabbling for access to the peephole.

Fluttering at my extremities, I groped along the wall in search of the door to the courtyard. No (I dented my head on the corner of some table), not there. Oh, the plum brandy made my head dance! I was frantic for a pee! Fumbling, I stunned my fingertips on stone. Then I gripped a handle of cold iron and passed through a doorway . . .

. . . into a second corridor. No matter. If I could advance quietly, ready to hide at the sound of footsteps, I was sure to find my way out. I felt pulled towards a third door like a bean of water sucked up a straw. I sensed the proximity of the wondrous alrauns, of the basilisk made harmless by Death's mirror. The Emperor's collection of paintings, original works by Dürer and the Flemish masters: how close these marvels must be! But this was no time to look for them. I turned the door handle, hoping to feel the night air on my face – and found myself in a small carpeted chamber which, though uninhabited, enjoyed a blazing log fire. Chestnuts impaled on pokers wheezed and whistled in the flames. My head spun; I was close to vomiting, and only a bite of something would settle my stomach. Therefore, creeping on tiptoe as though braving hot coals, I crossed the carpet with the intention of stealing a chestnut.

Another door burst open, flooding the carpet with candle-light. Mortified, I cowered behind a chair. A huffing, gasping figure – in the counter-light as black as the Devil – ran towards me. He stopped as though a rope had tautened behind him and turned to face the yawning doorway. Something was chasing him, some ravenous beast that snorted and champed on coils of phlegm.

'Your Majesty!' The terrified man wrung his hands, like a strolling player. 'Your Majesty must control himself!'

Beyond my vision, the courtier's assailant slowed. '*Monstruo! Aborto pérfido! Voy matarte con mis manos!*'

The hunted gentleman fell to his knees, his face contorted with such dread that it inspired the same in me. He clasped his hands imploringly. 'Mercy! Oh, mercy, my lord! Whatever I may have done—'

'*May* have done?'

The door was kicked against the wall and a fury landed on him. 'Guards!' the wretched courtier cried. 'Guards!'

Two men fused in the pool of light. I could hear the attacker's murderous frenzy. His victim, not daring to defend himself, gargled and kicked the carpet with his heels. 'Help . . . *gah* . . . help . . .'

I knew then how Semele must have felt when Zeus revealed himself to her in thunder. My blood chilled with holy dread. I was watching the Emperor Rudolf murder one of his subjects.

Looking to flee, I discovered a door to the right of the fireplace. It opened abruptly and admitted four guards with their swords drawn. 'For God's sake,' hissed the struggling courtier, training his fat and glaucous eyes upon them. The guards, failing immediately to distinguish the Emperor from his victim, pulled the two men apart. Rudolf fell heavily on to his coat-tails. The other man hacked and gasped.

'This *traitor*—' the Emperor yelped, and stopped to regain a semblance of composure. 'This man means to kill me. He means to kill your king.'

With impeccably bad timing, a chestnut in the fire behind me exploded. The Emperor screamed as though shot. All eyes, save the bulging jellies of the prisoner, flew to my shadow.

I leaped to my feet and bolted for the open door. My head start would not help me for long. I could hear cries and clamour of arms as I sped down a final corridor into the Royal Palace. I ran with the swiftness of Hermes, my route an inversion of courtly progress. Through the Green Chamber, of which Spranger had spoken three years earlier, I attained the dimly lit cavern of Vladislav Hall.

'*Wer ist das? Halt!* Halt!'

A guard snapped out of his exquisite yawn. I turned right into the Bohemian Chancery, where studious clerks looked up from candlelit ledgers to see a terrified midget pursued by soldiers.

Dead end! The Chancery led nowhere!

One lusty volunteer tried to block my access to the great window. My momentum proved sufficient to knock him off his feet. The fatal tusks of halberds were nearing my rump. Had it not been for the imminence of death or injury, I should have balked at clambering through an open frame in the latticed glass. There was no time to think, however. I mounted a paper-spewing table and, in tribute to my earlier ingression, squeezed myself halfway between disasters.

The guards halted and lowered their weapons.

'Easy, lad,' someone said.

Not for the first time, my infantilism spared me a mauling. I felt wretchedly cold, my skin a sweating surface of ice, as I balanced on the lattice frame. I could see the drop far below. The moat was a dense black bog.

'Come back inside, boy. You'll only kill yourself.' Clumsy fingers clutched at my shirt. I cried out, 'I'm sorry!' And then I had broken free. My fingers caught at vegetation; my feet floated in the cold nocturnal air. Managing to take strong hold of the ivy, I began my clambering descent, while above and below me torches flared and wept. I slipped, betrayed by broken tendrils, and almost lost my fingers attempting to save myself. There were cries of dismay, of futile warning, and the ground was rushing up – a dark unending wave – to swallow me.

7

Dalibor

Though God sees everything from His celestial vantage, yet had He sent one of His fiery lieutenants to watch me more closely. So it seemed when, lurching from Lethe, I found myself confronted by a ball of flame. I wanted to shield my eyes with my hands but I was manacled to a wall. All that I could do against angelic glory was shut my eyes and pray for the Lord's mercy.

'Shit, I think he just blinked.'

'About bloody time. Easy, Wolff, don't blind him.'

The glow inside my skull diminished. Pale blots and animalcules floated through an oily sea. A calloused hand slapped my cheek.

'Wake up, sunshine.'

Two human shapes crouched above me. One held a torch. His colleague – a black mask with gleaming hints of eyeball and teeth – nudged a bird's beak into my face. 'Don't struggle, lad. It's water.'

Indeed, I was afflicted by a scorching thirst. I took the beak between my lips and drank willingly. Singular damage, I realised, had been done to my backside and my shoulders felt sorely bruised.

'There now – feel better?'

One of the prison guards wet my brow with a cold flannel, dragging me clear of sleep's undertow.

'I'm not dead, am I?'

The gaoler with the torch scoffed. 'Not for the time being.'

The two men watched me with an expression almost like

pride on their faces. I had seen Gonsalvus and his wife smile thus to witness their children's play.

'Welcome,' my gaolers said, 'to Dalibor Tower.'

They came back later with a customarily stale loaf. I picked slowly at what had once been the soft: it felt like the marrow of old bone. I tried to make sense of my surroundings, and listened in vain for another's breathing. I was lost in blackness, backed by sweating stone, with damp straw beneath me. Given the hopelessness of my situation, I drifted almost serenely between sleep and waking. For I was relieved of responsibility to act. Chained in Stygian night and blind as a worm, I was too exhausted to contemplate my future. My gaolers, therefore, were keener to acquaint me with my circumstances than I was to learn of them.

'Tell him, Hans. Tell him how he survived the fall.'

'You got about halfway down. On the ivy. We found shreds of it in your fists.'

'Nobody was going to catch you. Not where you were heading. They just waited for you to fall.'

'Into the moat.'

'You can thank your stars you didn't meet any broken glass.'

The gaoler called Wolff smirked and plugged his nose. It seemed that human ordure had saved my life – the moat being swamped with Castle waste.

It was then I noticed the absence of my clothes: that costly frippery which had so pleased me. Somebody, while I was unconscious, had washed and scoured my body. I was dressed in rags cut from sackcloth, with sleeves too long for me attached to the torso by frayed, black stitches. There lingered an unspeakable taste at the back of my throat. Gagging, I strained to evacuate my nostrils.

'Don't foul your cell,' said Wolff. 'You'll only have to sit in it.'

Time was shapeless, an elastic quantity, in the dungeon. Days of agonising slowness might pass before my gaolers called on me; or else I had barely the chance to swallow a yawn before they were back with their affable taunting. My mind, cut from its moorings, floated in a sunless sea. Sometimes it invoked remembered faces, transparent like jellyfish, which trailed in their wake unanswerable questions. I wondered what had become of Hrabal and the twins. Had they escaped with Moosbrugger's loot? Or did they languish in a Castle cell some yards of stone from where I lay? Sequestered from the bustling world, I began to take journeys in my head. I ambled through baking Florentine streets, closing mantis wings with my fingers as though they were scutcheons and sheltering beneath my nurse's skirts. My tutor lifted the skirts – now a heavy green tapestry – and scolded me for having ink-stained fingers. Sandro Bondanella and all the grey heads of the Academy prodded me in the ribs with their mahlsticks. They hauled me screaming up the nave of Milan's cathedral, where Gian Bonconvento waited with the bleeding skin of his catamite, Vittorio, draped across his arm. Slowly, eyeing me with malice, the corpulent Maestro licked his butchering knives . . . Other apparitions came wreathed in sorrow. My dear Arcimboldo knelt beside me, silent as the grave whose cerements he wore. He trailed an odour of rotten fruit which made me abhor his company. Sometimes he appeared with battered Piero and Mosca, with Giovanni cradling his shattered hand and dead Růžena frigging coins. Together they produced a low murmur, which sometimes threatened to subside and sometimes swelled to howls of grief and consternation. There was no getting used to these recurrent horrors, no first light when ghosts fade beneath the melting moon; so that, when Petrus Gonsalvus appeared before me, I clapped my hands to my ears and implored him not to start howling. Gonsalvus, to break the spell, pressed my fingers into the matter of his beard.

'Don't vanish,' I whimpered.

'I will not vanish.'

'Or leave me.'

Beneath the greying veil of his affliction, Petrus Gonsalvus smiled. He took my unchained feet and rubbed a soothing ointment into the weals. 'As though you might be capable of escaping,' he said. 'Do not feel abandoned, Tommaso. You are in grave danger, I cannot lie on that score. But in spite of recent events you still have friends in the world who will see to your welfare. Here, I've brought you an apple. Caterina picked it for you in the Hasenburg orchards.'

In the glow from his lantern, I admired the yellow fruit – its delicate blush of red on one side, the still-fresh, solitary leaf like an ensign on its stem. As I caught the apple in my palm, it made a rich snapping sound. I bit into it and nearly wept for delight at the dribbling flesh.

'The children ask about you. Carlo is growing tall. I think he will overlook me soon.' My situation must have been bad, for Gonsalvus to attempt humour. 'You must want for spectacle in this place.'

I disagreed, thinking of my phantoms. All that I asked was a *lack* of spectacle: a total darkness where I could skulk unvisited by the howling dead. Gonsalvus watched me devour the apple to its stem – and then consume the stem as though it were liquorice.

'Tommaso, you are accused of being a spy.'

'A *spy*?'

'Were you not discovered in Rudolf's palace?'

'Yes, but . . . am I being accused of spying and nothing else?'

'Is not that enough?'

So Hrabal and the twins had succeeded. Perhaps by

my incautious wanderings I had rendered them a priceless service? My weary and deluded heart quickened as I pictured them in the Golden Dumpling, drinking to the health of their sacrificed friend.

'What were you doing in the palace, Tommaso?'

'The assault I saw—'

'What assault?'

'By the Emperor. On that man.'

Gonsalvus was confused; so I told him what I had seen, omitting only my reason for being there. His chest sank with every word. 'I had feared there might be a connection. The man you saw arrested was Wolfgang Rumpf, the Emperor's chamberlain.'

'How do you know?'

'The following day – the day after your arrest – it was announced that Wolfgang Rumpf had been imprisoned. He is here, in Dalibor. Charged with plotting treason.'

'He didn't look like a traitor to me.'

'They say that Rudolf is convinced of plots against him. There have been fiery bodies in the sky, winged dragons in southern Bohemia. A Jewess gave birth lately to a live bear.'

'*You* don't believe that, do you?'

'It is what the Emperor believes that matters.'

The silence between us was leaden with apprehension. We shared forbidden knowledge of majesty degraded. The god Vertumnus, Bohemia's fruitful king, was worm-eaten by melancholy madness.

'Had the guards not come, I think Rumpf would have died.'

Gonsalvus chewed the overdroop of his moustache: a gesture borrowed, without his knowing, from my late Milanese mentor. 'Imperial Chamberlain one day,' he mused, 'disgraced criminal the next.'

We heard the distant howling of an imprisoned wretch. Gonsalvus with his eyes confirmed that he guessed, like me, its origin. 'I must go,' he said when my gaolers, grown restless, hammered on the cell door. He left behind, like fragrant petals, his promises of support.

Thenceforth the conditions of my incarceration improved. Gonsalvus, on a return visit, denied any hand in the matter, while sharing my gladness at the provision of a chamberpot and the absence of too many weevils in my bread. 'No wonder about the weevils,' I said. 'They'd break their teeth just trying to get in.'

Every day Gonsalvus nudged me towards confession and every day I tried to evade him, offering curiosity as my only motive for entering the Palace. He wanted me to speak of my own volition, since penitence compelled has no redemptive quality. Finally, sensing me stuck fast in my shame like a toad burrowed in the earth, he confronted me with his suspicions. 'There has been a theft in the Castle. Ottavio Strada has discovered the absence of rare coins and some jade cups from their cabinets.'

'I didn't take them!'

'Clearly not, since your pockets were empty. Furthermore, several days separate your capture and the theft's discovery.'

'I know nothing about it.'

Gonsalvus nodded; he must have sensed that I was lying. 'The mystery runs deeper, Tommaso. Yesterday three men were dragged from the river. They had been dead several days. It seems somebody had broken their legs to prevent them swimming. They were your friends, I regret to say. Luboš Hrabal and the Mušek brothers.'

The dungeon lacked air. I seemed to have a damp cloth before my mouth, through which, however hard I sucked, I could not draw breath.

'Perhaps you were lucky to have been arrested in the Castle.'

'Moosbrugger,' I muttered. 'They told me it was just a *dare*. They didn't say . . . I didn't know exactly what they were planning.'

'Moosbrugger, you say?'

'Yes, Matthäus Moosbrugger. Do you know him?'

'I doubt that he exists.'

'He said he was working for a gentleman—'

'Whose identity was never revealed to you?'

'Not to *me*.'

Gonsalvus looked away from my weeping. 'I know,' he said, 'as I know my Redeemer lives, that you acted without malice. Stupidity, yes. You allowed yourself to be led astray and seduced by glory's shadow.'

'What will happen to me?'

'The Lord Chamberlain has jurisdiction over Castle employees. There is a date fixed for your sentence.'

'Pedro, they will *hang* me.'

'I do not believe it.'

'Yes! For what I have seen!'

'When sentence is passed I shall ask leave to appeal in your defence. Remember that your criminal friends were silenced. No man can implicate you in the theft. As far as your judge need be concerned, you succumbed to a surfeit of ambition – a boyish desire to meet the Emperor in person.'

'That's only partly true.'

'It is for God to judge and punish our deeper purposes.'

'You will *lie* about the theft?'

'That was not your crime, Tommaso. We need make no allusion to it.'

'And Moosbrugger?'

'I fear Moosbrugger and his inventor will never be discovered. We must be politic. The deaths of your friends cannot be avenged. For your own survival, we must throw ourselves on the Lord Chamberlain's mercy.'

My gaolers, Hans and Wolff, were discouraged by my stature from practising upon me their casual cruelties. Ordinarily they liked nothing better than to massage a prisoner's guts with their elbows, or to bring light to the dark regions of his anatomy with the aid of a tallow candle. Wolfgang Rumpf, to judge by his sobbing, received my share of abuse. Perhaps, too, the phantoms that tormented me had taken up residence in his cell? For with an oil lamp I was able to keep the dead at bay. The world, with only a little flame, was solid once more. Petrus Gonsalvus, at every visit, kept me abreast of the date and the weather. He nourished me with talk of Prague. I learned how the children walked with their mother to gather mushrooms; how Caterina would return with snails and jays' feathers, collected in remembrance of me. Recalling my interest in his anatomy book, Gonsalvus mentioned Prague's first public autopsy, lately performed by a Dr Jessenius at the University. He faltered, however, when it occurred to him that the cadaver had been a criminal hanged on the gallows. As though an untimely death were not enough to contemplate, my thoughts now feasted on the prospect of a final humiliation: the exposure of my deformities, even to my viscera, to the public gaze. What hope had I of Salvation if my parts were sundered for the sake of scholarly theatre?

'Do not think of these things,' Gonsalvus growled, angered with himself for introducing them. 'The Lord Chamberlain will give his judgement tomorrow. You must plumb your reserves of fortitude.'

When he had gone, the gaolers spied on me through a hole in the door. They produced a supper of gruel and cold beef. A decorative sprig of parsley gave it a touch of the condemned man's last meal.

I doubt that I slept much, trapped like a water spider in the bubble of my dread. As when, peeing in the middle of the night, you must touch cold stone to be assured that you are not being duped by a dream, I asked my gaolers for a morning slap. Gladly they obliged, and their smarting blows to either side of my face confirmed my waking state.

The Lord Chamberlain had concluded his deliberations. Though acquitted of spying, I was found guilty of *laesa majestas*. Sentence was declared by a court official from the top step of my cell. I recognised the fastidious clerk of the New Land Rolls. He that had arranged my first lodgings in Prague now announced my last; for I was to be detained indefinitely, confined to Dalibor Tower at His Imperial Majesty's pleasure. Hans and Wolff smiled inanely behind the Court herald. They did not trouble themselves to catch me as I fell into a swoon.

My eyes cracked open, stiff as mussel shells. Despair pulsed like a poison in my blood; it throbbed in every bone and sinew. Wherever he lay, like me, in the fastness of Dalibor, Wolfgang Rumpf howled, and I howled with him. Together we were damned, causes of shame to the courtiers who guessed our innocence yet dared not counter their Emperor's will. Sensing the new dispensation, my gaolers failed to bring me my daily bread, forgot to refuel my thirsty lamp and left my waste to fester. I begged them to transfer me to a cell with a window, a little gap through which, if I could see nothing of the glorious earth, I might at least glimpse the sky and follow a sunspot's odyssey across my dungeon walls.

I received no word from Gonsalvus. My confinement was solitary: not even my gaolers would soil their boots in my filth, depositing my meals, which looked like vomitous scraps, through an aperture at the foot of my door. You can imagine, therefore, my terror when after I know not how many days these same brutes shook me from a stupor. I feared that my end was come. They stripped me – laughing at my cringeing manhood – and scoured my flesh with stubble brushes. A new sackcloth shirt was dragged over my head; I panicked, expecting some kind of hood to blind me on the gallows. But my head emerged, tortoise-fashion, from the material; whereupon I was part pulled, part pushed, out of my cell.

'You're going to kill me,' I said while Hans made sinister music with his keys.

Wolff cuffed me sharply. 'Don't think you're that important, boy.'

At the tower's entrance, Hans was reluctant to chain my feet. 'He can't get away with legs like that.' So I was spared one indignity at least, before they opened the tower door and blinded me with autumnal gloom.

Never before had I felt the *consistency* of light, its pressure on the skin. My pores tasted the clouded radiance of the sun; my eyes ached and brimmed with tears. I saw my bare, filthy, etiolated legs, with the knees turned in, like crones gossiping. I felt pity for my body, this habitation soon to be void of sense – a pending husk.

'Come along, shuffle up,' said Hans, not unkindly.

As I faltered in custody along a narrow lane, nobody peeped out of windows to watch me pass; no nuns from St George's Convent crossed themselves at my frightful decay. How incongruous I felt amid such mundane calm. The Castle was too busy to trouble itself with some disgraced midget on his way to the gallows; the ornate, flying-buttressed chancel of St Vitus would no more lose its grandeur at my death than a mountain might flinch at a sparrow's fall.

We stopped beside a side door in the flank of the Royal Palace. An official in court livery opened the door and instructed us to wait. 'They're clearing the Diet of petitioners,' he said, as though that made sense, and proceeded to loiter halfway between the doorway and the street, straining a pink cord in his neck to ensure that everything within was going to plan.

Wolff nudged my shoulder. 'You must have done something interesting,' he said, 'for them to empty the hall.'

Briskly the official sprang to action.

'See *you* later,' Hans threatened as I was relinquished to the custody of palace guardsmen. Through the Riders' Staircase I was admitted to the Diet Hall. The great oak door that led to Vladislav Hall was locked, all petitioners excluded. A rumour of voices. Red plush benches formed three sides of a square about the imperial throne, which stood empty beneath a black baldaquin. I saw Petrus Gonsalvus sitting alone, magisterial in scholar's gown; yet before I could greet him the guardsmen had hemmed me into the wooden dock, where I found myself confronted by half a dozen gentlemen on the opposite benches. They eyed me with amusement, those unfamiliar courtiers, and whispered disparagements into their neighbours' ruffs. Cowed by my audience, I looked to Gonsalvus for some reassuring gesture. But he abstained stiffly from turning, and I sensed from the clinging of damp fur to his nape that he shared my trepidation.

From the side entrance the Lord Chamberlain emerged, flanked by two black-capped secretaries. All in attendance rose (with the exception of your hero, who languished on his feet already) while Authority assumed its seat.

'The case of Thomas Grilli,' declared the court official.

The Lord Chamberlain mumbled as he read from a parchment. I heard strange Latinisms, upon which the more learned gentlemen punned. One man's gaze, from the opposite benches, would not relinquish my face. I felt its malice on my skin and dared not look up to challenge it.

'I do,' said Gonsalvus, standing.

'What is the nature of your involvement with the prisoner?'

'I am his friend, my Lord Chamberlain. He lived with my family before gaining employment at the Castle . . .'

One of the nobility exploded in a sneeze. Ruffling his nose with a silken handkerchief, he apologised to the company. 'It is ever thus, my lord,' said he, 'when I am in the presence of *hounds*.' Immediately his companions roared with laughter; I watched them kiss their knuckles to quieten.

The Lord Chamberlain clucked his tongue. 'Continue please, *mein Herr*.'

'*Mein Haare*, surely?'

'Oh, har, har, har.'

Sensing official irritation at these quips, a darkly dressed gentleman tapped his colleagues' shoulders with a bodkin's scabbard. His face was obscured in shadow cast by the low October sun.

I felt shame and sorrow for my derided champion; yet Gonsalvus continued with new resolve. 'My Lord Chamberlain, I wish to vouch for the good Christian character of Tommaso Grilli, and hope to convince you that, while the committal of a misdemeanour is not in doubt, the punishment of perpetual durance is excessive.' (Licking his lips distractedly, my judge turned over the parchment in his lap.) 'My lord, he longs only to serve the Emperor with his talent . . .'

'For squeezing through windows,' said the dark gentleman to his acolytes.

'He is a gifted artist who has loyally helped catalogue the royal collection. I implore you, do not destroy his life because he succumbed to the fervour of his youth and tried to meet our sovereign in person.'

Bubbles burst in the Lord Chamberlain's gullet. Pressing his stomach with splayed fingers, he sank his chin into his neck. 'This appeal hearing is adjourned,' he said, 'for luncheon.' He stood up, obliging all seated to do likewise. The guard on my right supported me with a hand in my armpit when, a counterweight to the hall, my legs buckled. 'Take the prisoner to a holding room until we resume.'

'And someone throw the dog a bone!'

Petrus Gonsalvus stepped down, disregarding his tormentors, and touched my fingers briefly with his own.

There was to be no conference between the defendant and his spokesman. I was marched to a storeroom in the Bohemian Chancery and offered, if not a seat, at least a spot of floor cleared of clerical waste. Leaning together, my guards resumed a former conversation. I failed to listen at first, dazed as I was by hunger and weariness. Something, however, awoke my curiosity; perhaps the timbre of gruesome pleasure in their voices.

'. . . from the window ledge.'

'*On* the window ledge?'

'No, *from* it. Hanging out of the window. You see? His legs were dangling into the moat.'

'She won't get her widow's pension.'

'And she'll lose the cottage.'

'I wouldn't mind getting Bumm's place.'

'What about his ghost? You'd be afraid of that.'

'I'm *afraid* of not having four walls for winter. My name's on the list – what d'you reckon?'

'Not a chance.'

'Why not? I'm as deserving as the next man . . .'

The narrow doorway filled with a familiar figure. He was

dressed in his travelling greatcoat, with mud and leaf mould on his boots and a bag slung across his shoulder. I wonder today whether his attire was not a disguise, intended to give the impression of pressing official business; for he could ill afford to be seen dallying with his disgraced protégé. All the same, here he was. He came and delivered a letter straight to my hands, a letter much travelled, with the amber aureole of a tankard stamped on my floridly scripted name.

'This has been waiting for you several weeks. It's addressed to the Castle. I knew that you would wish to receive it.'

Jaroslav Meyrink coughed, betrayed by his nerves, as I took the letter. Conscious of the watching guards, both of us were embarrassed, with only platitudes for conversation. Looking in gratitude at a man who had assisted me without personal gain, I felt that, however long I lived, I would only ever shake my toes in the shallows of other men's souls.

'*Buona fortuna,*' Meyrink said – and left me to my unexpected letter.

Umb. Raimondi to Tom. Grilli at Imperial Court Prague
Via dei Calzaiuoli, Florence

It has required great expenditure of time and moneys for me to discover your whereabouts, my nephew, and I pray that this letter does not reach Prague only to find that you have eluded me a final time; for assuredly I shall not send my secretary to Bohemia in hope of recovering your spoor.

It was to such a purpose that I dispatched to Milan my assistant Piombino, whom you may remember as your first tutor, now a portly fellow with few teeth and nothing left of the scholar, yet loyal and most trustworthy. From information contained in your father's correspondence I knew of your apprenticeship to the late Gian Bonconvento, whose mother Piombino was able to locate in the hope of discovering your whereabouts. The old woman at her house expressed great bitterness towards the boys who, by their machinations, had hastened her son to his grave. At length, and somewhat incoherently, she extolled Bonconvento's qualities, describing how beloved he had been of his pupils and how grievously the world mourned his passing. Thereupon she took Piombino to an outhouse that served as a profane shrine to her son's industry, where he sifted among documents and sketches until he found a letter written by one Meyrine, art agent to the Holy Roman Emperor, describing the fortunes of his absconded pupil. In this manner I was able to discover your whereabouts, and write to you at Prague hoping that my letter finds you in good health.

In no sense do I mean to pass judgement, being too old to speak good or ill of a world which has almost finished with me. Therefore understand that I condemn neither my brother-in-law for allowing himself to slip from that public esteem in which he had seemed to stand when he married my lamented sister, nor my nephew for his doubtless inherited failings, though in his ambition he has trodden upon family and benefactors, insulting the sacrifices made to his advantage by the same. It remains my ardent hope, expressive of blood's enduring ties, that serving the Emperor has brought you worldly comfort, a stable if necessarily loveless life, and recognition of your undoubted talents.

In anticipation of your ignorance, my nephew, I must regretfully inform you of your father's death. It was Anonimo who wrote to me from Bologna shortly before consumption claimed him, explaining the circumstances of your estrangement. I do not know the extent of your acquaintance with the facts of your father's last years after Milan. He told me in his letter that none of his many letters sent by errand boy to the home of Gian Bonconvento had received a reply, leading him to despair of your obedience. Consequently he travelled to Bologna, which he considered to be the source of his art, and *having married a young widow there worked as a stonemason until disease ruined him. His widow, your stepmother, whose name is unknown to me, threw herself upon charity after his death. My secretary was incapable, while in Bologna on business, to locate the unfortunate woman.*

This is painful news, I imagine, for you to receive in the midst of your triumphs. I know not what occurred between you in Milan to sever the precious filial bond; but I feel sure that you will pray, as I do, for the repose of his soul that was so troubled on earth.

Please believe me ever, Tommaso, your respectful uncle,
Umberto Antonio Raimondi

*

We were summoned back to the Diet Hall. An impression such as had clouded my first sensible hours in Dalibor Tower, of Fate working upon me, dulled my pain, so that I walked between my guards strangely becalmed. In Vladislav Hall – where once knights had jousted on chargers and now, beneath rib vaulting and chandeliers, market stalls offered cloth, lavender and silver plate – a gathering of citizens parted to grant us passage. Weary petitioners waiting outside the Diet Hall seemed almost to resent me for the priority of my case, as though my manacled condition were an enviable privilege, far preferable to a broken hand or squabbles over rent. Heavily armoured soldiers opened the Diet doors and I resumed, to imperious and base mockery from the benches, my abject stance in the dock.

The Lord Chamberlain seemed much revived by his meal. His movements as he regained his seat had quickened; his cheeks glowed as though infused with new blood. He licked his still-greasy lips as he reconsulted the legal documents. 'I understand there is much business to get through,' he said. 'Do be brief, Herr Gonsalvus.'

So my fluent mathematician (that good man in wolf's clothing) summoned every syllable of his eloquence to rescue me from torment. He would have made a fine, though futile, apologist at the Resurrection, distinguishing between honourable motive and foolish or unreasoned action. His plea was simple: to insist that punishment be commensurate with my crime. Although I endeavoured to listen, the oration was faint in my ears, like the murmur of a bee beyond a window pane. I seemed to be standing on the precipice of another man's life: a spectator at my twin's trial. Gonsalvus spoke passionately of mercy and temperance, while to my soul's courthouse I summoned all the phantoms of my youth and begged their forgiveness.

A second voice wrenched me from reverie:

'My Lord Chamberlain!'

All heads turned on the dark gentleman now rising to his feet. The sun having travelled since midday, I was able to distinguish a virile, strong-boned face, not unhandsome, expressive of guile and power. 'My lord,' said the interjecter, 'we have listened patiently to this interminable verbiage, with its mawkish appeal to the emotions. Surely the fact stands that we know nothing of the dwarf's motives . . .'

Gonsalvus's blood was up: one might have fancied hackles rising along his nape. 'His motives, my lord, were innocent of malice, as I have shown.'

The Lord Chamberlain seemed greatly irritated by this time-threatening turn of events. Beneath his official gown, he shifted from ham to ham. 'Herr Langenfels, is this necessary?'

'Most necessary, my Lord Chamberlain. Let us consider the proximity of two events. On the one hand, we learn of a plot against our Emperor and King. On the other, valuables are stolen from his collection. Are we to believe that this malingering creature' (he indicated me with a black-gloved finger) 'is not in some sinister way implicated with these assaults on the Emperor's person and authority?'

'There is no *substance* to these allegations, my lord.'

'Indeed?' Langenfels flexed an imperious eyebrow at my defender. 'Are you suggesting, sir, that the traitor Rumpf was unjustly imprisoned?'

Gonsalvus hesitated: he was on politically dangerous ground.

'Herr Langenfels,' said the Lord Chamberlain, 'this line of questioning is holding up matters lamentably.'

Caught up in his performance, my self-appointed persecutor continued to amuse his fellows. 'Are we to make a travesty of Justice? For want of hard proof of their guilt, shall we allow those that must be guilty free hand to undermine the State?' The other courtiers jeered in agreement; slapping their thighs, they caused their sword-tips to flicker like wagtails. 'Is not the Empire menaced by unholy portents? Have we not seen fiery comets, monstrous births, freakishness on the streets of Prague?'

'Herr Langenfels, I am *tiring* of your theatricals.'

'Now these sinister creatures: a foreign dwarf, and *Cynocephalus* here' (shrieks of laughter from the benches) 'the fabled dog-headed man, pleading for his release. Here is proof, infecting the very air we breathe, of Nature gone awry.'

Amid uproar, the Lord Chamberlain felt the want of a gavel. Being seated without so much as a table to hand, he resorted, like an enraged child, to stamping with both feet on the floor. 'This may be the Diet, gentlemen, but under my authority it shall not be turned into a bear pit. Herr Gonsalvus . . . Guards, make the prisoner *stand* for sentence.'

'Um, he is standing, my lord.'

The Lord Chamberlain peered at me closely, perhaps for the first time. 'I believe he's slouching.'

'Stop slouching,' said my guard. With assistance from his covert hand, I rose to the quaking tips of my toes.

'By the authority vested in me,' said the Lord Chamberlain, 'the sentence of perpetual durance is commuted to banishment from the Kingdom of Bohemia.'

Langenfels offered his hands to the air in a gesture of dismay.

'The prisoner has three days to leave the city. After which time, if apprehended, he will be put to death, along with those that harbour or assist him.'

I was deaf to the Latinate closing formalities. The Lord Chamberlain, with a black temper upon him, swept from the hall, to the presumed frustration of petitioners outside. Langenfels scoffed and, barking dog-like at Gonsalvus, relinquished the benches with his pack in tow.

It occurs to me now, writing on this Tuscan hillside a seeming lifetime later, that circumstances conspired to rescue me. Had not the Lord Chamberlain been provoked by Langenfels, might he have taken the easiest course, for his own sake, and upheld the original sentence? Or was my release from Dalibor designed to salve the nobleman's conscience, offering an oblique riposte to the injustice done to his colleague Rumpf? Whatever the reasons for the Lord Chamberlain's judgement, the fact remained – in the form of exile – that I was free.

With Gonsalvus, my rescuer, walking behind me and the guards still at my sides, I was stopped in the Riders' Staircase by one of the court secretaries. His breast pocket bristled with quills. He presented me with a leather-bound Bible.

'Thomas Grilli, you must take a solemn oath, never to speak of what you saw on the ninth evening of September to a living soul, so long as His Imperial Majesty shall live.'

Reader, I placed my hand on the Bible and swore. It was an oath that I would keep precisely, to the letter.

After more than a month in solitary confinement, I had only two days to replenish my strength for travel. For years afterwards I would blush to think how Frau Gonsalvus had washed my naked body, without flinching at the crusted folds, and pulled her son's outgrown nightshirt over my head, while I sat groggily on the side of his bed, pining for near-eternal sleep. Carlo and Caterina, though they longed for some unfathomable reason to see again the friend who had spurned them, were forbidden to enter the darkened chamber where I was spoon-fed vegetable soup and sausages cut up for me by sullen Marta. I slept, I believe, for a day and a night: an oblivious absence, a black curtain drawn across the stage of dreams.

I awoke to the sound of Týn's bells, with farther chimes from St James and St Gall, and all the chorus of steepled Prague. Petrus Gonsalvus lifted his hairy chin off his palm, sat up at his son's table and greeted me.

'My young friend, you must leave Prague tonight. I have arranged a passage by ferry. It will bring you towards the Elbe. At Mělník you must take a coach to Dresden and meet contacts there. These letters of introduction to friends of Spranger and Meyrink ought to set you on your way.'

'But I can't, I *can't*. I'm too tired.'

'You have no choice, Tommaso. Besides the strict terms of your banishment, there may be someone in the city who fears you, someone who would, if he could, do you harm.'

'Moosbrugger?'

'Or Moosbrugger's employer.' Gonsalvus arose, with an audible creak of compacted muscle. I can only wonder how long his vigil had lasted. 'There are clothes on the chair beside you. Dress quickly and come say your farewells.'

Feeling sick in my stomach, I presented myself to the family. Frau Gonsalvus gave me several letters and a purse for transport; its contents totalled three ducats. 'A gift from your champions,' she said. 'They cannot afford to be seen with you but they contributed as they can. As for us, Tommaso, these few coins must speak of our affection.' Not to be outdone in kindness, Carlo insisted that I take a copper greshki which he had been saving. Caterina barely stirred, her large black eyes swollen with grievance.

Night approached and the city was preparing to exist without me. I felt like a spirit outstaying his welcome. Perfunctorily I offered expressions of gratitude, though my head was filling with all the uncertainties of my new life. Banishment from a kingdom not my own was an endurable prospect. Had I not exiled myself already, locking my language inside my mouth? Yet I feared the blankness of the road ahead and silently grieved for my aborted future.

I set out with Frau Gonsalvus, muffled inside Caterina's cowl, hoping to pass for a little girl in the eyes of a waiting assassin. Beside St Agnes of Bohemia we made our bashful farewell. I shrugged off my disguise, shouldered a small bag that contained my letters for passport, and took my lady's hand to kiss her surprisingly bony knuckles. 'I fear that I have damaged your family's name in the city.'

'Nonsense, Tommaso. My husband's health is failing – a return to Parma will do us all good.'

Marie Gonsalvus looked back down the path to where Petrus, her uxorious shadow, offered a final wave. 'Good luck,' she said. Then both were gone, back to their own story, to their lives and graves.

Picture me then, standing on the shore of the night-oiled river, listening to the plashing oars of my transport. There was a bank where the ferryman landed, the hull of his boat soughing in mud as it stuck. He held out his palm for payment, a mortal Charon, and I clambered into the stern, knocking my knees on wooden matter. The ferryman had been briefed on my destination. Pushing out the boat and then jumping aboard, he spat almost disparagingly into the Moldau and took up his oars.

It was right, as well as necessary, that I should leave. Reader confessor, I had abused the hospitality of strangers. My father had died believing himself betrayed, as I had betrayed his surrogates throughout my youth. Petrus Gonsalvus had opened his home to me and consider how I had repaid him. We all leave corpses in our wake, including at the last our own. Now, as I trembled in the ferry's stern, I imagined bodies heaped in the limbs of the water.

'My God! We have to stop!'

Rocking his boat in my agitation, I asked the ferryman to turn back. He refused, pretending not to understand German. I had remembered, too late, my uncle's letter. It fluttered far away behind me, left on Carlo's writing table beneath an open window, spotted by drops of rain instead of my penitent tears.

END OF BOOK ONE

II

The Library of Arts and Wonders

8

Nuremberg

Be seated. Careful – it's a long way down. Oops-la. *There* now.

We are sitting, on a May morning in the infancy of our present century, among the elderly beggars of Nuremberg. Our perch, a low brick wall, has yet to warm; nor can our bony rumps protect us from the night's cold residue. But ignore your agues (old age is its own Arctic) and watch with me the crowd as it passes, to and fro, beneath the Frauentor gate. Listen to the raucous bustle of hawkers and grinders, the brute percussion of livestock whipped to market and the fluster of chickens caged for slaughter. Sort carefully among the mangled, churlish faces, the perfumed dandies gagging behind the noxious fishwives. *There* – see – behind that sturdy farmer? The tall youth first, then his diminutive shadow, no more than waist high, excitedly talking. Hunched upon our walking sticks, we eye with slow, lizardly contempt that ill-matched pair. The adult, who is rudely handsome, saunters as though proud of his long limbs. His uncommonly white teeth form, when he smiles, a bright crescent moon. We despise this brash young cockerel, we old men half erased from the world; we imagine in sorrow his easy conquests, the cruel usage of girls such as we, in our time, failed to possess. By contrast, we are less offended by his young companion. This unlovely boy waddles like a gander. His clothes are ill suited to his frame: he must have pilfered them from his friend, for the sleeves absorb, in their yellow foliage, his animated fingers, while the stockings, though precisely cross-gartered, stubbornly wrinkle about his shins. One thinks of him as a boy. In fact his voice, when we catch it, sounds manly; and is not that stubble rather than shadow about his jaw?

Somebody hoicks and draws a heel across the phlegm. 'A dwarf. That's a filthy foreign dwarf.'

Oblivious to detraction, the young men make their way up Königstrasse. They come to a thatched house near Lorenzer Platz, at whose casement window the tall youth diffidently raps. Standing facing one another, they rock on their heels until the casement opens. There is no sound of greeting from without or within. A shapely, feminine arm produces from the interior a pouch made of wooden boards bound in leather. The handsome youth accepts the pouch and tucks it under his arm, while his ugly companion plucks at the strings of a purse. The soft, pale hand opens expectantly. Two coins travel from purse to palm. The tall youth kisses the air beneath his nose and the hand, being fed, retreats into the house.

Now Tall and Small (after stopping at a tavern for a fortifying drink) must cross the river. Upon the bridge that spans the Pegnitz, Small seems to roll a marble in his mouth while Tall stares, glum with apprehension, at the onion dome of the Frauenkirche. On the north shore of the river, in a quarantined annexe to the Holy Spirit Hospital, the lepers are singing the *Ora Pro Nobis*. To Tall it seems a sign of graceful dispensation; for God, like the ancient deities, smiles on those that punish fools. Small, on the other hand, shudders to think of so many stumps raised in prayer to the heavens.

'Slow down,' he complains, 'for pity's sake.'

Tall ignores the plea. He is carrying the pouch against his ribs, and so dictates the pace.

They reach the busy Hauptmarkt, where Small's nausea is made worse by the smell of raw meat – that chemical, gamy odour – wafting on the breeze from the Schöner Fountain.

'There it is,' says Tall, nodding into his shoulder to indicate an elegant house on the edge of the market.

'I know,' says Small. 'Just one twist, I beg you.'

With Tall's help to reach it, the dwarf leans on the grille of the fountain. He turns thrice, for luck as the locals say, the golden ring.

'Have you made a wish?'

'Indulge me, Ludolf.'

Fortified by wine and foolish ritual, they go to the wealthy citizen's house. A servant at the door permits himself the luxury of looking them over, until his master slaps him aside and with effusive greetings welcomes our chancers inside. 'Is that it?' the householder pants, indicating with a nod Tall's leather portfolio. 'You have them in there, do you?' A pudgy face, closely shaven, as though its features were assets to be proud of, squats above clothes of tarnished elegance. The gentleman's house, though richly furnished and kept clean by a troop of servants, might be said to evince a lack of womanly influence. (Bachelors make ideal customers, such is the focus of their acquisitive passion.) Tall and Small gape at paintings and engravings framed on the walls – at every object of art or utility – like a pair of innocent bumpkins. They are beckoned into the gentleman's study, where he serves them burgundy in silver goblets. The host can barely contain himself as these invited rumps spread on his furniture: he must look through his window at the market outside to conceal his emotion.

'Frau Dürer, the great man's wife, used to sell his prints, you know, the religious engravings, out there in the Hauptmarkt. My great-grandfather bought that print . . .' (he indicates, with plump fingers, a nursing Madonna) '. . . at Christkindle 1519.'

The gentleman's auditors emerge, bug eyed, from their goblets. The dwarf, the foreign-sounding one, takes the precious portfolio from his companion and places it across his knees. He tugs with his fingers at the ribbon, while his left foot impatiently rises and falls.

'Of course,' says the citizen, 'I will have to see the drawings with my own eyes to be assured of their authenticity.'

He nods to license the dwarf's fingers. Small begins, with difficulty, to untie the sclerotic knot. He says, 'We met this, um, antiguarian . . .'

'Antiquarian?'

'By the Town Hall. He wanted to see what we'd found.'

'My God – you didn't, did you? He hasn't *seen*, nobody else has seen, what you are about to show me?'

The dwarf looks up with an expression of good-natured bafflement. 'We thought we'd get them valued for you, sir.'

The gentleman laughs: he shakes without mirth, making a sound like stock doves mating. 'My friends, I must warn you, Nuremberg is full of unscrupulous dealers who would exploit your good nature. No, no, we need not trouble ourselves with intercessory figures. Show me the items – from your cellar, you say? Remarkable good luck, I must say, if they should prove to be . . .'

The rich man's blather is curtailed by the opening of the pouch. The dwarf, with pinching and inexpert fingers, lifts to the light an exquisite pair of ink-and-chalk drawings. The first is a study for the famous St Jerome print; its notable divergences from the ultimate masterpiece include the lion yawning and a skull enjoying pride of place, instead of the crucifix, on the scholar-saint's desk. The Nuremberg buyer makes a sound like sneezing; he rises, as though sprung, from his window seat. 'St Jerome!' he exclaims. 'And this is a study for *Melancolia*!' He profanes, with tentative fingers, the age-tanned paper. 'Yes, yes, it's the earthbound angel. And the *darling* putto.'

'In the corner,' says Tall, 'there's a funny symbol.'

'That is called a monogram. You see the initial A, like a tower, and D is a man strolling beneath it.'

The buyer spends some considerable time with these precious artefacts. He holds them to the mullioned window and traces with his fingers the pressure marks scored long ago (so he thinks) by the artist's pen. The dwarf and his colleague sit with gaping thighs, their goblets tilting on their laps. It is Tall who coughs into his fist to remind the gentleman of their presence.

'Well,' the fat man blusters, 'it's impossible to be *certain* of their provenance. You may have discovered imitations in your cellar. Look here, you see, haw . . . you see the cross-hatching is not typical of Dürer in his last decade . . .'

The dwarf looks aghast. 'It's a *fake*?'

The buyer does not answer. He watches the drawings with starry points of love in his eyes. 'I shall give you fifteen talers for both. I can hardly pay more, as I may well be – indeed probably *am* – taking forgeries off your hands.'

'We don't understand,' says the dwarf. 'Do you not like the drawings?'

'*Like* them?' The gentleman produces an alarmingly wide and mauve-gummed smile. He tosses a small purse of coin, which the recipients weigh between them. Thanks are exchanged in the hallway as the imperious servant shows the visitors to the door.

Willibald von Bartsch, as he returns to his study, rubs his loins with theatrical glee. He is doubly delighted with himself: not only that he possesses drawings by Nuremberg's greatest Master but also (a sugared cherry, this, on his fortune's cake) that he should have paid so little for them, easily duping those providential fools.

Later that day, in a cottage outside the city walls, Ludolf Bresdin will toast Tommaso Grilli on the sale of his latest forgeries.

And so we must begin afresh. You that have borne with me thus far, do not balk at the prospect. Life, between its constant gates, follows no straight path but is made of loops and tangents, bifurcations and resolutions and changes of heart. Is not every dawn, in the mind of the sinner, a fresh receptacle to fill with virtue? When I left Prague I believed myself to be my own pilot, and would have scoffed at the fatalist who dooms Mankind to repeat his errors.

Several years before this Nuremberg morning, a perilous journey had brought me from Bohemia to the outskirts of Dresden. It was deep winter. The coach, which I had boarded at great expense at Mělník, stuck fast in ruts of frozen mud and I was forced to conclude the last miles on foot, trailing my supposedly fellow travellers into the city. I felt my face, which was exposed to the wind, pucker and burn, until I ambled beyond pain, my nerves lulled by the opiates of bodily distress. Citizens no more real in my memory than figments of a dream pointed the way to my contact's house. Georg Spengler, discovering me slumped on his doorstep, guessed my identity and dragged me inside – where he attended, though howled at, to my swollen feet.

I hoped, in the throb of convalescence, that my travels might be ending.

Georg Friedrich Spengler (who would become, for many years, one of my most useful contacts in the art world) was by six years my senior. He was a genial, sandy-complexioned bachelor, stout in the powerful way that certain bulls are stout, with jowls like a dewlap expressive of latent energy. Prints were his trade: he imported from Prague, Vienna and Rome for the benefit of more provincial markets. Noble families like the Wettins of Dresden trusted and admired his tastes; for Georg Spengler had travelled in Italy and the Low Countries, and trailed like magical dust his familiarity with more inventive cultures.

Thus Bartholomeus Spranger had delivered me to the one man in Saxony who might find me employment in spite of my disgrace.

In Dresden, where after a few weeks in Spengler's disorderly home I was able to take lodgings beside the Elbe, I designed twelve woodcuts to illustrate a book of sententious poems. The commission, from the local printer, Ambrosius Becher, had been secured, of course, by Georg Spengler. In the spring of 1602, I travelled north to Moritzburg, where a mighty hunting lodge needed decorative paintings, in diverse chambers, on panels of Baltic oak. Truly I was my father's son: a commercial utility all but invisible to the buyer, offering my services like a peasant selling turnips at market. Returning each evening with my fellow painters to the servants' quarters, I remembered my Uncle Umberto's study in Florence, with its eye-duping motifs for Art and Learning. My own commission in Moritzburg was for vague and idealised landscapes: verdant arcadies where stags impaled themselves on hunting spears and savage boars expired at the first nip of a muscleman's arrow.

It was at Moritzburg that I encountered Ludolf Bresdin, that most decorative of decorative painters. He was by several years my junior and wholly unconscious of his good looks. My talk in the evenings was provocative, a verbal swagger of such absurd sexual assurance that Bresdin trusted every word. Conscious of his provincial training, he attached himself to me on account of my seeming expertise. He might as well have come, cap in hand, to seek advice on how to be tall.

Our allotted task took a long time to complete. Confined

for months to that marshy region, where mosquitoes keen and midges dance, in rapturous formation, above the reed-hatched waters, Ludolf Bresdin had only the servant girls on whom to practise his charms. I, for my part, basked as best I could in the glamour of this broad Adonis, trusting to my eloquence that, once girls were fluttering in the ambit of his flame, I might catch the weakest of them, as a bat snatches a moth.

Returning to Dresden the following year, I discovered Georg Spengler flush with love and engaged to be married. His bride-to-be – the most unlovely daughter of a Dresden bookseller – was readying herself on her chaperoned visits to Spengler's house to rid his rooms of my presence, which despite my best smiling was poisonous to her. Just as Georg Spengler was beginning to share his beloved's prejudice (such is the zeal of the recent convert), I received an invitation from Burg Weissing, in that region called Saxon Switzerland on account of its wild landscape, to oversee the decoration of a summerhouse.

We agreed to exchange letters, Georg Spengler and I; whereupon I departed from Dresden for many years.

At Burg Weissing I met again my young friend Ludolf Bresdin, and worked with him on the depiction of yet more pastoral slaughter. For a week we travelled, on special dispensation, to visit the Bastei rocks – great jagged slabs which rise abruptly from the forest, like towers built by Appennino the mountain god himself. I recalled that Roelandt Savery had produced grotesque capricci here for the Emperor Rudolf, discovering monstrous faces in the rock formations. One day I would do the same – fabricating wonders in the hope of pleasing a wayward patron.

As our time in Burg Weissing dragged to a close, Ludolf Bresdin and I discussed a partnership. It was he who suggested we decamp to Nuremberg, for he considered his home town to be a place of rich pickings. In those years before the war, Nuremberg was still a place of Learning: a broad tree shedding leaves of print, a grove where Art could fructify. Here Maximilian, the Wise King himself, had danced all night with the city matrons; from this house on the corner of Burgerstrasse and Obere Schmiedgasse the renowned Dürer had dazzled the world. My handsome companion was incapable of doubts concerning our future. He was like a lover kneeling at the foot of a bed, admiring the prospect of Europe spread out before him. Yet consider my stature, *my* trepidation; imagine me sunk below the mattress, unable to glimpse so much as the lady's toes, and you see clearly the circumstances wherein I agreed to his proposal.

That pale and downy arm of an accomplice at the window belonged to Ludolf Bresdin's mistress. Gunda Nessler – a beauty straining at the constraints of 'buxom' – concealed her native cunning beneath a snorting laugh and girlish, almost nympholeptic eyes. It was not the case that Bresdin had seduced Gunda: quite the contrary, she had netted him, her concupiscent eel, and so enchanted his quivering senses that even his roving eye was stilled. At first this infatuation suited my purpose. Gunda hid my forgeries in her father's house (it seemed prudent to keep our little foundry void of material that might incriminate us) and, impelled by love of Bresdin and small remuneration, could be relied upon for her secrecy. Furthermore, the delicious Fräulein baked sweetmeats much to my liking and revealed to me, when in frustration I rounded on my happier friend, the whereabouts of certain women, purveyors of easement, upon whose costed favours I might squander my ill-gotten pay. Both my grand, evolving passions were catered for in Bavaria: ingestion and emission became the chief preoccupations of my life.

Alas, like most felicitous arrangements, ours contained the seeds of its undoing. Gunda's father, conscious of his daughter's charms, was planning to marry her to the highest bidder. There was no shortage in Nuremberg of eligible bachelors, young men just come into their vocations and anxious to confirm their status with a wife. Gunda Nessler was indifferent to these courting blacksmiths, glovers and bakers; she amassed their gifts of rings, gloves and loaves with all the ingratitude of a pagan idol – the divine goddess on Lorenzer Platz. But Ludolf Bresdin grew jealous of his hopeless rivals; he moped and drank, alternating between despondency and outrage at the prospect of losing his life's adornment. It was impossible for him to marry. Herr Nessler, the foreman at Nuremberg's foremost glassworks, would never consent to a decorative painter becoming his son-in-law.

Ah, reader, how few of us escape the storyteller's bag of commonplace tricks! Gunda and Ludolf, like countless lovers before them, in romance or reality, prized their illusions above security. I learned about their elopement in the street, wandering past Nessler's house in a daze of perplexity at Bresdin's absence, when I overheard the father's inconsolable grief.

'She's dead to me! She's dead and buried, the bitch!'

Your narrator was none too cheerful either. Ludolf Bresdin had left two Griens and an Altdorfer beneath his beloved's bed. I had to bribe her little sister, at immoderate cost, to return the papers to my keeping.

With the unexpected disappearance of my colleague, whose chief virtue had been an intimate knowledge of his native city, I contemplated heading north to the Netherlands, where according to Georg Spengler a growing class of citizens spent prodigiously on portraits. Haarlem and Utrecht were exposed to Viennese art chiefly through engravings by Bartholomeus Spranger. Was not my old Prague friend of Flemish origin? So might I not appeal to him for a word or two of introduction?

Scarcely had I blown the ink dry on my enquiring letter than Fortune made it redundant.

I was dining alone in the Phoenix tavern near Bergstrasse, sucking every last nutrient from a blandly boiled pig's trotter, when my attention was drawn to a sloppy-vowelled, weakly consonantal voice behind me. It sounded like the gibberish of some halfwit, an indecipherable droning.

'One under any nine. Prince Thetis. Parlour jovial museum at Como.'

'How much?'

'Waffle?'

'For the Paolo Giovio prints.'

'Harmony?'

'All of them.'

'Pff. Snot gunner be cheap.'

'I don't care about the cost. I want every print Tobias Stimmer ever sold. And that includes Giovio's famous persons.'

Unable to resist, I turned my head at the jingle of coins. My view of the patrician buyer was blocked by a bent grey back. This belonged to the drunken salesman, whose voice conveyed a valiant battle for sobriety.

'Your Grace, I'll dry my puss.'

'One expects nothing less. I trust this may serve for incentive?'

The bald head respectfully dipped. From my disadvantage I could not see beyond the wheezing mountain. 'Most kind, your Grace. You won't regret dealing with Fritz Winkelzug.' With remarkable unsteadiness, the grey mass stirred. Winkelzug (if that really was his name) pushed his

183

chair into mine and thumped the table with his fists. A complicated set of manoeuvres, reminiscent of a fat grub squeezing itself through a bore-hole, restored the man to his feet. His listing departure revealed a whey-faced man of indeterminate age who was busily jotting figures with a stubby quill on a torn rag of parchment. Being absorbed in his calculations, he did not sense my eyes upon him. I noted his formal and old-fashioned clothes, the tousled luxuriance of his dark hair and the beard, very thick, whose greased moustache he caressed absent-mindedly. From where I sat his eyes seemed to strain, like those of a dormouse, in their sockets. His nose, which having been broken once had set awry, was pitted with a single pox scar. Big though unmuscular – like a scarecrow padded with suet – the man seemed not fully to occupy his body and clutched his quill so fiercely that, with a cartilaginous shriek, it shattered.

I felt inside my waistcoat pocket for a charcoal. 'Might this be of use to you?'

The man unclasped his eyes from the bleeding nib and sought my voice.

'I see that your quill has given up the ghost,' I said. 'For want of a better substitute, might this butt of charcoal serve your purpose?'

The man gaped in the throes of cognition. His lips were plump, dark crimson like plums in a stew. He moistened them with the pink bud of his tongue. 'Yes,' he said, 'that should be helpful.'

At once I transported myself – pig's trotter in hand – to his table. The stranger's fingers flew to his beard as though to hide it. I leaned against the back of my chair, sensing the discomfort that my proximity caused him.

'Keep it, sir,' I said of my gift.

'Very well.'

Our eyes converged upon his spidery calculations. His left hand transferred itself swiftly to the parchment; his right hand, to compensate, ascended to the lustrous beard. He poked himself in the cheek with my charcoal.

'I have plenty more of the same at home,' I said.

'Really?'

'Oh, a great many. Quills too, should you be short. And, uh, chalk.'

'Ah – chalk?'

'Yes, white mostly. To draw with. On tinted paper.'

The pale gentleman, his face seated on his hand, tugged with his lower lip at the base of his moustache. He stopped tugging a fraction of a second after I saw the moustache move.

'A collector of fine prints are you, sir?' (Beneath his beard, my neighbour turned crimson.) 'I could not help overhearing your conversation with Herr Winkelzug. How much, might I ask out of curiosity, is Wink, er, is my colleague charging you in commission?'

'Colleague?'

I swept the pig's trotter above the table. 'Tommaso Grilli, your servant. Purveyor of prints to the quality – portraitist – engravings at a most competitive price. I also do history paintings, if that's your fancy.'

My interlocutor's teeth (the blackened stumps of a privileged diet) gritted in a nasty smile. 'Has Moritz put you up to this?'

'Uh . . . Moritz?'

'Winkelbach.'

'Did he not just leave . . . ?'

'Winkel*bach*! Don't play the innocent with me, I have a nose for cheats.' My face was a mask of incomprehension and the man relented. 'Forgive me. It is difficult to carry out transactions when all the time one is being . . .' His eyes fixed on a distant spot near the tavern's entrance. 'Thunderstorms – he's found me.'

'Who has found you?'

The curious fellow endeavoured to burrow, with his belly for leverage, under the table. I tried to make out, among the drinkers, the cause of his alarm. A long, stoatish gentleman stood on tiptoe by the door, peering above the customers' heads as though searching for someone.

'What did you say your name was?' the bearded man whispered below the table.

'Tommaso Grilli.'

'Are you Italian?'

'Florentine.'

'Then you will value what I value. That man over there is looking for me. I'm just an amateur of beautiful things.' I watched avidly as he slid a silver coin along the table-top. 'I'm going to escape through the back door. Will you help me, Signor Grilli – as a kindred spirit?'

'In whatever way possible,' I assured the silver coin.

The man emerged from hiding. He hitched the beard above his nose, and lowered his entire scalp with a tug on his forelock. 'Get in his way, signor. *Block* him.'

With that instruction, the art lover fled. I pocketed the silver coin and considered for an instant staying put. It was no concern of mine what became of the man; nor did I care to implicate myself in any dangerous intrigue.

Drinkers swore at the rear of the tavern. Half blinded by his black hair, my stooping escapee had crashed into a table. The commotion alerted his sinister pursuer. Eyes of iridescent blue focused on their prey, who balanced on the fulcrum of a drinker's fist, babbling apologies. The hunter leaned into a run – and I flung myself from safety just in time.

The buckle of a belt struck my mouth. My eyes watered and filled with refulgent spots.

'Get out of my way!' The man tried to push me aside; yet I clung to the pommel of his sword.

'So sorry – have I spilled your drink? You must let me buy you another.'

Glancing back, I saw the escapee squirm loose of his detainer and run, with the zeal of one mortally endangered, out through the back door of the tavern. Even in the heat of intervention, I recalled my own frantic and unaided flight through the benighted Castle of Prague.

'Let go of my sword, damned midget!'

Fearing a blow, I took three steps back; my opponent claimed the vacated ground. He stepped right to pass me. I stepped to my left. He stepped, to compensate, to *his* left. Snickering coyly at this time-honoured dance, I stepped to my right. The exasperated weasel unsheathed his sword – whereupon your diminutive Horatio, judging his commission amply fulfilled, retreated from the fray.

I escaped the tavern through its main entrance, anxious to be elsewhere when the huntsman returned without his quarry. Midget or man, I knew the taste of my own blood and had no appetite for the sapid nectar. I paced in the direction of the river, turning the evening's profit over in my hand. Below imposing Kaiserburg, the wealthy citizenry was savouring its leisure. I would have no difficulty losing myself in their midst should vengeful cries gather at my back. Over time my thumping heart settled. The external world receded – its living apparitions moved behind a flimsy veil. I returned in my head to an imaginary street in Haarlem, whose fictional topography was acquiring detail with each new, fancied visit. Gables were honeyed by the sun. Weeping willows swept the dusty street. A cat draped a stoop with its tawny forepaw. I heard, above the liquid murmur of wine served in a crystal glass, the bass approbation of a customer. ('Psst.') Yes, the phantasmic Dutchman nodded, yes, at an exposed canvas, as he reached with gloved fingers for the ripe purse at his waist . . .

'Psst! Signor Grilli – over here!'

A man, whose face was obscured in shadow, emerged by a tentative step from behind a cabbage cart. He lifted both hands to his mouth and flickered his fingers – like the frothing mandibles of a crab – to beckon me over.

'I want to thank you for your assistance,' he said. 'You've not been followed?'

'Not to my knowledge.'

I marvelled at the young man. His beard had vanished, exposing a chin which, in its retreat, was partly absorbed in the dough of his throat. The dark thatch of hair had bleached and grown so thin that a pink scalp was discernible beneath it. The boiled-plum lips remained, however, below the warped nose and protuberant green eyes.

'I did not recognise you,' I said, 'with your face removed.'

'Was it not an excellent disguise?'

Between us, reader, it was not. A fringe of the wig peeped out from beneath his collar, as though the young man were a Gonsalvus from the neck down. Small tufts of black wool clung to his stubble.

'Close by,' I ventured, 'is another tavern where we might talk.'

The young man hesitated, taking a quick look up the street as though hoping for instructions there. 'We cannot stay long,' he said.

'Are you in danger?

'Well, if I want to enjoy a comfortable night's sleep, I shall at some stage have to turn myself in.'

We settled at the sign of the Bear opposite St Sebaldus. Cannier, from sore experience, than when last you knew me, I suppressed my curiosity and trusted the Kornbranntwein to loosen the boy's tongue. Evidently he had never tasted strong liquor. He huffed dramatically above the amber liquid, offered his trembling upper lip as a sacrifice to its fire and aspirated the faintest sliver – which caused him to shiver and cough.

'You are inhaling the spirit of the drink,' I said. 'The body goes down, I assure you, more easily.'

Making light of his innocence was a mistake. The young man's alcoholic tears evaporated, his nostrils dilated with fury. I had to absorb my perceived offence. 'Tobias Stimmer,' I said, though the name meant nothing to me. 'Naturally you are familiar with his, er, his illustrations— ?'

'Illustrations to Livy? They had them in Heidelberg. I was at Heidelberg, you know. And his *Ages of Man*, I saw that also.'

'Stimmer is a great engraver.'

The young man knotted his brow. '*Was*, you mean?'

I invited him, with my glass raised, to have another go at the whisky. 'What *is* death, to the eternal artist?'

Before his mind could catch up with my nonsense, I turned to my more certain talents. I asked whether he had any paper; whereupon he produced his numbered parchment, overturning it to expose a dirty underside. I asked him for the loan of my charcoal. Then, with deft strokes, I committed to that scrap a passable likeness of its owner. It seemed politic to forget the bend in his nose and to strengthen his jaw with shadow. When the cartoon was finished (with the hastily invented monogram 'TG' for imprimatur), my subject patted his hand with the back of his fingers.

'You are indeed an artist,' he said, looking with new eyes at this quizzical gnome: Court Painter to His Caesarean Majesty the Emperor of the Romans, sometime employee of the most gratified Wettin and Sonnenstein families, woodcut illustrator and portraitist for hire. Those already familiar with my career will require no transcript of the approximate history with which I regaled him. My father metamorphosed, to suit my present purpose, into Giambologna's favourite pupil and a most solicitous nurturer of his son's talent. Members of the Florentine Academy – with Sandro Bondanella their guiding star – dressed themselves as wise tributaries and gathered with gifts about my crib. As for pious Bonconvento (that venerated patriarch), he packed me off with a tearful kiss to greater triumphs at the Court in Prague. Not immediately – in that first oral draft of my life – did the Emperor Rudolf assume his mythical proportions; yet I could not resist, seeing how my admirer's eyes glistened at the name of power, telling fat lies about my imperial connections. Oblivious to great Rudolf's decay (he knew less about the intrigues and corruption of the Castle than your humblest Prague tapster), the young man cawed to hear me describe the Emperor's accomplishments and begged that I describe the paintings in his possession.

'I wonder,' I said, 'does Herr Winkelzug boast contacts capable of finding the prints you seek? Do you live in Nuremberg?'

'Lord, no. I'm only passing through. It is one of the last stops on my *nobilis et erudita peregrinatio* . . .'

'I see,' I lied. My scalp tingled; I was glad of a sip of Kornbranntwein. 'And the gentleman whom, by my intervention, you evaded earlier was—?'

'Oh, that was Count Winkelbach. My protector. He has no business interfering in my affairs. But then he's only obeying the Duke my father's orders.'

'The Duke, you say?'

'I try to remain anonymous, Signor Grilli, when conducting fine art negotiations. I am Albrecht, heir to the Duchy of Felsengrunde.'

I dropped my head in deference. 'The honour is mine, your Grace.'

It was a game of hide-and-seek played, in accordance with ducal wishes (on Count Winkelbach's part) and ducal expectations (on Albrecht's), within the saving parameters of one abiding rule: that neither participant, once habitual roles had been resumed, should acknowledge in conversation the *fact* of the chase. This was in deference to each player's status as, respectively, loyal retainer and heir to the Duchy.

'The aim of the game, so far as I am concerned, is to move freely among common men. Do you know Michelangelo's *Last Judgement*, engraved by Giulio Bonafide? I should like enormously to return with it to my homeland. Felsengrunde, apart from the presence of one shabby fraud, lacks a shred of artistic life.'

'But why this pursuit with Winkelbach, your Grace?'

'Oh, my tiresome father is close to his treasure. Money that I am supposed to squander on dignitaries I prefer to spend on things that please me. Felsengrunde is a desert for the visual arts. We have barely any native talent – none at all, I would say. Beauty is prized at naught. And even in the castle it is a starvation diet.' Albrecht's face darkened with purpose. 'But I mean to remedy all that. Winkelbach tries to restrain my spending, of course. I am *supposed* to be attending university. Even for that, the Duke let me go only with great reluctance. He is a mountain rustic, Signor Grilli. He values nothing if it hasn't got antlers.'

'University, you say?'

'I wanted Wittenberg but my father forbids it. A Feldkirch (that's our family, you know) attending *that* heretical swamp? So when the summer ends I shall be going to Ingolstadt – at sufficient proximity to my father's wrath.'

When I asked Albrecht what he hoped to gain by his

studies, the young man shrugged and burbled into his drink. I sensed already that curious tension within him between indolence and ambition. It was a blending of tempers whose outcome, should either force ever exceed or yield to the other, could only be inaction or failure. Here was Power without Will; Will without Power, such as characterised your narrator's existence, was its natural complement. Therefore I assured the Marquis – while in the Hauptmarkt he concealed himself, a threadbare Proteus, beneath his moulting beard – that I would serve his interests better, far better, than agents like Winkelzug. I had Georg Spengler and Meyrink and Spranger for contacts. 'I can help you to broaden your collection,' I said, 'and refine your appreciation of European artists.' Quoting my (hastily invented) agent's fee, I assured him of such riches as would astonish his parochial subjects upon his accession. But the Marquis was as changeable as mountain weather: one moment sunshine and the next a tedious mizzle. Instead of accepting with delight the offer of my undivided services, he grew withdrawn and melancholy, and spilled ambiguous vowels into his false beard. I surmised – correctly, as it turned out – from his reluctance to answer my questions, that Albrecht of Felsengrunde had yet to acquire a single print. Pseudonymous meetings with drunken dealers had so far been the summit of his achievements. I felt it my duty to translate these fraudulent acts of rebellion into action. It would be my task to keep the flame of his enthusiasm burning. I had to make myself indispensable to the Marquis of Felsengrunde, so that I might outlast in comfort the oncoming winter.

9

Anna, Gretel, Favour

I used them at first for my own pleasure: lithe, dark Anna of the brisk hand, plump gap-tooth Gretel, my accommodating blonde. It cost me little effort (my hair childishly coiffed, my dress endearingly formal) to overcome their aversion. I made myself familiar to them – played the precocious infant, the exotic horror, decorated my German with Italian flourishes – until my money disappeared, sunk by quick fingers, into their corsets. Between these two whores a man could know the poles of sexual pleasure. Anna was all lean and muscle, swift as a loom and fiercely gripping. Her companion Gretel was mountainous; floundering below, I was a spectator at private pleasure, clamped between quivering thighs.

'Where's this money coming from?' Anna enquired in the spent calm after our second tryst. 'What are you, a court jester?'

'Of sorts.'

'A conjuror?'

'In a sense.'

'What – a magician?'

'A painter.'

This met with frank scepticism. To prove myself I extracted pen and ink from my sack. Anna, wary of this mysterious dwarf, yelled for Gretel to join us; which she did, though still attached to a startled customer.

'What would you have me draw?' I asked.

Anna, double-chinned as she peered from the bed, shrugged. 'Whatever pleases you.'

Cautiously I dipped my pen and proceeded, with Anna's

permission, to draw upon her belly. Gretel laughed. 'What's he doing?' It might have proved a grave mistake to pursue my conceit. I traced lightly the outline of a womb – as Arcimboldo had done, years before, in imitation of Leonardo. The canvas rose and fell, tremulous at the scratch of my pen. Anna giggled (a revelation to my ears: such girlish gaiety!) as I engendered the bowed serious head, the softly curving back, the clenched fists and gathered knees. Before I could make a start on the shading, Anna sucked in her breath and sat up to see. The fetus flinched and shrank; lines of ink streaked into the folds of her belly. 'Is that— ?' she gasped, staring at the upside-down image. 'Is it— ?'

I was seized by doubt. Had I insulted her terribly? Anna's face looked stretched and bloodless. She stroked the baby's skull.

'It's beautiful,' she whispered.

From that day I enjoyed favoured status with Anna and Gretel. 'It's our little monster,' Gretel would shriek, tucking her fists into her breasts in mock terror when I knocked on the door of their shack. 'Come give us the creeps, Thomas.' Then Anna would appear, hitching her skirts, from the adjoining room. 'Little beast,' she called me. 'If he's naughty, Signor Baby gets a spanking.'

'Don't spank him, Anna. He's our little sweetie.'

'Sweet enough to eat.'

I suffered this infantile play: it endeared me to them. I became the women's pet, hidden in their skirts, tickling them with my tongue or scratching their thighs with my fingernails until they fell upon one another in fits of laughter. After a time, for a reduced fare, I was permitted to spend the morning in their pungent bed, wedged between them as they snored and scratched. Sometimes, to my delight, Anna might rest her hand on my chest. Gently not to wake her,

I would place my fingers across her knuckles, feeling the bones beneath her skin. Or Gretel would fold her plump knee across my groin and sigh, complacent with slumber, into my hair. I lay awake, with the sun peeping at the shutters, imagining that these were my wives – or rather, that Anna was my wife and Gretel my concubine – or Gretel my wife and Anna my concubine – no, they were *both* concubines and my wives, all nine of them, lay jealously excluded in a neighbouring chamber. Come lunchtime, to thank my whores, I would produce ink-and-wash portraits from my sack.

'What's with the antlers?'

'That's me. I'm Actaeon turning into a stag.'

'Boaster.'

'You're Diana, the goddess. Look: Actaeon is a handsome Greek. He's out hunting deer one day when he stumbles on Diana bathing . . .'

'What's *that*?'

'It's a flannel. Actaeon is punished because he—'

'Do goddesses use flannels?'

'*Yes*. Actaeon is punished – he gets transformed into a stag and torn apart by his own hounds. Because no mortal can see Diana and live. She's too chaste.'

'Anna? My arse.'

Anna set aside my dawdle and reached across the table for Gretel's picture. 'Oh, now, that's Leda and the Swan.'

Gretel beamed. 'Am I the swan? I love swans – they're so graceful.'

'You've got eyes, Gretel,' said Anna. 'You're the *girl*.'

'Oh.'

'The mighty Zeus used to covet mortal women. He came to them in many shapes and sizes: a bull, another woman, floating gold. In this story he ravishes Leda in the shape of a swan.'

Gretel gaped, suitably impressed. Anna tore a crust of stale bread. 'If you ask me,' she said, 'that's depraved.'

Glad as they were of my useless gifts, the two whores would kick me out soon enough after lunch. For a time I would pace the muddy street outside their hovel, suspiciously sizing up passers-by, waiting for some oaf or lame-brain to knock on their door and, for a banal exchange of metal, to usurp my place. So many lusts – one for every citizen – itching to be scratched! Thinking about this, wallowing in the numbers, bathed me in misanthropy.

But my plan allowed for no such emotion.

I had to win the Marquis's favour.

Albrecht wore heavily, like a coat of rusty mail, the illusory shame of his virginity. Any man, encountering him, would have sensed the incubus weighting his shoulders; he would have remembered from his own youth the discomfiture of ignorance and want, the tide of yearning that seems to maroon one on a grey and boundless shore. I inferred from scraps of self-revelation that moral qualms, contracted of Albrecht's tutors in childhood, inhibited him from seeking the usual remedy to his affliction. Nor had Felsengrunde granted its future lord the peremptory lessons learned (by most heirs to power) of some dutiful chambermaid. The seemingly impenetrable mystery of the feminine sapped his confidence. One evening, after I had delivered a bibulous lecture on Italian art, I watched from afar my pupil – whose tastes, to my financial gain, I was carefully forming – surrender himself to his pursuer. Confronted by Moritz von Winkelbach, Albrecht could only simper and wipe his lips, when by rights he should have reprimanded the brute for his presumption. Where could the young man turn in his need? Winkelbach was supposed to be his guide and confidant; yet he failed utterly, being the father's spy. I perceived the nature of my vocation. I would be a genial, corruptive foil to the dour moralist: procuring such delights as the noble Count prohibited.

It was important that I gauge the Marquis's preferences. To ask outright what inflamed him would have been impossible. So I sketched my ladies of easy virtue, making studies for portraits that would never be painted, and showed these to him in the chaste context of artistic instruction. I looked for dilation in Albrecht's pupils as he compared the images. He expressed admiration for Gretel as Magdalene, whose weeping tresses failed to conceal her formidable breasts. Anna's Lucretia, pining in ecstasy as the dagger pierced her delicate bosom, unfastened his lips – with an audible pop – and dropped his epiglottis from the cave of his chin. How fetchingly the Marquis coloured when I told him that live models had posed for these studies. He hid his face in his tankard, the more easily to boil there.

'If it pleases you,' I said, 'we might dine with these ladies at my cottage.'

'No, that's *impossible*.'

'Impossible, your Grace? Females must eat as we do.'

'I mean that I cannot – could not – leave the city without Winkelbach knowing.'

'What is it to him that you should dine with gentlewomen? Such creatures were good enough for an emperor to dance with. And where, think you, did Dürer find his models for the Holy Mother?'

The Marquis stared longingly at my drawings. 'Did they *really* pose for you in the . . . ?' He cupped his hands before his ribs but courage failed him and he abandoned the lewd gesture.

'Did they pose in character, your Grace?'

'Yes, by God!'

'They posed exactly as you see them.'

Albrecht was sold. He gathered up the sketches and thrust them beneath his collar for later perusal.

'Their names,' I said, 'are Anna and Gretel. They complement each other pleasingly, do you not agree?'

I considered my chances of failure. Would not Anna frighten him with her cunning and wit? Or Gretel's size prove too daunting? A virgin wants to be taken in hand, to abandon himself to experience; at the same time he must believe himself to be the first conqueror. Therefore I needed (to be certain of success) a combination of knowing innocence and depraved maidenhood. Anna and Gretel were common vessels, pots for the public to spend in; yet they were also skilled actresses who could suppress their shudders and disguise derision as yelps of rapture. When I told them of my plan, they seemed glad of an easy night (deflowering a boy is swift work, entailing few dangers) and they relished the chance to dress like ladies, in costumes hired for the occasion from a Venetian dressmaker – a casual acquaintance – whose tales of low adventure on the Ponte delle Tette I endured in the vain hope of reducing his fee. The whores twirled and clasped to their breasts the green-and-scarlet bodices. Ordinarily, thrilled by my power, I would have paid for a tumble. But lust was eclipsed in me by ambition. I envisioned Albrecht with a golden key, standing beside ramparts and gilded turrets, promising me a share in his great fortune.

We met outside the hospital church of St Martha, on the evening of the seduction. I was dressed in my best coat and leather jerkin. Albrecht came disguised as usual, though by now Count Winkelbach must have been familiar with his woollen extensions.

'The ladies are waiting,' I said. 'Your Grace may dispense, in their company, with the beaver and thatch.'

Sullen with trepidation, Albrecht found a stick of ash and threshed with it the cowslip and nettles, burdock and grasses that lined the road to my cottage. Arriving at our destination on the edge of wheat fields that rolled like the sea, Albrecht reprieved a quaking poppy to take in the scene.

'Is this *it*?'

'A humble dwelling, I confess. But clean. And comfortable.'

'Very rustic.'

'Imagine a swain wooing his lover at the window.'

Albrecht, in the failing light, was blind to the pots of flowers that I had hired for the occasion. I saw his nose wrinkle at the leaning timbers, at the lone window whose gable I had so expensively restored for his visit. A treacherous breeze laced the pine-sweetened air with rumours of the privy. Inside – please God – the cottage would smell of fruits and spices and my lovely aides would be sitting on borrowed cushions, fingering perfume between their breasts.

'Your beard,' I said, poised to rap on the door. Albrecht, with manly resolution, tugged off his wig. 'And the *beard*. What need have you to hide your face?'

Albrecht growled, 'You know very well.'

The women, hearing our voices, called for us to come. We left the black lambs of Albrecht's disguise on the stoop and entered my amorous den.

Beneath the hayloft (now my bedchamber) there was only one room to speak of, where not long ago a farming tenant would have sat with his hens and his dogs, devouring, let us imagine, the flesh of a rabbit snared in the woods. The floor was of packed earth, though the straw, which I had inherited rotten, was newly laid down for the Marquis's visit. The ladies, good Anna and Gretel, were plumped upon mock damask cushions, their less than dainty feet tucked into vair slippers whose secret undersoles were worn bare. The ancient carpet (which my Venetian stage furnisher had tried to sell me) marked the confines of that colourful island set in a dun and driftwood sea. The table, which was set with choice dishes and *tafelwein* transposed to bottles of *qualität*, gleamed in candle glow. It was intimate theatre, a stage-play luxury into which one could sink one's teeth.

'Ladies, may I present Albrecht, Marquis of Felsengrunde.'

I nudged the stultified boy, who stepped forward and made his reverence. Anna rose to her feet and Gretel followed (stowing a toffee apple behind her rump). The whores curtsied as daintily as could be hoped, and rising from their genuflection sized up the evening's custom. Albrecht stroked his ribs and turned a full circle, pretending to take an interest in the shadows.

'Let us begin,' I said, 'with a toast.'

Anna sank back into her leavened dress and poured sweet white wine into Venetian goblets. With my hand cautiously raised to the small of Albrecht's back, I steered him to his cushioned seat.

'To Felsengrunde.' The others raised their glasses, a three-pitched echo. 'Long may she prosper under wise government.'

'Oh, *b*ollocks.'

Gretel's hand flew to her throat as she tried to catch a spilling thread of wine. It was too much for her – the liquid flowed in converging streams from her chin into the plunge of her corset. Anna glanced in dismay at the Marquis. (His own glass, which he held in suspense inches above the table, had been drained in one draught.) His mouth was open, his plump lips glistening. Over his eyes – which were fixed on the flustering whore – a telling glaze had settled. Gretel apologised, dabbing at her breasts with Albrecht's napkin, and from the slur in her voice I knew that she had fortified herself for our arrival.

'Sorry – oops – your Majesty, I'm such a clumsy slut.'

'*Your Grace*,' said Anna, 'lives up in the mountains, I understand?'

'Hm— ?'

'It must be . . . is it very – er – cold up there?'

'Very,' said Albrecht. 'I'm sorry, what did you say?'

Anna repeated her question, grimacing at its inanity. As her noble interlocutor struggled to articulate an answer, I perceived the tug of a smile in the corner of his mouth. ('Only, madam, when it isn't hot. I mean when it's not . . . not cold . . . it is hot.') Gretel, taking advantage of the distraction, claimed my eyes with a deep and shameful look of apology.

'Should you ever visit my duchy, madam, I would show you thunderstorms on the High Plateau, and the peak of Adlerberg which is covered in eternal snow.'

Now Albrecht (to my great and happy surprise) undertook a verbal ramble through Felsengrunde, with Anna nodding and mindfully providing her own facial weather (now augustly serene, now stormily frowning) to the peaks and chasms. I had worried, until this moment, that my honeytrap whores would prove too vulgar to seduce him. Instead they set Albrecht at ease because they were *not* high-born ladies: neither the courtly schemers nor saleable innocents he had encountered at court but powdered strumpets – a gift that need not be acknowledged from his diminutive employee. Beneath the still untouched display of cold meats and fruit, I patted Gretel's thigh.

'And that, madam, gives but a little sense of Felsengrunde's variety – her changeable, er, beauty.'

I charged our glasses. 'To Beauty, then, let us drink.'

With everyone refreshed, I broke a leg off the crisply tanned fowl. Gretel laughed from sheer relief and smacked her lips. We began to eat. Whenever silence threatened, yours truly spoke of Art and Food and Love, 'all things given by God to make our earthly stay endurable.' The wine flowed freely (Albrecht must have known that I was refilling his glass) and the company feasted with abandon, licensed by pretence. From a butcher near Lorenzer Platz I had bought strings of plump, greasy white sausages, with an earthenware pot of sweet mustard sauce which his porcine wife mixed for customers. Elsewhere in the Hauptmarkt I had bought a pot of brown lentils, a dozen salted herring in thick cream (the onions to accompany which I grew in my own patch of soil by the privy), several loaves of wheat bread softly exhaling from the oven, a chicken for slaughter, and liver dumplings, which Gretel, in a distracted moment about my thighs, had informed me was her favourite dish. Lastly, from my farming neighbour, I had bought some pears in brandy, a jar of toffee apples and some red cabbage oozing in its own juice.

The Marquis was not, it transpired, a prodigious eater in my own image but rather a dainty picker, more likely to contemplate than to devour the little mound on his plate. In this respect he resembled my dark Anna; for though she ate with peasant manners, sucking on her fingers' ends, yet she did so sparingly, being loath to cram her belly like her bloating colleague. Gretel, on account of her few teeth, was obliged to suck her food into a pap, which rendering she did with a greedy deliberation fit to enflame an ox. A creature of base appetites, hungry reader, I knew which of these two performances pleased me most to watch. Albrecht, however, had sloping eyes only for Anna – who was well aware that she had been selected.

Through all our talk and merriment, one problem remained: how to transport the Marquis from secret desire to desire's fulfilment. A corridor of air separated him from Anna's polished shoulder, which no amount of sweet white wine could bridge. Thank goodness, then, for Gretel. Twice, unwittingly, she rescued the meal from stalemate. The second occasion, when the tablecloth carried more food in scraps than the borrowed pots and dishes, she strayed in the foolish labyrinth of her mind on to the subject of blemishes. Albrecht, reminded of his own, fumbled with his broken nose. He was on the verge of retreating into himself when Gretel giggled and showed 'the Duke' a mole on the underside of her left breast. Neither Anna nor myself could prevent her from exposing that great mammary.

'You can't see it in the candlelight, your Majesty. There's two hairs sticks out like bristles, look.'

'Thank you, Fräulein, I think we can take you at your word.'

But Gretel was glad of an airing and refused my soft entreaties to return her breast whence it came. She even threatened – for the night was balmy and the candles hot – to expose its twin. Anna rose from her seat, still every inch the lady of manners, and with stern and matronly gestures pressed Gretel's breast into her corset. Gretel sighed and made no attempt either to help or hinder. I reached for the last drops of table wine, trying to cause a distraction, when a stifled moan escaped from Albrecht's lips. He was pressing against the table, his arms crossed beneath its shambles as though he were gripped in the belly. His eyes bulged under irreducible pressure.

'I must—'

'Your Grace?'

'*Please*,' said Albrecht. He gripped my hand with unspeakable significance.

Gretel, by her lack of manners, had brought the evening to its crucial instant. I jumped up – snapping that first physical contact with my patron – and announced in what I hoped was a casual manner my intention to retire.

'Gretel, my dear, will you accompany me? We can savour the soft hours of the night together. In the *guest* room.'

Anna understood first, and pinched her friend in the folds of her wide-hipped skirt. Gretel complained: 'Ow!' Then, catching on, she arose from her cushions.

'Your Grace, I bid you goodnight.' Albrecht chewed his lip with soiled, infantile teeth as he watched me receding. 'Gretel?'

'Coming, coming.'

A swift round of bows and curtsies excused us. I leaned in mock drunkenness with my arm beneath Gretel's backside. Gretel steadied the bucking floor by pressing on the top of my head. We must have looked a grotesque pair as we sank into the shadows. What better licence can a virgin be given than to see such imperfect beings lumbering towards pleasure? At the door to the 'guest room' (which had been until recently the adjoining stable), I watched Anna resettle beside Albrecht and raise her own glass to his lips.

'Don't be offended,' I whispered to Gretel. 'There's no accounting for taste.' But my explanation of Albrecht's choice went unheeded. Gretel had stepped out of her deflating dress and was rootling into a clean patch of straw.

There were no convenient spyholes in the wooden boards through which to watch Anna's progress. No sound came from the banquet save a single chime from a wineglass. Then I heard, quite distinctly, the sullen percussion of feet ascending the stairs to my vacated bedchamber. I had shaken my straw mattress vigorously and picked out the fleas one by one, sitting in poor light, until I had thought my eyes would fuse and leave me squinting. Ludolf Bresdin and I had slept for months on that mattress together, so I doubted not its capacity to accommodate more athletic recumbents. Gretel behind me snored: a sonorous noise like barrels rolling down a gangplank. I had slaved since daybreak to prepare for the evening. This little whoremonger's work was done and he sank like a stone in the waters of sleep.

I woke to find the day already advanced. An oblique shaft of sunlight anointed my forehead. I propped myself on my elbows, rising out of celestial favour, and cocking my head to void my nose I saw the discarded heap of Gretel's clothes, and a Gretel-shaped nest in the straw where she had slept. I spoke her name without reply, then crawled on my hands and knees to the door.

The table in the centre of the cottage was heaped as we had left it. A party of mice somersaulted at my approach. They bolted for shelter, shooting across the floor as though pulled on strings.

I climbed the steps slowly, on fat feet, not to waken voices in the wood (for a very starveling on tiptoe will sound like an ogre) and pushed open my bedchamber door to discover – in sequence – a pair of white stockings splayed on the floorboards; shoes heaped one upon the other; Albrecht's crimson breeches, sagging like a fallen plum; and the gaping ribs of some devoured carcase, its hide the colour of Anna's corset. Six feet peeped naked from a sackcloth blanket. Gretel's face and nose were crushed into Anna's neck; Anna's small breasts sagged, cold pancakes, on her ribs, across which Gretel had thrown her plump and downy arm. I recalled, from my own mornings beside them, the whores' shallow breathing, a fenland air which I would inhale as though it were sweetest perfume. Now, instead of myself in their midst, Albrecht of Felsengrunde was laid out as stiff as a corpse, robbed of his clothes and confined to the very edge of the mattress by Gretel's jutting buttocks. The women had taken the blanket between them, chewing it away with their ruminant heels until it only covered Albrecht below the groin. I found myself inspecting the placid mollusc of his sex, the surprisingly luxuriant hairs around the taut scrotum. Goose pimples pricked the skin of his arms, and I saw a shiver pass like a ripple across the surface of his belly. (Perhaps my gaze was icy on him?) I was tempted to go closer – to inspect the sheets themselves for signs of success. But the telling of lubricious tales was included in the whores' price: I had only to be patient, and should not risk Albrecht's waking up to find me staring at his manhood. Therefore I withdrew, backwards, with a courtier's deference before an emperor, and shut the door until the latch softly clicked.

The women were still sleeping when Albrecht came down an hour later. He had dressed himself and attempted to flatten – perhaps with his own spit – the stubborn duck's-tail curls on his nape. I opened wide the cottage door to welcome in the sun and saw, in the sober light, the Marquis's disenchantment; for the table looked like a plundered ossuary, the carpet was chewed by a mange, the cushions that I had hired of the Venetian furnisher were spilling their guts of eiderdown, and over everything a film of straw and dust was spreading.

I said nothing, busying myself with a last loaf of bread. Albrecht sat without a word on the cushioned chair. I gave him some bread and cold chicken, which he discovered almost with surprise in his hands. 'I didn't touch them,' he said.

'I believe you. Though there is no harm in touch. Beauty must be shared, your Grace, and since men cannot be beautiful, they must possess it from women.'

Lord – a Roman pander, I winked at the boy! Albrecht looked from his glass to my chest, from my chest to the stairs, then back to his glass. Later, on my return to the cottage, I would learn from Anna the specifics of his debauching – how, once Gretel and I had withdrawn from the scene, Albrecht had followed Anna to bed, tugged by the hand like a child obliged out of duty to meet a fearful relative. The wine and Anna's skill had delivered the young Marquis in a state of readiness from his clothing – so ready, indeed, that Albrecht fired his volley the instant Anna was naked. Voided of his essence before term, the Marquis had seemed inconsolable. Not with all her considerable art could Anna rouse him for a second attempt. The female country, its comely uplands and fruitful valleys, seemed to him no longer worth knowing. He shrank from exploring, with even a finger, the cave of her sex, with its false and true entrances, its yielding depths. 'And I could have left it at that – quite happily – only *you* wouldn't get your money's worth. So I came downstairs to fetch Gretel.'

Reader, I could have asked, nay begged, on my bare creaking knees, for my doves to repeat their Sapphic cooing. Hidden, so he thought, behind the veil of their passion, Albrecht had rediscovered his potency. He had put it to solitary work, until all three participants, whether in true or mock satiety, had subsided. This perversion would take seed in the Marquis's imagination. Prompted by dissembling whores, it would become the founding myth of his erotic life, with myself in the background as its sower.

Albrecht's chest sank with relief when I bolted the door to my cottage. Dread of the women descending to greet us had soured his nauseous breakfast. It forced me, though famished, to abandon a cold sausage.

'The gods are smiling on us,' I said, regarding the blue sky.

The Marquis grunted and barely glanced upwards. Side by side we retraced our steps of the evening before. I kicked from the flowering verge his abandoned stick of ash but Albrecht ignored it: no weeds or poppies would lose their heads today. Twice the Marquis faltered, contemplating the

207

rumbles of his stomach and popping open his lips. The third hesitation culminated in a necessary purging. Propped against an oak tree, he heaved and retched, expelling great quantities of anonymous matter – so much animal slaughtered for nothing. I left him gasping beside his supper and hurdled through tall grasses in search of a stream. But Albrecht, marvellously, called me back. Pushing himself up on his knuckles, he announced that he was well again, thank you, very much restored.

Half a mile from the Frauentor gate, I prepared to recite my practised confession. I had learned from Luboš Hrabal and the Mušek twins that a crook, to win trust, must take his victim into his confidence. Had I not compromised Albrecht with the secret of his near-deflowering? So should I not, out of solidarity, expose to him a secret of my own? 'Your Grace,' I said, 'I have other skills, supplementary to those of artist and agent. On occasion I have had to live by them . . .'

Albrecht looked at me askance. Was there a spark of fear in his eyes – an expectation of ambush or blackmail? I hastened to reassure him.

'I am a master forger, your Grace. When the need, or demand, arises. But whereas a journeyman may be mistaken for any number of similar beasts, this forger is a perfect marvel.' From my waistcoat pocket I produced a sketch of Baldung Grien's *The Groom Bewitched*.

'I know this,' said Albrecht. 'I've seen it.'

'You have seen the *woodcut*, your Grace. What has become, in this drawing, of the horse? And notice, the witch at the window has no firebrand.'

'This is *your* drawing?'

'Once familiar even with a sample of his work, I can recognise an artist's hand. Each painter, your Grace, has his unique style – even the nonentities. It could be the application of light and shade, the bulge of a figure's eyes. Whatever the trait, it is as distinct and revelatory as a signature. I can attribute a painting as readily as you can put a name to a face. And recreate it more skilfully than any counterfeiter living.'

I had timed my speech to perfection, concluding as we entered the shadow of the great archway – where you saw me earlier, attentive reader, in the company of a previous investment. Albrecht offered no response to my revelation. I wondered whether he might denounce me, and pictured myself fleeing the region pursued by howling dupes.

Only at the bridge did I realise that he was not wearing his disguise.

'Damn it,' the Marquis whispered.

Upon the bridge, leaning their rumps against its wall, two stocky men dressed as tradesmen, with daggers in their belts, were sorting through the passing traffic. Albrecht slowed but there was nowhere to hide. The Felsengrundians saw him before he could place a toe above the river. One of them came towards us; the other turned and whistled across the fork of his fingers.

'Winkelbach,' muttered Albrecht, indicating with his nose the darkly dressed gentleman running towards us from Lorenzer Platz. The Marquis set off to meet his captors on the bridge. 'It's all right,' he called. 'I have not come to any harm.'

Uncertain how to behave, I fled. Footsteps sounded at my back. I felt the breath of encroaching anger, and turned before Count Winkelbach could whisk me about. '*You*,' he said.

'Me?'

Winkelbach's nostrils flapped; his thin lips were compressed almost to nothing. 'Stay away from him, midget.'

'I'm sorry – are we acquainted?'

'You know who I am. I ought to crush you under my boot.'

'With your weight behind it, I should be crushed.'

Moritz von Winkelbach gripped his sword and exposed the blade shaft. 'It is a point of honour with me,' he said. 'I will see my duty done.'

'Herr Winkelbach!'

My confronter turned, surprised by his master's voice. I saw Albrecht running back to join us, the portly soldiers puffing in his dust. 'Herr Winkelbach, you may stand down.'

'Your Grace need not concern himself . . .'

'Stand down, I tell you.'

Winkelbach's mien changed utterly. 'My lord, I am trying to save you from vermin.'

'His name is Tommaso Grilli. He is an artist – he will have your respect.'

'Respect? For this profiteer?'

Albrecht made a soothing and placatory gesture. 'Herr Winkelbach, I am returned safely to your keeping. You perform most commendably your duties to my father.'

Incredulous noises died in Winkelbach's throat. His soldiers, having caught up with us, tried not to watch a scene that intrigued them. Albrecht of Felsengrunde had grown in stature. Was it by my friendship, or his carousing with Nuremberg drabs, that he seemed to inhabit pockets of himself previously unknown? Moritz von Winkelbach rooted about inside his narrow, predatorial head for a means of saving his honour. The Marquis, meanwhile, wished me good day and strolled off towards the bridge with the soldiers in tow.

Count Winkelbach glared down at me. 'I am wise to you, little man. You had better watch your step. And mind your back . . .'

*   *   *

Five days followed without news. The trees were putting on their late summer glaze. Oak leaves grew waxy; the beechwood crackled underfoot; it would soon be time for the Marquis to depart. Would I pursue him, I wondered, though unbidden, like a loping fox to Ingolstadt? On the sixth day I began to despair, being short of funds, with my cottage cleared of its borrowed luxuries and neither Anna nor Gretel willing to touch me without pecuniary reward. For want of food I went to gather hazelnuts in the forest. Prising the still-green nuts from their ruffs, I contemplated crushing them into a paste – a bitter mush fit only for mules and bankrupt chancers. Having filled my blanket, I was trudging home, my mind all pestle and mortar, when outside my cottage I recognised one of Winkelbach's soldiers.

'Open up! Open this door!'

The hazelnuts scattered – they hobbled, animated by their fall. The soldier turned and saw me on the grass verge. He tugged the brim of his cap and waded through his brawn towards me.

I found myself backing away, my hands imploring. Surely Winkelbach had sent this brute to punish me?

'Wait! Where are you going?'

Roots and mole-hills tossed themselves under my feet. I turned with the intention of fleeing to the trees but a powerful hand seized my collar. I barked, strangled, and lost my footing. 'Please!' I scrabbled in the grass, like a man looking for a dropped jewel. 'Mercy!'

The soldier relaxed his grip on my collar. 'Easy, lad – I'm not going to hurt you. The Marquis sent me. I'm to deliver a message.'

A single hazelnut offered itself to my grasp. 'Ah-*ha*.' I gulped down a restorative breath, then clambered to my feet. '*Found* it.'

The soldier glimpsed some precious object in my blinking hand. 'Do you want to hear the message?'

'Message?'

The soldier drilled a finger at his skull. 'In here,' he said.

'Yes – why not?'

The soldier parted his legs and stiffened to attention. 'His Grace the Duke Albrecht the Twelfth of Felsengrunde is grievously sick he is ailing alas.' The delivery halted, waiting for its rear. 'His loyal son the Marquis must return to Felsengrunde at once he is going . . .' The effort of recollection nudged the soldier's eyebrows. '. . . to leave Nuremberg.'

'Is he not going to Ingolstadt?'

'Hold on, there's more. The Marquis requests that Thomas Cricket accompany him to his homeland our beloved Duchy where he shall be found worthy employment . . . worthy employment . . . That's it.' The soldier looked at me with soulful eyes. 'It's not my usual line of work. Only the Count doesn't trust errand boys. Was I all right?'

'Fine, yes.'

'I learned it by heart.'

'Very succinct.'

'Your name isn't really Cricket – is it?'

I shrugged. 'Grille, Grilli. What's a vowel between friends?'

'We're leaving in two days. The southern gate at dawn.' The soldier rubbed his flanks and looked, with a sniff of disdain, at my cottage. 'You'll be having to settle your affairs.'

'I don't have many to speak of.'

'No, well – you won't need any food or money. The Marquis says. Just bring the tools of your trade.'

'Thank you.' I smiled. 'I most certainly will.'

10

Felsengrunde

We had no time to stop and visit Munich. Instead we turned our horses westward. Clinging to my soldier's waist and buffeted on the cruel hump of his saddle, I dared not protest against our haste; for Moritz von Winkelbach longed to see himself reflected in the still-living eyes of his lord – to pay homage to the father before his questionable son could profane with his flab the ducal throne. Albrecht, for his part, sealed himself behind a sullen mask, his jaw set against his horse's mane.

At the inns where we stayed, I was obliged to share beds with strangers (none of whom appreciated the gnome in their ribs) while the Marquis slept in comfort with his entourage. Saddling up at dawn, in the clucking yards where mongrel dogs loitered and cocked their legs, I attempted to ingratiate myself with Count Winkelbach. I was moon faced for his approval, inviting instructions with open palms; but no instructions came and by the time we reached Augsburg I guessed that he would always despise me.

A letter awaited us at the inn from Count Winkelbach's brother. Albrecht found me to convey the news that his father's condition had stabilised. 'That's encouraging,' I ventured. 'And several days old – he may be even better now.'

'Indeed,' said the Marquis, 'he *may* be.'

To dissolve my patron's gloom, I suggested a visit to the Fuggerei estate, which Jacob Fugger built to house the poor citizens of Augsburg. 'Jacob Fugger,' I said, paraphrasing a local coachman whom I had grilled for information, 'was not only a patron of the Arts. He was also a father to his people.'

Albrecht shrugged. 'He could afford to be.'

So while the Count busied himself with our lodgings, the Marquis and I set out with one of the soldiers – Klaus, my sometime messenger – serving as our watchful shadow. Guardsmen outside the Fuggerhäuser uncrossed their halberds when Albrecht flourished his letters of transport. The Duchy of Felsengrunde, you should remember, is of scant importance to the wider Empire: a mountainous scab on Bavaria's rump. Even so, Albrecht was of ruling stock and a flustered hen of an official tumbled down a staircase to greet us – whereupon he began, or perhaps resumed, an elucidatory monologue concerning the palace. We walked dutifully through arcaded courtyards and peeped at the locked art cabinet of Friedrich Sustris. I confess that I absorbed little of what we saw, resenting our guide's patter and eyeing my distracted patron with the glum preoccupation of an unacknowledged lover. There was general relief when the tour ended and we returned to the sunbaked streets.

We ambled wearily to Rathaus Platz and stopped at the statue of the Emperor Augustus, whose name the city still bears. Albrecht noted the casual-fingered gesture of power and, with a dreamy and supercilious smile, stretched out his arm to mimic the Roman. He reminded me of a man trying on another's robe.

'Your Grace is not quite there yet,' I said.

Albrecht caught his arm as though stung. 'What the Devil do you mean? Not quite *where*?'

'I . . . sir . . . I simply observe that your impersonation lacks a butterfly.'

The Marquis looked again at the statue of Augustus, upon whose bronze finger a peacock butterfly had settled. It was – I lied – my fancy that the Emperor was extending his arm to provide the insect with a perch. 'Power transfigured to meekness,' I said.

Albrecht, accused in his own mind if nowhere else, uttered not a word to me for the remainder of our visit.

The Duchy of Felsengrunde, from outside her borders, seems an impregnable fortress, where sheer cliffs burst from forests of ash and sombre pine and the green slopes are scarred by rockfalls. Standing beneath those ramparts, one can scarcely imagine the existence of lush valleys, the Wintertal and Grosse Weideland, beyond. To reach these one must negotiate either of two passes carved into the rock by the same river – the one leading from Bavaria and the other, alongside foaming rapids, into the Swiss cantons.

After four days in the saddle, we dismounted at the Pass of Our Lady.

Our throats were ticklish from the dust of the road and we stopped to cup water from a nearby stream. As I knelt to drink, I found my gaze compelled by the mountains. Storm clouds loured upon their crowns and made me regret the gentler slopes of Tuscany. Albrecht clunked down beside me; he pointed to a snow-capped peak on the Duchy's sombre table-top. 'Berg Mössingen,' he said with significance. 'And that greater mountain to the east is Adlerberg. Do you remember Adlerberg?'

'I recall the occasion upon which you mentioned it.'

'It simply *teems* with eagles.'

I received this improbable news with an appreciative pout. The first drops of rain plashed on my cap; I caught one, as fat as a berry, in my palm. Weary grasses aslant the stream began to nod and the pebbled water shivered. 'Take cover,' called Winkelbach, and the soldiers led their horses under the trees. I rushed to join them but the Marquis remained in admiration of the eagle's peak. He stood impersonating the Man of Destiny: too absorbed in contemplation of his duty to take heed of the rain. The more Winkelbach called after him, the less Albrecht was able to relent, though I could tell from the bitternish hunch of his shoulders that he felt his soaking. Moritz von Winkelbach swore under his breath and unrolled the blanket from his horse. 'I'm not having *him* die this year as well,' he muttered. Braving the downpour, the Count stretched his blanket above the Marquis. This conferred the necessary authority. Albrecht could leave off contemplating his destiny and join us beneath the whispering trees.

After an hour in that leaky tent, I saw a small troop of horsemen riding towards us along the track. Our soldier Klaus belched and rose to one knee. 'It's the welcoming party,' he said. 'They've been waiting for us.'

So the Marquis received an escort over the pass into the Weideland.

As our way steepened the clouds dispersed and the sun began to huff on the mountainside. Here branches and trunks were lazared with pale lichens. Rotten logs were banks of papery coral; the dust of felled trees furred the glistening soil and mossy rocks appeared to weep, spilling water all about us. I caught the flash of a redstart as it dashed from glade to cover. A black woodpecker yelped in alarm and fled, dipping and rising on its invisible pulley. 'Altdorfer!' I declared to my rider's back. This was the landscape the old Master had painted, where larches and pines, immensely long in their chase for the light, clung precariously from every lump of soil, while others, which had survived their partial falls, were rising again, bending concupiscently towards the sky. Far below us, the river had dug itself a deep trench, where it frothed and churned, achieving the colour of eggwhite battered in a blue bowl.

Now the Pass broadened out and the gorges sank behind

us. We were back in the world of men, among wild-flower meadows and fields of oat and barley. On every side of the Weideland – the Great Pasture – green mountains stood. I would come to know them all by name: the oyster shell of Saint Andreas which divided us from the Wintertal valley, the grander peaks of the Felsungründische Schweiz to the south and, domineering the eye, the vast expanse of the Augspitzer Wald with the High Plateau beyond it, like a ship's prow in Europe's ocean. Such dwarfing grandeur was relieved on the Weideland by weathered farmsteads, whose peasants dropped their forks to watch us pass. Fly-misted cattle dozed under clusters of sweltering oaks. A little boy, naked from the waist down, escaped his mother's clutches and stood bandy legged on the grass verge, watching the progress of his future master.

We passed without fanfare through the village of Kirchheim. I write 'village' – it consisted of a few wooden shacks with sloping roofs clustered about a muddy lane. Villagers emerged from smoky interiors, their poverty manifest in shreds and patches. A few women possessed clogs; most of the men wore lime-bark shoes. They barely flinched when our clattering horses flung muck at their breeches. (Was Winkelbach smiling, I wondered, to be returned where his person inspired dread? The Marquis seemed barely to notice his tenants, fixing his gaze on the as yet invisible castle.) At the fringe of the village, a muddied wretch lay sprawled as though drunk by the roadside. A bundle of damp faggots was scattered about his knees and a scrawny mongrel with scabs on its rump rested its head on his thigh. Sensing us, the beggar raised his left hand for alms; seeing armour and the fluttering banner, he snatched it back. 'Wilderer,' said the captain of the guard. The beggar raised his head and I saw that his cheek had been branded with the letter W – the sign of justice meted out to poachers. Somebody tossed the beggar a lump of rye bread. It landed in a puddle some yards from where he lay.

One mile farther south, we saw the glinting body of the Obersee spread out like a mirror at the foot of Felsengrunde Castle. One of the soldiers pulled a hunting horn from his saddlebag and sounded an alarum. Klaus geed up his horse and clapped his comrade on the arm. '*Heimat!*' he said joyfully. We rode behind a wooded escarpment and lost sight for a time of castle and lake. The ground rose steeply on the approach. Now we were on the flat of a ridge, with the forest withdrawing like the curtain from a stage. The whole company (with the exception of a certain Florentine) cheered to hear a belated echo of the sounded horn. Fields cultivated in tidy rows, with enclosures for goats and pigs, opened out before us. I glimpsed a small town, more prosperous than the last, with stone houses and a church spire, gathered about the castle's southern ramparts.

I cannot pretend, being acquainted with the great Hrad of Prague, that I was overcome with admiration for this old-fangled keep, whose fortified walls, dirty grey and choked in places by besieging ivy, were slowly eroding. On the ramparts a few soldiers waved to greet us. I looked in hope of seeing a flag at half-mast; but the ducal banner floated proudly above the gatehouse.

Resplendent in plumes and armour, we soared along the ridge above the Obersee. A grilled gate retreated into its stone gullet; the wooden tongue of the drawbridge rumbled beneath our mounts and we passed beneath the gatehouse where soldiers hollered and shook their caps. I saw a buttressed chapel – stables – sombre buildings – as we entered the Great Courtyard to meet the welcoming party.

A bewilderment of faces. I was left high and ridiculous on the horse while the riders dismounted. I watched the Marquis greet his officials with a perfunctory flourish.

(Women were regrettably few and kept back to the fringes of the party.) I saw Moritz von Winkelbach embrace fraternally a pastiche of himself, shorter and plumper than the original. Nobody, after the courtly formalities, embraced in like fashion the returned Marquis. There was a deferential and loveless space around him, maintained by false smiling. His father the Duke was absent.

For want of instructions, your narrator played the scholar, reading a dusty and most improbable *History* (itself at least a century old) *of the Duchy of Felsengrunde*. There were few vernacular books in the Duke's Library and I erred from pages of dense Latin to contemplate the panel paintings between the bookshelves: clumsy depictions of wild men from the Silver Age who, dressed in lion skins and muscled like Hercules, clubbed and broiled and devoured one another in a general wash of moss and mucus. Every so often a sigh would gather beneath my ribs and take a long time escaping. It was my fifth day in Felsengrunde and the novelty of arrival was wearing thin.

I had been given a tiny cell in the East Wing above the servants' quarters, where I dozed and drooled and butted the pillow with my face, waiting to wash down with small beer the ignoble meals brought to me by surly and suspicious pantry boys. After two days I had despaired of receiving a summons and begun to explore, quite unchallenged, the so-called Great Hall: a labyrinth of time-pitted stone where voices murmured behind closed doors and footfalls echoed down passageways that never revealed a living soul. I could walk (as I was doing now, leaving the *History* to Latinate ghosts) around the oaken gallery of the Great Hall and peep into the Council Chamber where dust lay like a carpet, unscarred by the movement of any chair. For all my wanderings, familiarising myself with the corridors and stairways, with the mystery of the Duchess's Apartments which the Duke had sealed up, in grief or relief, at his wife's demise; despite my licence to duck below the glassy stares of the sentries and climb the ramparts, where I admired the greensward and the purple mountains and the humble skiffs beetling on the surface of the Obersee; despite these seeming freedoms, I languished in uncertainty. None but servants sought me out. I dared not approach Martin Grünenfelder, the tall and morose High Chamberlain (last representative of a noble serving family) whom I heard giving orders to the servants; nor could I address the wild-haired Treasurer, Wilhelm Struder, who chewed goose quills at his desk and emerged every so often, with the resolve of a ravenous shrew, from the holt of his counting house to interrogate or reprimand spendthrift ministers. As for my Albrecht – the Marquis, rather – he was constantly engaged, locked in counsel in the Duke's Apartments (to which the whispering business of government had long ago withdrawn) or else praying in the chapel for an end – one way or another – to his father's sickness.

My own purpose, my reason for being here, had not been made public. From the tucking away of courtly elbows at my passing, I could tell that my person met with disdain. Contemptuous glances made the short hairs on the back of my neck stand on end; my ears, which until now had always enjoyed equanimity, burned in proximity to heard or imagined slander.

'Herr Grilli, is it not?'

I had wandered to the Chamber Gallery, thinking myself alone. I turned in surprise to hear my name. 'Yes?'

A man in a fusty gown doffed his cap, exposing a bald and speckled skull. His breath smelt of vinegar. 'My name is Altmann,' he said, 'Theodor Altmann, at your service.' How very like a pear his nose was! It went so far as to feign a split in the rump, with a deep furrow between the eyebrows to represent the stem. The nose by its ripeness seemed to compress his lips, which formed a pale line between a white moustache and a prominent chin. Milky, rheumy-cornered eyes scrutinised my face, no doubt making similar discoveries. 'I see you looking at the portraits,' Altmann said. There were two paintings on the wooden partition that entombed the Duchess's Apartments: likenesses made without skill, the faces waxy and wanting even points of light in the eyes to suggest animation, the clothes vague and afflicted by a mange intended, no doubt, to represent folds and creases. 'This lady is our late Duchess, blessed in memory. And this' – he indicated a darkly tousled bull of a man – 'is the present Duke. In, uh . . . depicted in happier times.' Theodor Altmann furiously scratched the scalp beneath his cap. 'You . . . you are from Florence, I understand?'

'I was born in Florence. But I have lived in many places since. And you?'

'Felsengrunde, born and bred. In the town here. Of course, I have travelled abroad in my time. *You* are – uh – friendly with the Marquis.' (The bland grin disappeared; the pear nose loured.) 'He's, he's, how, how have you, what uh, *what* is the . . .' (I dared raise my eyebrows in expectation of a complete sentence.) 'I mean, *why* are you here?'

'I begin to ask myself the same question.'

The old man made a vexed, rasping sound in his throat. I wondered was he a clerk of some kind? Or a spy for the Treasury, which feared having yet another salary to pay? I determined to give no quarter to his questions. I was troubled, however, by the existence of these portraits, concerning which I failed at first to make an obvious and significant connection.

'Might I ask you, Herr Grilli, how old you are?'

I told him. Theodor Altmann licked the inside of his

cheeks as though rummaging for crumbs. 'The same age,' he said, 'at which I began my service.'

'And what service would that be?'

'*Loyal* service, young man.'

Theodor Altmann reined in the horses of his fury and invited me, in a falsetto of good humour, for a stroll on the ramparts. Together we walked – Altmann in sunlight, your narrator in crenellated shadow – above the Grosse Weideland. For all his probing, the old man could learn nothing of my profession; yet I, exploiting his desire for revelation, gleaned some information from *him*.

There existed, it seemed, a tradition of rivalry between each duke and his heir. The present incumbent – for whom Altmann professed his undivided love – had always shown little affection to his son. I wondered aloud whether the death, in the Marquis's infancy, of the Duchess had not soured the love between them? 'Look there,' said Altmann, changing the topic, 'that rooftop. Do you see? It's the house of my parents. I was born there.'

On the southern ramparts of Felsengrunde Castle, I learned of the Duke's strong affections for certain 'inferiors' – imported favourites, Altmann called them, with a significant glower that I feigned not to notice – which exceeded the love he showed his own flesh and blood. The worst example of this concerned Josiah Koch, a stable boy grown retainer who, in the flush of his beauteous youth, had bowed to the Duke's desire. The resentment of the Winkelbachs and Grünenfelders ran deep. 'Our ruling families,' Altmann concluded, 'do not appreciate upstart outsiders.'

North of the gatehouse, as we approached the dungeon tower – a miniature Dalibor – and Theodor Altmann showed me Vergessenheit Strasse ('where criminals walk on their way to oblivion'), he exhumed the rumour that Albrecht's nose had been broken by the Duke his father. 'It is common knowledge, though I forget what offence the boy committed.'

Our walk accomplished, Theodor Altmann attacked the ascetic lice on his scalp. He asked me, testily: 'What did you make of the decorated panels in the Duke's Library?'

'The savages, do you mean?'

'Yes, the, uh . . . well, not savages exactly . . .'

I had solved the riddle of Theodor Altmann. Recklessly, I gave him my opinion of his paintings.

For a fortnight, the Court at Felsengrunde seemed to hold its breath. Conversations overheard in the course of my explorations touched on platitudes and avoided mention of the Duke's sickness. Everyone was waiting, careful not to act before the outcome was certain.

One morning I received a summons from Martin Grünenfelder, the High Chamberlain, to attend the Duke's review of his troops in the Great Courtyard. With trepidation and not a little excitement, I dressed in my Nuremberg finery – straining into my taffeta doublet – and joined a line of courtiers and attendants already forming outside the chapel. From the guardhouse tower on Weidmanner Platz came the sound of marching boots. Theodor Altmann, the neglected Court Painter, scurried next to me looking ill kempt, with the laces of his collar awry.

'Does this happen often?' I whispered at his elbow.

Theodor Altmann ignored me. I repeated my question and was fanned by his inky fingers to be silent. Now the guardsmen marched into view. They were a small troop of perhaps thirty men (I recognised my friend Klaus among them) dressed in light armour, carrying spikes and halberds and measuring their steps to the beat of a scrawny drummer boy. Flamboyantly plumed, as though returning in triumph from a war against ostriches, Maximilan von Winkelbach, my enemy's younger brother and Captain of the Footguard, played fugle to his troops.

'Halt!' The guardsmen stopped (only the back four crashing into one another) and turned about. Maximilian von Winkelbach confronted the audience with a stony face and bisected his nose, as it were, with the flat of his sword. Now the Duke's party emerged, unheralded for want of a trumpeter, from the Great Hall. My heart galloped at the sight of my patron elegantly dressed, with a military air, wading out of his depths in cordovan thigh-length boots. He accompanied the Duke's intimate Josiah Koch, the High Chamberlain Martin Grünenfelder, the Lord Chamberlain, our favourite Winkelbach, and two aged physicians whose own decrepitude gave poor advertisement of their professional skills. The Duke's page – a most womanly boy, high cheekboned and aloof – was pushing a bath chair whose occupant, concealed beneath an Ottoman rug, commanded the world's attention.

I was under the impression at first that, being troubled by a lump in his cushion, the Duke was fumbling behind himself to press it out; for he was awkwardly twisted at the waist and leaning to his right side. It had been a mighty body once, as Altmann's portrait suggested; but brawn had become a burden that weighed down his spirit. Dressed all in black, as though in mourning for his life, Duke Albrecht XII of Felsengrunde approached his guardsmen, the wheels of his bath chair chirruping like sparrows in a thicket. How wretched he looked, needing Josiah Koch to turn his head as the bath chair progressed along the line. I could not hear his comments about a soldier's dress; nor, it seemed, could the soldier in question, and Josiah Koch was obliged to translate. This humiliation angered the Duke. With his right fist, where power still resided (the same perhaps which had broken my patron's nose), he struck the armrest. A martial drum roll slowed from exhaustion as the inspection continued, and when the Duke had seen enough I sensed our own, civilian line ruffle and tighten.

'Ndwhoziss?'

'You know Herr Altmann, Father.'

'Whoziss? Nextim!'

The brute's face had turned sloppy; my eyes were level with his. The voice, no doubt sonorous once, now wheezed like air from a rusty pump.

'My name is Tommaso Grilli, if it please you.'

'Cricket?'

'No, Father – Grilli.' Albrecht, my Albrecht, with whom I had exchanged no word since arriving in his homeland, spun a thread of conspiracy between his eyes and mine. 'He's a friend of mine, Father.'

'Easer midger.'

'A friend from Nuremberg. A most noble gentleman.'

'Fuggin *midger*.'

Was it distaste for me or for his weary life that made the Duke's fallen countenance so bitter? 'Woise for? Brech – temmy woise *for*.'

'He is my tutor, Father. My Latin tutor.'

The Duke's eyes lost their ireful glow: interest seeped out of him and the page pushed his chair down the line. I thought,

'Latin tutor?'

'*Latin* tutor?'

I was returning to my guest room in the East Wing when Theodor Altmann leaned into me, pressing against my flesh as though to trip me up.

'He *had* Latin tutors when he was a boy. I knew them, they were my friends. Why should he need a Latin tutor now?'

I picked up my pace towards Vergessenheit Strasse, wanting to be alone. 'Answer me. Why are you so mysterious?'

'I am not mysterious, Herr Altmann. You heard what the Marquis said.' Musty, vinegar-breathed Altmann knocked his cap to the ground, such was the itching of his scalp. 'Have you lodgings,' I asked him, 'in this part of the Castle?'

'Lodgings? I, uh, formerly, yes . . .'

'Oh, *formerly*. And so you're accompanying me out of – what – nostalgia? You live in the stables.'

'Beside. I live *beside* the stables . . .'

'Then you have no reason to be following me, have you?'

Theodor Altmann turned sour with fury. His nose filled with old man's blood; his lips turned white to compensate. He shouted accusations at me in fluent-sounding Latin. I could not return fire in kind (it was not *my* fault that Albrecht had invented so poor an excuse for me) and opted instead for vulgar German. 'I am,' I said, 'exactly what you have always feared.'

'Uh,' said Altmann, 'what?'

'I am a painter. I am the Marquis's favourite. How greatly are *you* loved by the power to be?'

Without waiting for a response, I left my dumbstruck opponent in the Duchess's Courtyard and regained my quarters.

In the afternoon, hoping to dispel my boredom, I decided to visit the town. I had no idea what I might find there (apart from a certain painter's birthplace) but, stirring the few coins left in my pockets, I dared to entertain the hope of certain pleasures the appetite for which had been too long suppressed by the bruising memory of a saddle.

At the gatehouse, good soldier Klaus was the duty officer. I expected him to wave me through with a laugh. Instead I was treated to an intimate view of his soiled palm. 'Surely,' I joked, 'you are supposed to prevent people from *entering*?'

'I am sorry, sir. I must ask you where you think you're going.'

'I *think* I'm going for a stroll. Do you know, Klaus, I've not yet set foot on Felsengrundian grass.'

Klaus was humourless, as though the coldness of his helmet had seeped into his face. 'I have express orders, sir.'

'Orders?'

'You must turn back. I am not allowed to let you leave.'

At first I feared that I had caused the sickly Duke some displeasure. Had harsh words been exchanged in private about me, the fuggin midger? Still no communication from the Marquis, who according to rumours seemed never to leave his father's side. What sign of enmity was there in this filial devotion? I began – for the last time in many years – to doubt that my luck would hold.

A fortnight after my encounter with officious Klaus, I was summoned in haste to the Duke's Apartments. It was Josiah Koch himself, the ruined beauty of Albrecht XII's prime, who stood at my door and wept my instructions.

'Has it— ?' I asked, my heart stumbling. 'Should I dress up?'

'For God's sake, just come.'

I followed him down to the servants' quarters, where pantry boys and maids snatched up their excited whispers and stood to attention. Weeping still and muttering to himself, Josiah Koch ignored them. Instead of taking the long way round to the Great Hall, we cut through the Revenues Office to access the courtyard.

Ostentatious grief was spreading throughout the castle. Servants bowed in condolence as we passed and then resumed their chatter. Handkerchiefs, kept spotless for the occasion, were dabbed at dry eyes. From the lobby of the

Great Hall we entered straight into the Duke's Apartments. As in the courts of greater families, at Felsengrunde one made a gradual approach to the seat of power, advancing by degree of favour from room to room. The last time I had found myself in a setting of such political loading, I was being pursued by palace guards. Now only glances nipped at my heels.

In the First Apartment, where no natural light penetrated, the castle servants huddled together according to hierarchy, with masons, carpenters and chamber servants nearest the door to the Second Apartment and dish-scrubbers, stable boys and scullery maids consigned to the farthest wall. Guardsmen clapped their hands to their swords as we entered the Second Apartment. Here a blazing fire did the work of the excluded sun and warmed the rumps of the higher servants: those who worked in the Revenues Office, huntsmen still in riding boots with greyhounds at their thighs, cooks from the Banqueting Hall stroking flour from their chests. I glimpsed for the first time the crescent moustache of the Sheriff, a sanguinary dandy, propped beside the hearth in conference with his three-man brute squad. Everyone assumed a bashful countenance when Josiah Koch appeared. His true grief reprimanded their shadow of emotion. Some enterprising gentlewoman tried her hand at a wail but stifled it promptly. I felt all eyes disdaining me and was glad to exchange this crowd for the Ritterstube, the official audience chamber.

'Koch, what *is* going on?'

'Why can we not be admitted?'

'We've been languishing here for two hours!'

The nobility did not content itself with silent reproaches. Howls of protest accompanied the realisation that I – a scoundrel according to Count Winkelbach – was being ushered into the ducal absence before them. Martin

Grünenfelder stamped his long foot like an exasperated child. The Treasurer tugged at the shock of his mane, receipts and bills tumbling from his pockets. Even the Lord Chamberlain had to await his summons, dagger points of loathing in his eyes.

In the deserted Private Chamber, Josiah Koch waved aside the last guardsmen. The door of the Duke's Bedchamber was opened by his beauteous page, whose face I met innocent of tears.

It was dark within. My eyes adapted to make out a four-poster bed, turned catafalque by the stark and cavernous-nostrilled corpse upon it. Albrecht was praying at the bed-side, his hands clasped above the blanket.

'Thomas Grilli,' Josiah Koch whispered, as though to speak loudly might trouble the corpse.

'Leave us.'

I heard Josiah Koch and the page withdraw – and saw in the shrinking light the monstrous decoration on the dead Duke's walls.

'He is gone,' said Albrecht.

'My condolences, your Grace.'

Albrecht staggered on all fours, like Nebuchadnezzar put to grass, and threw himself at my chest. I was embraced so tightly that my breath was trapped; I hardly dared move, my arms hanging limply at my sides. Surely it was my task to comfort the boy whose shoulders shook so violently against mine? Then I understood that he quaked not with sorrow but laughter. It was a muted, hiccuping sound, squeezed from ugly spasms. I leaned back, as lovers do to contemplate the faces they are kissing, and watched the Duke's saliva-webbed lips part in jubilation.

11

A Book of Virtues

Before the entombment, townswomen hired for the occasion had wailed and beaten their breasts until tears, tricked by feigned emotion, had started from their eyes. In the gelid gloom of the chapel, however, better-fed countenances were kept from melting by the cool laws of ceremony. Albrecht himself seemed impervious to his sorrow; several times during the liturgy I watched him stretch out his legs to admire the polished ghost of his reflection in his bootcaps.

They laid the Duke to moulder in the family vault, compounding him with the clay of so many former Albrechts. (When the Last Trumpet sounded, who would not mistake his grandfather's femur for his own?) The nobility bowed to the gaping vault, whose cloying breath would soon be stopped by a granite seal. Below their ruffs of goose-feather white, the Winkelbachs and Grünenfelder, Wilhelm Struder and the weeping Josiah Koch wore crimson shoulder capes and mantles of black velvet. Each man was invested with a chain whose pendant resembled a pair of shears: emblem of the sacred Order of St Bartholomew, which the lamented corpse had founded in imitation of France's Ordre du Saint-Ésprit. Thus accoutred, the noblemen seemed insensible of their absurdity. They paced through the ceremony with sombre faces, looking like actors in garments which, being seldom worn, retained a gloss of theatrical newness.

I followed the mourners from the antechapel back to the nave, where Albrecht was to put on caparisons of power. He lifted his arms, like a child waiting for his nurse to clothe him, and Moritz von Winkelbach hoisted the late

Duke's mantle over his head. It sat most ungainly, like the pelt of a great beast, on Albrecht's shoulders.

Now the chaplain appeared, flanked by his pageboys; he salvaged his hand from the sleeve of his surplice and made the sign of the Cross. 'I hereby name you—'

'*Stop.*'

Pious fingers withered on the chaplain's hand. 'Stop, my lord?'

'I will not adopt my ancestral name. Albrecht the Thirteenth is ill omened.'

'But,' said the chaplain, 'your Grace was christened Albrecht.'

'My grandfather Wilhelm changed his name, did he not, to claim the dukedom? So I can do likewise.'

'And . . . so what would your Grace be called?'

'In tribute to our glorious Emperor – to whom each of us owes his debt of duty – my name will be Albrecht Rudolphus.'

By God! My stories had fermented in the young man's imagination: he was drunk on them. He raised imperiously his misshapen nose, defying the Order's disapproval. But there was too much ancestral mould in the chapel for dissent to catch fire. Obediently the chaplain, with all the Order of St Bartholomew, bowed and hailed Albrecht Rudolphus, 13th Duke of Felsengrunde, Defender of Spitzendorf, Prince of the Holy Roman Empire, Scourge of the Infidel and Several Other Things Beside, which in my stupor of self-congratulation I omitted to hear. There was profound unease in noble ranks about this innovation; yet silently I congratulated my patron for attempting to wrest his creation from others. He had an actor's sense of timing in his gestures which would not stand him in good stead – displaying it later in the Banqueting Hall at the feast for his accession.

It was Maximilian von Winkelbach who, as Master of the Table, ordained the seating of guests. Naturally, he and his fellow nobles dined within arm's reach of the transverse table where my patron sat, a lodestone to the general eye. All the worthies of the dukedom were assembled for the feast, along with a few guests from beyond the mountains: a portly, dimple-cheeked ambassador from Bavaria, two Venetian timber merchants, a one-man delegation from the nearest Swiss canton and a bishop from I know not where. So many people – a number of them barely known to the Duke – sat closer to him than I. My sense of grievance was so enthralling that I failed to notice the guest dining on my right.

'Not so high and mighty after all, are we?' Theodor Altmann looked down his nose at me (an easy trick) and pinched the water in his finger bowl. 'You must sit with the servants, it seems. Whose favourite are you? The chamber-maid's?'

The Revenues clerk on my left scrutinised his mutton chop, the better to train his ears on our exchange; for such it became, my injurious rival provoking me greatly. 'I have been in Felsengrunde three months, Herr Altmann. It has taken you thirty years to achieve the same eminence.'

'Not true, not *true*. I once sat higher—'

'Was it your own cushion?'

'Nearer to the Duke, I mean. I tutored his son.'

'It is a shame they have no musicians playing.' I turned to the clerk. 'I have a shrill blast in my ear which sweet airs might dispel.'

'We have no music in Felsengrunde,' said the clerk. 'Save the singing of coins.'

Several diners laughed at that; gristle and tattered bone were jabbed in my direction. Theodor Altmann tried, without success, to suck up a thread of meat juice. In appearing to be the old fool's rival, I was tarnished with the same contempt. Eyeing me coldly, my fellow diners belched 'dwarf', they muttered 'midget' and splayed their greasy lips.

It was then that our new Duke sprang his surprise. Could he possibly have overheard those jibes, at such a distance, through the hubbub? Or did some invisible spy relay to his table the inanities of his subjects? It seemed that way, I tell you, for he struck the board with the force of one personally slighted.

'Friends, noble lords and ladies, Felsengrundians. I stand before you in grief and gratitude, your new Duke.'

No table-thumping or chiming of struck glass greeted this pronouncement.

'I have always known my duty. As you, my noble friends, value and observe yours. It is my belief that other men – men from humbler backgrounds than ourselves – may also learn the dignity of service. So there is one among you who does not sit where he ought.'

Heads turned. Though no man within my vision dared move his lips, yet the air filled with whispering.

'This gentleman,' continued the Duke, 'belongs in more exalted company. Though all of you . . .' (he looked vaguely along the ladies' chests) '. . . are well loved by Albrecht Rudolphus.' The Duke gestured to a non-existent gap between the Treasurer and the High Chamberlain, three yards from his table. 'Arise, Tommaso Grilli, and assume your rightful place.'

Before that sullen assembly, I flung my left leg from the bench, hopped to liberate its trapped brother, then, taking with me a glimpse of Theodor Altmann's white knuckles, his bowed and furious head, began a walk of a dozen yards which seemed a mile long. Thank Heaven (I thought this once) for my deformity. None of the diners on my table dared look over their shoulder to scowl at me, while the ladies on the opposite side of the hall could not see past their hunched husbands. The Treasurer, Wilhelm Struder, and Martin Grünenfelder, our High Chamberlain, gathered up their venerable hams at my approach. Bowing left and right, simpering to the Duke and pressing a hand to my breast like a Mahometan, I assumed my place among the nobility of Felsengrunde. Once my reluctant second foot had joined its pair beneath the table, Albrecht Rudolphus led the assembly in applause. I glimpsed the gaping Venetian merchants, curious no doubt to hear my Italian name. I grinned some more, my head swimming, until the applause petered out and the Duke returned to his seat. Conversation resumed among the lower orders but my neighbours refused to speak. There would be years, I told myself, to atone for this moment. Any enmity that my promotion inspired would fade to familiarity and, at worst, its proverbial twin, contempt. A plate and goblet were placed before me, into which I deferentially nodded. Both were made of silver.

It became customary for me to visit the new Duke in his Private Chamber, where I would attempt to regale him with descriptions of the Emperor Rudolf's art collections. My flair for invention was matched by the Duke's appetite for such stories. I omitted accounts of Rudolf's weaknesses: the poor finances of Court and Realm, the neglect of public duties. My patron sought a role model and turned away his Treasurer, Wilhelm Struder (whom I crossed in the Ritterstube with thick ledgers in his arms, blotted with ink and worries), to receive his Tuscan fibber. 'Again,' said Albrecht Rudolphus, lolling on cushions and pushing the balls of his thumbs into his eyes. 'Tell me more.'

'My lord, there is so much. The Emperor is both merciful and wise. He has exquisite taste and will go to enormous lengths to enhance his collections. I remember when he bought Dürer's *The Feast of the Rose Garlands*, how four men were paid to carry the painting, carefully encased and slung between poles, for hundreds of miles across mountains, that it might not suffer the slightest knock. His Majesty will permit no one to look at his works – unless a man has earned his special favour. I personally was invited several times to admire his objects of art – the prints and drawings and paintings. There were natural wonders too, among the artificial.'

'Show me, Tommaso.'

There existed in the Duke's Library a small but choice selection of books bought long ago by Albrecht IX. These included Sebastian Münster's *Cosmographia*, which I brought to my patron's attention, harpooning with my finger the monsters that bristled in its vellum seas. I described the specimens that travellers had sold to our delighted Emperor. From a literary source which I failed to acknowledge, I described how a sea bishop, having been landed by Baltic fishermen, had begged leave of the King of Poland to be returned to its salty parish. Rudolf had acquired a similar creature, I believed, though alas it had been dead on arrival. In the margins of the *Cosmographia* I drew the Emperor's mandrakes, which the earth had shaped in the likeness of men; I forged the mysterious signature which had apparently been left in a slab of granite by Nature's hand. For hours I embroidered these legends, until I became, by my own account, a close familiar to the Duke's namesake.

'I shall write to the Emperor,' said Albrecht Rudolphus, 'as one of his Electors and express my gratitude that I should have acquired your talents.'

'By all means do, your Grace. His secretary in artistic matters is Jaroslav Meyrink. You should address your letter to him.'

My unofficial role as forger to the Duke was not yet

determined; officially, Albrecht Rudolphus appointed me Librarian of the Hofbibliotek (it took me one afternoon to catalogue its contents) and purveyor of his mental pabulum. Beyond free board, I did not yet receive a salary. In hope of cementing my position – and finding more comfortable lodgings – I resumed contacts with agents of my acquaintance, through whose intercession I might extend the Duke's collection of fine prints. So far, in all the expanse of the castle, I had found only one picture.

'*Two Followers of Cadmus Devoured by a Dragon.*' Albrecht Rudolphus blinked as he read from the frame. 'What do you make of it, Thomas?'

I replied that I admired the cruel picture for adhering to Arcimboldo's unwritten Law of Detail; a reference which I was bound to explain. So many mythical beasts, I argued, want a convincing shape, seeming to have been assembled by the artist from the slops inside a knacker's pail. Our lazy expectations are met by dragons with lizard beaks and scaly hides; they have not the fierce particularity of Nature. Yet in this print so cherished by the late Duke, the dragon's face disturbed us by its oddity, having about it something of a lamb; while the teeth that sank into its victim's cheek were like the teeth of a famished child. I marvelled, scowling, at the dismembered victims – at the torn head with its windpipe exposed – at those cords of flesh trailing and the agony printed on a lifeless visage. What precision of horrid detail! See how the flesh of the second torso ravels up beneath the gripping talons; how the wretch's untrapped leg juts out on the impulse of agony. Albrecht Rudolphus giggled.

'I was frightened of my father's chamber when I was a child.'

'On account of this image, your Grace?'

'The dragon has all the malice of Hell in its jaws.'

'It is Nature indifferent to Man.'

'I think Nature despises him.'

'Do you intend to keep it here, your Grace, watching over your sleep?'

'I say we move it to the Ritterstube. Let us share our treasures with our loving servants.'

As soon as the cheerless image had been transferred, it was necessary to find a replacement for it. I sat for two days composing letters to Jaroslav Meyrink in Prague and Georg Spengler in Dresden, acquainting them with my remarkable good fortune and requesting their services. These letters sat on my desk, pressed beneath a polished stone, until spring thawed out the mountain passes.

Josiah Koch, the dead Duke's favourite, was sent into retirement in Felsengrunde town. His roles as Cupbearer and Doorkeeper were awarded to the pretty page; and it was this boy (whom gossips called the Cupbearing Dowager on account of his womanliness) who would come to my door with summons to visit the Duke. I noted the shadow of fluff at the corners of his lips and wondered how long his special favour would last.

Many times on my way through the Great Hall, I passed the painter Theodor Altmann. Alone as ever, shunned by his fellow aspirants to favour, he muttered into his beard. 'Old men cannot control their rages,' Albrecht Rudolphus said when I told him of Altmann's distraction. 'You should hear him stamping his foot in the Ritterstube and demanding an audience.' (Careful not to deride a colleague, your narrator amiably smiled.) 'He poisons the general ear against you, Tommaso.'

'Against *me*?'

'Do you know what he calls you?'

'I fear your Grace is about to inform me.'

'The Upstart Dwarf.' (I failed to descant on my patron's laughter.) 'Do you not think that comical, coming from such an arse-licker? All the same, sooner or later he may try to ingratiate himself with you. He mumbles of commissions, and would like to paint a fresco in the chapel if only I would let him. But he lacks paints and brushes. So he may come to you for his necessities.'

In the event, Theodor Altmann did visit my workshop. He stood near the door, his fingers grubbing in his collar and his face contorted by the effort to smile. His chest in turmoil wheezed and bubbled. 'Are these your drawings, Herr Grilli?'

'They are, Herr Altmann.'

'This medallion portrait of the Lord Chamberlain is most faithful.'

'It is the Duke.'

'Uh – quite so. An excellent likeness. And these are your lovely paints . . .' I suppressed a shudder of sympathy as he warmed his hands above the precious colours. 'Is this mummy? Where did you get the pig gut?'

'From a pig, Herr Altmann.' I perched on my stool and watched the old man muttering into my pots. I was tempted to offer him work as my assistant. After a time, chilled by my silence, he bowed and retreated from my lair without having advanced his cause one jot. I myself, you see, had no need of Theodor Altmann. I had received my patron's endorsement to create a *Book of Virtues* – a celebration, in thirty-two woodcut prints, of the young Duke's qualities.

My immediate task was to produce ink and chalk drawings that an engraver might translate to wood. I began with a depiction of the Duke's admirable father riding to hounds, whilst in the distance, beneath the castle ramparts, his beloved spouse stroked her pregnant belly. The next print showed the Duke's sainted mother (I had modelled her face on Altmann's clumsy portrait) nursing in her arms her infant son, who in turn gripped a goldfinch with pudgy fingers, in the manner of certain dandled Christs. The third picture showed Albrecht comforting his father over the death of the Duchess; the fourth recorded the father's own lamentable end. Henceforth, the privileged reader would admire my patron's manifold talents. Now he was a scholar, a king of boundless thought presiding over ancient books; now a statesman, attending with his retinue the Imperial Diet; now a huntsman impaling a stag, or an angler slinging a pike from the lake, or a swordsman trapping his opponents in the fret of their swords. When the actual Duke – inspecting his guardsmen with your obsequious narrator at his hip – suggested that a print containing the bust portraits of the entire Order of St Bartholomew be included in the publication, I dared express the hope that, given my labours, a place might be found in the picture for my *own* likeness.

'Certainly not,' said Albrecht Rudolphus; and there the matter rested.

Armed with the Duke's authority, I secured the obedience of my courtly superiors and sat in their offices attempting to draw them. Maximilian von Winkelbach, who seemed to be engaged in a contest with his older brother to outhate me, insisted that I sketch him in the Sheriff's chambers. Though Master of the Table and Captain of the Footguard, Maximilian took no duty more seriously than assisting with his fists in the upkeep of the law. He lunged and grunted while I sketched, and the Sheriff's brutes buzzed about my head, chuckling at my unsteady hand. Maximilian looked up, a drop of sweat plummeting from his forelock.

'Are you including the prisoner in your drawing?'

'No, my lord.'

Maximilian shook his hand at the wrist and wiped his

239

knuckles on the seated gentleman's sleeve. 'Nor should you wish to commemorate a villain. I just want you,' he said, 'to keep in mind what you have seen today.'

After this encounter with his brother, my effort to smooth out Moritz von Winkelbach's brow was almost a pleasure. Clearly the Count despised the venture ('A book of praise, indeed. What need has my lord of paper virtue, when the observation of custom would suffice?'), yet he was careful to master his tongue lest I relay its contumely to the Duke.

My other subjects gave me less trouble than the brothers. Martin Grünenfelder, seated with documents at his desk, pretended not to notice me, while his assistant grinned like a dullard at the scratching soliloquy of my pen. In the Revenues Office, I captured Wilhelm Struder's baffled likeness and requisitioned one of his clerks. This young man – I forget his name – was set to work transcribing the dull Latin prose of Hans Vögel's *Illustrious History of the Duchy of Felsengrunde*. I cared not that he was a slow writer, who took an artist's deliberation in fulfilling every curlicued letter (as though his copy were for any other purpose than to guide a printer's fingers), for I would require at least the year to complete my print designs and expected not to travel to Frankfurt with them until the following spring. As days passed, the Treasurer made ever more irate requests – first in person to myself, then in writing to the Duke – for the return of the clerk to his office; yet Albrecht Rudolphus backed my insistence that the boy's services were required for a little while longer.

Thus passed my first year in Felsengrunde. I had free rein of the town and country. Preceded by rumour, I was glad to accept the discounted hospitality of innkeepers and plucked, as one might chance berries, the respectful bows of castle employees. Meanwhile my cultivation of contacts abroad began to bear fruit. Our irregular postilion delivered letters and prints from my old friend Georg Spengler in Dresden. He wrote congratulating me on my success and describing the blessings of family life (it seems his wife was prodigiously fertile) for the enjoyment of which he held himself to be the happiest man alive. Upon this first delivery of prints, I was able to present the Duke with the *Stoning of St Stephen* after Rosso Fiorentino and the *Martyrdom of St Lawrence* by Cort after Titian. Albrecht Rudolphus enjoyed the billowing smoke of the martyr's fire, which filled the grey heavens like heavy drapes. He seemed amused by the two cherubs floating over Titian's scene, their faces illumined not by celestial light but by the flames below, wearing the unshakeable curiosity of dirty-fingered and sublunary boys.

A single letter came from Prague, and that five months after its composition, in which Jaroslav Meyrink wrote obliquely of the Emperor's troubled mind. The letter hinted at dark intrigues involving Rudolf's ambitious brother – all disquieting news which I kept from the Duke, burning Meyrink's letter as soon as I had sucked out its nutrients.

To distract myself from my efforts on the *Book of Virtues*, it became my habit to go for long walks in the town of Felsengrunde, or else to seek out the green shade of beeches and delicate larch (whose needles in early spring look like tight green heads of paintbrushes) along the shore of the Obersee. Many times I endeavoured to lose myself in the contemplation of Nature. Twittering birds hid from my sight in the overhanging canopy; squirrels curled behind tree trunks and plopping fish sank into the murky depths, frightened by my shadow. Always I felt a nagging need to return to my workshop, or regale my patron with tales of the Emperor. My eyes grew dull to Nature's displays: they brightened only for human creations.

*   *   *

It was my Revenues Office clerk who brought me the letter – one copy out of several, it transpired, each written in laborious longhand, for the correspondent had a great deal of time to occupy. My good spy was thanked for his pains with a small purse and sworn to his customary secrecy.

'That is his signature,' I assured the Duke a few hours later, 'and that his seal. The letter cannot be a forgery.'

Surreptitious Grilli had slipped the offending missive beneath the Duke's official papers, so that it might have been placed there quite accidentally by a clerk of the Treasury. The lords and ladies of Felsengrunde had all received the same letter: so its author assured the recipients, keen that none should conceal his opinion for want of communal support.

' "His Grace the Duke's mind is softened by fancies," ' read Albrecht Rudolphus, angrily gripping the head of his throne. ' "You know as I do the source of this infection. Grilli the dwarf has made our lord contemptuous of the hunt; it is he, with his Italian vices, who weakens the Duke's appetite for government . . ." By *God*, I shall have him flayed alive!'

'Perhaps,' I volunteered, 'it is meant in jest?'

'He calls you a disease to be purged from the state. And so by imputation *I* am corrupted.'

'I am confident, your Grace, that your loyal courtiers will not hesitate to bring this letter to your attention . . .'

'Let us hope so.'

'. . . once they have read the matter.'

The Duke gasped and struck the letter in his exasperation. 'I am sorry that you must hear this old goat's slanders.'

'Alas, I fear Herr Altmann is no longer in his right mind.'

'Let him be *insensible*, if he shall escape flogging.'

Poor Theodor. Like the proverbial old dog, he had shown himself incapable of learning new tricks. In his letter he stated explicitly what others in the castle must privately have thought; in so doing he obliged men who might have sympathised with him to denounce him publicly. I was, therefore, confident when I concealed myself – with my patron's knowledge – behind an arras in the Private Chamber. The pretty page (whose voice now croaked and squeaked) was sent to summon the painter from his room beside the stables. I could hear the old man's excited chatter as he approached, anticipating a commission perhaps after so many barren years.

'Banishment?' the old fool piped moments later. 'On what grounds, your Grace?'

'From *my* grounds.'

'But I was born here,' Theodor Altmann sobbed. Had he not tutored the Duke in his boyhood? And was there to be no mercy for an aged retainer? 'Please, my lord, I beg you, I *beg* you . . .'

Grovelling penitence embarrassed a little mercy into the Duke. 'Banished from the castle, then,' he said.

'I may stay in the town?'

'No, no. I banish you from the town also.'

'But your Grace, how can I live elsewhere? Without any patronage?'

'Do not cast *me* as a villain, sir. These seditious letters that undermine my authority are in your hand. You have ousted *yourself* – I will no more weep for you than Michael did for Adam.'

Thus the matter was sealed. Albrecht Rudolphus instructed his guards to drag Theodor Altmann, my defeated rival, out of the Private Chamber. He had just three days to be gone.

I had wanted Klaus but it was, instead, with his youngest colleague that I travelled to Frankfurt in the spring of 1606. The soldier, whose name was Jörgen, was not the sharpest witted of fellows, yet he guarded my print designs as though they were etched in gold and bore uncomplainingly my tyrannical moods (I was rapidly, reader, casting aside my humble carapace). I shall not encumber this narrative with an account of our journey, which took us, alas, far from Nuremberg and the soft remembered charms of Anna and Gretel. There was a faint odour of juniper shrubs as we journeyed through the Swabian Alb, whose densely wooded slopes stirred Jörgen to remembrances of home.

Arriving finally in Frankfurt I met my contact, Lucas Detmold, at his printer's shop on a corner of Römerberg. For the next four months I would oversee the cutting of wood blocks for my *Book of Virtues*. I was so overcome by the ubiquity of publishers in that beauteous city that I surprised myself by spending most of the Duke's money on those items for which it had been intended. I bought the *Last Judgement* by Bonasone after Michelangelo, Annibale Caracci's *Susana and the Elders* and my favourite print, Cornelis Cort's *The Practice of the Visual Arts* after Stradanus. I informed Jörgen that we would need a third mule to carry the books that I bought: chronicles, biographies of the saints, two cookery books, a wonderful herbal by Fuschius, and novels by Reineke Fuchs to complement Albrecht's copy of *Tristán*, which my patron in his enthusiasm for familiar stories had clawed to tatters.

Word of a spendthrift midget spread rapidly through the city's fraternity of printers and booksellers. It reached the handsome ear of a certain Ludolf Bresdin, who burst through the doors of Detmold's shop one morning and, with his bellowed greeting, drove a chisel into its manipulator's flesh. Once I had assured myself that no damage had been done to my woodcut (and the *formschneider* had patched up his bleeding thumb), I mounted a stool to embrace my former colleague.

'My word, you *have* filled out,' I told Bresdin, 'and your beard is most becoming.'

'You're no starveling yourself, Thomas.'

The block-cutters hissed across their fingers for us to be silent. So Tommaso Grilli, the Tuscan patron and Ludolf Bresdin, the printer's assistant, walked out in sunshine and ambled towards the Main. I did not reprimand my old friend for having abandoned me in Nuremberg, since Destiny had made his betrayal its benevolent instrument; instead I congratulated him on his marriage to Gunda Nessler. (Brought face to navel with his daughter's swelling womb, Herr Nessler the foreman had moodily consented to a wedding.) 'Now I smell of baby puke,' said Bresdin. 'And I'm constantly tired. But I wouldn't change my life for anything.'

Whatever ambitions my friend used to nurture had been put to bed by domestic life. Now Gunda Bresdin's husband worked cheerfully as a nameless craftsman, untroubled by longings for fame, finding sufficiency in fatherhood. 'I lack your determination,' he said, 'and your desire to please.' He pitied me, I think, for my ambition. I reciprocated, lewdly patronising my poor, clambered-upon Ludolf.

Despite these divergences in our stories, we agreed to resume our former alliance. Bresdin anticipated ever more hungry mouths to feed, while I needed a printer of assurable discretion. Ludolf Bresdin pledged to cut and print whatever designs – be they originals or pastiches – I might chance to send him. Our undertaking would be in no sense dishonest, I hastened to assure him, since my patron knew perfectly well what he was paying for.

We departed from Frankfurt in late summer, with Jörgen devoting much of the journey to whipping the flanks of our mules, who resented the demands made upon them and offered us the grandmotherly obstinacy typical of their kind. The first beast carried books by diverse authors; the second bore prints and ten fresh copies of Vögel's *History of Felsengrunde*. The last mule had sole responsibility of my published masterpiece, the twenty copies of the *Book of Virtues*. Properly motivated by Jörgen's birch (I had to intervene only once when, in a fit of inventiveness, he attempted to violate the creatures with his goad), our mules made tolerable progress. The silence of my human companion allowed me to formulate my next project, drawing fanciful plans in my imagination until we entered Felsengrunde – this time without escort or trumpet's clarion – to be joyfully reunited with our beloved Duke.

By chance we arrived on the morning of my patron's birthday. He received my books with such delight – impressing copies upon his lords, and ordering me to clear a shelf in the Hofbibliotek for his own – that the celebrations to which he was treating his people seemed almost to be in my honour.

Thus, within hours of my return, I found myself seated on a dais above the commonage in the castle grounds, flapped about the head by Felsengrunde's banner and steeling myself to propose my great undertaking.

Beside the chapel a bonfire cracked its knuckles. I could feel the heat of the flames on my face – an invisible web pulled tight across the skin. A substantial crowd had assembled to witness the afternoon's entertainment. Old women sold apples from baskets suspended at their waists; young men pushed and shoved, puffing out their chests like courting pigeons to the flattered derision of chaperoned daughters. I watched a group of tumblers present their heels to the sky, as though they had newly arrived from the Antipodes. A small band of urchins stood on the edge of the castle well, clutching the winch and fixing their eyes on the smouldering pyre.

'They love me today,' the Duke said, reaping the crowd's acclamation with a lazy hand.

'What is the entertainment, your Grace?'

Perhaps my patron did not hear me. Tabors and fifes

struck up a raucous music – so suddenly that I jumped in my seat – and the crowd cheered to see the Sheriff, with six of his brutes, mount the rickety scaffold. I saw the men shimmer, like insubstantial phantoms, in the haze of the flames. '*Maleficium!*' the Sheriff cried, and the people heartily responded: '*Hexenbrenner! Hexenbrenner!*'

I turned, grimacing, to the Duke. 'Witchcraft, my lord?'

'Shush!'

Now the Sheriff opened a basket, around which his assistants gathered. To gasps of admiration, they plunged their arms up to their elbows into the basket; then, straightening, they brandished what they had captured. Thirteen black cats twisted, shadow-boxing, on their pinched scruffs. In vain they kicked out their hind legs and opened their pink mouths.

'In Frankfurt, your Grace, I did some thinking.'

'Did you indeed?'

'Er, yes.' I noticed that my left knee was quaking and pressed my heel into the floor to stop it. 'Consider the acquisitions of your fellow principalities. We saw the Fuggerhäuser in Augsburg, did we not, and its cabinet of arts? Duke Philip of Pomerania has commissioned something similar – a world of wonders in a single cupboard.'

'Do you propose to create one for me?'

'My ambitions are on a somewhat grander scale.'

Over on the scaffold – egged on by the baying crowd – the Sheriff and his assistants dropped the cats on to an iron griddle. The cats yowled and bristled in mortal fear. Their feet, I suspect, had been mutilated to prevent them escaping. Besides, like people clinging to a raft in perilous rapids, they preferred the dread of the griddle to the flames and faces below.

'Once when I was a boy, we burned forty cats in one day.' Albrecht Rudolphus, as he leaned towards me, failed to notice my sickly pallor. 'For a mere dozen,' he said, 'one might as well not bother.'

But the people of Felsengrunde had no objection to the waste of kindling and their Duke was acting to please them. At his command, stokers plied their bellows to rouse the fire. When the executioners had dropped the last animal on to the suspended griddle, the Sheriff invited a scullery maid on to the scaffold. The brutes groped beneath the girl's armpits to hoist her – to general applause – while the master of ceremonies made great comedy of stroking his moustache.

'I see no reason why your dream of emulating your great namesake might not – to all appearances – be realised.'

The Duke's attention was torn between the merry spectacle of the burning and his grave, frowning dwarf. 'What do you mean?'

'Why should emperors alone have great collections?'

'Money, Tommaso, money. Felsengrunde could not support such ambition. Look at this measly bonfire.'

'In so far as means allow, your Grace, I continue to buy prints and books and even paintings. But there are *other* ways of acquiring works by dead Masters.'

Albrecht Rudolphus would not turn his face from the spectacle; but his ear was devoted to your narrator.

'We have the beginnings of a library,' I said urgently. 'I propose to extend it, to fill it with wonders and, er, automata . . .'

'Ought *what*?'

'And you shall have drawings and paintings by great artists – works of which the world knows nothing, rediscovered by our efforts. Dürer, my lord, and Cranach and Baldung will live again, creating new works, as it were, from the grave.'

My patron licked his boiled-plum lips. 'And the world,' he said, 'need not know the *provenance* of these masterpieces?'

'You understand me perfectly, your Grace.'

Exposed on the scaffold, the scullery maid, being promoted for the only time in her life to public attention, could not resist the exhortation of the crowd. With timid smiles, she tugged a priapic lever and set a machinery in motion. Cog wheels spun, tooth locked on tooth, and jerkingly the griddle, with the cats upon it, descended.

'I could transform this castle into a palace,' I said. 'I would have these old stones dragged into our present age, until your fame extends beyond these mountains.'

How the crowd whooped, how the nobility shrieked with laughter, to watch the cats burn! It was hard to hear their agony for all the human noise. Even Moritz von Winkelbach seemed entertained, opening and closing his mouth, like a man blowing smoke rings, to emit low hiccoughs of merriment.

'I would need,' I yelled, 'to ship talent into Felsengrunde.'

'What?'

'Talent! I need talent!'

Suspended inches above the flames, the cats became leaping torches. Townspeople profited from a holiday's licence to clutch one another in lustful agitation. The moustached showman waggled his tongue in the scullery maid's ear and servants pushed themselves in laughter until they retched and gripped their sides. Even when the last cat had stopped twitching – and thirteen corpses boiled on the griddle – the noise continued. I glanced across my shoulder at the Duke. He was stifling a yawn behind his white gloves.

'Forgive me,' he said. 'I do not gape at your proposal. On the contrary, it agrees with some ideas of my own.'

The wind on its invisible salver presented us with a stench of burning. Portly ladies gasped into their pomanders and grimaced until their painted faces cracked. From behind the petals of a scarlet handkerchief, Albrecht Rudolphus gave his approval.

'I would ask you to draw up detailed plans,' he said. 'Then, if I like what you have to show me – as I am pleased with my *Book of Virtues* – I shall provide you with all the moneys you require.'

12

The Library of Arts

And so we stand poised to enter the happiest – at least the most gratifying, that is, the most lucrative – years of my life. These veins ought to pulse with invigorated blood, the chambered muscle in this grey trunk should beat with a little of its former vigour, as I return to the scenes of my provincial triumph. Yet my body aches with weariness. Of ten years in power I can recover only episodes, instances, to help preserve the memory of my creation . . .

Proud of their stink, of their bare arms tanned to leather and their language thick as horse piss, the stable boys were unaccustomed to visits from the Duke and adopted a silent industry more resentful than courteous when I embarked on my prepared speech.

'Imagine this transformed, your Grace, into a palace of Art. Hang your banners, your candelabra of gleaming bronze, from these cobwebbed rafters. Today they are smoked as black as Dis. Send twenty painters up their ladders and behold! a blue heaven fretted with golden stars.' (I was aware of the stable boys watching me through their horses' legs.) 'Take this stall, my lord. Conceive in its place an alcove draped with dark velvet, where a cup fashioned from rhinoceros horn – or mother-of-pearl, or purple hydra of Indies coral – stands. Now fling open these doors! Here, in this swirling dervish of straw . . .' (The Duke rested his ankle on his knee and grimaced at the sole of his boot.) 'Rotten straw, your Grace. It is the general air that smells.' (Scarcely reassured, the Duke tried to clean himself.) 'Here, you – stable boy. Fetch that brush. I don't *care* if it's for the Lord Chamberlain's horse.' (A surly youth, flushing vermilion under the Duke's elbow, scrubbed the underside of his boot.) 'Now, uh . . . fling open these doors! Picture, in this whirling straw, the dresses of visiting ladies. Make the tinkling of these stirrups their laughter, turn the horses' tails into the flay and splatter . . . the splay and flutter of dainty fans . . .'

'I should not admit women,' said the Duke. 'Not in my library.'

'Quite right, my lord. There are some things to which they are not suited.' The invisible barbs of the straw were pricking at my nose. My face bristled as if I had just tugged a hair from a nostril. 'Look at these gawking stable boys,' I wheezed. 'Dress them in livery – of the design that I showed you – and see what a retinue of craftsmen waits on your pleasure.'

'It is too dark,' regretted the Duke.

'Dark? Why, do they not make mirrors in Venice as clear as God's conscience? These walls are blind, but say the word and they will see. It would be child's play for carpenters to build apertures in the rafters.'

Albrecht Rudolphus lifted his feet from the straw like a man wading in surf. He reasoned with an angel on his shoulder; he craned his neck to consider the rafters, and peered into recesses of the stables as though soliciting their opinion. I sensed the encroachment of stable boys, closing in like little fishes on the receding tail of a pike, to watch the pale Duke cogitate. Or were their eyes trained on *me* – on this escapee from fairy tale, gaudy in ostrich feathers and funnel boots, the *Gnom* who threatened their livelihoods? Horses burred and farted; their hoofs dragged on the straw. Duke Albrecht Rudolphus admired his Lord Chamberlain's horse – the sheen of its hazel flanks, the enormity of the head with its black liquid spheres. Then he turned to face me, his unlovely face calm and resolute.

'My Treasurer Struder is worried about the cost. I want you to reassure him.'

The architect had other concerns. A ruddy, practical-minded fellow, with a bearing as strong and tightly fitted as a master builder's joist, he listened politely, his arms crossed and his woolly head bowed, to my vision of an eye-deceiving palace. A Felsengrundian by birth, though resident with his skills in Augsburg, he was better used to constructing minor palazzos from scratch than transfiguring stables into labyrinths. 'Like in dreams, you say?'

'Yes. Do you never dream of such places?'

'For getting lost in?'

'To wander from one dark room to another, unsure of your whereabouts. A palace like an enchanted forest, where everything seems possible.'

'You wish me to design a place where men can lose their way?'

'The *Duke* will know his way. I need trapdoors and secret panels for him to slip through. I want him to seem a magician to his visitors. I want dark caves and moonlit groves, and alcoves such as you might find in a garden of yew . . .'

'Herr Grilli, the space is not *that* big.'

'Why, then – we broaden it with mirrors. We eke it out with corridors. We build little staircases and each room stands on a different level from its neighbours.'

'But you are asking me to break all the rules of decorum.'

'If you wouldn't mind.'

The architect pursed his lips as though chewing a sweet. 'These drawings remind me of a rabbit warren,' he said.

'Why, thank you.'

'I would need to bring in thirty of my most capable men.'

'I've already ousted servants to make room for them.'

'And I expect assurances from the Duke that he approves of my designs . . .'

'Naturally.'

'. . . as well as regular payments, in cash, to my quarters, to compensate for any custom I may lose by my absence from Augsburg.'

'Will florins do?'

The architect nodded, his expression solemn with the contemplation of technical quandaries. 'I can make a house of wonderment for you. But the structure alone is my business . . .'

'. . . its *contents* you can leave to me,' I said.

We shook hands above the table in my chambers, where my fanciful diagrams sucked up the pearly evening light. I had paid a spy to follow the architect since his arrival at the Castle and was able on the strength of his observations to spoil the gentleman with a bottle of his favourite alicant. He emptied six glasses before I could manage one, then spread himself on a couch and enquired into my history. I told him earnestly whatever it would please him to hear and spoke of the Emperor Rudolf's grand collection. 'Our Library of Arts,' I said, 'will pay homage to his everlasting achievement.'

The architects' men arrived in June the following year and would return to Felsengrunde twice more before their work was completed. (Some cynical members of the Court would accuse them of delay, of diluting their efforts on a project that ensured them material comfort; for the builders enjoyed most excellent hospitality, overseen by Martin Grünenfelder, who was compelled to oust even the best servants from their dormitories in the Great Hall. These unfortunates had to sleep in corridors and on stairwells, shrinking like snails from the boots of their usurpers as they rolled, heavy with drink, to their beds.) I spent many days on the work site, watching the builders as they measured and sawed and joked in the yard. I found myself envying the height from which they swung their hammers and tried to imagine how the physically complete man must feel when, aching, he takes his potent rest. More practically, I oversaw, in my official capacity, the provision of their refreshments. Perhaps I was attempting to placate a ghost? For I remembered seeing my father cut stone on the Corso di Porta Romana – how he grimaced from thirst, his skin pounded by the implacable sun. I even provided soaked towels for the workmen, as if to chase away a vision of my father blanching his brow with the dust-milky sweat on his arm.

Although I pampered the architect's men, there were harsher forms of motivation on the work site. Infuriated by the languor of our local workers, whom Maximilian von Winkelbach had rounded up from the taverns, the architect equipped himself with a foreman whose puggish features, constantly oiled with sebum and boiled in sunlight as mauve as a phallus, are lodged most unwelcomely in my memory.

The foreman's name was Kussmaul – though everybody called him 'Küsseman' on account of the pleasure he took in kissing men with his whip. Küsseman's dog, a malevolent yapper of indeterminate breed, was endowed with teeth so sharp that I imagined the foreman labouring each night in the brute's maw with a filing blade. Standing in the stables with Cerberus at his knee, Küsseman's purpose was twofold. He kept the menials working despite their inadequate pay, while to his Augsburg colleagues he served as a mascot and drinking partner. Nightly, in taverns like the Ram on Fleishstrasse, wagers were placed on his capacity – ensuring that Küsseman never had to pay for a drink. He had a powerful cure for hangovers which required neither raw eggs nor emetics but a plank of birchwood to be broken over his head. Several times I saw Küsseman stagger on this physic with bloodied splinters jutting from his brow. His colleagues would shuffle along behind him, ready to catch him should he fall. But the hardy foreman merely shook himself, like a dog after swimming, and returned unperturbed to the work site. In my childhood, as you can imagine, I would have shrunk from such company. Yet the architect had confirmed to his men what my elegant clothes suggested: that I was the father of the project, 'Court Painter', 'Undisputed Master of Arts' and 'Learned Friend to His Grace the Duke'. Never again would whole companies of men – each of whom was powerful enough to crush me like an apple – bow in unison or doff their dusty caps when I passed. Even Küsseman acknowledged me, with a nod of his parboiled head, and nudged his dog to stow its growling.

As well as the regard of Augsburg builders, I enjoyed the deference of my apprentices. I write 'apprentices', though of course I never had any intention of training those timorous boys to be artists. (They were the excess skimmed from bloated households. Being ignorant of the arts, they did not know a forgery from an original. I had nothing to fear, by way of exposure, from that quarter.) Three boys joined me in my workshop in the castle's southern tower, where they learned to perform the simpler tasks that Gian Bonconvento had taught me. They mixed paints and kept them from drying; they learned as I had done how to assemble canvases, how to colour paper and mix quicklime with skimmed milk cheese to produce casein glue. A few of the boys would attempt, on the sly, to learn the rules of perspective from my work, or else sidled into my workshop when they believed I was absent to sketch my studies and compare their talents with my own. But the majority were simply grateful to be housed and irregularly beaten, brightening at deliveries of expensive mummy from Venice, or when smoothing the grounds of my canvases with sharkskin. I taught them – alas! – nothing about how to *see*. I only pray that a few stole nourishment from my tyranny, and that one day I might hear a familiar name bandied about these Tuscan hills, uttered in the same breath as Raphael or the blessed Michelangelo.

As, with maddening slowness, the Library's interior moved towards completion, my patron refused to visit the site until at least one room was furnished. So I invited Ludolf Bresdin in Frankfurt to pay me a visit and, for excellent remuneration, to help me paint the panels in the Duke's Study. Bresdin – whose wife had just been delivered of screaming twins – hastily agreed. Our subject matter was to be the amorous conquests of Zeus. We settled down, with brushes and paints, as merry in our task as we had been all those years ago in the hunting lodge at Moritzburg or the summerhouse at Burg Weissing, to transform Zeus into an amorous quail, a bull, a swan, a shower of gold, an eagle. Around us as we worked the din of industry resounded. Every oath and gust of laughter glanced off the cross-beams and gathered in the rafters, so that Bresdin and I, being conditioned to secrecy, whispered in conversation. In the evenings I would report back to the Duke with news of our progress, finding him in the Private Chamber sunk in dreams or contemplating his prowess in the *Book of Virtues*. I cannot tell what more clearly proved my patron's illusions: his belief that my graphic eulogy was true, or his conviction that future generations would believe it.

'Future ages,' I assured him, 'will have forgotten our soldiers and statesmen. Only the patrons will be remembered.'

Early in the history of the Library of Arts, as winter tightened its grip on the mountains, news reached the Duke of his former tutor and court painter, Theodor Altmann. Kussmaul the foreman was showing me the carnivorous barbs on his whip (within hearing of its shivering beneficiaries) when Albrecht Rudolphus dashed unannounced through the courtyard. Aiming to grip my arm, he unwittingly pinched my neck. I followed him to the fountain, grinning through my pain.

'Altmann,' he said. 'They found his body near Spitzenberg.'

'Where?'

'In a ditch outside the village.'

'Dead?'

The Duke looked at me oddly. 'He had no money to pay for his lodgings. All that he could offer was drawings. It seems the innkeeper tired of gods and satyrs – Altmann never *was* skilled for likenesses.'

'How did he die?'

'Frozen, probably. The village elders couldn't tell if he was dead before the wolves set to work on him.' Albrecht Rudolphus joined his hands and huffed down the spire of his fingers. 'I did right to banish him, did I not? It was not . . . capricious?'

'A man creates his own fortune, your Grace.'

'I mean, my Lord Chamberlain and his brother endorsed the measure. They never loved him while he *lived*. But now that he's gone – oh, I hear the rumours – he will become a sort of martyr.'

And so it proved. From the lofty vantage of my workshop, I could feel the mounting resentment of the Winkelbachs and Grünenfelder, as though a swamp were sucking at my tower's foundations. The Duke sank into a guilty melancholy. I went in search of women to mask with perfume the cadaverous stink of our dreams.

Yes, I was the Duke's whoremonger. Not content with

overseeing the construction of his Library, with curating his museum and assembling his books, I was also the agent of his baser pleasures. The town of Felsengrunde was poorly stocked for the provision of carnal sport, so that I had to seek farther afield, visiting Krantor (which, despite its name, boasts neither a tower nor any cranes on its leaning chimneys) and Spitzendorf on the slopes of the Augspitzer Wald, to find a little talent. Most of the girls of suitable age were hardy and big boned, unshapely great pods for mountain seed. But even the peasant stock, in these villages of kissing cousins, produced a few beauties: flowers blooming among the weeds, whom parents, afflicted by common poverty, traded for pouches of chewable gold. To every weeping mother and jaw-clamped patriarch, an elegantly dressed if somewhat undersized Italian promised a life of dignified service for their child. What noble employment I had in store for Ursula and Lotte, for Maria and little Ilse! To ease their apprehension as our covered wagon rumbled back to town, my trembling assistants adorned the girls' breasts with mantles of fur and forced bronze rings on to their fingers.

Albrecht Rudolphus, who dared not inspect this feminine harvest in person, feasted on my descriptions of his Duchy's fruits. To avoid the scandalised breaths of courtiers, he paid for the girls to be lodged on the outskirts of town, two hundred yards from the castle's western ramparts. Thus it was possible to winch the evening's fare up the garbage chute (a conjunction that would please a moral sermoniser) and whisk her to the Duke's bedchamber without drawing unwelcome attention.

Marooned by a whispering tide of respectable townspeople, the four girls in my care grew sad and fat. They sighed away the days in sleep, or bickered over glass-jewelled trifles. I considered for a time sending an emissary to

Nuremberg in search of my old doxies. (The years that had elapsed could not have been kind to Anna or Gretel: they might have been glad to work as bawdhouse madams.) But somehow my courage failed me. It was not moral scruple, since at the time I had none. Perhaps I feared to learn what my emissary would discover concerning the fate of my old flames. Instead I trawled through Taubenstrasse in the Meierei district, where Klaus informed me the town's only practising whores might be found: sour creatures with sloping eyes and corrupted breaths who, though unsuitable for the front line, might at least keep the infantry in order behind it. With an almost sober matriarch in charge (a woman of no more years than I, under whose dirt and degradation there moved the delicate skeleton of a milking maid), I set about furnishing the courtesans' residence.

The whole procurement business was a tiring distraction from my primary concern. I needed permanent staff – a select band of inventors – to replace the carpenters and workers once these had departed, grumbling on the fuel of bad pay, back home. To this effect, I wrote to several agents in foreign cities, including my trusted friends Spengler and Meyrink, hoping with their help to lure artists, gardeners, authors of masques – whatever crafts or comedies might entertain the languid Duke.

I sat beside Albrecht Rudolphus on the morning of the first interviews, in the tapestry-draped and darkly mirrored penumbra of the Duke's Study. My patron, nostalgically renewing the disguises of his mock-student days, divested himself of his official insignia and issued orders that none of the candidates should know his identity. He did not wish sycophancy to distort their performances. Therefore he swapped his creaking throne for a chair like mine (though without my heap of cushions) and requested that I conduct the interviews while he silently watched.

Several hours passed in which our spirits gradually sank; and indeed the first day fizzled to a belly-aching end without a suitable candidate. We had to wait a further twenty days until the next, equally dismal, batch of amateur botchers arrived . . .

The guardsman who announced him cast me a look of such significance that I was roused from my torpor. After so many scribblers, daubers, third-rate conmen; after the debacles with the knife thrower (whose teeth were still being discovered in the floorboards three weeks later) and the bearded woman who strapped his member between his thighs: after so much disappointment, I was ready to hope again.

'Come in,' I called.

The gentleman who followed was entirely void of hair. His blue eyes looked peeled without their lashes; his eyebrows were pencilled on to a barren ridge of flesh. As though to atone for his striking physiognomy, the gentleman – a Calvinist perhaps – confined his body to sombre black. Albrecht Rudolphus sat forward, intrigued. I wanted to set down on paper this merman's head, which gleamed in the torchlight as naked as a foetus.

'I have an assistant, signor,' the man said. 'Is it permitted for me to— ?'

'Bring him in.'

The gentleman smiled and made small bows as he summoned a little Negro boy to follow him. The boy was dressed identically to his master. He pulled a trolley whose contents – two spheres topping a mound – were concealed beneath a sackcloth sheet. 'Hurry up, lad. Careful you don't knock the wall.' The gentleman smiled and advanced, his little assistant scurrying behind him with the shrouded trolley. Its wheels squeaked and warbled like the castors on the dead Duke's bath chair.

'What is your name, sir?'

The gentleman pouted and twisted his lips, as though tasting his mouth; he cleared his throat with a medley of grunts and sucked the ridge of his finger to attenuate the delay. 'Adolfo – uh – Adolph Brenner.'

'You hesitate, sir.'

'I, uh?' The gentleman covered his mouth with his entire hand as though suppressing wind. 'Hesitate, signor?'

'You seem not to know your own name.'

'My name?' The visitor laughed: a breezy noise, almost girlish, better suited to a lady's chamber than this dark study and its inquisitors. 'Does a dog know it is a dog?'

'Come, no riddles.'

'No riddles, signor. I mean, without a name and the knowing of it, a man is little better than a dog.' The gentleman shook his head at himself. Decisively, with a faint stamp of the foot, he said: 'My name *is* Adolph Brenner.'

I could not keep from smiling. A poor charlatan makes reassuring company. 'You're quite sure of that, are you?'

'Quite sure, signor.'

The Duke strained in his chair, fascinated by the hidden object at the Negro's back.

'What is your field of expertise, Herr Brenner?'

'*Monstrorum artifex*, signor. I am a maker of monsters. And artificial men, women, children. Lapdogs. A mermaid. Once, a flying dung beetle.'

Albrecht Rudolphus gaped. 'Dung beetle?'

'Trickery for a play. Like Dr Dee in England. Only his flew without the use of strings.'

'Herr Brenner,' I interrupted, 'you speak too opaquely. Tell us plainly, in transparent German, what it is you make.'

'Automata, signor.'

My patron's hand fell heavily on my wrist. 'Tommaso –

261

that's what you promised me, remember? That time with the cats, on my birthday.'

Adolph Brenner's smile grew fixed as he guessed my colleague's identity. This overgrown child was the *Duke*? Our visitor sought confirmation from my eyes – and received it. 'Your Grace,' he said, lavishly bowing, 'I have an example of my work here on this trolley.'

'Show me, by God!' Albrecht Rudolfus punched my arm in his excitement; I bit my lip to stifle a whimper as Adolph Brenner scurried behind his invention.

'If you'd be patient for a moment, your Grace . . .' Covering his head and shoulders with the sackcloth, the bald inventor twisted some sort of mechanism, making a ratcheting, cicada sound. 'On my word, Kaspar.' The little Negro boy trembled; he bowed his head in the presence of authority and insinuated his fingers under the sheet to pinch the edges.

'I've not seen *this* before,' whispered the Duke, lodging a pearl of spit in my ear.

'NOW!'

The boy Kaspar pulled at the sheet. Two heads nodded with the momentum of their discovery. They were stuffed balls of cloth with painted features: red parabolas for mouths, black triangles for noses, copper-blue buttons for eyes and as little hair on their yellow heads as their creator sported on his. There was a gaping, baffled hiatus, filled only with a mechanism's chatter. Adolph Brenner sucked on his finger, little Kaspar looked as though he might cry, while the uncanny twins considered the possibility of movement.

'I give you,' said the clockwork-maker, 'the Embrace of Amity.'

Suddenly, as though Brenner had uttered a magic formula, the automatons turned their heads to face one another. The torsos followed the heads with a jarring motion, rattling and emitting faint creaks, like farts into furniture. Some kind of umbilicus stretched out between them. At its centre two cotton balls had been sewn together, representing clasped hands. This fused appendage trembled in a kind of hand-shake, while the clumsy heads lolled and nodded. Adolph Brenner's hand settled on Kaspar's shoulder; his bald eyes darted nervously between his invention and the Duke.

'Wonderful,' said my patron.

'It is a little rough and unadorned, your Grace. But appearance is secondary. It can wait until the movement is perfected.'

Now the dolls began to tremble and the castors on the trolley to gibber as the clockwork unwound to its rest. The nodding heads bounced furiously. The conjoined arm tightened, dragging the torsos closer together. Kaspar's face inflated, it became puffy with trepidation, as the lifeless heads collided – bounced off each other – then collided again. Albrecht Rudolphus giggled with childish glee. 'The Head-butt of Amity,' he exclaimed, and slapped his thigh, like Harlequin in a comedy.

Adolph Brenner was canny enough not to contradict the Duke's laughter. Even little Kaspar grinned, peering with mirthless eyes at his upturned palms, while the poorly calibrated heads bashed together. When the clockwork at last whirred to a halt and the automatons, still swaying with residual motion, resumed their neutral pose, my patron fairly leaped from his seat to embrace his new servant.

'Welcome,' he cried, his fat lips gleaming, 'to my Library of Arts and Wonders.'

Two years before he would write with news of Rudolf's dethronement and the division of his collections, Jaroslav Meyrink sent me a letter that refreshed memories of my Bohemian disgrace.

'You may have heard,' he wrote, 'of the dramatic fall of Philip von Langenfels, also known as Langenfelsu. That criminal Jew was imprisoned last year and languished in the White Tower for many months until the ultimate punishment righted his wrongs. Langenfelsu, whose conversion in my opinion was ever but a ploy to advance himself in court, confessed to stealing over many years from the Imperial Collection. In his houses were found old coins, jewels, jasper vases. He confessed to employing common thieves to perform his bidding and that he used a pseudonymous agent to preserve his own identity. Furthermore he pretended to possess alchemical powers, duping credulous men with the copulation of his lies. These crimes and many others Langenfelsu confessed to under duress.

'One particular assault on the Emperor's property took place in November 1600. Masterminded by his lieutenant, the sometime Moosbruder, it culminated in the drowning of three dupes. I am sure that you will know what conclusions to draw concerning your own misfortunes at that time . . .' Meyrink went on to spice his letter with details of the scoundrel's corpse 'sunk like a dog's in the Moldau, his head exposed on the bridge for all to spit at'. He concluded from these facts that crime is always found out; that a man cannot grow into power if his roots inhabit poisoned soil; and that the Jew in all his disguises can never be trusted.

The unmasking of my Prague enemy and details of his painful demise necessitated a consoling antithesis. Meyrink compared the villainous conduct of von Langenfels – that ruthless upstart – with the kindness shown to me by Bartholomeus Spranger. I was not to believe that my most influential benefactor in Rudolf's court had abandoned me at my hour of greatest need. 'Bartholomeus Spranger was a politic man; you may owe your liberty to his caution.' It had been Spranger who had arranged for the material improvements in my incarceration. The better food, the potable water unsoured by rust or the furry corpses of drowned slugs, were his doing; likewise the candles, by whose flickering light I had watched my dear friend Petrus Gonsalvus.

'Thus Vice and Virtue may inhabit the same epistle,' Meyrink concluded. I was more grateful to him for these revelations than I would have cause to thank him for his future interventions.

I had no desire to revisit my youth in memory. Over a decade I had managed to excise most of it, plucking the dry roots from my heart and living only for my advancement. Being gone, my ignoble past did not exist. A respectable gentleman at last, I would have nobody in Felsengrunde learn of my mistake.

When, early in the summer of 1610, the cells and ante-chambers of our labyrinth had been completed and the Augsburg carpenters (to the relief of all but tavern landlords) had departed from the dukedom, I was glad to begin work on furnishing the Library. I ordered tapestries from Brussels and Aubusson; goldsmiths were shipped in from Augsburg to fashion bronze candlesticks and picture frames; for stone-work I attempted to revive my allegiance to my mother's family, the marble-exporting Raimondis. To this purpose I wrote to my former tutor Piombino in Florence, and learned in his reply that my Uncle Umberto had died of heart stoppage in his exemplary study on the Via dei Calzaiuoli. So the instigator of my adventures – the man whose boot had so nearly collided with my rump in the Piazza della Signoria, and whose efforts to honour his sister's memory had hastened my conversion to a performing freak – existed no longer. I was inconsolably sad for a day, deprived of a chance to impress upon the old man the amplitude of my success.

Custom, for my Florentine relatives, must have been poor; for Piombino sent me two more letters in quick succession, detailing what generous accommodations I could reach with the company should I make use of their expertise. I was obliged regretfully to end our correspondence, following a shrill confrontation with the Treasurer, Wilhelm Struder.

The costs of the project were mounting. A little invention, a touch of duplicity, was required of your narrator. And lo! within the month, a humped and rattling cart lumbered through the Castle gates, yoked to mournful nags. The cart was protected from the elements by canvases slung between brightly painted poles; ribbons of canary yellow and barber's red gave the supports a festive air. Articulated puppets – dwarfs, magicians, white-haired kings – jigged on their halters. A dog chased the muddy wheels, barking furiously at the tantalising and entirely wooden sausages that trailed from the rear. The cart clattered, it jingled, to a halt on Weidmanner Platz and a troupe of strolling players emerged. I introduced myself to their taciturn leader. Over bottles of Rhenish in my workshop, to the melodious chatter of florins on wood, I negotiated with him for his assistance.

The money was intended to buy their discretion: never a cheap commodity with actors. What I needed was the expertise of men who, though possessing only limited resources, could transform a bare platform or corner of a banqueting hall into a forest, the Roman Senate, the Trojan shore. With muffled candles and torches we entered the barren Library, our feet making the raised boards creak. Excited as schoolboys, the players carefully avoided the trapdoors whose presence I indicated with a downward-thrusting finger. My theatrical guests, delighted by the dips and turns of the Library, by its true and false and secret entrances, agreed to contribute to the faking of its splendour.

They stayed in Felsengrunde Castle, sleeping on their cart at night (my Lord Chamberlain would not have rapscallions and whoremongers under 'his' roof) and working by day on the manufacture of antique busts and hollow statuary. It was a joy for me to work alongside these self-taught craftsmen, transforming, with veins of pink and white paint, their wooden pillars into marble columns. Ludolf Bresdin's skills as a painter of false perspectives were required again (it would be our last face-to-face encounter: ten years later, a stray bullet doing God's work would dash out his brains) and he worked ungrudgingly beneath the players as they added volutes and tympana and Roman-style friezes to the walls.

In order to keep the Duke ignorant of our makeshift inventions, we treated him every night for three weeks to performances in the courtyard. Twice, when it rained and the skies were overcast, the Duke overruled Moritz von Winkelbach's objections and gave up the Banqueting Hall to the players' revels. He liked low comedies, our high-minded patron, and requested a dumbshow of the Faust legend every night for a week, sniggering and slapping his thigh to see the Pope kicked or the Spanish King plucked by the beard. The requests only ceased when the players, tiring of routine, replaced the King of Spain with the Emperor; whereupon their fat-lipped host stormed back to his apartments. Mephisto gripped Faust's shoulder, Faust hugged the Emperor, the Emperor sucked his beard – the whole company frozen with horror. But your narrator acted swiftly and managed to cool the offended Duke's rage.

At the end of three weeks, many of the lesser interstices in the Library had been filled: either painted with scenes from the *Eclogues* and the Duke's chivalresque favourite *Tristan*, or else draped with gathered material – stage cloaks, backdrops – in anticipation of objects as yet unknown. Tapestries arrived from Aubusson, which we installed in the entrance hall and reception room. Suddenly my stage-makers were free to go; which they were glad to do, having wearied of the courtyard and its gloomy walls. After bidding them all farewell (and seeing my last of dear Ludolf Bresdin), I waved from the battlements to their retreating colours. I was still waving, clenching down a sense of utter loneliness, when they had vanished into the forest and their chatter was snatched away by the ungracious wind.

My last guests arrived on the evening of the players' departure. Rolling in in a closed carriage, they were followed by two goods wagons and a small armed escort. I received them in Weidmanner Platz – alone this time – instructing the stable lads to attend to the horses and commiserating with my visitors as they complained of exhaustion and wounded rumps. Both men were sallow, lean and middle aged, their faces pock-marked and traced with yellow veins where sweat had run through their face powder. Born Venetians, they were better used to the swell of boats and the slap of water on canal walls than the bruising jiggery of horse and cart.

'Does the Duke expect to see us?' one of the men asked.

'The Duke is unwell and does not wish to pass his ailments to his honoured guests. Please, allow me to offer you and your men some refreshments . . .'

They had come all the way from Venice, bringing the sorts of fineries which even humble citizens of the floating republic will hire for their daughters' weddings. I had to reward the gentlemen very handsomely for their sacrifices and insinuated two extra purses from the Duke's fortune to assure myself of their discretion; for I could not have tolerated the prying and pinch-nosed meddlers of the Court sniffing out my sources.

After I had seen to the feeding of their escort, I smuggled

the Venetian dealers into Vergessenheit Street and guided them up the narrow staircase to my former apartments. Surely the damp could not have appalled them; yet they skewed their jaws and pinched their shoulders to keep from touching its grimy walls. 'Tell us what you require, Signor Grilli, and then let us leave.'

There was no solidarity of countrymen between us. Tuscans and Venetians are breeds apart – the former bronzed by the sun, exalted by hills and the shift of clouds; the latter conceited, amphibious and greedy.

'Show me what you've brought,' I said, 'and I will not detain you.'

I can recall precisely the bill of fare. It included carved chairs of Mugello oak, jewel-patterned Ottoman rugs, damask cushions, ornamental mirrors in frames encrusted with ruby-coloured glass, a map of the world after Ortelius, eternal roses and lilies and tulips woven out of silk, four terracotta lions in need of repainting, a parrot cage, a celestial globe seated in its cradle, gold-embroidered napkins, lengths of blue kersey cloth and a dozen other things beside. Fairy towers of coins sprang up on the negotiating table. The Venetian dealers were unaccustomed to parting eternally with their clutter: they pulled faces and twisted the rings on their fingers, they muttered together in lagoon slang – rivals made colleagues by adversity – and sighed as though each transaction were a noble sacrifice.

'Thank you, gentlemen,' I concluded, blessing them with inky fingers. I pinched out the shrinking candle and we sat exhausted in the blue wash of dawn. The Venetian dealers left the Castle much lighter than they had come, preferring to sleep against the bucking walls of their carriage rather than endure another hour in this smiling midget's company.

The Duke was unaccountably sunk in gloom. He dragged

himself from chair to chair in the Private Chamber, his breathing shallow and his clothes awry. His fat round face looked heavy on him, his reticent chin was shadowed with stubble. When, in my attempt to rouse him from his torpor, I described the Library's progress, he turned his leaden gaze to my knees. 'Leave me,' he murmured.

'. . . and in the Long Corridor we'll display . . . your Grace?'

The Duke's eyes filmed over with weariness. 'Please,' he said, 'go away.'

Swallowing my pride, I bowed and withdrew – trusting that my rump would find the door. In the Ritterstube, Moritz von Winkelbach flagged me down. His weasel face bristled with malicious humour. 'Has the Duke dismissed you, Herr Grilli?'

'For the time being, my Lord Chamberlain.'

'Unhappy, is he?' Sprawling across both arms of a chair, his brother sniggered and wafted his fingers beneath his nose.

'I was not,' I replied, 'so impertinent as to enquire.' I ventured past, attempting an air of disdain.

'Then you have not heard?'

'Heard what?'

Moritz von Winkelbach pinioned me with his eyes. 'About our Emperor?'

'A grievous loss,' Maximilian simpered, 'a happy gain.'

The Winkelbach brothers pursed their lips: I would have to crawl on my hands and knees to elicit more matter from them. 'The Duke,' I said, 'seems to me in excellent spirits.' I scurried to the door and waved for the guards to open it. Behind me, in the dark pool of the Ritterstube, Moritz von Winkelbach laughed. I heard him address his brother as the door closed. 'Grilli's tall stories,' he called, 'look set to crumble about his ears.'

Kicking cobbles, I returned to my workshop in the south tower and tried to concentrate on my projects. My assistants, chary of their master's temper, defensively raised their shoulders. I summoned them over to my desk – meted out coins – and sent them to the East Wing to lubricate servants who might have overheard matters of state. When, after two hours, my honest spies came skulking back, they returned the bribes to my keeping.

'What, nothing at all? Not a whisper? From anyone?'

Like scolded puppies, my informants raised their eyes and whimpered. I saw to it that their rations were cut for three days.

Unable to approach my melancholy patron, I loitered outside the Treasury and the Revenues Office, busily going over my sketches (so it appeared) of the Castle's architecture. I listened to a clerk from the Office of the Lord Steward gossiping with a servant as they pissed beneath the Duchess's Apartments. Castle rumour weaved around me; I dared not believe it, until confirmation came in a letter from Meyrink.

Rudolf had been dethroned by his brother Matthias.

Up to this date, Meyrink's letters had kept me informed of the gradual erosion of the Emperor's power. Weakened by the storms of his own misgovernment, humiliated by the Turk and the Czech Brethren, Rudolf had divided rule with his brother, keeping for himself Bohemia, Silesia and the imperial crown. Civil and religious war had followed – a foretaste of much madness to come – with the result that even the Bohemian crown had passed to Matthias. Spurned by the Estates, hidden away in the Castle and clutching his objects, Rudolf had found solitude at last. I prayed to the nameless gods of my own malice for the powerless husk of an Emperor to die: for the wind to scatter his dust, leaving me free to embellish his myth.

The Duke had lost the model for his invented self. Did he suspect that Tommaso had been less than truthful with him all these years? I seasoned my account of events in Prague for his consumption. Rudolf had been deposed by a malicious faction, I said, to the detriment of all Bohemia. The myth of Vertumnus, of the Fruitful Caesar who bestowed riches on his subjects, could survive a few years longer.

'Think of yourself, my lord, as a continuation of Rudolf's achievement. Like Constantinople shoring up the dream of Rome.'

For weeks the Duke's sickness persisted. He would not touch his courtesans and refused to have them sent to his study. He was ordering food every hour and sat masticating, with an air of indescribable melancholy, his cold roasts and sugared fruits as though attempting to plug some gap in his nature. He was growing fatter, it seemed, by the hour, like a corpse becoming waterlogged. I tore myself anxiously from my arrangements for the inaugural festivities to visit him in his bedchamber. Sometimes he would stare fixedly at the Persian rug, or into a dish of stewed prunes, to avoid having to acknowledge my presence; on other occasions he railed against the waiting imposed upon him by 'the damned slowness' of my labours. Alas, I could not bring forward the inauguration date, to which the nobility of Felsengrunde – along with a few prominent citizens, merchants and minor foreign dignitaries – had received official invitations; so I urged Adolph Brenner, the maker of automata, to help me rouse with amusements the Duke from his sickness.

'I have nothing new to offer you, Herr Grilli.'

Adolph Brenner lived in a single room above the Revenues Office, where he shared a bed with his taciturn assistant and spent the days scrawling designs for his future marvels. There was a fetid, closeted smell in the room; I wanted to plug my nose against it.

'Come, dear colleague,' I said. 'We live to serve our patron. You must have *something* in your armoury.'

Adolph Brenner exchanged a look with his assistant. I turned too late to be certain that Kaspar had shaken his head. 'We,' said Brenner, 'we do have something.'

'An automaton?'

'No. We found them – that is, I bought them – in Padua.' At my back the little Negro sighed. 'I had been hoping to keep them in reserve.'

'Why?'

'For whatever need might present itself.'

Adolph Brenner's selfishness angered me. I had authority over his tricks. '*Now* is the need,' I said. 'The Duke must be distracted from his melancholy. Whatever it is that you bought in Padua, it is needed *today*.'

Brenner mournfully nodded. By making vague promises of improved pay and lodgings, I was able to quash his reservations. All chancers must stow a trump card or two up their proverbial sleeves. Mine was to borrow his.

*

'The astronomic lenses of Galileo Galilei . . .'

Adolph Brenner's eyes swelled to owlishness as he held the lenses on either side of his nose; he must have seen the Duke distending on his throne, a deliquescent form oozing towards him, octopus arms outstretched.

'Bought in the astronomer's shop in Padua, your Grace.'

The fingers of Albrecht Rudolphus lost their appetite before they could grasp the lenses. 'Have I heard of this inventor, Tommaso?'

'Galileo, your Grace,' said Adolph Brenner, cradling the lenses as a child saves a pet mouse from the ardour of his cat, 'is the celebrated author of *The Starry Messenger*. And these belong in an instrument which is called a telescope, such as Herr Galilei presented to the Republic of Venice.'

'Are they for disguises?'

'Through the telescope, your Grace, a man may see a ship two hours before it is visible to the naked eye, steering full sail into the harbour.' Adolph Brenner looked expectantly at the Duke. When no expression of amazement was forthcoming, he turned to me for succour. 'The Venetians,' he joked, 'love a new-fangled device when it helps them to win battles.'

'Have you got one?' said the Duke.

'My lord?'

'A telescope.'

'Only the lenses, I'm afraid.' Brenner looked across the Ritterstube to where his dismal boy stood, running a hand through his black-burred scalp. 'Galileo has disproved the belief in the spherical perfection of the moon. Like Felsengrunde, your Grace, the moon has *mountains*.'

The Duke, whose eyes, pellucid globes floating in aqueous misery, had drifted towards the oriel window, showed little interest in Brenner's second novelty, 'a geometric and military compass'. When he straightened on his throne, it was only to facilitate the passage of wind. Adolph Brenner produced from a walnut casket a hollow bulb and tube used for measuring a liquid's temperature. Like the calibrated device for mathematical observations, like the telescope lenses, it was cast away on the barren soil of the Duke's understanding.

'Perhaps,' I endeavoured, 'his Grace might like to invest in one of these telescopes?'

'What on earth *for*?'

'To watch the stars swimming in the firmament.'

The breeze of an idea stirred between the Duke's ears. He raised himself off his knuckles and focused on the middle distance, as though attending to his borborygmi. 'Go on,' he said softly.

'I understand that Galilei, by means of celestial observation, has named the spheres the "Medicean Planets". With such a telescope, your Grace, the fame of Felsengrunde could extend all the way to the stars.'

My patron's eyes widened. 'Really?'

Adolph Brenner queasily nodded. 'Why not, my lord?'

Even this conceit failed to cheer the Duke for long. Adolph Brenner had squandered his only portable novelties. But he had won favour with the Court Librarian, who in turn reconciled himself to his patron's gloom and inertia. Like a dense fog, it would clear of its own accord, dissolved by the sun of some unknown impulse.

Unseasonable weather soaked us at the outset; so that, instead of admiring the honeyed splendour of the beechwood lobby, with its frieze of Attic dancers and false-perspective ceiling where cherubs floated towards a canvas Heaven, the guests chattered in a gloomy grotto, blowing raindrops off the tips of their noses and sweeping water from their sleeves. Ladies disconsolately patted their headdresses, which the squall had left tangled, like rampant honeysuckle. Gentlemen fanned the dank air with broad-rimmed hats whose plumes had degraded to fibrous pulps. Duke Albrecht Rudolphus stood apart from his guests, propping himself on the lintel of the decorative fireplace and furtively demolishing an oatmeal biscuit. I sidled up to him, bobbing and smiling, and observed how fine the Order of St Bartholomew looked.

'They smell of wet dog,' replied the Duke.

'Might I suggest we equip the servants with torches?' I whispered. 'It may serve to heighten the mystery of their visit.'

And so (after several humiliating entreaties for silence) I managed to promote myself, in the crowd's mind, to the status of a diminutive Virgil tasked with guiding them through the depths. Laughing and flirting and discreetly pushing one another, the intrepid explorers cast off in my wake. Shadows swam and evaporated on the walls of the Kammergalerie, where guests could admire my designs for the *Book of Virtues*, or commiserate with the lugubrious subjects of Theodor Altmann's portraits, in anticipation of replacements as yet unexecuted by his successor. Though we were separated from the Long Corridor, where a feast awaited us, by a mere inch of polished oak, yet I had no intention of revealing the concealed panel that would permit immediate passage.

'Mind your heads,' I cried.

To enter the neighbouring cell we had to climb five steep steps. Ladies gasped as people trod upon their trains; gentlemen tucked in their swords and flustered to rescue their tilting hats. The third room was higher still, the fourth a narrow corridor in which the company was distilled to single file. A momentary panic greeted the smouldering of a theatrical drape, which a servant had caressed with his torch. I heard Maximilian von Winkelbach issue stentorian orders and nervous giggles rippled back and forth along the corridor as disaster was averted. Now we descended: the carpeted floor adopted a sharp incline, which pressed chests to shoulder blades, crotches to rumps, and made the Duke behind me splutter with unlooked-for merriment. (As for me, I protected my fluttering taper behind the cup of my hand, and instructed my patron to hold my collar tightly.) The sloping corridor opened on to a larger, blue-draped, oval space. It was like some ancient tomb, I heard someone mutter. The low wooden ceiling had abruptly evaporated, leaving us exposed to the cavernous vault of the stable rafters, where banners floated like ethereal kelp beneath the lulling chutter of wind-gusted rain. There was a strained hush as the laggards joined the fore, filling up the space and obscuring the false mosaic painted on the floor. I assured myself of the Duke's fingers on my collar. It was time to cozen these sycophants, to beguile them in the labyrinth.

'*Now*,' I said.

I dashed through one of five doors on offer, with Albrecht Rudolphus following. My taper blinked and lashed out in the darkness. Together we turned and locked ourselves in. We could hear sharp cries of surprise and dismay as genteel palms beat against the bolted door. Grinning to reassure the Duke, I shouted instructions to our abandoned guests to use the other exits. And so we listened as they rushed into a theatrical dungeon, where a paper skeleton was playing cards with its own shadow; as they stumbled into a glaucous pond from whose ceiling floated carved pike and sturgeon; as they entered an intimate bedchamber where Brenner's automaton conducted its amicable embrace. Beyond our hearing, a fourth party of baffled explorers emerged into the skylit expanse of the Long Corridor, where servants from the kitchens must have been as startled by their emergence as the guests were themselves.

Albrecht Rudolphus squeezed my shoulder. His courtiers were beginning to laugh, eager peals of merriment announcing their appreciation of the Duke's waggery. He was only disappointed to find himself in the servants' quarters instead of some enchanted cell, and stepped disdainfully over carcasses of straw mattresses, over chamber pots and food bowls and a game of chess whose pieces had been carefully carved by a servant's hand.

Back with our guests in the Long Corridor, I found myself surrounded by the Winkelbach brothers, who tauntingly observed that my grand Library had nothing much *in* it. 'Not as yet, perhaps,' I replied.

'I see,' said Moritz von Winkelbach. 'The best is yet to come?'

'Precisely, my Lord Chamberlain. And if you don't believe me . . .'

Piqued by their sour faces, I took the brothers on a private tour of the less visible parts of the Library. The entire purpose of concealing these rooms, which lay hidden to the south of the Long Corridor, was lost on account of my crowing pride. I asked the brothers, as though we were allies in conspiracy, to keep a lookout, lest nosy diners see me pull back a tapestry and open the secret panel that led into the Duke's Study. (The only other entrance, at the side of the building, would soon be closed off by an annexe between the former stables and my tower.) Once inside, the Winkelbach brothers sniffed about the half-furnished shelves. There were other rooms beside, I explained, which were not, as yet, ready for use.

'I've seen these books before,' said the Lord Chamberlain. 'In the *old* library.'

'Is that your achievement, Herr Grilli? One can train a monkey—'

'—to cart furniture around.'

The brothers sneered to thank me for my pains, then sauntered back to the feast in a Long Corridor which – save for a few prints and the books that I had bought in Frankfurt arranged on the lecterns – was also unfulfilled.

I joined my preoccupied Duke. Most of his guests had recovered from their surprises, and were noisily devouring what the kitchen staff had sweated for two days to produce. (I had watched the cooks flaying and broiling meats, stripped to the waist and gleaming with sweat, their hips maculate with the prints of floury hands. Spiced fruits, sweetmeats and honey-glazed cakes had tumbled from the ovens; pheasants that had wilted on the gun-resounding hills had recaptured their former splendour in plumages of carrot and onion and parsnip. The bill of fare would, I knew, far exceed the capacities of the guests' bellies. No matter: we had to impress our visitors, there could be no shrinking of ambition.)

After the feast – while servants wavered beneath long poles to close the shutters in the roof, and the bloated guests launched themselves warily, though less mischievously guided, back into the labyrinth in search of an exit – I accompanied my patron to his study. Here he stood contemplating the books, including the Vögel manuscript, which I had transported from the old library in the Great Hall.

'One day,' I said, 'the whole Library will be as finished as this study. It will be a lifetime's vocation. And I its lifelong servant.'

The Duke contemplated the empty spaces, his chin melting in his palm. 'You call this *finished*, Tommaso?'

I replied honestly that it would take years to fill even these shelves.

'Years!'

'Well, not years. A long time.'

'But they're so *bare*.'

'Unless we buy in bulk. Collectors are always dying. My agents in Germany can bid in auctions, if you wish it.'

Albrecht Rudolphus would never care actually to *read* those books whose weight and insulation he so enjoyed. He turned to me with the fixed jaw of a determined child, hungry for more of everything.

'Yes, Tommaso. As you say, I wish it.'

When, less than a year after his political emasculation, the Emperor Rudolf died and perfected his dissolution, I attempted to rescue works from his collection. King Matthias was anxious to trade his brother's objects for cash; without sufficient funds, however, and obliged to conceal my identity from the Prague authorities, I failed to secure the meanest thumb sketch.

'The Emperor died a few days after his lion,' I told the Duke in his study. The pleasing shape of this conjunction did nothing to console him.

In February 1612, the treacherous Matthias was crowned Emperor. Although officially Felsengrunde was one of the Empire's principalities, Albrecht Rudolphus received no summons to attend the coronation.

'Tell them we scorn their ceremonies,' the Duke shouted at my quill. 'Albrecht Rudolphus refuses to sanction this travesty!'

'Good,' I said, 'very good,' and read the letter back to its dictator. Matthias was accused, without restraint or euphemism, of having hounded his brother into his grave. The Duke was proud *not* to have attended the coronation: he alone remained Rudolf's kinsman – though they had never met in person – loyal to him as he travelled into Stygian darkness.

'I see the blood returning to your Grace's cheek,' I said when the letter had been sealed and stamped. I reverenced elaborately, wafting dust into the air with the sweep of my hat – then torched the letter in my workshop and set to work forging a reply from the Emperor's Secretary.

Felsengrunde was my New World. Living on my wits, by talents I had discovered long ago in the lane they called Neu Welt, I prospered like Pizarro. In many courts of Europe, both petty and grand, the mechanical view of artists as craftsmen prevailed and painters superior to your humble narrator suffered the status of workmen. Not I, in the court of Albrecht Rudolphus. I was his tutor, the arbiter of his tastes: procurer, painter and spinner of dreams to his Fantastical Lordship. 'You have built a kingdom,' I told him, pouring sweet liquor of suggestion in his ear. 'Now you must let me *populate* it.'

By my sole efforts, the expenditure of Felsengrunde Castle doubled in six years.

I will tell you shortly (and keep the telling shorter than my pride would have it) what craftsmen I imported to fill with wonders the strange rock pool of the Library; what paintings spread across its walls; what desiccated creatures made their mausoleums in its cabinets. For a moment – if you please – I wish to bask in recollection, to bathe in the glowing memory of my easeful years, when my craft was my only concern . . .

Hardly any political scheming was required of me, as my peripatetic good angel (who had abandoned me briefly in Dalibor, and would do so again one day) had surely intended. I devoted myself to Art – to the creation of matter where none had existed. I assembled, using my existing contacts, a network of agents in Italy, Germany and the Netherlands, who sought out books, prints and paintings at auctions. Two or three times each year, a consignment of books would arrive – titles in Latin and Greek and several vernaculars – on every subject under the sun. (Those with illuminations the Duke would cradle and cosset back to his study.) I compiled books for my own education as much as the Duke's acquisitive pleasure: books on astronomy, rhetoric and mechanics, mathematical prefaces to Euclid, herbariums and treatises on philosophy and Books One and Two of the *Adventures of Don Quixote de la Mancha*, which with my vestiges of Milanese Spanish I was able slowly to decipher. On one occasion, in the sixth year of Albrecht Rudolphus's rule, a Genoese chancer offered us the *De Revolutionibus* of Copernicus – which an excited Adolph Brenner insisted that I purchase – and a *History of*

Monsters by Ulisse Aldrovandi, in which I discovered, with a ripe effusion of emotions, the woodcut likenesses of my old benefactor Petrus Gonsalvus and his prodigious, hairy children. Aldrovandi's book both fascinated and disgusted my patron, who kept it, to my sorrow, in the fastness of his bedchamber.

As well as books, I bought in these prosperous years a great number of prints. Giovanni Orlandi restored and reprinted ancient plates in Rome; Georg Spengler kept me stocked from Dresden; Jaroslav Meyrink did all that he could in a gloomy and diminished Prague. From Rome an engraving of Dürer's *Head of the Twelve Year Old Christ* afforded me a timely reminder of the Master's style. From Dresden came engravings by Jan Muller after Adrien de Vries, perfectly suited to my patron's tastes. Mercury carried off Psyche, mounting her high, a prodigious erection, on his chest; a plump and pale Cleopatra nursed wormy asps on her breast; a Sabine woman with the musculature of an Amazon wrestled with her Roman abductor. From Bohemia came Sadeler's print of Vladislav Hall at Prague Castle. The Duke was thrilled to see, in such detail, the centre of the imperial palace, where Art was the hub of commerce, as evidenced by the print stalls along the walls; whereas I scarcely dared to look at the print for fear of recalling, with ripe blushes, the scene of my humiliation.

From a disposable young painter I commissioned landscapes of Felsengrunde: rocky gorges with supernumerary cascades and scattered tree trunks, ramshackle cottages from the backwaters of the Wintertal, the craneless chimneys of Krantor to the north and the emerald rapids near Winkelbach to the south. Ordinarily I would have executed these studies myself, sitting on my stool in a luminous glade while my assistants stretched a sheet above my head to give me shade, or ran into the forest in pursuit of water to slake my thirst. But I was too busy in the lofty rotundity of my workshop to attend to the embellishment of tatty nature. The landscape artist, when he had delivered his drawings, was strongly discouraged from seeking residence in Felsengrunde. I had him escorted by sturdy Klaus beyond our northern border.

In six years I spent eight hundred florins importing works of sculpture. These included bronze casts from my father's master, Giambologna – his *Lion* gilded in fire, with its great head tousled and its tail, alas, broken in transit; his *Sleeping Nymph and Satyr* auctioned from a notable Bolognese merchant's estate; and a second lion, this one clawing a horse, in bronze with a light brown patina and red smoke glaze. (See what remained of my father's craft in his son's memory? I wondered whether a young Anonimo's hand had not contributed to Susini's casting.) The Duke loved this last statue especially, comparing the ravenous head of the lion, and the flesh of the agonised horse forever pinched by the lion's fangs, to his frightful print of the dragon devouring the followers of Cadmus. From Georg Spengler I gained several curios: a crab-shaped inkwell reminiscent of the one my father owned, its claw raised to pinch – and steady – the inserted quill; a miniature elephant in bronze from an unknown workshop, the beast deeply engrossed in its wrinkles; a drinking vessel shaped like the jutting underlip of a satyr; and several gladiators, elegantly frozen in postures of defence, as though the ultimate vision of their diminutive lives had been the Medusa's petrifying glare. It was Georg Spengler who sent me the ever popular *Mercury in Flight* by Giambologna, which formed, at the Duke's extraordinary insistence, the dynamic centrepiece of his sculptural collection.

Keep up, keep up, breathless reader!

My efforts as a curator were tireless. I travelled frequently in Germany, equipped with ever more substantial escorts, in pursuit of collections to be disbanded at auction. Yet the powers of expenditure of the greater patrons – the Duke of Bavaria most notable among them – tended to reduce me to the status of a scavenger, bidding eagerly for minor scraps. The limits of my florins and influence in the wider world placed the onus of responsibility on my own forger's skills.

Let me tell you what I made.

In the creamy, long-limbed, erotic manner of the late Bartholomeus Spranger (as a private tribute perhaps, a Lazarene act), I painted the Duke's favourite courtesans in the guise of Callisto seduced by Jupiter, who to conquer the obdurate nymph had taken on the shape of Diana. Albrecht Rudolphus was reassured by the classical allusion that his private painting was not obscene. I smoothed out the goose-pimpled flesh of the courtesans (they had lain pressed together on my workshop floor for several chilly hours) and altered their hair colour from russet to blonde, from brown to black, to remind the Duke of his carnal induction, at my expense, in Nuremberg all those years ago.

Subsequently I painted two nudes by Lucas Cranach (Elder or Younger), a version of St Anthony by Hieronymus Bosch and a shaggily verdant Altdorfer, inspired by the Pass of Our Lady, where a brightly armoured St George rescued a damsel so pasty and insipid that only a German patron could have admired her. Snickering to myself, I revived the dead hand of Gian Bonconvento and gave a new Mary Magdalene to the world, forging the work of my first patron as though to exorcise myself of his corpulent ghost. For the Kammergalerie, I painted portraits of Albrecht Rudolphus, of his parents (improving on Theodor Altmann's waxy busts) and, to placate the nobility, of the Winkelbachs with their wives and children, and Martin Grünenfelder, whose ledgers were his only progeny.

All of these paintings were, I believed, accomplished; yet the merely formal challenge of mimesis is not the limit of the forger's art. I had also to *age* the newly dried forgeries: painting on muslin which could be rolled after completion to produce the veins and cracks of time, and then fixing the muslin on to suitable panels. Two agents – cut-throats prised from the rotten wood of Felsengrunde's roughest tavern and made serviceable by the threat of pending convictions – loped through Bavaria in search of worm-eaten old pictures over which I could repaint. When such materials were not forthcoming, your scrupulous perfectionist would bore the holes of fictive woodworms into pristine panels with a fine drill and auger. I made gravediggers of my apprentices, who hooked out the corpses of those hungry burrowers from their tombs in old beams and then squinted to insert them in the forged holes. At last, when the painting had been cracked and perforated, and fly-specks of dust had been added with glue, I would smoke the panel in my chimney, tempering its too fresh colours with soot, until the mock Dürer or Bosch (as crammed full of horrors as a wasp's larder!) acquired a worn and antique appearance.

Nor did I stop at these activities – entrusting wood-block designs, attributed by faked monograms to Grien and Burgkmair, to my friend Ludolf Bresdin in Frankfurt and making countless drawings (some 'studies' for extant paintings, others free inventions in another man's style) on every theme, biblical or Antique, that I could summon to memory. These drawings, supposedly rescued from the deliquescent estates of obscure German bankers, formed the papery body of the Library; the Duke's greatest delight was to peer at them through a magnifying glass, skullcapped and mumbling like some dusty antiquarian.

How difficult it was, with so few examples of their work, to draw in the manner of Dürer or Baldung or Spranger. Those who are not compelled to live by Art imagine that eternal delight accompanies its practice. The mind ought, as one draws or paints, to be as loose and easy as the mind of a gardener, when in fact it is assailed by worries and doubts. Perhaps I did force my hand a little, and strained my impostorous hatchings? Yet the Duke professed himself pleased with every new addition to his collection; and I could bask for an hour at least in the glow of achievement, until the restive urge to stain paper returned.

But I was not alone in engendering the Library's contents; there were some crafts that I could not hope to master. Lodging them as best I could in the East Wing of the Castle, I added to my staff a clockmaker and a goldsmith, a young sculptor in *pietre dure* who endured the mountain gloom for a paltry month, and Mordecai ben Ezra, an astronomer from Cracow. This last, being in possession of a full telescope, managed to stay for a year by naming celestial bodies in honour of the Duke – whose own astronomical ignorance blinded him to the deceitful renaming of previously discovered stars. (This was no great treachery. The naming on Earth of a distant sphere does not make that sphere any more or less itself. What cares that blinking diamond for its sublunary name? If a worm, escaping by luck the tread of my boot, praises me with the name of king, I should hardly be a monarch in the world of men.) These itinerant gentlemen made little inroads into my affections. Only the ballard Adolph Brenner became a colleague. We chatted together in rude Italian, the only language in which his boy Kaspar appeared comfortable to laugh, revealing white and perfect teeth: a lovely illumination of his tawny face. Over time, Adolph Brenner's *Embrace of Amity* was followed by a dozen cheerful puppets, each one brought to a spasm of feigned life by chirring cogs and wheels. The automaton-maker would dote on his clockwork beings as though they were made of his own flesh – fussing over them most shrilly when his clumsy boy dropped them on their heads or snapped their winding keys. So much effort was vindicated when Albrecht Rudolphus – our ever more reclusive patron – requested a 'party of clockwork children' to regale him in his hours of leisure.

'A formidable task,' Brenner confessed, haggard at the prospect. 'But we shall do our best, shan't we, Kaspar?'

And so every 'Librarian' under my authority devoted himself to his craft. Ignoring the fears of the Treasury – or the call for new soldiers to enforce the mounting rates of taxation – Albrecht Rudolphus retreated ever farther from public life, taking even his meals in the Library and neglecting the Order of St Bartholomew, which sat forlornly in the Banqueting Hall and toasted the health of a vacant throne.

As for me, Tommaso Grilli, I was feared and hated in equal measure. Those garish insects, the nobility, resented me for distracting their Duke with sterile encounters from his duty to produce an heir. Knowledge of my dual function as painter and procurer had long entrenched my power in the Castle: it was a public secret, an insubstantial seal of office. But now demand for a marriage was growing, while the Duke's appetite for his courtesans appeared to flag. He had grown weary of his furtive and unsanctioned spasms; and so, by extension, might one day tire of me. Therefore, on the last day of my fortieth year, I took out paper and ink and sharpened my quill. It was time to procure a wife for the Duke.

13

Annus Mirabilis

'Frankly now. Between friends. Is this portrait honest?'

I was sorry to ask the question: a momentary paralysis of Meyrink's face, an ineptitude of the muscles, revealed how it pained him. 'You must take my word,' he said, 'if you will not trust the portraitist.'

'I trust *you*, Herr Meyrink.'

'Her picture belies her beauty only in falling short of it.'

I looked again at the medallion portrait. Elisabetta Zbyněk, as small as a fairy, met my gaze through a glass dome. She was a peachy-complexioned girl of eighteen, almond eyed and Roman nosed, with golden tresses that tumbled to her shoulders. Was she demure? I wondered. And obeisant?

'So far as I am equipped to judge in these matters,' said Jaroslav Meyrink, 'a kind husband will prosper.'

Satisfied on this point, we fell to the weightier matter of the lady's dowry. It was uniquely suited to the Duke's tastes. '. . . while to *her* family comes a name and land for her progeniture. There is currency,' said Meyrink darkly, 'in placing one's children beyond the troubled borders of Bohemia.'

Elisabetta Zbyněk, youngest daughter of Bedřich Zbyněk, Chamberlain of the Hunt in Prague, had been raised in Hispanized Czech circles to the highest levels of courtliness. Her summers spent with the daughters of Polyxena and Zdeněk Lobkowicz, Chancellor of the Crown of Bavaria, at their castle in Raudnitz, had mixed Spanish to her repertoire of German and Czech. 'She is honest and God-fearing,' said

Meyrink with flagging zeal. 'No rebellious Hussite blood in those veins, if you see my meaning.'

'I see it clearly,' I said, and replenished the old man's glass.

We had convened upon Dresden as a safe mid-point to conduct our negotiations. Jaroslav Meyrink must have sensed that it was his last mission: no longer as the Emperor's agent but as a matchmaker, the conduit for a dowry and a name. I found him greatly diminished, stooped almost to my level by a crumbled spine. There was little strength in the degenerate claw that clasped my wrist as we parted outside Georg Spengler's house.

'If ever life becomes untenable in Prague,' I said, 'you would find a hospitable friend in Felsengrunde.'

'You are kind, Tommaso.'

Meyrink's carriage door swung open and a liveried page elbowed him up to his seat. He leaned forward to see my face. 'I don't expect to leave Prague again. I mean to stay there whatever happens.'

'God be with you.'

The driver jeered – he thrashed the flanks of his horses and the carriage rumbled off towards the Elbe. Meyrink would convey my letters to his employer. With such ease and assurance had the marriage been brokered.

Adolph Brenner gaped at me. I could see the pink tip of his tongue.

'Whatever *for*?'

'To lodge his arcane objects.'

'But . . . surely . . . he's going to be married?'

'All the more reason. Husbands need a place of refuge.'

The maker of automata stared at my plans for a revolving platform: the inner sanctum, hub of our Duke's universe. My conceit was simple, though I meant to leave its execution to more practical minds. Next to the Duke's Study, in the hidden back reaches of the Library, an empty space awaited its numinous purpose. I dreamed of a tunnel running below floorboards, from trapdoor to trapdoor, in a fashion guaranteed to thwart an intruder. Only the Duke would know how to use this secret tunnel. Leaving his study at one end, he would emerge at the other in a barren cell. Stooping beneath a wooden dome with one low aperture set in its blankness, the Duke would operate some sort of lever; whereupon the cell itself, being fixed to a system of pulleys, would turn a full revolution. In the aperture the Duke would see, at intervals, three wooden doors. It was up to him to decide which of the cells he would visit. They would contain his rarest objects: 'Artificialia', 'Naturalia', 'Erotica'. The Arcana Mysteria.

'And what is that, exactly?'

'The Arcana, my dear Brenner, improves on the arts cabinets of Pomerania and the Fuggerhäuser. It represents all the wealth of Creation.'

'What, *all* of it?'

'*Multum in parvum*. Greatness in lessness. With unique access to his Arcana, the Duke will feel like a deity, whetted above the blunt wits of ordinary mortals.'

'I'm not sure, Tommaso. It looks difficult.'

'And your clockwork children? Are they not progressing?'

Brenner groaned. 'They would, if only Kaspar would stop dropping them on their heads . . .'

'Our patron must be stimulated, Adolfo. All the time his melancholy threatens to engulf him. If things keep still we lose our purpose.' I pushed towards Brenner's fingers a purse of florins. 'I should think, compared to mechanical putti, building a revolving cell ought to be child's play.'

So began the last great programme of building at Felsengrunde Castle. (What has become of its dusty arches and cold, gritted passageways since, under an aged Duke and Duchess, I do not care to imagine.) Adolph Brenner set aside his clockwork children, to the evident pleasure of his Negro, and furrowed his brow over my drawings. From Augsburg we reconvened a small band of carpenters: a few familiar faces, some new blood also, Kussmaul the foreman having died of plague the previous summer. Sworn to secrecy about the Arcana, these men struggled to build it under Brenner's supervision, while I attended to more public matters.

It was time to reopen the Duchess's Apartments. Felsengrundian workers smashed down the flimsy partition; their pasty, birth-slackened wives washed the floors and scrubbed the carpets. In this manner the apartments were swiftly restored. A Tafelstube was its point of entry, then two anterooms, each with a great fireplace and long chairs to recline upon. Forever indulgent towards my superiors, I ordered that a water closet be installed in the outer wall of the Duchess's Bedchamber. This innovation raised eyebrows. I overheard Maximilian von Winkelbach suggesting to the Sheriff that, from his dungeon tower, he would be able to observe the parting cheeks of our future Lady.

On the same theme, I designed a house of easement for the courtyard behind the Banqueting Hall. 'They have built them in all the great palaces of Europe,' I protested when the Winkelbachs confronted me in my tower. 'Progress, gentlemen. It will improve the quality of the air.'

'That, Herr Grilli, is precisely the insinuation to which the Order objects.'

'Insinuation, my Lord Chamberlain?'

'To explain would be to make explicit the insult.'

My assistants leaned intently at their work, the better to overhear us. 'I wish that I followed you, my lords.'

Maximilian could not contain himself. 'Years of *waste*.

You, dwarf, squeezing our coffers dry. And taking our Duke away from us.'

'Your house of easement betrays a lack of tact, Thomas Grilli. It seems we must confine our waste to your perforated dungeon. Contemplate how we shall dispose of *you*, when you are ripe for dropping.'

I acknowledged the menace and persisted with my building. (But what if the Duke became ill? Or died? Who would protect me then?) Albrecht Rudolphus was enflamed like a toad at the prospect of marital life. He strode from room to room, addressing his courtiers with wooden good humour, and began to take an interest in the affairs of his dukedom. Sometimes he would make appearances at the Treasury or in the Lord Chamberlain's Office, obliging the servants to stand to attention and parrying their astonished glances with obtuse questions, turning up the corners on documents as though he might, if time allowed, settle down to read them, or sympathising with the clerks for the feeble light in which they worked. After a time, the Order of St Bartholomew began to rally, like a wilted flower newly watered in its pot. The long, childless years of the Duchy were coming to a close. All would be once more as Albrecht von Feldkirch, the first Duke of legend, had intended. The Winkelbachs and lonely Grünenfelder would be able to don their velvet fineries for a wedding (in whose preparations I was careful not to participate) and then, nine months later, to attend the first of many baptisms, baptismal feasts, celebrations of First Communion . . .

Elisabetta Zbyněk, having consented at her parents' strenuous entreaties to marry the Duke, was scheduled to arrive in early autumn. So thoroughly did this news revive my patron's spirits that for a time I feared he might lose interest in the Library. I was greatly relieved, therefore, to learn that work had been completed on the revolving chamber.

*　　*　　*

As you will appreciate, it was unsound for a man in my position to accomplish things. To dispose of a project by completing it was to run the risk of becoming disposable in turn. Thus, while I took credit for having found the Duke a bride and continued to buy prints and forge paintings for his pleasure, I was in no hurry to furnish the inner sanctum.

'We must be patient,' I told my patron, 'for as long as the Emperor took to gather his objects. We have agents in Italy and Germany. Let us trust in them to stock our mystery, though it seem a protracted business.'

At its completion three years hence, the 'Artificalia' would consist chiefly of mathematical instruments: a directional compass, a gilt brass gnomon shaped like a dragon on a cubic dial, an astrolabe of walnut with silver fittings, a celestial globe from Padua, a nocturnal clock from Prague and a *Planetolabium* that demonstrated the course of the planet Jupiter. (After the expulsion, demanded by the Winkelbachs, of our Jewish astronomer, nobody in Felsengrunde would have the faintest idea how these instruments worked, nor sometimes to what purpose; yet ignorance would only heighten their potency in the Duke's imagination.) Quadrants, compasses, protractors; ivory syringes; some baffling device called a theodolite – I remember them all, for I have sketched and noted down their qualities. Other items in this miscellany include a Persian sherbet spoon, carved along the handle, the spoon itself as brittle as a dry laurel leaf; shoes from Mongolia embroidered with lace like delicate mosses; a rhinoceros-horn cup carved to resemble a hibiscus flower; Moorish spurs pointed at their tips like bodkins; and a shety, or *abacus indicus* of Muscovy, whose counting beads were made of walrus ivory.

Mention of walrus leads me to the next cell, and the 'Naturalia' . . . But you fidget, good companion. Please, arise and stretch. Rub those aching eyes, gather yourself a bite to eat, while I fetch a document.

Now. Do you see this? Along with my *Thesaurus hieroglyphicorum* (upon whose boards I write these words), a single parchment is all that remains of my collecting years. The parchment is covered with a faded script: the brisk and upright ancestor of my senescent scrawl. Let me transcribe it for you.

Items, a monkey's claw from Africa, reputedly magical;
two shells of Brazilian tortoises, with unhatched eggs;
an ostrich egg from Jan Fux's plume shop in Prague;
a Nilus crocodile, stuffed;
two samples of bezoar, said to be deposited in the guts of an ibex, shaped like human faces;
shark's tooth, salvaged from the rudder of a fishing boat near Naples;
a sea-turtle's shell from East Indies, with silver timepiece inserted by Ettore Marpurgo, a goldsmith of Genoa;
some jewelled beetles;
a dodo's wing feathers, also its skull, rendered & boiled;
a unicorn's tusk from Ultima Thule;
a piece of *glossopetrae*, or 'tongue stones', considered by some to be emanations from the sky

And there the document ends. I can picture myself at the instant of writing, seated in my last room in the East Wing, leaning forward to refresh my thirsty quill and scraping my left breast against the high table-top. I have, as I work, many of these objects about me, placed on the table or resting on my bed, each item nestled in a crate of straw.

There are sketches also, strewn as though by some artful wind in every corner. Blithely I begin a fresh page, little knowing that it will be lost for ever—

But I must not run ahead of my story and risk losing you, kind reader. The hour has not yet sounded for my humiliation. You must forget this untimely glimpse of misfortunes to come (though they have passed for your narrator). Now is the year 1618. War has yet to begin in Bohemia; an accursed Englishman is still in Bavaria, hoodwinking the gullible gentry. Elisabetta Zbyněk will arrive shortly – and I am basking in my remarkable year.

Our Bohemian guests were welcomed with garlands of flowers. The air on Weidmanner Platz was heady with the scent of doomed roses and the cobbles were slippery with their crushed flesh. Bells rang out from the chapel as the carriage doors opened. A small welcoming party, consisting of the Lord Chamberlain and Martin Grünenfelder, guided several ladies into the Great Hall and thence to the Ritterstube, where the Duke was waiting with his dwarf at his side, rocking on his toes to keep his terror at bay.

A portly chaperone appeared first. Horror consumed the Duke at the sight of a bulldog chin and white hag's moustache; until he realised, with a sigh of relief, that she was not his betrothed. Elisabetta Zbyněk was ushered forward, eased by the ladies from their midst. She was not quite as her portrait had suggested. Her cheeks, rose upon peach in the painting, were in the flesh more pale and gaunt. Her ceruse-painted lips were uneven, ripe above and starved below. As for her tresses, they were closer to straw than gold, and owed their buoyancy to curl papers rather than dainty Nature. Yet this should not mislead you into picturing a sow. Elisabetta Zbyněk was lovely enough for an ageing bachelor – a sublunary beauty rather than Meyrink's watercolour Venus.

'It is an honour, Fräulein,' said the Duke, reverencing as low as his paunch permitted.

Elisabetta Zbyněk's face fell. Her eyes scrabbled and she had to fix them on her shoes to keep from betraying her dismay. Had she really expected the Adonis depicted in my courtship portrait? If so, the living Albrecht Rudolphus must have come as a shock, with his belly straining at a gaudy waistcoat, with his flabby chin like a pelican's pouch and his boiled-plum lips – which she would have to kiss – lubricated by a sallow tongue. 'Your Grace,' the girl sighed. She curtsied and her ladies followed, bobbing like swimmers on a wave.

Now the portly chaperone conveyed the respects of her employer to Albrecht Rudolphus, Duke of Felsengrunde. When she had finished the eulogy (whose recipient smiled, caressing his chest and bowing at the envoy) our Lord Chamberlain unfurled his own speech of welcome. A chant of praise warbled from the chapel's indigent choir; whereupon the couple were swept up in ceremony.

At the Banqueting Hall neither Albrecht Rudolphus nor Elisabetta – separated by their referees – made great show of appetite. The members of the Order of St Bartholomew beamed approvingly at the ambulant womb of their future Duke and chattered loudly, heated by wine and succulent meats.

Later, and somewhat fortified, the Duke sat with Elisabetta in the Private Chamber, watched by an audience of worthies that included, at a slight remove, your matchmaking narrator. Verbal niceties – the ballast of uneasy society – kept the courting couple afloat for a time. Albrecht Rudolphus admired his betrothed for her Bohemian upbringing. Had she met the late Emperor? he wondered. Had she dined in his company, or been granted a glimpse of his art collections? Unconscious of any error (Elisabetta would have been twelve years old when Rudolf died), the Duke sidled closer and moistened his lips. He regurgitated, with embellishments, my fanciful stories of the dead Emperor, while his eager hands, like puppies that have slipped their collars of restraint, nuzzled Elisabetta's own entrenched in her lap.

'We have the profoundest respect for Rudolf – for his wisdom and sound governance. How I envy, madam, your familiarity with his world . . .'

The young woman, retreating from his breath, seemed to watch the Duke with wry humour. Her dark alluring eyes trembled. I did not like what I saw in them – I did not like it at all.

'You will notice,' said the Duke, 'the similarities between his achievements and mine.'

Elisabetta Zbyněk laughed. It was a musical eructation that burst forth charmingly, chillingly, before she could stifle it. 'Forgive me,' she fluted. Her fingers danced in the breeze of her laughter. 'Forgive me, your Grace.'

The chaperone interjected. 'Do not take this badly. My lady is overwrought by the occasion.'

'Yes,' said the Duke, 'of course.'

Elisabetta Zbyněk struggled to quell the paroxysm. She pressed a prophylactic finger to the welling corner of an eye. Its neighbour deliquesced. She sniffed at a sudden rheum and prodded her burgeoning tears. 'Lord,' she wept, 'oh Lord.' A pearl gathered at her left nostril – I watched it grow – then she snuck it back, quick as a limpet, into its shell. 'The journey has tired her,' said the chaperone, slapping open her fan and patting the Fräulein's knuckles. She endeavoured to screen the girl's emotion with her taffeta rump. 'These are tears of happiness, your Grace. Please accept our thanks for your most kind reception.'

'Not at all,' said the Duke. He clambered to his feet beside the young lady, averting his gaze from her averted face. At the door to the Ritterstube, where Martin Grünenfelder waited to show our guests to their quarters, the future Duchess regathered herself. 'He was not so wise as you think,' she said. 'I met him only twice but my father and my uncles served him.'

'Away,' said the chaperone.

Elisabetta allowed herself to be spun towards the door; she spoke over her shoulder. 'He was not the man you imagine.'

Then they were gone. The nobility of Felsengrunde clenched their stomachs and withdrew, tapestries curling about their breeze. I was left with the aroused and bewildered Duke.

'What do you think she meant, Tommaso?'

'A woman's blather, my lord. What can it ever mean but noise?'

'Mind your tongue – that's my wife you're insulting.'

'I apologise, your Grace.'

Albrecht Rudolphus stared admiringly at the Ritterstube door, as though her beauty had left a ghostly outline lingering there. 'Damn me, though, she is lovely.' Elisabetta Zbyněk had been my discovery; yet I felt a pang of envy and had to swallow my cavils about her overbite or the pallor of her skin. 'What's more,' marvelled the Duke, 'she's to be mine.' I wanted to pinch the unworthy dreamer. Instead I smiled and sniffed my hand.

'I am delighted to have served you, my lord.'

The wedding was a resounding success, although the Duke lamented the absence of automaton children treading on his bride's train and my own failure to create (in three whole months!) a triumphal arch of a hundred prints for him to pass through on his way to the chapel. The Order of St Bartholomew grinned throughout the service, as did representatives of the commonage – wool tradesmen and village elders, farmers and timber merchants – who forgot their mundane grievances and, proud to have been invited, cast about for a neighbour's recognition. The Duke looked splendid in his father's mantle, with his head served up on a Spanish ruff and his boots buffed to gleaming. Elisabetta paid him no glancing compliment. She fixed her gaze on the altar's crucifix and seemed to ignore her husband, until he battered her finger with the wedding ring. No sighs of encouragement came from her family, represented on this occasion by a tearless mother and a mashing, toothless uncle. Elisabetta's father was at Karlstein Castle attending to the Archduke Ferdinand; his absence might have caused offence had it not been for the dowry.

'Tommaso – you are a *magician*.'

It appeared, from the objects on display, that Bedřich Zbyněk had profited from an early pruning of Rudolf's collection. Or perhaps the Archduke had wanted to reward him with some baubles found lying around the disordered galleries? My spirit shook Meyrink's ghostly hand as the Duke admired a sea-turtle clock. He moved on feverishly to three drinking vessels with caryatid stems, a set of knives and forks in a case made by the Haban Anabaptists of Hungary and, most enchantingly for Albrecht Rudolphus, two cameos of his namesake from the Prague workshop of Ottavio Miseroni (who trod on my toes one evening on Bridge Street). Both cameos, cunningly fashioned in agates and jasper with onyx and silver gilt, depicted Rudolf in his maturity, crowned with laurels like a Roman imperator. The Duke pressed the objects to his breast, his lips melting with emotion as he thanked his Bohemian bride. So my choice had proved doubly judicious. It promised not only good sport in the bedchamber – gratifying with its fruit the Order of St Bartholomew – but also contributed to the Duke's Library and the myths that sustained it. An ecstasy of self-approval carried me, like flotsam in a mill stream, through the stilted speeches and forced carousing of the wedding feast; it filled my belly with sweetmeats and burning wines and sent me elated, long after the newlyweds had retired to their pleasure, to my own bed in the southern tower. There were cries of mirth in the Great Courtyard. I lay in my bed, watching the heave of the ceiling and trying to breathe the succubus of drink off my chest.

I awoke with a jolt. My stump of a candle was almost consumed. I listened, tensed on my elbows, for another sound at my door. Had I imagined it? Or was it an emanation from my dreams of brocade and edible dowries, where Albrecht Rudolphus had stood, naked and keen membered, holding my hand at the marital bedside? In the poised stillness I heard one of my assistants gasp in his sleep, knocking the partition with his elbow as he turned over the page of his dream.

Reassured, I grunted on to my side and hooked the blanket behind my ear.

Somebody knocked at my door. I bolted across the cold suction of the floor and, without my usual precautions, lifted the latch.

I was pushed backwards, my nose nipped by a button on a familiar waistcoat. The Duke leaned hard to shut the door, as though he were pursued by tigers. 'Uh – my lord, what's— ?'

'*Shh.*' The Duke's face was glazed with sweat; an unfamiliar blush streaked his cheeks. 'Can your boys hear us?'

I took up my guttering candle and led him into the workshop. The Duke breathed heavily through his mouth, like a dim-witted child, as he peered into the shimmering shadows. Beneath a tent of drying canvas, I sought an outward semblance of calm. 'Is everything well, my lord?'

'Does it *look* that way to you?'

For a terrible, drunken instant, I searched the Duke's hands for signs of blood. 'How . . . how fares my lady?'

'Sleeping soundly.' The Duke looked along his shoulder at the somnolent workshop, seeing the sheen of candlelight on a fake Dürer, catching the lustreless eyes of a charcoal Madonna. He appeared to seek his bearings, like a sleepwalker coming to his senses in an unfamiliar room. 'She was tired, Tommaso. My lady was very tired after the celebrations.'

'Which passed off excellently. Would your Grace care for a little refreshment?' I indicated a flagon of wine – filmed no doubt with dust and insects – left to sour on the workshop surface.

'And go back to my wife with the stink on my breath? No *thank* you.' The Duke noticed his trembling hands. 'Perhaps just a glass, then.' He drank thirstily, making rude hawking noises. A trickle of crimson stained his paltry beard. 'I couldn't do it, Tommaso. She was like a saint readied for martyrdom.'

'Did she . . . refuse you?'

'Quite the contrary – I *think*. I had been looking at those drawings you gave me. When I came into our chamber she pulled back the bedclothes. Then she lifted her nightdress . . . just above her hips.' The Duke grimaced, a dismaying sight to behold. 'And she just lay there, Tommaso. Cruciform, with her knees pressed together. She would have been . . . my God, she *would* be obedient to my will.'

'But your will . . . ?'

'It—'

'Wilted?'

'Like a flower.'

Now both of us were grimacing. A virgin untouchable in her purity, a puppet to be manipulated by its master, offering neither resistance nor encouragement: what man could press on with his marital duty in such circumstances? Tommaso Grilli was powerless to assist his patron in this intimate dilemma. Over several more fortifying glasses of Rhenish,

I described how the Soul's intimacy must write itself in the Body's book. 'Desire may follow affection over time,' I said. 'It is the auxiliary of tenderness.' Albrecht Rudolphus quickened from desolation to anger, from anger to sullen determination. He left after an hour of my amorist's counsel (I that have never been loved) and pledged to go to it.

My spies reported to my workshop at dawn. They informed me that the Duke had not returned to his bride. Instead, a clumsy bird, he had built himself a nest of cushions before the Ritterstube's embering fire.

Later in the day, I found my patron full of good cheer. I was careful to believe his lies, until by force of persuasion he convinced himself of his own prowess. (It is difficult for a man, even one of low cunning, to live for years in the presence of a dissembler without acquiring some of his style.) So the marital linen was exposed at the window, displaying three petals the colour of rust. At supper, which the newlyweds enjoyed in the company of courtiers and guests, I could not help noticing the bandage on the Duke's left index finger.

In public the couple grew fond. Sentimental glances pursued them as, hand in hand, they socialised with the castle. Moritz von Winkelbach impressed himself upon his mistress as a wise and loyal counsellor; she smiled on his piety, on the devotional squareness of his jaw and the potency of his swagger. It was he, in his capacity as Lord Chamberlain, who suggested a ducal progress through Felsengrunde.

'New hope has come to the Duchy, madam, and new vigour. You stir our hearts. Let the people offer their blessings to your union.'

Albrecht Rudolphus seemed less than enthralled by the proposal; it was Elisabetta, the duteous consort, who by her insistence brought it to fruition.

Thus, in the summer of 1619, while I busied myself in the Arcana Imperia, the Duke and Duchess set out on their travels. Advance guards were necessary in every village to exhort the inhabitants in their displays of gratitude. Elisabetta reaped her acclaim as the embodiment of a people's hopes; she held her tight-lipped smile against the reeking cries of peasants as they flung their dirty caps into the air. Only once did her even temper falter, when, in the Wintertal Valley, she learned of a Calvinist preacher who was permitted to spread his poisons unchallenged.

'This indolent government,' she reportedly declared, 'must be shaken from its slumber, before all our souls are blackened.'

As for me, relieved of sycophantic duties, I resolved to emulate my patron by taking a wife. An actual marriage, complete with public ceremony and prayers, would of course have exposed me to intolerable ridicule. Instead I had to satisfy myself with a clandestine affair, unsanctified by holy rite, in the manner of Europe's landless thousands. I considered taking one of the courtesans left yawning with redundancy in Felsengrunde town; but these had been compelled by extremity to offer their services to the townsfolk. I was a man of power now, no longer satisfied to pick up the scraps of other men's lusts; so I opted for a peasant girl, Magdalena, whom poverty had driven to the castle in pursuit of employment.

There has been no Madonna in my life, at least until now, too late in the day. Whores, on the other hand, have occurred in various forms, literal and figurative, in bountiful supply. Some of these have behaved (it must be said) like their antithesis; yet I cannot claim to have encountered purity, nor sipped its unpolluted waters. In Magdalena I came closest to my ideal – but came there only by theft. Every man is familiar with his odours and secretions: being his own, they cause him no repulsion, so he cannot imagine himself feeling alien or corruptive to a woman. If only I could have impressed upon my darling that she was adored by a charming fellow! What an honour, to be known by one whom I held in great esteem! Magdalena cupped her shame with her fingers but I nuzzled them away. I broke down her resistance with gold coins. I devoured her wounded mouth. Even after many months, when she was familiar with the tricks of love, Magdalena lacked the art to hide her displeasure at my embraces. Yet I treated her well, giving her a room of her very own above the servants' quarters in the East Wing. Magdalena never expressed any gratitude for the maid who washed her clothes and refreshed her linen and kept her abreast of back-stairs gossip. My darling was pampered like a sultan's cat (if sultans keep cats) with no obligation to struggle, like most beings on Earth, for her survival. What then gave her the temerity to flaunt her unhappiness? Not once did I strike her, as most husbands will strike their wives when they turn shrewish; nor did I humiliate her with perverse practices. Most nights all that I asked of Magdalena was a gesture of tenderness: her hand resting on my chest, a breast that withstood the cold kisses of my adoring ear, or the veiling of my hideous features with her lustrous hair. It took me weeks of wrangling, of arm-twisting and bribery (the lot washed down with mutual tears), before she would consent to my holding her fingers as she slept. For three nights I could sense her waking beside me, rigid with disgust at my clammy grip, until I released her from a contracted intimacy that had brought us only sleeplessness. I remember those bleary hours before dawn when, my brain scoured with lassitude and remorse, I hurried myself in contemplation of her turned rump, or faded in and out of dreams that brought Magdalena and her predecessors to my chamber, their paps grotesquely engorged and their faces as void as Brenner's automata.

Horror dissipated, dissolving like dew as the sun rose, so that by the time of Magdalena's waking I had forgotten my remorseful resolutions and our misery continued.

Shall I pretend that the sanctified marriage of Albrecht Rudolphus was more felicitous than my illegitimate own? Upon their return from the tour of Felsengrunde, a smiling chasm had opened up between husband and wife. The Duke offered a steadying hand to the Duchess as she descended from their carriage. Extending a token finger, she barely touched her husband's skin. Elisabetta's face had acquired shadows, almost bruises, of sorrow. In repose it was desolate, a mask whence all mirth had fled. She brightened only at the compliments of her attentive Lord Chamberlain.

'I am very glad to see you well,' I cried after the couple as they breasted the Castle's welcome. Elisabetta pressed tighter against her husband, the better to freeze me out. Was I not the dauber responsible for having duped her with his portrait?

'They seem fond enough to me,' said Adolph Brenner.

'Why, so they *seem*,' I replied. Such a front would have to be maintained in public; yet in private, as my informants noted, few words were bandied between them. The Duke took refuge in his Library, whence wife and counsellors were excluded; Elisabetta withdrew to the Duchess's Apartments, where she conversed in Spanish with her companions, received fawning tributes from Moritz von Winkelbach and turned for solace to her Jesuit confessor.

The propitious year shivered into its successor. Like water beneath a mantle of ice, news trickled through to Felsengrunde of rebellion in Prague, of a newly installed Protestant king and his electors' triumph over imperial rule. Bedřich Zbyněk had fled with his family to Vienna, where they would wait patiently for soldiers of the True Church to restore their authority. As soon as the mountain passes had thawed, Elisabetta demanded leave to visit her father. Albrecht Rudolphus seemed quite happy to relinquish his wife; yet form and the patent frowning of the Lord Chamberlain compelled him to go with her.

'The Duke will be glad of the chance to speak with his father-in-law,' I told myself, while ostensibly addressing Adolph Brenner. 'The gentleman served Rudolf, after all.'

'Is that a good thing? For us, I mean?'

My silence was eloquent. Brenner sighed and stretched himself, wincing as the little crystals crunched in his back. I watched his boy Kaspar, now become a man, hug his knees on the pallet bed in the corner of the room. How sullen he had grown, his timidity curdled into surly resentment. With his master I discussed the grim prospects of war.

'The newly minted king cannot prosper,' said Brenner. 'And the Protestant Estates will pay in precious currency for their crimes. They tried to kill the Emperor's men when they tossed them out of the chancery.'

(Had it been, I wondered, the same window from which I had made my own, scarcely more volitional, defenestration eighteen years earlier?) 'Surely,' I said, 'whatever follows cannot hurt us in Felsengrunde? We are like an island fixed in rough seas.'

Brenner sucked in air through his teeth. '*Tua res agitor, patries cum proximus ardet*,' he said. The automaton on the bench echoed my blank stare. Behind me, plain-speaking Kaspar tutted.

'You will have to translate,' I said.

Brenner lowered his voice to a whisper. He spoke in Italian. 'All are threatened when a neighbour's house is on fire.'

Good Adolfo: how slenderly I knew him. For years I had enjoyed his company without seeking the pith of him, without plumbing the depths of his quiddity. Perhaps it was the comical gleam of his glabrous head, or the finicky effeminate gestures with which he pinched at the world, which endeared him to me as a harmless clown? He was pompous, certainly, a self-regarding taster of his own eloquence. Yet now my curiosity flamed, lit by a heavenly spark – a lightning glimpse of another man's mystery. Who *was* Adolph Brenner? Where was he heading? And why should not this inventor know more than Tommaso Grilli about the capricious turns of Fortune? Our actions breed consequences, he once asserted, which spread beneath our toes like the white veins of a fungus and sprout a sudden mushroom for us to trip upon. I had laughed at the metaphor; and yet, would that I had sought the ballard's counsel. He might have advised against marrying Albrecht Rudolphus to an emissary from my past.

Immediately upon his return from Vienna, the Duke summoned me to his study.

'You lied to me,' he said.

The very atomies of the air seemed to freeze in their course. I swallowed a sharp knot in my throat. '*Lied*, your Grace?'

'Yes, lied. Fabricated. Deceived. Even now you play the innocent.'

He had found me out. All precautions taken before my meeting with Meyrink, my cultivation of pseudonyms, had availed me nothing. Bedřich Zbyněk, struck by my name as it flitted through the Duke's prattle, had revealed to him my Bohemian disgrace. ('Cricket, you say? Oh – Grill*ee*. I remember a thief of that name. Imprisoned in Dalibor. Yes, and here's the strangest thing. *He* was a dwarf as well.') I wiped my lips with my sleeve. Would banishment suffice? Or humiliation, canted over in specially tailored stocks on Weidmanner Platz?

'Please, my lord, I beg you. Tell me in what way I have offended.'

'My father-in-law served the Emperor Rudolf.'

'Yes.'

'Whose praises you sang. In whose emulation I have lived.'

'So you have, my lord.'

'*He was not the man you imagine*. Do you remember those words? And who uttered them? My wife, Tommaso. Before all the court, laughing at my conceit. The late Emperor was not the man you said. He was weak, impressionable, surrounded by thieves . . .'

'*Thieves?*'

'Bedřich Zbyněk told me about his mad fits. How he lost his dominions, lending his ears to the calumny of cheats and frauds. Men like Lang . . . Langen . . .'

'I've never heard the name!'

On this dangerous lie the Duke did not pounce. 'He was corrupted. He failed to marry and produce an heir. God damn it, why did you keep these things from me?'

'About . . . Rudolf? Why did I not tell you . . . ?'

'The *truth*.'

'. . . about the Emperor Rudolf?'

Oh, jubilation, sweetest of nectars, coursing through me! This disillusionment I could redeem, so long as my shame remained hidden. 'My lord, the Emperor's decline, of which it grieves me to learn, must have begun *after my time*. There was no hint of his melancholy while I was in Prague. I have always spoken the truth, according to my lights.'

The Duke chewed his underlip. 'You made me want to be like him.'

'And rightly so, my lord. As a *patron*. In that regard, his collections remain when Rudolf is rotten.'

'But as a ruler, Tommaso—?'

'As a ruler you emulate his triumphs while avoiding his disasters.'

14

Jonathan Knott

A bubble of doubt had formed between the Duke and his dwarf which I would need all of my art to smooth away. He no longer trusted my word as before and seemed to watch me as though at any moment I might reveal myself with a blush or fluttering eyelash. Suspicion became the unspoken watchword of the castle. My spies reported furious rows (a rare occasion for verbal exchange) between the ducal couple. Moritz von Winkelbach was too attentive, the Duke complained. Did Elisabetta mean to mock him, flirting with the Lord Chamberlain and flaunting to the world the emptiness of her womb? The Duchess in response to these accusations was much given to prayer. She called on God to teach her forbearance; she prayed for her husband to fulfil his duty. As a last resort she took to condemning his solitary and unnatural vices: these were responsible for his childlessness, not her receptive and dutiful body.

Albrecht Rudolphus stormed across the courtyard (shedding a shoe and hobbling back to retrieve it on green-stockinged toes) and confronted my colleague Brenner in his workshop.

'Where are those damned automata? I've been waiting ten years to receive them! Nothing but clockwork to occupy your days, when I have a *dukedom* to govern.'

Stammering Brenner wrung his cap. 'A long jest . . . a long gestation, my lord. Technical demands. Never before attempted.' Later, as though to assuage the sting of his scolding, the inventor extended it to his inferior.

'What *use* are you to me, Kaspar? I'm trying to make

these children live and you break them. You spill soup into their working parts – you drop them from your full height. Are you trying to ruin me?

Poor Adolph: his troubles ran deeper than the Duke could have imagined. It seemed that his young Negro, whom I had watched grow into ungracious manhood and with whom, finding myself troubled by a flame in his eyes, I had exchanged barely a word in all these years, had sprung from his coiled rebellion and, stretching to the apex of a nameless anger, attempted to seduce one of Elisabetta's maids. Adolph Brenner was informed of this misfortune by the *Hofdame* Maria and subsequently, with gentler vehemence, by Martin Grünenfelder. Kaspar was forbidden to visit the innocent child. 'The Duchess,' Grünenfelder explained, 'would be loath to dismiss one whose services she so values.'

'But what power have I over the boy?' Brenner swept the perspiration from his brow. 'What influence can I bring to bear?'

'Warn him of the dangers,' I said, 'if you will not thrash him.'

'Thrash Kaspar?'

'If it's a tumble he needs we can point him to some drabs in town. But Elisabetta's maid? It places all of us in danger. And to produce what – a bastard mulatto?'

Adolph Brenner tugged at the wraith of hair above his head. 'I cannot scold him for that,' he said.

'If the Duchess should complain to the Duke, when he himself is incapable of the act . . .'

Brenner tried to change the subject. 'At least my commission is almost fulfilled.'

'Can they move yet?'

Brenner grimaced at the infinite pains a creator must take over his inventions. 'Very nearly,' he said. 'But their faces . . .'

'. . . lack something . . .'

'Your father was a sculptor, was he not?'

I understood the appeal in Brenner's eyes. 'I'm a painter, my friend, not a sculptor.'

'Wax features would be best, of course. But painted ones will do.'

So we agreed: though we could not control the living, at least the childless Duke would have his toys to dandle. Parting at the threshold, we heard the leaden footsteps of Brenner's assistant on the stairs. 'You *must* satisfy Grünenfelder,' I whispered.

'I cannot fight the dictates of Kaspar's heart.'

'Damn his heart, man. Let it break, if he wishes, in the confines of his own chest. As for tupping, he must obey his master.'

'No, Tommaso.' Brenner sadly shook his head. 'It would be rank hypocrisy: to warn a bastard against the sin of bastard-making.'

While the inventor struggled with his servant and his clockwork children yawned through their bellies – the copper stars and springs of their viscera flourishing like rank summer weeds – I accepted stolen goods to ease the Duke's impatience. One day in early June 1620 (a month before a mob of zealous Christians met in the streets of Nuremberg with the shared purpose of dashing out the brains of my dear friend Ludolf Bresdin), on a fine afternoon beneath a limpid and swallow-scything sky, while the Wiedeland was lush with new life and every detail of pine and rock on Berg Mössingen was as clear to the eye as a stone magnified in a globe of water, I received a Moravian salesman in my tower and invited him, with a lordly wave, to lay out his wares before me. The salesman kissed his wrists and set out his trinkets on a Persian rug. 'These are *glossopetrae*. Very rare.

From Malta. Look, look, look.' I inspected a ten-inch lump of sandstone in which were lodged four arrow-shaped teeth. The Moravian gently bit the tip of his tongue; I could sense his eyes measuring my reaction. 'Some say that lightning strikes the rocks and these are the teeth of the sky. Others that dragons left them, or that St Paul fought the serpents of Malta and then hid them in the rock.'

'Serpents' teeth.'

'Or lightning tongue. *Glossopetrae* are tongue stones.'

I paid almost full price for this curiosity and several lesser items. The Moravian salesman sucked his fingers, as though he had dipped them in gravy, and hurried the soldiers who escorted him from the castle. The cause of his haste was revealed when, two days later, a sunburned rider clattered into the courtyard and begged to know whether anyone had seen a thief fitting the Moravian's description. I was quick to offer the man some meat and drink and to send him in the wrong direction – refreshed in body though frustrated in his mission – towards the Rapids Pass and Switzerland. It was shameful of me, I know, to commiserate with him for his wealthy patron's loss while all the time those stolen objects were hidden in my bedclothes. What can I say in my defence, save that Needs Must? Albrecht Rudolphus received with pleasure the petrified teeth and – in a temporary fog of acquisitive joy – endorsed my suggestion of a new commission.

'A portrait, your Grace. In the manner of my first and best tutor.'

'Bonconvento?'

'Arcimboldo. He of the composite head, of beasts and fishes and firebrands that combine to resemble a man.'

I had for several years been rolling the dough of a conceit between my fingers. It would be something so ingenious and strange that only the Comus Palatinus himself – or a respectful forger and former pupil – could have hoped to execute it. The painting would no more be a mirror of surface reality than the portrait of the Emperor had been when Arcimboldo transformed him into the Etruscan god of harvests. For two days I could not keep from smiling at my own cleverness, until my face duped my spirit and I was suffused with a kind of happiness.

Albrecht Rudolphus came to my workshop at the appointed hour. Recalling the conditions in which my long-ago tutor had painted, I seated him in my candlelit studio. The air quaked with the heat of so many flames, which attracted and then consumed the light-lorn moths. I placed myself at a preset angle to my subject and draped a grey silk curtain across his shoulder, exposing in the open window the obscurity of the night-drowned valley.

'Should I look at you?' enquired the Duke.

'Away, please, as I demonstrated.' Never again would I have licence to study so closely the features of my employer. I needed less the particulars – that patent constellation of warts and blemishes – than the gist of a likeness, a graspable impression of Albrecht Rudolphus. Within an hour I had completed my sketches and could respectfully dismiss the sitter.

The Duke shrugged off his curtain-cape. 'And when should I return?'

'No need, your Grace.'

'What – have you finished already?'

'Only with my need of you. Your lordship has been most still and patient.' I could address the Duke in this manner only in the fiefdom of my workshop. He departed without protest, stifling his desire to peek at my drawings. I listened to his heavy feet punishing the wooden steps of the passageway that newly linked my tower to his study. As soon as he was gone, I returned to my studio and barked instructions at my bleary-eyed assistants.

'Bestir yourselves, boys! There's more to life than bursting pimples.'

Work began on the stretching out and grounding of a canvas; paints were mixed to pre-determined colours. I planned to fuse my studies of the Duke's face with my elaborate conceit. I arranged twenty or so books of diverse sizes – some of white calfskin with gold filigree engraving, others with beige or red leather bindings – into a discernible shape on a table, and so began to trace the outline of a pyramidal torso. As night deepened, I felt as though I stood alone, the unique engendering being in a world of sleepers. Across the blent and huddled rooftops of Felsengrunde town a profound hush had settled, troubled only occasionally by the coughing of a dog or the barbed ecstasy of copulating foxes. My buzzing ears were attuned to every rasp of my hand on canvas – to the muted pealing of a water glass when I struck it with my bleeding brush, whose stiff bristles found their echo-image in the short hairs that stood up on the back of my neck. The creative urge consumed me, rapture descending, in ripples, my spine from nape to lumber and my heart beating with such ardour that it began to hurt. Years later I would experience the same jolt of primary power when, upon the barren crest of a mountainside, a bolt of lightning grounded itself inches from my feet. That black night, working late in my tower, I felt talent welling up inside me. Surely, I reasoned with my soul, though this painting be a forgery in the strict sense of imposture, yet shall the end product prove of equal quality – and so, by rights, of *value* – to an original?

Ah, yes. 'Forgery'. Nine years after that nocturnal rapture, sitting on this Tuscan hill with blunted fingers writing, I see things otherwise. Perhaps something had failed in my creative faculties long before this final commission? Capable as I saw it of imitating the strokes and mannerisms of others, I had allowed whatever faculties might have helped me to evolve a style of my own to atrophy. My attempts to paint independently of formal models – as evidenced, long ago, by my portraits of the Gonsalvus family – resulted in flatness, mere parodies of physical matter unsparked by imagination. 'Better to imitate an established artist than to labour obscurely in one's own manner.' For a few more years I would manage to suppress all doubts about the worth of my endeavours, convinced that the Library of Arts was ample monument to my Pickpocket Muse.

Within a fortnight, I had only the features of the 'Librarian' to complete. Four brown leather volumes were used to represent the head, with a black ribbon undulating for eyebrows and two further ribbons, fortuitously catching an improvised light, doing service as the monster's eyes. A salmon-pink ribbon tied to the book of his cheek became the Librarian's left ear, while two small copies of Euclid represented plump lips emerging from a beard (flatteringly made fuller than the subject's own) of sable-tail dusters. An eighth book served as a long proboscis jutting on a diagonal from the face. It was impossible within such constraints to convey the human blemishes of the Duke, though I did brush in, as an afterthought, a red-buttoned clasp to suggest the wart that nestled alongside his nose. Finally I had only to solve the problem of hair. The greasy straw which seemed, for shame, so eager to escape the Duke's speckled scalp could find no counterpart in my caprice. My solution was to paint an open book (a ledger pilfered from the Treasury on account of its silk-beaded markers) resting on the impassive head. This ledger rounded off the stolid construction of the painting, rather as a dome or cupola solidifies the columns that support it. Its wafered pages lent a bird's plumage to the effigy – a creamy crest which yet suggested the headgear of a scholar.

In a mood of jubilation I sent word to Albrecht Rudolphus that his painting, my master forgery, awaited his approval. The Duke in his enthusiasm swallowed three steps at a stride. He rested, panting for air, on the workshop landing, then greeted each of my assistants by name, to their open astonishment. We approached the alcove, honeyed with sunshine, where the painting stood. My assistants scrabbled to their places; on my nod they pulled back the grey curtain from the canvas where it was immortalised. Albrecht Rudolphus shouted 'Bravo!' and, having shed his kid gloves, beat them together like a seal's flippers. 'Wonderful,' he exclaimed. 'A work of genius.'

I seemed to flutter in Mercurial shoes. 'I'm honoured, my lord.'

'Honoured? You should be *ennobled*.'

'Oh, your Grace.'

'It's a marvellous creation.'

'You enjoy the likeness?'

'Likeness?'

'Only Arcimboldo could have managed a transformation like it – if you will permit me the boast.'

'What likeness?'

The Duke, in his instant admiration of the painting, had forgotten the hour spent sitting for his portrait. Now the delight leaked with the blood from his cheeks. An invisible hand smoothed all expression from his face. He became, for a pendulous instant, a man of clay. 'This is supposed to be *me*?'

'Why, yes.'

'Is it some kind of jest?'

'Ah – in a sense, your Grace. It alludes to the breadth of your learning.'

'This dead thing? It doesn't even look like a man. And what's that supposed to be?'

'A wart. A *clasp*.'

The Duke glanced across his shoulder. Accustomed to a courtier's proximity, he needed someone to endorse his opinion. 'I'm bereft of words,' he said. 'So much skill and so maliciously applied. It seems deceiving me about my namesake was not comedy enough for you. Well, I will not stand for this.'

Albrecht Rudolphus turned heavily about. I gasped after him, hopping from toe to toe as he bolted down the stairs. 'What have I done to offend you, my lord?'

The Duke sank into the penumbral well of the stairs. 'I leave you to mull over the question. When you've found an answer – if indeed you need to search – you may find me in my study. And bring your apology with you.' The door between our worlds (as substantial a divide as existed between my patron's mind and mine) swung open and then closed.

My assistants had fled by the time I returned to the studio. For an hour, perhaps two, I sat in a daze of bewilderment. At some point I was alerted to a faint scrabbling, like the twitching of a mouse, which seemed to come from my assistants' chamber. They were hiding there and listening, expecting a cry of rage from their diminutive master. I did not stir or scold them. I sat forward and began to understand. Deprived of sunlight, the painting had turned sombre, ashen veiled. The longer I saw it the more I felt, with a low visceral pang of despair, that I had betrayed the Law of Specific Detail. This *seemed* a brilliant forgery in Arcimboldo's manner; yet the Duke himself had disappeared from the artful confection. Vertumnus the Etruscan god had gleamed in the Master's studio, fearfully alive, as though at any moment he might saunter into the breathing world.

Something of humanity had survived, also, in that original painting – something of the Emperor. In my forgery no such spark of life existed. This was a grim portrait, the likeness of an automaton, an emissary from the Underworld of Dead Objects. No wonder Albrecht Rudolphus had hated it with such passion. The Librarian was a sterile being. Its books clasped shut, its eyes unseeing, it could breed *nothing*.

Damn him, I thought. Damn his ignorance. Damn his plum-juice misted eyes, which could see nothing through the rheum of his self-obsession. 'What about a menagerie?' said Adolph Brenner suddenly. He had abandoned his nervous pacing and was leaning now, with a solicitous frown, on the back of my low chair.

'A what?'

'Buy him some animals. At least you won't be to blame if he doesn't like the shape of them.'

'That's a stupid idea,' I said.

Within a week I had drawn up my plans. Never mind its rumours of discord: the Empire was surely awash with growling, fluttering and scaly beasts, real live naturalia to complement the Duke's present ossuary. (Albrecht Rudolphus spent too much time in the hush and stare of inanimate objects.) Taking the menagerie in the Royal Gardens at Prague for a model, I had soon convinced my sceptical patron to give me leave to depart, with a suitable retinue of soldiers, porters and assistants and whatever moneys I could require to make my purchases.

It was of course folly to leave. Powers to the north were bristling with arms; unlikely alliances were being hatched to defend the Protestant King in Bohemia or restore the authority of the Papist Emperor. Though war's kindling had been sparked (and great burning was bound to follow as men plied the bellows of True Religion), I left Felsengrunde in haste, anxious to escape for a few weeks at least the poisonous atmosphere of the Castle.

No sooner had our clattering party entered the shining ambit of the Obersee than I felt my soul spread its cormorant wings. I breathed freely, my chest rid of its habitual congestion. Travelling had always lightened my spirits (especially when it was funded by someone else) and I engaged my underlings in frivolous conversation. If they doubted my leadership, they kept their doubts to themselves; for I made up our itinerary day by day, hoping to catch something as we drifted along. None of my contacts in the wider world could serve my purpose. I knew not what had become of Jaroslav Meyrink since the disasters in Prague; Ludolf Bresdin was soon to perish in Nuremberg while endeavouring to close his business there, leaving his family to expect his homecoming eternally; only Georg Spengler in Dresden would survive to bind my letters and the remarkable – if somewhat expurgated – biography they contained; but Spengler could not help me now.

I have no desire to bore you with my peregrinations, nor to repeat the countless words exchanged with innkeepers (pressing their fingers into the table and peering down at my panache) to learn the whereabouts of possible salesmen. Foolishly I wandered inland, when the ports of Italy (no, no, I could not venture there) or Holland would have teemed with seasick animals.

It was a last, flagrant gift from Dame Fortune that placed within my grasp an entire menagerie.

Karl von Langer, the 9th Count of Ulm and a most dissolute nobleman, had in the pursuit of alchemical returns incurred a most lamentable collection of debts. I learned of his urgent need for gold from an indiscreet drunkard, a footman to the Count recently dismissed for reasons of economy, who railed and roared himself sick in a Donauwörth tavern.

Scarcely crediting my luck (a talent I was to retain long after my art had abandoned me) and racked with anxiety lest we arrive too late, I kicked my porters where they sprawled in the grass and harried them towards the Count's estate.

One of von Langer's creditors, a corpulent man with a bearskin collar and great pink hams for hands, met us at the gate. He attended, with his bloodshot eyes trained on my lips, to my enquiries, and then brought me to a set of fenced enclosures in a dense forest of firs. The deaf giant scooped a rock from some quivering grasses and brought it to my nose. The rock sprouted a wrinkled head.

'Jesus – what's that?'

'A doordus.'

'Am I buying it?'

'The doordus is free. All the rest . . .' His unoccupied hand opened and clenched six times. When it had finished I lost my own hand to its clammy maw.

Thus I came to acquire two Brazilian tortoises, four ring-necked parakeets from Asia Minor, two peacocks a-courting, one dejected hoopoe and a brown bear with a threadbare coat which, though reputedly captured in the wilds of the Bavarian forest, was given to dancing whenever anyone struck a drum. My assistants flapped and fell, swallowing sawdust and turds, in their pursuit of the peacocks; fingers and thumbs were savaged by the shrieking parakeets; the bear growled and swatted the chain about its neck, refusing with all the ballast of its rump to be moved from its familiar squalor until hunger and the prospect of some salted pork lured it into a cage. As evening settled in the firs, there was much panting and cussing and nursing of wounds. The resentful glances of my subordinates landed on my cheeks without inflicting any hurt. I was exceedingly pleased with myself – for I had secured, from the creditors of the mad Count of Ulm, a stranger beast than I could have dared hope for.

It was a male dodo, the survivor of a pair shipped to Genoa by Dutch tradesmen. I was delighted by the flightless brute, and reinforced its cage with intermittent bars of iron lest it try to pluck its way to freedom using its savage beak. 'It's vicious,' I heard my assistants whispering. 'I reckon it could kill a fox.'

'Or a baby.'

'If it *wanted* to.'

The usefulness of the dodo (or dodar, as some men call it) to entertain even the most sullen individual with its peculiarities was confirmed that evening as we rested around our campfire. The dodo – a sort of giant pigeon with a headache – screeched like a crow and plucked at the bars with a tongue the colour of a blood clot. One of the young porters opened the lid of the cage and dropped a field mouse inside. 'He'll eat it,' said his colleague. 'A pfennig he won't.' 'Done.' Too frightened to squeal, the mouse took shelter, unnoticed by the dodo, beneath its rump. The dodo plucked at its breast with a grooming beak; it flapped its useless wings and blinked. It sat on the field mouse. 'Whoa!' marvelled the porters. The dodo, equally startled, stood up and peered between its legs, like a man inspecting his stool. Scrabbling to see better in a confined space, it plunged its rear talon into the mouse's belly. 'There! What did I tell you!' The dodo managed to turn. It sniffed at the mouse, from whose belly intestines peeped like a fairy's labia. 'It was an accident,' said the second porter. The dodo cocked its head speculatively – then, with a snap of the neck, caught the mouse in its beak. There was a high-pitched squeal. The first boy held out his hand to receive his payment. But the dodo did not eat the mouse: it dropped the furry pulp on the ground and seemed immediately to forget the encounter.

Observing the piteous issue of this experiment, and fearing that I might discover, one morning on our road, a parakeet choked with blood sausage or the hoopoe savaged by a ferret, I gave orders that none but I should touch the collection. Chastened, the expedition made good progress. The men trudged beside the laden cart, while I shared a donkey with our travelling bags. At daybreak and sundown the aged bear would sit on its haunches, like a forlorn dunce in a schoolroom, and watch me lumbering from cage to cage with the rations of food and water recommended to me, for the health of his darlings, by a tearful servant to the Count of Ulm. I was convinced that, all being well, the delivery of these exotic gifts would restore the Duke's faith in my qualities, and that he would credit once again my expressions of solicitude for his happiness.

We reached the green ramparts of Felsengrunde on a day of unwonted heat. The climb into the dukedom, with our cart so weighted by its breathing cargo, was slow and laborious. The packhorses strained at the incline; the drivers nodded and perspired; the garrulous parakeets seemed swollen in number by the mercilessly echoing cliffs. Filthy children lined the road down from the Pass of Our Lady – rickety starvelings balancing on the gudgeon of their bellies. There was time enough for me to indulge my sentimental companions by allowing them to display the birds and the bear and the snapping tortoises to those hushed urchins. At last we ascended the familiar slope – with the cages clanging and moulting and the languid old bear farting in its prison – and arrived on the cultivated level to find the familiar walls of the castle washed and renewed by three months' absence.

Albrecht Rudolphus smiled to see me again. He was

dressed in his Order's gown with a doublet of linen embroidered in silk thread and bobbin lace, very gaudy and handsome. Alongside his burnished chain of office hung what looked like a ruby pendant, which proved on closer inspection (made by your narrator while the Duke cooed at a shrinking tortoise) to be a phial containing a port-coloured liquid. The Duke chuckled briefly at the antic parakeets, sought loudly my agreement that a brace of peacock was essential to a nobleman's demesne, and commandeered some meat from the kitchens. With a pair of fire tongs manipulated at arm's length, he wedged a leg of pork between the bars of the bear's cage.

'Never mind, never mind,' said Albrecht Rudolphus. 'He would not be unique in the world to lose his appetite when travelling. This hoopoe looks rather sad. It needs a hole to nestle in. I hope you've clipped its wings, or it shall escape, you know. Now then – good Lord!'

The dodo appeared already to be ailing. Not even its keeper in Ulm had known what fruit or cereal to feed it. The Dutch tradesmen had included, as part of their original fee, two sackfuls of some mysterious tropical berry dried on the salt sea air but none of these had grown, as they were reputed to do, after passing through the dodo's gut, and I had been compelled to take the bird without one sample of its favourite food. Explaining these matters to the Duke, I reflected on my responsibilities. Heretofore my only concern in life had been my own survival. Now living things were dependent on my kindness to exist.

'A splendid gift. Well done, Tommaso.' The Duke patted me on the head. Before I could acknowledge his thanks, he had begun to wade, as through invisible molasses, back to the Library of Arts.

'Your work,' I said to the servants and slouching porters,

'is not yet done. Henceforth the courtyard of the Banqueting Hall will house the Duke's menagerie.'

How I thrilled to sense my old authority returning! Tommaso Grilli had only to dream of something for its construction to commence. I felt – as others must feel the pang of nascent love – that auspicious moment when the nebulous idea begins to take shape in the material world, and what had been imagined in part becomes the common cause and motion of a dozen or three score hands, all labouring to realise the mental form.

Adolph Brenner emerged from his workshop and flapped in his tatty gown towards me. He asked me in what condition I had found his Grace.

'Exceeding well. You have not shown him your automata while I was away?'

'No, of course not.'

'But they *are* ready?'

'All they need to be set loose is a lick of paint. Where are you going?'

'You should be proud of your achievement, Adolfo. Walking children. A subtle feat of engineering.' I was fairly marching now, despite the ache of my donkey-stretched thighs, to find the Duke waiting for me – with a bottle of finest Rhenish perhaps – in the sanctum of his study. The inventor caught me by the collar.

'Listen, Tommaso. There's a new . . .'

'Spring in the Duke's step?'

'Your absence from Felsengrunde . . .'

'Has breathed new life into our friendship? You were quite right, my dear Adolfo.' In this deaf and pontifical manner I made my way towards the Library. There was nothing out of the ordinary about the entrance. One of the guards clapped briskly to attention. I smiled in lazy greeting and passed by.

Inside the Library, where formerly the statues and prints had been kept, were a gaping hole, piles of sand and bricks, and all the tools of a building site at rest.

'What . . . what's *this*?'

'That's what I was trying to tell you. The Duke is moving his apartments here. To the Library of Arts.'

'Without consulting me?'

'The Duchess and the nobles refuse even to inspect the work in progress. She considers it an impious waste of time and money. They are forming a faction around her, Tommaso. She has become the focus of all their discontent.'

'Who,' I said, 'who . . . ?'

'Winkelbach, of course. And then his brother and Grünenfelder, and all the staff in the Revenues Office and Chancery.'

'No, I mean – who designed these new developments?'

'*Ah.*' Adolph Brenner plunged his chin into the pink folds of his neck. I could scarcely credit the information of my eyes and ran to assure myself that my works were still in place in the Kammergalerie (where statuary was piled in a corner beneath the portrait of a snub-nosed ancestor) and in the print room, where all but my erotic works had been scattered by insensitive, dusty-palmed builders. How could the Duke have smiled and welcomed me in the full knowledge that I would find my achievements degraded and piled up, like silt left by a tidal flood, in cramped corners of the Library? My conceited swagger took on a martial briskness until I flung aside the tapestry in the Long Corridor and operated the latch to enter the secret study. Who, I would demand to know, *who* had instigated these monstrous renovations?

The Duke obscured my view of the bass-voiced gentleman whose discourse I had interrupted. 'Oh – Tommaso. You have seen the alterations that I commissioned?'

'Who is this guest of ours, my lord?'

'A *guest* no longer but resident. His name is Jonathan Knott. Skryer, inventor, alchemist.' With the timing of a fairground showman, the Duke stepped aside and revealed the man.

Jonathan Knott made enthralling use of his blue-green eyes. He was evidently most proud of them and of the long dark lashes that enhanced their sway. Perhaps it was the potent straight nose, whose fleshy tip edged lower than the dilating nostrils, or else the broad visionary forehead beneath a tousled head of brown hair, which gave him strength, a steady pulse of intellectual fire which threatened, at any moment, to blaze forth and send one tumbling like Icarus blasted by the sun. Contained inside a smock-coat of black silk with the faintest sliver of white lace at the neck and sleeves, he stood a massive figure, with bullish shoulders and a stonemason's hands. At over six feet tall, Jonathan Knott could look down even on Moritz von Winkelbach. He released me from his appraising stare and performed a deep reverence. Then he restored to his head a black skullcap of the sort that university doctors and stage quacks wear.

'Young man,' I acknowledged him with an ingratiating bow.

'Signor Grilli,' said Jonathan Knott, and the voice was indeed suited to the frame: bass, authoritative, with languid self-regarding vowels. 'I've heard many interesting things about you.'

'Would that I could say the same.' With shrill interrogative eyebrows, I looked to the Duke.

'Your achievement,' said Jonathan Knott, 'in creating this Library is worthy of the highest accolade. I learned of its existence from Herr Zbyněk – my lord's father-in-law, the royal huntsman.'

'Bedřich Zbyněk?'

'In Vienna we conversed once or twice, at the house of a local worthy where I was giving demonstrations . . .' (What an ugly accent – so full of tang and drawl. And I thought my *Tuscan* inflections sounded badly in German.) 'That's how I found my way here.'

'And what demonstrations would those have been?' The newcomer prodded his throat and flaunted his mutism. 'Knott – is that a Swedish name?'

'English. I was born in Kent.'

'Knott is a philosopher,' said the Duke.

'Ah, *philosophy* demonstrations.'

'A philosopher in the alchemical sense,' said Jonathan Knott. 'One who transmutes base metals into gold.'

I looked over my shoulder at the Duke; he was abruptly fascinated by the yellow cuticles of his fingernails. Shaken as I was by the unsolicited changes to my Library, I still had not associated them with this, as I hoped, transitory chancer. 'A *subtle* philosopher, then?'

'One who reads deeply, with a spirit of utmost humility, in the Book of Nature.'

'Made any gold yet?'

Jonathan Knott hoisted a modest shoulder; he could not suppress a smile at my belligerent tone, and I realised that I was the weakest participant in the scene.

'That phial about your neck, my lord . . . ?'

'A phial of red tincture, Tommaso. The philosopher's medicine.'

'Does it taste of berries?'

Jonathan Knott laughed – a deep-chested spasm, ripe with self-assurance.

'Well,' I said. I could feel the sweat beginning to trickle down my back into the cleft of my buttocks. 'I hope you have enjoyed your stay in Felsengrunde. My lord, perhaps you will care to join me in the courtyard of the Banqueting Hall? I propose to install the menagerie . . .'

'He's staying,' said the Duke.

Jonathan Knott, without a glance or by your leave to its owner, folded himself on the Duke's reading seat. 'I hope you will appreciate, Herr Grilli, my plans for the new apartments.'

'*Your* plans?'

'Herr Knott is an architect as well as an alchemist.'

'And a skryer when the spirits take me.' The Englishman smiled. 'The foreman should be on site to show you round. In the . . . pottery room, is it?'

'Sculpture.'

'Anyway, the Ritterstube now. Do run along and you might catch him. He knows to expect you, so he won't be alarmed.'

The Duke picked gently at the flyleaf of a book open on the desk. He must have felt my accusing eye-beams, for a pink cloud formed on the dough of his cheek. 'I am tired,' I said. 'It has been a very long journey.' I bowed and almost ran from the study, bruising every knuckle in my left hand in my haste to shut the panel. How, in three months, had this unimaginable thing happened? I vomited in the drains on the south side of the chapel – pretended to search for a lost trinket when the Lord Chamberlain paced moodily by – then staggered into Adolph Brenner's workshop.

'Tell me everything,' I said. 'I must know who I'm up against.'

'Then sit down and accept a glass of wine,' said Brenner. 'For you won't enjoy the experience.'

Unheralded on horseback and trailing two donkeys that bore his equipment, Jonathan Knott had entered Felsengrunde a mere fortnight after my departure. He had presented himself, with reports of commendations from Bedřich Zbyněk, to the noble lord our Duke.

Adolph Brenner had watched him bow and doff his scholarly cap.

'He came into the world – he said – on the twenty-eighth day of April 1583. He was most particular about the date for its astrological significance.' Born under the sign of the Watery Trigon, which signified a prosperous era for England and the German states, Knott was a herald of glorious change. From the earliest age he had been aware of his spiritual gifts; these included the ability, in the eaves and hedgerows about his village, to perceive and converse with benevolent spirits. Angels in bright raiments favoured him with their secrets. It was his firm conviction that one day the Adamic language, the First and Original Tongue that denoted the primary material of Creation, would be revealed to him. In the heat of such wisdom he would dissolve the mysteries of alchemy; and earthy man would be transformed into the Heavenly Philosopher.

As though to give some weight to his claims, Jonathan Knott had introduced my patron to his selection of occult books. Those titles of which Knott seemed most proud, or which provoked the loudest gasps of stupefaction from his audience, included the *Secretum Secretorum* attributed to Aristotle on the nature of immortality, the *Liber Experiementorum* by Ramón Llull, the *Thesaurus hieroglyphicorum* – upon whose battered boards I am composing this confession – and Giovanni Porta's *Magia Naturalis*, which Knott considered his most valuable guide to avoiding the temptations of Unnatural Magic. Perhaps, good reader, you are already familiar with the metaphysical claims of alchemists? I, however, being innocent in such matters, could only gape like a codfish (as the Duke had done before me) to hear my friend's account of that super-fine pursuit.

'If he can make a patron's fortune,' I protested, 'how come this Knott's still mendicant and birching donkeys?'

'Ah.' Brenner smiled. 'There our young actor played for the Duke's sympathy.' The lords of Europe can be hard masters. Had there not been instances when searchers had been imprisoned and subjected by their gaolers to cruel abuses in the hope they might surrender their secrets? Could the red elixir be sapped in admixture with the more common fluid from an alchemist's veins? Or the philosopher's stone be drawn with his intestines, inch by inch, upon a windlass? *No*, the Englishman had cried, mopping the sweat of indignation from his brow. Brutes and tyrants cannot make gold because *they themselves* are moral dross. It requires the tincture of virtue in a patron to cause a transformation in the alchemical furnace.

'So,' I scoffed, 'he claims to be shunted from palace to palace?'

'Not for the reasons you might presume. Not for having duped his hosts and been discovered in the imposture. We must not hope to prove his malice, Tommaso. This Englishman is too strong.'

Like a magus led by a mischievous star, Jonathan Knott had come bearing gifts. From a purse of yellow silk thread he had plucked an arrow's tip which became, on closer inspection, the serrated tooth of a shark. From the pocket of his quilted satin doublet he produced a small walnut wood box which contained the desiccated armour of tropical beetles, each with its black spindles tucked away and its wing casings burnished to a metallic sheen. 'Observe and touch this monkey's claw but do not summon its magical properties.' (Adolph Brenner mimicked and mocked Knott's curious accent.) 'The claw will grant a man his wishes, though in a form he cannot imagine. Thus the lamented corpse walks from its grave aswirl with worms; or a fortune

attends the demise of a cherished parent. I do not dabble in
the dark occult, your Grace, and have managed to resist its
temptations. But I offer you this claw with a counsel – that
you maintain in your company a gentleman who is capable
of containing its power.'

'What nonsense.'

'Knott put the claw in the Duke's palm for him to
inspect it.'

'Was he horrified?'

'He giggled as though it tickled him, and declared it
worthy of a place in his Arcana.'

I reflected bitterly on the Englishman's good fortune.
He found my patron in the vernal bloom of good spirits.
Had Jonathan Knott arrived at another time, in the savage
winter of the Duke's melancholy, he would have been ousted
immediately for presenting so sinister a tribute.

Over the days that followed, questions about my opponent festered in my imagination. Who *was* this Englishman,
with his piercing eyes and exotic trinkets, who could so
impress the Duke? I was afraid of him, as afraid as the court
painter Theodor Altmann must have been when another
foreigner – as squat and ill favoured as Knott was tall and
handsome – had appeared unbidden in Felsengrunde and
threatened to usurp his position. I tried to imagine Jonathan
Knott in more desperate times, wandering through Bohemia
or Poland selling verjuice cordials, a veritable mountebank
spouting cod Latin to credulous peasants. When I returned
to my enchanted patron in the sweating hope of changing
his mind, I tried to detect the latent desperation of a
charlatan behind the Englishman's self-assurance. Surely
here was another Geronimo Scotta, a descendant of the
shabby fraudster who accosted me once on Prague's Old
Town Square? Perhaps he was a danger to my patron?
For a dead man had been found, washed clean of his

blood and snagged on rocks in the ravine below the Pass of Our Lady. The letters in his sack had been blanked by the rushing stream, so it was impossible to know his identity or provenance. I decided at once that the dead man had been a pursuer sent by some abused lord. Like the frantic rider whose hunt for the Moldavian thief I had knowingly frustrated, the pursuer had failed in his mission – murdered by the very man who now stood smiling before the Duke. I dared not voice these suspicions before the villain, though by talking at length and with idle speculation about the discovered corpse I hoped to confound his damnable ease.

Insinuation, generally, became my only weapon. 'I wonder are you acquainted, Herr Knott, with the Count of Ulm from whom I bought our menagerie?'

'Alas, no. Is he a friend to your Grace?'

'Never heard of the man,' said Albrecht Rudolphus, cupping a hand beneath his lips to catch the juice of a plum.

'He ran up great debts,' I said, 'in vain pursuit of an alchemical dream. He was preyed on by chymicks, or multipliers as some men call them.'

'A regrettable word,' said Jonathan Knott.

'It signifies also a coiner, or maker of counterfeit coins.' I watched to see if my words might lodge like barbs in my enemy's flesh; yet Knott responded tamely by taking his leave. Let me fumble for the Duke's ear – he seemed to say – I would never change his mind.

'He's no more than a *chemist*,' I protested as soon as he was gone. 'He's a drudge in magician's weeds. One of Geber's cooks.'

'He knows my wife's family,' said the Duke. 'I was honour bound to grant him an audience.'

'Now it seems he grants *you* one.'

Albrecht Rudolphus reared up, bloated with indignation.

Crumbs and a plum stone tumbled from his belly. I begged his pardon for speaking out of turn and sensed that I was repeating ancient errors.

'Herr Knott told me to tell you,' said the Duke, 'that your former colleague from Prague – Meyerlink is it? – has died in Vienna.'

I quite forgot my stratagems. All pleas and arguments fell like bats from the eaves of my brain.

'He was very old, Knott says. It was to be expected.'

I sat down without asking for permission and folded my hands in my lap. Meyrink. Dead in exile. He had looked his last on foreign spires – so far from his beloved Moldau and her chestnut hills. I pictured him shivering in alien soil, an outcast even from his grave.

'Jonathan Knott has come here to help me, Tommaso. And so restore my dukedom to health.' Almost coyly, the Duke showed me the phial about his neck. 'It is red earth. In Hebrew, *adom*. Extracted from the menstruum of the world. One touch of the powder whence this tincture is made and base material is transmuted.'

'Have you tasted the tincture, my lord?'

'It is *aurum potabile*, the elixir of life. Knott explained everything to me. How melancholia in the deathly stage of the opus is akin to what afflicts me. Man, you see, Man is the vessel in which the transformation takes place. Alchemy is an art that can surpass Nature. It is not sufficient to copy, as you do, its imperfections. In the heat of the athanor we hope to *perfect* it.' My patron's need simmered like water in the heat of Knott's metaphors. He explained that Knott possessed, most carefully hidden among his retorts and alembics, a sample of this *adom*, the philosopher's stone, a mere grain of which when added to the *opus alchimium* could affect a transmutation. This medicine was the panacea to cure his wife of her dryness. Just as sulphur and *argent*

333

vive, the male and female seeds, copulate to produce the philosopher child, so with the Englishman's aid Albrecht Rudolphus might at last produce an heir.

How, you may wonder, could the Duke have been seduced by this occult verbiage? It seemed that his mistrust of me did not extend to my competitor. When Adolph Brenner described the tricks with which the Englishman had weighted his claims, I despaired of proving Knott's falseness. 'Three things he performed using the red earth. First he heated lead in the Vas Rotundum. Then he added a grain of powder and stirred the water with a sort of wand. When he took the vessel out of the fire, we could see scales of gold at the bottom.'

'Which you tested?'

'Nobody in the Castle knows how to assay gold.'

At once I was reminded of the Mušek twins in Prague. 'I'd wager that wand was hollow,' I said, 'with a few ounces of gold sealed inside by a layer of wax that melted in the foam.'

Adolph Brenner looked at me with surprise. I asked him about the second trick. 'He appeared to produce gold from a lump of coal.'

'Did you *see* the coal?'

'The whole Court was in attendance. I haven't Kaspar's height for peering over heads. The opus *seemed* genuine – at least, everyone else was taken in.'

It was the last trick, however, which had sealed matters for the Duke. Jonathan Knott had requested a musket, loaded the breach and then dropped a grain of red powder down the barrel. He asked the Duke to shoot him – which the Duke refused to do – whereupon the Lord Chamberlain volunteered and, placing Jonathan Knott at a distance across the room, fired straight for his heart. Knott fell backwards with a cry. There was a great tremor in the Ritterstube. Smoke and the stink of powder. Then the Englishman picked himself up and, opening his shirt, revealed a bruise where the bullet, made safe by the philosopher's stone, had struck his breast.

'How— ?'

'An amalgam, I'd swear it. I heard of an actor once, in Padua, who shot his own brother with a bullet that disintegrated in flight. But Jonathan Knott's a more subtle performer. Minutes after he was shot, a servant found the bullet rolled into a corner of the Ritterstube. Still warm from the firing. Now the Duke hangs from the Englishman's lips like a love-struck girl. He has been promised everything. The ducal marriage brought to fruition, the bruises healed in his own soul. How can your drawings – or my automata – protect us from that?'

15

The Flesh Sculptor

The Duke, immured in his amazement at Knott's powers, could not readily be persuaded to visit my menagerie. Everywhere he perceived symbols of his own condition: in the pining hoopoe and eremitical tortoises, in the haughty indifference of the hen to the peacock's shimmering fan. The parakeets wearied him with their chatter and their feathers irritated his throat. As for the bear, my claims for its wildness were belied every time the kitchen staff banged pots together in the caverns below. Hearing the ghost of a summons, the dew-eyed brute rose mournfully on its hindquarters and performed a desultory dance.

'Have the keepers been teaching it these tricks?' asked Albrecht Rudolphus, his eyes hooded with suspicion. I hastened him to the last and rarest exhibit.

The dodo let me down most grievously of all. Though by now its mate was an eel-twisting heap of bones at the bottom of the ocean, yet the bird was desperate to breed. Moved by curiosity (of the callous sort which results in eviscerated field mice), one of the keepers had placed a looking glass against the fence of the enclosure. The Duke and I contemplated the amorous bird – its futile displays and reciprocated kisses, its leaps for joy when it received an encouraging wink from its own reflection. The Duke pressed his chins into his palm and I imagined our concurring thoughts twining like creepers between our heads . . .

Such futility.

On his next visit, the Duke to my surprise brought the Lord Chamberlain with him. A command was given for the looking glass. The Duke nudged his adviser's elbow like a mischievous schoolboy, and instructed him to look, *look*! Moritz von Winkelbach disdainfully regarded the dodo in its tangle of guano-spattered straw. The bird opened the coffer of its beak and emitted a malevolent hiss; then it scratched its rump, plucked a feather from its breast with the fervid self-contempt of a desert ascetic and hunkered down to sleep. A reluctant keeper was ordered to prod the bird awake.

The Lord Chamberlain rushed the boy to the surgeon while I followed with the bloody ball of his finger wrapped in a handkerchief.

After the mutilation of the keeper's hand, the Duke lost all interest in his menagerie and dedicated himself to more occult pursuits. My own enthusiasm for the creatures waned: I had to adapt myself to the exigencies of the time. So I slaved away painting alchemical motifs on the walls of the new Ritterstube, which doubled now as a laboratory. At Knott's entreaty I depicted Sol and Luna bathing, the Beheaded King, scatterings of black crows and a sun-headed Hermes Trismegistus. Shortly thereafter, I was instructed to relinquish the southern tower to my competitor.

'He has more need of it than you,' said the Duke when I confronted him. The stridency of my protest (so reminiscent, I *knew*, of the futile appeals of my own predecessor) made it easier for my patron to enforce his command. So I carried my equipment and belongings in a barrow all the way to Magdalena's quarters in the East Wing. My reluctant wife, as you can imagine, was less than delighted at this invasion. For three days and nights she sustained her counter-assault, shifting my encampment from her belongings whenever I absented myself and greeting my returns with such hot invective that I fled the bed of our supposed love for a bundle of cushions arranged beneath my desk.

My other dependants abandoned me. Jonathan Knott welcomed them as his own apprentices, asserting his authority by dressing them all in corvine black. Spurned, humiliated, I continued as best I could to work for the enrichment of the Duke's collection, concentrating now on erotic pastiches of Primaticcio. These piled up on my workbench, weighted face down to avoid Magdalena's prim fury: spied-on Susannahs and masturbating satyrs, Judiths swinging heads as though they were lanterns, a dozen Lucrecias dying on the pricks of their honourable blades.

During the winter my menagerie perished. First the hoopoe, which never once in captivity had hoisted its strawberry crest, was found limply hanging from its nesting hole. The Brazilian tortoises followed. Unaccustomed to our temperate seasons, they died on a night of savage frost and were found by their keeper in the hibernal straw, withdrawn into their shells like hermits dying in contempt of the world. On Saint Nicholas's Eve the frigid peahen choked to death on a cherry stone which one of the kitchen staff had carelessly discarded. The peacock, lacking even the disregard of its unrequited love, pined away in the warmth of the bakery and left, for its entire posterity, a foul stink and enough rancid droppings to fuel the hearth for about a minute. In a culture of official indifference, the Chief Cook must have known that he would escape grave censure for wringing the necks of the parakeets, whose shrill and incessant garrulity had driven him to the edge of reason. One gaudy feast, with roast swan and suckling pigs, on the occasion of the Duchess's birthday, proved sufficient to restore the murderer to favour and consign his feathered victims to convenient oblivion.

I received the news of all these deaths with a kind of grim humour. 'What are you laughing at?' Magdalena would scold from beneath her frowzy sheets. 'Mad old fool.'

But I could laugh no longer, even bitterly, when the bear contracted whooping cough. Since there were no rooms in the castle to which one could safely confine a bear whom sickness deprived of its winter slumber, the Duke suggested (no doubt advised by Jonathan Knott) that the animal be shot. No indeed, it is not unreasonable to suspect my English rival of hastening the extinction of my project. What more potent symbol could there be of power's transference?

The dodo died on Christmas Day when its keeper failed to secure the cage door. It escaped its prison and ran, warbling with excitement, into the Banqueting Hall and then down into the kitchens, where the drunken staff quite forgot their duties to its owner and merrily hacked the bird to a pulp. The corpse was returned to its enclosure and on the morrow I was assured by all involved that a fox had attacked it.

'A fox? How did it get into the enclosure?'

'It, uh, it flew.'

'The fox *flew*?'

'No, the bird.'

'Oh, I see. How silly of me. The *dodo* flew.'

'That's it – into the courtyard.'

'Where a fox just happened to be loitering in hope of catching a large, flightless bird.'

'We rescued a wing. And the head's in good shape, look.'

'It's *dead*, you bastard.'

'Not many dukes,' Jonathan Knott consoled me later, 'can boast a dodo's skull among their treasures. Why, man, you can add it to the heap of his naturalia . . .'

The four-fingered dodo keeper was flogged at my orders (over such lowlifes I still had authority) but the sight of his blood spraying across dirty snow did little to ease my fury. I worked hard to preserve the corpses for their inclusion – as a pile of beaks and bones and talons, as peacock feathers

339

and the blunted claws of a senescent bear – in the deathly still cabinets of the Arcana Mysteria.

At least (at last) the automata were ready. I had spent the yawning hours of an afternoon in Adolph Brenner's workshop painting their moonish faces. The heads were balls of twine, with sackcloth for skin and string for hair. I asked for a demonstration of their dancing, as Brenner called it, but my colleague, being fogged in deep gloom and unspoken apprehension, mumbled his refusal. I should wait, he said, that my amazement before the Duke be unfeigned on the morrow.

'What names shall we give them?' I wondered, stepping back to admire their rag-doll features – the lopsided grins and pink button noses, the tentacled suns for eyes. It seemed somehow immodest to make their faces lifelike, though to his credit Adolph Brenner had excelled himself in the proportions of their bodies. Only their heads allayed one's fear that these were infants propped dead on a table.

'Primus,' said Brenner, 'Secundus, Tertius. And now, if you would be patient while I replace these sackcloths.' The inventor peeled the painted faces from their skulls of twine and replaced them with three blank sheets of cloth. 'After so many years perfecting their movements, I will have convincing faces, if you please.'

I cast a long glance at the masks shed on the floor. Brenner's eyes simmered with emotion. Without saying a word, I dipped my brush in expensive mummy and resumed work.

Angry silence buzzed about us.

'I don't see your bastard hereabouts,' I said, meaning to wound. Adolph Brenner slammed shut his toolcase and feigned deafness. I worked on, through the blaze of afternoon to the glimmer of candles, giving a spark of illusory life to Brenner's inventions.

The next day, when the Duke was expecting to see the automata unveiled in his new apartments, I found Adolph Brenner weeping in his foundry. He greeted me with a blockage in his throat, left the door ajar for me to enter if I would and lumbered back to his primped and lace-collared children. 'My God,' I whispered at my fingers. 'Are they broken?' Brenner shook his head. I watched him fret and reach for air over the tousled heads. 'What then?'

'Kasp,' he gasped. '*Kasp*.'

'Kasp?'

'Kaspar . . .'

'Kaspar's broken them?'

'. . . was abused. Yesterday. Seeing him in the yard . . .'

'Kaspar?'

'The *Duke*, seeing Kaspar in the yard from his window, rushed out to abuse him. He was carrying a length of carpet.'

'The Duke was carrying a length of carpet?'

'No, *no*. His finger was pointing as if it were a lance. I saw everything from my window and heard the Duke's words. "*Nigredo!* Impure matter! Keep this blackness from me!" And with that, surrounded by Knott's men flapping like crows, his Grace was ushered back to the Library.'

'It is the asafoetida,' I said, 'the smell of graves that emanates from the Englishman's pot. It drives the Duke mad.'

'Whatever the cause, its consequence is simple. He has threatened to do it ever since his girl was banished.'

'The Duke has banished Kaspar?'

'He has run away.'

Not today, oh, Lord, not *today*. I looked for soothing assurances. 'Surely the boy will come home. Where can he go in these pale-favoured lands?'

'To Prague, of course. To your blessed damnable city in

the midst of all its broils. To find her – Elisabetta's maid. And my money taken withal.'

'Let me call out the guard. We'll drag him back a thief.'

'No, Tommaso, you don't understand.'

'Or let him fly, if you must be milk-livered. My God, man, he has betrayed his master!'

Something in my voice, or the prodding of his guilty spirit, made the inventor weep again. 'I mistreated him. Fussing over *these* . . .' (he swept a contemptuous hand above the dolls) '. . . when my own flesh and blood went unrecognised. No wonder he used to drop them. His mother was headstrong alike. All African fire . . .'

'Adolfo, we have a task most urgently to perform.'

'Oh, my boy . . . my boy!' The inventor slapped his brow, making a sound like an apple tossed and caught in the palm. 'I never acknowledged him. And now he's *gone* – my son, my Kaspar!'

I withdrew backwards, like an obsequious servant quitting his king. Adolph Brenner continued to weep, bent double with his elbows on his knees like a constipated man. He must not have been aware that I was leaving, so terrible was his desolation. I felt sick and sore afraid in the presence of such unhappiness.

Sleep has crept over the ramparts into the castle – sleep, benign stealer of men's eyes. The Duke sleeps in his study, a consoling cushion pressed to his heart. In the southern tower the Englishman lies ungnawed by conscience, a tripwire running to a panel of bells above his bed. Now the Duchess sleeps, watched by Our Saviour above her pillowed head, while the Treasurer dreams of pregnant coffers and the Winkelbachs scowl beside their flatulent wives. All, it seems, have been touched by Morpheus, dismissed for the night from their burdensome roles. Even the guards are cocooned in blankets on the battlements, or else lie drowned in ale in the guardhouse. Only I stand vigil. A fat tongue of flame sits like the Holy Spirit above my oil lamp. Behind me, diagonal in our bed, my wife and quondam lover scratches and sighs. Surely now she will leave me, turning her somewhat rancid charms on a better-favoured patron? Through weariness I close my eyes – only to find the dreadful memory waiting beneath my lids. I see again the audience gathered about the impatient Duke while Adolph Brenner, pasty from having swallowed too much grief, readies his clockwork children. There stand Primus, the boy, with a golden cherub's face, dressed in Kaspar's former clothes; and Secundus, a pretty dimpled girl with string hair in ringlets, clutching a posy of real mountain flowers; and Tertius, with a rattle in one hand and pap in the other, smiling for ever at the vacant air.

'Your Grace – my lords and ladies – after many years of labour and perplexity, I have emerged at last from the labyrinth with the marvels that I sought there.' Adolph Brenner held little Tertius by the shoulder. With his left hand he gripped the butterfly of the winding key in the automaton's back. 'These children are of a complexity never before attempted in the world. They are my life's work, the very pinnacle of my achievement. And I humbly offer them to your Grace, with gratitude for your unwavering patience.'

Brenner released the spinning key and Tertius waddled forward. Like a child newly learned to walk, it plucked its knees and dropped its heavy-seeming feet. At every tenth step it hesitated and dipped its buttocks, as a toddler wary of its own progress considers the safety of sitting. Then the head began to nod, as though agreeing with its legs to continue, while the mechanism inside its belly clucked and purred. To my surprise, the automaton stopped three yards from the audience and extended its hands with the rattle and pap, as though offering these infantile things to an adoring parent. I almost expected the painted head to speak, as Tertius dropped its arms and resumed, at a slowing pace, its toddle towards the Duke.

Albrecht Rudolphus received his gift with a startling yell. He kicked out in horror at the approaching doll. Tertius flew backwards – its left arm shattered and the rattle sped across the room.

'You *mock* me!' cried the Duke. He stood up on his chair as though escaping floodwaters. The automaton traced a circle on its flexing legs, as a mutilated fly spins to death on a window sill.

'Out! Everybody out!'

There was at once a tumble of bodies. Guards at the Lord Chamberlain's prompting flung back the sluice gates of the new Ritterstube. Dresses billowed and gushed in urgent confluence; sword-tips clashed and feet tripped on the felled automaton, treading its face or kicking it tartly in the guts. 'Your Grace is not well,' I heard the Duchess protest, before she was caught up in the whirlpool of her faction. Hiding beneath a vacillating chair, I saw Adolph Brenner dive into a thrashing forest of legs and clutch Tertius to the safety of his breast.

The sound of feet washed away and the doors were closed upon us. Jonathan Knott stood unruffled beside the Duke.

'Knott,' said the Duke, 'I need my medicine.'

'In your study, my lord.'

'I can wait for it no longer. You should not make me *wait* so.'

The Duke, after his outburst, remembering the burden of his flesh, tumbled heavily into the Englishman's arms. Without so much as a glance at the injured automaton or its maker, he retreated towards the Private Chamber, clutching at the alchemist's elbow and calling him 'comforter, my only comforter'.

Adolph Brenner gathered up his boys, leaving Secundus to my care. Without uttering a word, he carried his automata and Kaspar's length of carpet across the deserted courtyard to the greasy clouts and instruments of his workshop. I followed him into the shuttered darkness where, after a period of untenable silence, I flung out words that might console him.

'You have shown yourself a master of your craft. Whatever mad fancies may have informed the Duke against you . . .'

'He was right, Tommaso. As were you to give them dolls' faces. The more lifelike our inventions, the more dead they seem.'

'It was the Duke's desire to have clockwork children. Why should you suffer because his wife is barren?'

'Oh, Tommaso. If you knew the number of my sins. If you knew the *weight* of them—'

'Please, friend. Don't tell me.'

The man was determined to make his confession. 'I am a thief as well as a cruel father. Those lenses from Galileo's shop in Padua, which I used to gratify the Duke. I stole them from their display case. And the other devices also. The shopkeeper saw me thieving. He would have testified against me, though I was poor and could barely feed my son . . .'

'Need is no worshipper of property. Besides, it was long ago and in a different country. Your work here is not yet done. The Library needs upkeep – and with your mechanician's talent . . .'

Adolph Brenner heard my attempts at persuasion calmly, as though drained of all grief. He fetched three coffins of rough pine into which he lowered his automata. 'You cannot help me,' he said. 'We are living in a new dispensation. Henceforth we must shift for ourselves.'

After the famous Battle of White Mountain, in which the combined armies of Catholic Europe set the Protestants in Bohemia to flight, I tried and failed, for want of means, to secure part of what remained of the Emperor Rudolf's collection. Meantime Maximilian, Grand Duke of Bavaria, a gruesome pike in the murky pond where my tadpole-patron swam, acquired one thousand five hundred *wagons* of precious trophies to ballast his triumphant homecoming.

'Those are victors' spoils,' said Jonathan Knott when, denying me access to the Duke, he compelled me to tell him of my dead letters. 'What claim could you possibly have for them?'

'We might send a representative at least, to salvage some of the more negligible items.' I winced at my infelicitous phrasing. 'I don't mean by that to denigrate his lordship.'

'Of course not,' said the Englishman, stretching into a yawn. His tongue curled luxuriously: I saw uncommonly sharp incisors and a bleached shred of meat in an interstice. 'I shall bring the matter before the Duke. You might wish to visit Prague yourself, perhaps?'

'*No*. Ah, no – not necessary.' I had to humiliate myself to conceal worse. 'What would a city in turmoil make of a midget tugging its sleeve? No, what's needed is someone with authority.'

'For you,' said Knott, 'lack that entirely.'

It was too late for the treasure; nor did the Duke greatly covet a gem or medallion from his discredited namesake. Meanwhile the angelic dictations were progressing: the Englishman claimed to have a whole book of arcane symbols in his tower, transcriptions in the Adamic language of alchemical recipes.

I retreated to my quarters, where a new task awaited me.

A record was needed – in sketches that could be transferred to prints – of Albrecht Rudolphus's collection. Did not most great curators publish lists of their belongings, complete with illustrations that could spread their fame abroad? It was Jonathan Knott who made the suggestion; he secured our patron's endorsement and then handed down my official commission. It was the most precise of insults: that I, past usefulness, should sketch the symbols of my former power. The dull, cold implements of the artificialia bored me to moaning (functionaries must have thought they had a bull for a neighbour). Then one day Knott's apprentices brought me the remains of my menagerie. I would preserve these creatures – which had died in my supposed care – in a paper museum. Every stroke of my pen would constitute my indictment. I would draw up a most detailed record of failure, an inventory of lifeless things. Pluto's scribe, I surveyed petrified jungles, calcified seas.

One more participant is poised to grace the stage in this drama of my demotion. Given my stature one might quip that I had not far to fall; yet fall I could, much farther, into the cold depths of public disgrace. This last actor in the Morality, having been lured to Felsengrunde by Jonathan Knott, would precipitate the final collapse of my ambitions.

His name was Jakob Schneuber. I was present when he floated the length of the Ritterstube and reverenced before the Duke. He was dressed in the dull leather of a gentleman riding to hounds. A very pale countenance, unremarkable and bland, as though his creator had tired of making heads at the end of a long day and left this one in the standard mould, undistinguished by personality. Though I would see Jakob

Schneuber's face several times (and read some fearful things there), yet I cannot summon so much as a mole to memory. Perhaps you should imagine an amalgam of faces, a dilution of particularity, in order to gain a sense of him. His body looked perilously thin without seeming frail. Like a Toledo sword, it contained menace without recourse to might. 'Your Grace,' he said, 'I have worked as a scrivener, an apothecary and a merchant's clerk. I was a soldier at White Mountain. I watched the rebel army routed and saw the punishment of its leaders. Now that True Religion is restored in Bohemia, I have resumed my wandering vocation.'

The Duke, out of politeness (for he knew already), asked the nature of Schneuber's vocation.

'I collect mysteries, signs that have fallen to earth of an ingenious God. I am also an embalmer. I preserve matter from corruption. Might I— ?' The lean Saxon took a step closer to the ducal presence. 'Might I present you with some tokens of my admiration?'

Albrecht Rudolphus smiled and nodded, his fat lip quaking.

Reader, our new rival, allied with Knott in the degradation of our patron, bought his admission to the Duke's inner circle with the ostrich egg and the lumps of bezoar (stolen for all I know from the late Emperor) which survive to this day in faded ink in my catalogue fragment. Next he produced, from a casket made of lead, the shrunken head of a Jivaro tribesman. It was no bigger than an artichoke and stained brown like an apple boiled inside its skin. I would have occasion to admire, with a delicious shudder, its savage workmanship: the eyes and mouth sewn tight with vine, the wispy hair tied to a wooden stake, the nose disapprovingly wrinkled, as though death were no more than a cloacal breeze.

Jakob Schneuber's last gift interested me particularly. It

was a copy of the anatomy book by Vesalius, *De humani corporis fabrica*. Considering Schneuber's origins – a ghoulish figure in the dark passageways of Prague's Old Town – I was convinced immediately, with a feverish shiver of hope and desperation, that it was the very copy that Petrus Gonsalvus had permitted me to study under his roof. There ought to survive a stain of ink in the left-hand corner of the frontispiece. 'Your Grace,' I piped, 'might I take a look?'

'Why?'

'Because . . .' I looked up the nostrils of Jakob Schneuber. 'Is it a first edition of Vesalius?'

'It is,' said Schneuber, feigning ignorance of my identity.

'Did you acquire it in Prague?'

'I did.'

'And the owner sold it to you?'

'Herr Grilli,' said the Duke angrily, 'what's the meaning of this interruption?'

Jakob Schneuber, though many years my junior, addressed me with avuncular forbearance. 'You are asking me how I came by this gift for the Duke? I bought it from a Kleinseite bookseller.'

'And where had *he* acquired it?'

'From a werewolf.' Schneuber smirked and shrugged. 'How the devil should I know?'

The Duke set down the Vesalius in favour of the shrunken head. Perhaps he disliked seeing his own inner workings so comprehensively exposed. Consequently I was allowed to leaf through the heavy volume. It was the same edition as Gonsalvus had kept. There was no stain, however, on the frontispiece, no equivalent of the birthmark that distinguishes a man from his twin. Foolish as my hope had been (what would the stain's discovery have signified, save the annihilation of its previous owner?), I could not suppress my disappointment. The sensation, so oddly akin to indigestion, subsided as I admired the familiar prints, until I realised with a guilty start where I had seen Adolph Brenner before. His entire head, so raw and parboiled in appearance for want of any hair, reminded me of the dissected figure in Vesalius.

I returned to the East Wing disquieted, eager to dismiss the newcomer as a feeble fraud whose presence to amuse the Duke suggested a weakening of Jonathan Knott's powers. I might have worked longer at these fancies had not Magdalena chosen that very day to leave me.

Necessity is a cruel dictator. I had known my betrayal was due: I could no longer afford to keep her. Yet the expectation did nothing to ease my pain when the inevitable happened. Lassitude prevents me from recounting in detail the hours of desperate pleading, the clutching of elbows and ankles and the offer that I made, with a parched grimace where formerly tears had flown, of a generous share in my dwindling pension if Magdalena might consent, just occasionally, to betray her new protector and relieve me of my solitude. As a last resort I made myself pitiful, hoping for the mercy accorded by its master to a whimpering dog. 'You never showed much pity for *me*,' Magdalena replied. With cold, hard fingers she prised my own from the folds of her skirt. I begged her to choose another man – the Treasurer if needs be, or that old bachelor Grünenfelder – anyone by whom to be cuckolded but that moustache-twirling brute. I warned her that she would suffer, that his violence would make my feeble lust seem a paradise by comparison.

I hid when the Sheriff's men lumbered up the stairs and presented themselves, with obscene nods and winks, to their employer's doxy. Their booming, manly voices and the insinuations they bandied between them as they carried away our bed and my cherrywood chest filled me with the murderous fantasies of a caged ape. When I emerged from the closet, Magdalena was gone.

I slept for several days on my cushions beneath the desk, distracted by the dusty absence at the end of the room where our bed used to stand. I failed to shave or wash. I worked with glacial slowness at my tedious drawings.

One evening, I heard the East Wing stirring from its torpor.

'Where's everyone going?' I asked a neighbour. A senior clerk in the Revenues Office (whose room reeked always of burned cheese) hollered down the corridor: 'To the Library. The embalmer's going to show his work.'

What, I wondered, had Jakob Schneuber found on his travels? A dog's head stitched to a pike, perhaps? A hen fitted with kitten's teeth? Locking the door to my lodging, I descended the steps to Vergessenheit Street. The entire castle seemed to be on the move, impelled by curiosity. I glimpsed towards the chapel Count Winkelbach's faction, lumbering in an attempt at swagger, their hands rocking on their swords' pommels. Elisabetta's *Hofdame*, the portly Maria, overtook me like a galleon and nearly tripped me in the wake of her dress.

In the Second Apartment of the Library, guardsmen held off the crowd with halberds crossed. Court employees bobbed and performed dainty leaps on their toes to comprehend the obstruction. Lost at the rear, I could see almost nothing. I was a child again, tugging at coat-tails, though with no father to hold me above the fray. 'Well,' I told the buoyant rumps, 'I won't put up with *this*.' I took a deep breath, like one about to dive underwater, filled out my chest like a menaced toad and pushed through the crowd. Arms and hands fell in my way like branches in a wood. Hips flinched, buttocks clenched, as I burrowed forward – emerging at last – having carved my thigh on a gentleman's sword – three feet from the Ritterstube door. Here the nobility stood, thrilling with indignation. Grünenfelder gritted his black teeth; the Jesuit confessor Wackenfels huffed and blushed. Moritz von Winkelbach, invoking his official status, deplored this dishonourable treatment. 'Let me through, I say! I am the Obersthofmeister! President of the Court Council!' But the guards held their ground. They were no longer directly in the Treasury's pay. And I guessed what was happening, I tasted it on the air. Jonathan Knott, Chief Librarian and Adviser to the Duke, was asserting his power.

The Second Apartment where we waited was tenebrous, its high windows bleared by damp autumnal gloom, and the groves of candles on the walls, which bowed reverently to their own heat, cast trembling shadows over angry faces. Adapted to this penumbra, we flinched at a sudden explosion of white light. The door of the Ritterstube had been flung open, like the gates to Heaven, transfiguring our infernal antechamber. Howling like the damned, we blinked and averted our eyes from the doorway, in whose effulgent centre stood Jonathan Knott, imposing in white robes and astoundingly tall. My heart tightened as he extracted, from the folds of his archangelic gown, a translucent scroll.

'By solemn decree of Albrecht Rudolphus, thirteenth Duke of Felsengrunde, Prince of the Holy Roman Empire, Protector of Spitzendorf, Scholar and Patron, the following shall be admitted to see the exhibit . . .'

There followed a dream-slow recitation, each courtier having to await the enunciation of his name. Servants of the Duke, his guardsmen and Revenues officers, were granted admittance before their superiors. Elisabetta's faction had to wait until last. '. . . Martin Grünenfelder and their lordships, Maximilian and Count Moritz von Winkelbach.'

Here the list ended. Jonathan Knott's gaze met mine as

he prepared to withdraw. His functionary's dispassion-ate expression faltered; a provocative mirth flashed, most unnervingly, in his eyes. 'And lastly,' he said, 'let us not forget the Duke's archivist, Tommaso Grilli.'

My nomination provoked the anticipated protests. Winkel-bach's men tried to restrain me; the Sheriff hooked his fingers about my collar while the other guests filed through into the light. I managed to squirm loose and squeak through the Ritterstube door moments before it closed.

The Ritterstube shone with a white, metallic light. Focused on a single point at the centre of the hall, it cast long spidery shadows across the ceiling. I approached the light's source and found the guests assembled about a shrouded case. It was a low, square box, placed on a pedestal and draped in the Duke's Persian rug. A dozen spherical mirrors surrounded the display. In crucibles bracketed in front of each mirror, a blinding white powder smouldered.

'An ingenious fellow, your Brenner,' said Jonathan Knott, inclining at my shoulder to indicate the mirrors. 'You remember how accommodating he can be. How hard he works for his friends.'

I pretended to ignore this comment and remarked upon the room's transformation. It had been cleared, you see, of alchemical materials. Knott's retorts and crucibles, his flasks and bellows and glass cucurbits, had been swept from view, their odoriferous fumes dispersed; yet the smoke-tinctured walls continued to exhale a tart chemical breath and the once elegant stone paving (with my curlicued fleurs-de-lis) was blighted by stains and smudged with ashes.

'His Grace,' said Jonathan Knott, 'has discovered a new passion.'

'Alchemy failing him, is it?'

Jonathan Knott smiled and retreated, trailing a gelid sort of draught, into the ranks of his assistants. The crowd had surged ahead of me and I stood once again at the coat-tails of my superiors. It was difficult to see anything of the exhibit with so many bodies in my way. The light clung like a moonlit fog about their nodding heads.

Suddenly, to the fart of a single trumpet, the door to the Private Chamber opened and Albrecht Rudolphus appeared. He was splendidly attired in black silk and taffeta. Marooned inside his own blubber, he had not shaved for at least a fortnight.

The ducal audience bowed and curtsied. Spotting me in gaps between the reverential legs, the Duke flung his arms into the air. '*Il miglior fabbro!*' he exclaimed. Heads turned in my direction. '*Maestro mio.* Such an honour.' Stepping crabwise through his subjects (few of whom cared to grant him easy passage), Albrecht Rudolphus sought me out. I noted from the hang of his belly that he had grown even fatter. 'Tommaso, old friend. Let me kiss your hand.'

Horrified, as if I were leaking bile, the courtiers parted about me. The Duke seized my hand – my left, the sinister – and, falling upon one knee, smothered its knuckles with wet kisses. 'You know it is *they* that keep you from me,' he muttered. 'I would have you in my Library. But they tower over me so.' I tried to extricate my hand but the Duke clasped it firmly. 'They are incapable of kindness.'

The quicker assistants surrounded us, anxious to screen the Duke from view. Jonathan Knott tried to grip him by the elbow but Albrecht Rudolphus shook him off. 'Don't *hoist* me. I will rise of my own accord.'

With all the castle watching, Jonathan Knott had no choice but to fall back.

The Duke panted to his feet. He tried to lift me to his height – forgetting that I stood as tall as God (or the Devil) had made me. 'Get up, get *up*,' he said. Blushing with shame,

I trembled on to the tips of my toes. The Duke relinquished my hand and, nearly recomposed, shooed Knott's assistants from his path. 'Signor Grilli,' he said, 'will stand beside me for the unveiling.'

Jakob Schneuber stood at a remove from the scene, studying his fingernails. Unlike the assistants, who were trussed up in black robes to offset their master's magical white, Jakob Schneuber wore flamboyant crimson. His doublet and hose were blood red, his sleeves gashed and the shirt beneath scarlet, like exposed muscle; even his waistcoat of black velvet seemed to have haemorrhaged spots of flame, which echoed the ginger (never before noticed) of his beard.

'Ah, Schneuber.'

'Your Grace.'

'You know Signor Grilli – my, uh . . . a very fine painter?'

Jakob Schneuber gave a faint, notional bow. I reciprocated with sarcastic effusiveness. 'We had the pleasure of meeting, your Grace,' I said as my hand, from its brief flight of fancy, returned to my side.

'Herr Grilli used to be Chief Librarian, did he not?'

'His Grace has seen fit to make use of my talents in other fields.'

'Indeed? What office do you hold now – Lord High Homunculus?'

The assembly burst into prim, nasal laughter and I tried, with acid in my lips, to force a smile. The wry, conspiratorial glance exchanged between Schneuber and Knott did not escape my attention.

'Signor Grilli is my archivist,' said Albrecht Rudolphus. 'He is producing a visual record of my entire museum. Isn't that true?'

Jonathan Knott, behind his barricade of assistants, nodded in confirmation.

'Yes,' I said. 'It is essential, for the fame of the collection, that it be amply documented. A visual record preserves and knits the objects together. It guarantees their posterity.'

With a gasp of approval, the Duke began to clap. He flicked the backs of the fingers of his right hand against the heel of his left. It was a wet, slapping sound which failed to elicit any wider applause. I grinned fixedly through my mortification, until the Duke, abashed at the silence of his courtiers, curled his fingers into his palm. 'We ought to begin the, ah . . . Kunstmeister, if you please.'

Jonathan Knott separated from the corvine mass of his assistants. 'Your Grace,' he said. 'My lords and ladies. Herr Jakob Schneuber will now unveil the exhibit. His discovery, made in the course of perilous travels through the Empire, will move the hardest of hearts. It is a thing of great beauty and strangeness – a herald of wondrous Nature.'

The curious crowd pressed forward. Footmen tried, without conviction, to hold the bodies at a distance from the exhibit, which Jakob Schneuber had begun, with teasing slow tugs at the Persian rug, to expose.

Liquidly, with a muted thud, the rug fell to the floor. 'Noble ladies and gentlemen, I give you . . . the Dwarf Venus.'

It seemed, in the first seconds after its unveiling, to be the body of a child: a small girl fixed in briny opalescence. The long blonde hair, cleared from the face, was gathered about palely glowing shoulders. Braided locks had been arranged over small, adult breasts. 'How beautiful,' whispered the Duke. His fingers floated up towards the lighted glass. 'Doesn't she look alive?'

'You're too kind,' said Jakob Schneuber. The courtiers tried to press forward, distending the line of footmen. Promoted from their ranks, I felt with horror their curious eyes slither between the exhibit and this live specimen. 'I have perfected new ways of preserving the capillaries. A subtle combination of wax and resin and cinnabar pigment . . .'

'The eyes – what colour are the eyes?'

'Blue, your Grace.'

The dwarf was duck tailed. Her heavy, blanched buttocks sprang directly from behind the knees yet the torso, from the stunted legs upwards, was normally proportioned. Closer inspection revealed no seam or skilfully dissembled sutures. Those infantile limbs belonged to the pubescent beauty, were of a piece with that virtuous trunk of womanhood. Her privates were concealed, in a foretaste of Schneuber's displays to come, behind an Edenic fig leaf.

The Duke stared at the placid, sealed face. He approached his nose to the glass, as though to tempt open the effigy's eyes. His mouth bent in unconscious mimicry of the pickled guest.

'Perhaps you would care to hear how I came by the object?' Jakob Schneuber did not wait for the Duke's assent before continuing. 'I was travelling, in my capacity as Provider of Wonders to their Majesties of Europe, through Dresden when I learned of this dwarf's existence. It had been glimpsed by a gentleman of my acquaintance in woodland to the north of the city. Intrigued, I followed his directions to a village – a small huddle of huts – where I made enquiries.

'Imperial troops, on their way home from Bohemia, had recently visited the region. I was compelled, alas, to bribe some locals and show them my good intentions before they would talk to me. Yes, it transpired, the creature existed. It was a sad affair, a dark matter. She was the daughter of a peasant woman, now dead, whose progeny had been cursed with deformities.'

'Cursed?' interrupted the Duke. 'By whom?'

'By a witch. For her refusal to lie with the witch's familiar.'

'Which took what form?'

'A wolf, your Grace.'

The audience stirred, impressed. There was no theatrical murmur, no words spoken – just an audible exhalation, the collective weight shifting to another foot.

'In the event,' continued Schneuber, 'the creature was easy to find. Villagers were in the habit of leaving food scraps on the edge of the forest to keep it away from their houses. I had merely to wait for it to appear. Then, as night fell, I tracked it down to its dwelling.

'The monster lived in a cave, a small outcrop of rock among the trees. It drank from pools, picked berries and scavenged. It was simple to the point of brutishness – yet almost beautiful, in the face and hair.' Jakob Schneuber grinned. 'Had I presented you with the head alone – enveloped in these blonde tresses – your Grace might have demanded which *princess* I had pickled.' (This quip played surprisingly well. The ladies tittered behind their hands; the gentlemen hummed to show their good humour and peered at the exhibit's nipples.) 'It was impossible to approach the dwarf – I mean, openly. One had sooner tame a doe. So I made contact with a garrison in Meissen, a small company feeding off the land. I poached a couple of officers on their way to the village and, with their assistance, managed to acquire the exhibit.'

There followed a lengthy and yawn-inducing lecture from the embalmer concerning his revolutionary methods for the preservation of corpses. Nobody paid him much attention, being captivated by the floating monster. For days afterwards I would hear exchanges on its subject. Grandly coiffed ladies quivered with pleasure as they evoked a doll's repose, the woven flax and pallid limbs, the staring and unseeing eyes fixed in lifeless amnios. Now they confided to their winnowing fans how odd they considered the Duke's behaviour – how very odd and unseemly. Was he really going to welcome the *Tuscan* back into his favour? They shuddered at the recollection of that frightful gnome: how the Duke had tousled his ghastly head and (ugh, *ugh*) kissed his hand. It had been, they all agreed, a most revolting display of affection. And what had the dwarf ever done to merit such love?

Addled by the fumes of Knott's experiments, the Duke seemed to be falling back on his old affections. Though ceremony pretended otherwise, his marriage had become a sterile void, filled for Elisabetta by her Jesuit confessor and exploited for their own advancement by the loyal Winkelbachs. Surrounded by such feigned affection, was it any wonder that his Grace pined for our former understanding? Had I not unburdened him, all those years ago, of his troublesome virginity? Or given him a mythology, a star to guide him on the lonely vessel of his authority? After the mawkish scene in the Ritterstube, I found myself courted with gifts of coin and silverware, delivered by a fearful page in strict contravention of the Englishman's orders. And so I began to dream about my restoration. Though there was no resurgence of the Duke's emotion, our conversations were cordial and instructive. My lies concerning the Emperor Rudolf had been merely embroidery, the embellishment of certain facts to make them more pleasing. Should a father be condemned for trying to delight his son's imagination, though it demand the withholding of less than enchanting contradictions? Look, gentlemen of the jury, what achievements had sprung from the Duke's illusions. A modern palace where previously a draughty keep had withstood the mountain rain! A resplendent bird in place of a hardy crow! To capitalise on the improvements in my status, I hastened to produce some more drawings for the Duke, putting aside my clerical tasks. He received, in the space of a month, two heads of Christ by Dürer, a devilish Walpurgisnacht by Hans Baldung Grien and a Leonardo Passion, complete with buckled earth and tumultuous wind spouts to mark the instant of God's sacrifice.

A year passed in which my fortunes improved; a year in which Knott's power lost some of its dazzle, beginning to tarnish for want of a triumphant opus. Jakob Schneuber had left us for many months and was now returning – as I surmised from the chattering of ladies in the Duchess's Courtyard. The modest improvements in my relations with the Duke, though by no means a recovery of my former status, had made me complacent again; so that I suspected nothing when greasy Kurt, one of my former dogsbodies and now Knott's smiling minion, extended an invitation from the Lord Chamberlain to join the Duke in the Audience Chamber.

I crossed the Great Courtyard with barely a twinge of apprehension, my fatigued panache drooping into my eyes. 'So,' I said, for conversation, 'Schneuber's back?'

Kurt barely nodded.

'Have you seen his new monsters?'

Kurt shook his head.

'Are you enjoying your new life?'

'Are *you*?'

I was determined to keep my good humour, however, and murmured an old Florentine song until we reached the Library. All people of quality were gathered in the Ritterstube: Moritz and Maximilian, the new Treasurer, Schaffner, and Martin Grünenfelder, even the Sheriff and his grimacing apes. The Duchess was surrounded by her ladies, while the Duke sat gloomily with Jonathan Knott in attendance and looked everywhere to avoid meeting my eyes. I bowed, receiving barely a reciprocal nod, and accepted the bowl of dark lustrous cherries pressed into my hands by a servant.

Jakob Schneuber stood beside his new exhibits. He was dishevelled in his riding clothes, still reeking of the saddle, and I almost expected his boots to be thatched with horse shit. 'How long has he been back?'

'Quiet,' said Kurt.

'Your Grace – my Lady – my Lord Chamberlain and gentlemen.' Jakob Schneuber spoke softly, confident of his hearers. 'The Procurer of Wonders to their Majesties of Europe has returned from his encounters with darkest humanity. The world beyond these happy mountains is riven with strife yet I searched it tirelessly. I sought proof, physical proof, that God's invention is not yet exhausted. That Creation can surprise us with new forms.'

Knott and his assistants led the applause. I nearly swallowed a cherry stone, so startling was the flight of their hands. 'Thank you,' said Schneuber. 'In Thuringia near Erfurt – in the heartland of devilish Luther – I found this hideous sign of God's displeasure.' He swept the crimson cover from a glass egg, whose visible yolk made the audience gasp. 'The mother, my lords and ladies, died in parturition. Some claimed she was torn to the navel – others that the sight of these stillborn heads drove her to madness and self-slaughter. You will notice, your Grace, my preservation of the veins – how they show through the flesh as though it – as though *they* – were alive.'

'Uh, yes,' said the Duke, very pale. 'Excellently lifelike.'

'And now my Lord—' (a second cover slumped to the floor) '—a pig born to impious farmers in the Thuringian forest. No sooner delivered from its dam but this monster fled into the wild. It attacked children who were foraging for berries. It fought a bloody battle against its enemies. They say it developed a taste for human flesh.'

'How did it run?' asked Moritz von Winkelbach.

'On these four legs, my lord. The other pairs stood erect, like quills, upon its back.'

Everyone closed in on the exhibits; rank and rancour were set aside in the mutual hunger for abomination. I stood my ground, watching the distracted Duke and sucking my cherries.

'Lastly,' said Schneuber, 'I have prepared an allegory – a little capriccio of my own composition – that may satisfy our indignation at the depravity of the Lutheran states.'

It was a skull, a woman's skull, according to Schneuber, with tufts of red hair still clinging to patches of scalp, very cruelly frittered about the nose, with the frangible palate eaten away by the French Disease. Fixed by some means in the preserving fluid, a dimpled baby's leg was poised to kick the rotten skull.

Jonathan Knott laughed. 'Thus Innocence brains Corruption!'

'A whore's head, my lord,' said the flesh sculptor. 'It is a composition for you to add to your museum.'

How crude these rustics were to be seduced by such horrors. They gaped and shook their heads with great satisfaction, their faces made monstrous by the distorting jars.

Affecting indifference to Schneuber's exhibits, I looked about the Ritterstube. A doubt smuggled itself into my thoughts. I searched the room with more attention and discovered to my dismay that nobody else had been eating cherries. At once my throat constricted. Poison! My palate seemed to lazar, drying up like cracked mud in a river bed. I needed water. I needed air. The cloying fragrances of the courtiers, the acrid dust of the ladies' farded cheeks, seemed to infest my lungs and nostrils.

Adolph Brenner swept at me through the mist of my fear. 'Tommaso,' he said. 'You've been denounced.'

'What?'

'Your assistants and spies have informed against you.'

'But the cherries . . .'

'Don't you understand? They've brought you here to condemn you in public.'

My escape from the Ritterstube was impeded by Jonathan Knott. 'Leaving us so soon, Herr Grilli?'

Adolph Brenner removed his incriminating fingers from my shoulder.

'I . . . I, uh . . . my throat is parched.'

The Winkelbach brothers turned about to watch the scene; the Duchess and her entourage did likewise.

'Why,' said Jonathan Knott, 'what have you been eating?'

As though commanded by an invisible power, the entirety of the Felsengrundian court turned its attention on my spilling plate.

'Enjoying the fruits of your questionable labours?'

'I was given . . .'

'Felsengrunde has always been a Land of Cockaigne for you, has it not?'

I looked in desperation to Albrecht Rudolphus. I knew that I was done for when he refused to lift his downcast eyes, and I watched the Lord Chamberlain unfurl my indictment.

'Your erstwhile apprentices,' Moritz von Winkelbach began, 'whom it appears you treated contemptuously, have testified that you paid them to spy on his Grace the Duke. Do you deny this?'

'. . .'

'You maintained, using money given to you in good faith by the Duke, a network of informants throughout the Castle. You broke the bond of trust between yourself and your patron, even going so far as to pry into the intimate affairs of our Duke and Duchess . . .'

Scandalised breaths were snatched up on my right; the Jesuit Wackenfels, like a comedy priest, opened his palms and raised his eyes to the heavens.

'These are allegations, my Lord Chamberlain,' I said. 'It's plain, your Grace, there are people in our midst who wish to blacken my reputation.'

'Corporal Jörgen Suhl, who escorted you sixteen years ago to Frankfurt where you printed Vögel's history, has sworn on oath that you embezzled funds, lavishing upon yourself, for your carnal pleasures, money entrusted to you by the Treasury for the purpose of acquiring books and objects of art. Do you deny *this* accusation?'

I tried to circumvent Moritz von Winkelbach, straining to catch the eye of the Duke. 'Am I on trial, your Grace?'

'You don't merit the *expense* of a trial,' said the Treasurer, Schaffner.

'Nor its dignity,' said Grünenfelder. I was beset on all sides by leering jackals. Only clever Knott – having commenced proceedings – stood back, neutral behind his crossed arms.

'I did spend a very little amount of your money, my lord. A very small sum on necessities. I do not recollect exactly what, I confess, the amount was so trifling and the offence – if it *was* an offence – so long ago.'

'So long, your Grace,' said the Lord Chamberlain, 'has this Tuscan been abusing your hospitality.'

Shame and fury made me incautious. 'What of Schneuber, then? What of Knott, who has so craftily taken my place? You can all see *my* legacy. We are standing in it. My work for the grandeur of the ducal name. Can't you see – it's these new arrivals who have been abusing the Duke's trust.'

'*Silence.*' The Duke wiped his lips. 'I will have silence from the accused – and less insolence . . . Continue, please, my Lord Chamberlain.'

'Thomas Grilli, you have lied to his Grace about your

circumstances in Prague under the late Emperor. You alleged a familiarity with kings which, quite rightly, you have never enjoyed.'

'How . . . ? What makes you think . . . ?'

'Your imprisonment in Prague Castle you kept a secret, which is tantamount to lying.'

'Withholding is no lie. It's a sin of omission.' Adolph Brenner scowled at me from a distance to be quiet.

'You have insulted your superiors,' continued Moritz von Winkelbach, reading from his charge sheet, 'and betrayed the trust of him who gave you everything.'

'And my punishment?' Let it come, I thought. Let the worst befall me, that the worst be over and done with.

'Had I my way,' said the Lord Chamberlain, 'I should have you flogged and kicked out of the Dukedom.'

'No,' cried the Duke. 'I will not have him hurt.'

Elisabetta remonstrated with her husband. 'He has not even attempted to offer a refutation, my lord.'

'He has served me,' said the Duke. 'He has made some . . . and procured many . . . beautiful things. For which I cannot be unmerciful.' Staring at my planted toes, I understood that our shared secret, the forgeries that both of us had sworn to uphold as originals in the eyes of the world, would remain secret a little longer. They were the glue that would keep me in Felsengrunde; for the Duke to have banished me without hope of a pardon would have meant risking his own exposure.

'He is to be stripped of his titles and fined. His wages shall be cut. But he is *not* to be persecuted.' Albrecht Rudolphus closed his eyes. He sat, bloated with sorrow, against the back of his chair. 'Let him go now. I have spoken.'

Courtiers closed ranks above me. They hissed and booed like the Winds personified on a map. 'Shame! Cozener! Cheat!' I pressed through yielding gowns and fled the

Library. I crossed the desolate courtyard. Guards wafted me like a malodour under the gatehouse. On the murmurous bridge my feet peeped above the horizon of my belly. Left now, down the hillside into town, where houses shrank away from the Castle as pebbles dwindle towards the grinding sea. Had news of my disgrace travelled before me? Were these idle cloaks really snatched up against the contagion of my passing? Only in the dregs of the town, it seemed, might this hermit crab outcast from its shell find shelter. A few coins jangled in my ballock-purse. I ought to have mustered them as my security, a strip of rind to carry me through lean times. But I was to lose them all. I wandered through narrow gabled streets, sidling into filthy taverns where formerly I had recruited labourers. Every stale blast of laughter, every spilled slop beside my stool, I took for an insult, an imputation against my honour which only my size prevented me from defending with my fists. Dejected, piteous, I hid my snout in greasy tankards. Foam and snot limed my sleeves. I remember the day, long muted in that dismal tavern, sinking at sunset and the custom thickening: men reeking of the forge or the leafy stink of carted vegetables. So long as I was seated the drink – a mixture of sack and warm beer – worked honestly on my brain, numbing its agues and boxing up the world in cotton. But when I tried to stand the floor fell away, like Tantalus's water, and the walls began to swim. I was cast out to sea in the midst of a hurricane. The ground rushed up to greet me like a passionate dog. I remember vaguely being hoisted aloft. Fingers not my own rummaged inside my pockets. My purse was taken. Then someone deposited me on the blue dunes of the sky. Somehow lust declared itself. I staggered at skirts and remember clutching a piece of taffeta while some angry birds flapped and pecked at my face. Anna, I protested! Gretel, *mein Herzensau*! A husband at last put an end to the affront. A cane, or an uncommonly spherical fist, struck my cheek a savage blow. Sobriety came with the pain. I remember the cherry-flesh that had to be flushed from my nostrils, passing into the vomit before my splayed and steadying fingers. I staggered into an alcove where some halfway clean straw had been delicately fragranced by a crate of peaches. Tomorrow, or the day after tomorrow, I would have to return to the Castle to see what I could salvage there. For now my eyelids were leaden. Sleep fell like a hood. I awoke from a dream of my life.

I returned to the Castle very penitent. I had nowhere else to go. On a wafting from the indifferent guards, I walked in the shadow of the East Wing up Vergessenheit Street and climbed the lesser staircase to my quarters.

It was heavy dusk in the corridor. Someone had closed the shutters without bothering to light a single lamp. 'Damn servants,' I muttered, and felt inside my pockets for a flint that was no longer there. The corridor gaped ahead of me. Nobody stirred in the adjoining rooms. I felt suddenly afraid.

'Who's there?'

I strained to hear breathing, some involuntary whisper of clothing, a faintest ting of unsheathed metal.

'Adolfo, is that you?'

Nothing. *Bah*. Was I going to frighten myself on vacant air? I advanced, stumbling on blind mole feet.

Jakob Schneuber was sitting at my desk. He had left my door ajar so that, if my fright were not greatly mitigated, at least I might not wake the neighbours by my screaming. '*So*.' I tried to speak carelessly. 'It seems you have my key?'

'I have plenty of keys.'

He was inspecting the Jivaro shrunken head – which I had been sketching for posterity – as though it were a fruit to be thumbed at market. A faint blue light came through the paste of the window pane. I asked him what he was doing in my chamber.

'I want to tell you about my life, Herr Grilli. Where I've been. And whom I've met.'

'I'm sure Wackenfels or the chaplain would be delighted to receive your confession.'

Jakob Schneuber laid down the head. His voice sounded gentle, intimately cadenced. 'I fought among the Germans at White Mountain. We faced the right flank of the Czechs under Joachim Schlick. Afterwards I slept in an orchard. It was very cold. We ate rotten pears. The next day we entered Prague without firing a shot and cheered when Maximilian received the enemy's surrender.'

'Good,' I said with the impatience of sickness. 'I'm very glad for you.'

'In the spring I put my former life as a scrivener to good purpose. I was hired as secretary to Karl of Liechtenstein. It was our job to draw up a list of ringleaders to be arrested and tried.'

'Really, Herr Schneuber, I am feeling most dreadfully *tired*.'

'It was last June. A huge scaffold had been erected against the east wall of the Old Town Hall. You know the place well – it was opposite your schoolhouse . . .'

Through sickness and exhaustion, my blood summoned the courage to run cold.

'Go on,' I said.

Without stirring at my desk, Jakob Schneuber described the executions. The names of Bohemian nobles meant nothing to me; the story of their suffering only compounded my nausea. 'I watched them execute Dr Jessenius. You have heard of *him*?'

'He was . . . the anatomist . . .'

'He negotiated with the Hungarians in Bratislava.'

Poor Jessenius. What had they done with his corpse? Does his skeleton ramble on a rope in Charles University?

'But I wasn't only a witness on that day of judgement,' said Schneuber. The world outside was darkling; I could make out the white gloss of my enemy's eyes and the glistening ivory of his teeth. 'I personally drove the nail that pinned Mikuláš Diviš to the gallows. By his tongue. '

'I think *yours* lies.'

'But I was kind and gave the boy a chance of recovering his speech. I instructed the family to hold up his head, to keep his tongue from splitting.'

'Damn you, Schneuber.' I gripped the wooden frame of the door for support. 'Why must you tell me these monstrous things?'

'Because you wrinkled your nose at my exhibits. Because you smile and poison the world by your smiling, then flinch before a pock-eaten head and think that makes you a Christian. Have you never used a whore?'

'Get out.'

'A true artist relishes horror.'

'You call yourself an artist? *God* made those bodies you display.'

'God made those bodies you draw, Herr Grilli.' Schneuber picked up the tongue stones from my desk and tossed them at my chest. 'God made that. He made these, all these curiosities. We *both* record matter. Only I try to preserve it.'

'By killing it first.'

'You despise my methods. And yet you import mummy for your . . . shall we call them paintings? The only difference between us is that you daub flesh, while I save it. You create illusions, I celebrate the thing itself.'

'Cheap gimcracks.'

'At least they're genuine.'

'What?'

'One cannot *forge* human flesh.'

Cold sweat welled up from my pores. 'I sense an insinuation, Herr Schneuber.'

'Let me speak plainly, then. You are a forger, Grilli. You have no art of your own but steal from better men. And Duke Albrecht is tired of it.'

'Duke *Albrecht*?'

'Of course, it has yet to be proclaimed. His Grace has relinquished the assumed part of his name. With my help – with the help of Mister Knott – the Duke has reclaimed his true identity.'

I felt extravagantly sick; my bowels were stabbed with ice.

'It was Albrecht who told us about your inventions.'

'He would not have done so. Denigrate his own Library? His life's achievement? It's inconceivable.'

'The guiding spirits can reveal nothing to a man who lives by deception. The Duke has made a clean breast of his failings.'

'So why did he not denounce my forgeries in public, yesterday, when I underwent my verbal bastinado?'

'A private confession has satisfied Knott's angels. That's right, Grilli. You sit down. Have a rest.'

My cushions were cold, lumpy, dishevelled. I was aware that my left knee was trembling, as it had done decades ago in the dark stairwell of a Kleinseite tavern.

'But I haven't told you,' said Schneuber, 'what I did for a living *before* White Mountain.'

(Oh God.)

'I worked for a man called Moosbrugger. Matthäus Friedrich Moosbrugger. I believe you met him once or twice in your youth?'

'Nonsense. You can't have been more than a boy.'

'Philip von Langenfels – yes, you knew *him* too – employed me as his page shortly before he was imprisoned. Moosbrugger kept me on. After Langenfels was exposed we travelled from place to place, through Saxony and Thuringia. I learned many valuable skills from my master. And he told me of his former intrigues. Which must have been how I came to learn of your shame.'

My throat was raked with pain as I tried to swallow. 'He didn't get *me* into the river,' I croaked. 'Your murderous benefactor.'

'Though he tried to have you swallowed up in Dalibor . . . I'd forgotten about that particular intrigue, of course. There were so many to remember. Then my good friend Jonathan Knott described you in a letter and I wondered if you were not the same dwarf. Is it not heartening to learn of one's existence in the correspondence of strangers?'

'So Knott brought you here – to expose my guilty secret and discredit me.'

'The Duke retains some misplaced affection for you. It took a long time for him to credit the charges. Even now he protects you from banishment.'

'Lucky me,' I muttered.

'His Grace seeks to refine himself. In order to purify his soul and restore his body, he must remove the impurities from his life. That includes those who surround him.' Jakob Schneuber stood up quietly, with barely a creak from my ordinarily loquacious chair. 'You are a hindrance on his path to healing.'

'It is your colleague who makes him sick. What opiate is he giving him?'

'Herr Knott applies alchemical laws to everything – and everyone. You had to be removed from the Duke's life.'

Kind reader, it was almost a relief. My lies had been

exposed like a fish gutted on a slab. My name before the Duke lay in tatters.

'Goodnight, Herr Grilli. May you dream sweetly of success.'

Jerking in satirical reverence, the flesh sculptor withdrew. I followed him to my door and listened to his diminishing footsteps. I feared no knife swooping at me through the darkness. Jakob Schneuber, though he may have coveted me for his collection, had no need to cut my throat.

I was stuffed already.

16

Manheim

It began with a horseman. Tommaso Grilli, banished curator of the Library of Arts, was drooling into a pillow, his left ear bathing in a cold dew, when news came clattering into the yard. A clarion sounded from the ramparts, and invisible trumpeters took up the call from east and north and south.

I woke with the echo's dying.

From the pounding in my head and the crawling nest of pain in my shoulders, I knew that I had overslept. It was a common failing since my denunciation. Sleep had become a refuge for me, as wine is for other men, and like them I surfaced from an excess of it in a state of alarming decrepitude. Where is the poet who will sing the body's agues, who will fit words to the agonies of the imprisoned spirit? Nothing can be said or written that has not been said or written before, one hundred times in one hundred tongues, about the mayfly, Love. Yet if ecstasy of the blood is a fit subject for poetry, why not its distemper also? All of humanity experiences the latter; the former passes many of us by.

Sitting in my cushions and fizzing like a stale mug of beer, I heard people rushing about the Castle. Voices were raised in surprise and alarm. I yawned lionishly, letting my eyes melt and stretching my jaw until it clicked and gave me gristly earlobes. I was no longer interested in the world outside. Dispatch riders were common enough, even in our misgoverned backwater, while Felsengrunde was replete with men whose salaries were dependent on their rushing

373

to and fro. An illusion of purpose must be upheld when all purpose is lacking.

Having to observe this principle myself – for I could not give in to despair – I broke the green mantle of the washbasin and soaked my crumpled face. In my haste to dress I scattered thick wads of paper. Kicked in the spine, a portfolio vomited sketches of dodo claws and wrung-necked parakeets. I scraped a knuckle on the corner of a fake Dürer and then, withdrawing my injured hand, toppled a bronze gladiator with my elbow.

I went back to bed.

'HAVE YOU HEARD?'

'Shh! Not so loud.'

'Have you heard?'

'This way . . .'

The voices came closer, right up to my door, so that my sleep gained nothing from their hush. 'It wasn't just a brawl gone wrong. The Duke would never have been told if the death was accidental.'

'Killed, then?'

'Worse.'

'Worse than killed?'

'There's killing and there's killing.'

'And?'

'This was worse.'

I had meant, as I jumped out of bed, to silence the servants with a blast of invective. Before I reached the door, however, my intention changed.

The men snatched up their elbows. 'Christ – you gave us a fright.'

'What are you talking about?'

The men's surprise turned to glee at having virgin ears to corrupt. 'Have you not heard?'

'Heard what?'
'About the farmer.'
'What farmer?'
'Murdered.'
'By soldiers.'

'They came out of nowhere and demanded food with menaces. When the farmer resisted they dragged him into the forest.'

'His brother found him twitching . . .'

'Eyes taken.'

'. . . head first in an ant hill.'

Feeling very stupid, I asked a number of questions which received withering replies. I understood that armed men had entered Felsengrunde from the north. Over the next few days they began to plunder the Weideland, using the great forest as their redoubt, from which they would make violent incursions for supplies and then melt back into the trees before any defensive force could be sent to meet them. Felsengrunde had scarcely the resources to protect itself from such plunder. Fields were going untended, cows and goats unmilked. Nobody knew the fate of the sheep in their summer pasture on the High Plateau. One evening, the Sheriff returned to the Castle haggard and dishevelled, his horse bleeding from its spurred flanks, to announce that one of the rogues had been captured. Since no screams could escape the fastness of the dungeon, I learned from scraps of rumour that the captive was a Protestant mercenary, a veteran of White Mountain, and that his comrades were the last and most loyal followers of the Lutheran mercenary Jörgen Manheim, taking refuge from the Catholic League in our mountain fortress.

The news must have chilled courtly blood. The routine of government was shattered. According to Adolph Brenner, who alone braved official displeasure by meeting me in my quarters, the factions were more clearly marked than ever. The nobility had gathered about the Duchess. Inspired by the Jesuit Wackenfels and eager to prove themselves men of action, they spoke of blood and True Religion. The Duke meanwhile hesitated. He had retreated to his Library, where he was rumoured to be seeking angelic advice through Jonathan Knott, while Knott's assistants sweated over their vessels to keep Albrecht supplied with elixir. Noxious fumes seeped from the tower like spores from a mushroom. Elisabetta herself was heard pounding on the Ritterstube door, demanding action against the enemy.

'Suppose we did fight back, Adolfo? Suppose we could train enough tradesmen and farmers to complement our guards?'

'A few shopkeepers against a desperate and battle-hardened foe? The Church has laws against self-slaughter.'

Finally, under pressure from the Duchess, Albrecht sent a courier to Manheim requesting that he restrain his men. This outraged Elisabetta more than the Duke's inaction. She wrote on his behalf – pleading her husband's illness – to the Emperor for help.

'These fugitives from Bohemia have come here because Albrecht is feeble,' said Brenner. 'Are not Calvinists allowed to live and worship in the Wintertal? This is almost a Protestant stronghold.'

I agreed. 'By the time this crisis is resolved, all that may well have changed.'

We shared a perilous glance. The castle would fracture – we felt it clearly – under the weight of this emergency. Meanwhile people continued to suffer, and the forthcoming harvest looked doubtful. Farmsteaders, abandoned by their lord and protector, were said to be defending themselves with staves and pitchforks; so it was almost a relief when Maximilian of Bavaria – the big fish who stole Rudolf's treasure and could not leave a little scrap for me – announced by herald that his army would be entering Felsengrunde to finish once and for all with the fugitive Manheim. The Duchess in particular was delighted when Catholic soldiers – numbering several hundred by all accounts, formidable with their muskets and pikes, with their horse-drawn cannon and champing steeds – marched up the Pass of Our Lady and billeted themselves in the villages of Kirchheim and Krantor. True Religion, it seemed, would prevail over heresy. A room in the Duchess's Apartments was cleared and refurbished to receive the Bavarian Grand Duke.

'Of course, he won't come,' said Brenner, whose constant gloom would have wearied Job. 'To this backwater, for a skirmish in the woods? Elisabetta can always dream. There will be no glory for her, nor for anyone, in the days that are to follow.'

Perhaps, unimaginable reader, in the world far in the future where you have discovered this document encased in lead deep within the Tuscan soil, Mankind has cast aside war and its causes? Perhaps greed and misgovernance and the ravages of religious strife no longer exist for you, where you sit in the shade of a spreading oak, surrounded by concord of ethereal music? I pray that you will not comprehend what I am about to describe.

The Bavarian troops (few of whom had ever lived in Bavaria) were welcomed by many Felsengrundians as liberators. There was a flaw, however, in this hope. Like their enemy, the terrible Manheim, the Bavarians lacked means for supporting themselves. No soldier, however wretched his origins, will fight if he is not fed. So the Catholics fuelled their campaign of liberation by plunder also. It was a kind of tribute to be paid by the peasantry for its salvation. Manheim's men hid themselves in the forest. To deprive them of cover, the Bavarians set fire to the Wald.

Felsengrundians, escaping from the flames, were killed by the Protestant rebels to be assured of their silence. The Catholic liberators, hunting Manheim, killed Felsengrundians for protecting the enemy. Unable to distinguish between the two sides, the peasants had to take pot luck in declaring their allegiance, when in fact they owed none to either.

In the fastness of the Castle, the Duke continued to consult with spirits, while the Duchess held masses to pray for victory and commissioned a splendid dress in which to hear the anticipated *Te Deum*. I tried to ignore events beyond my chamber. There was comfort in drudgery. To prolong my employment, I had decided to colour the Duke's botanical books, and was about to start in watercolours on the vast cabbage in *De Historia Stirpium* when my curiosity betrayed me. My whiskers twitched at rumours. I ventured forth.

As you can imagine, I was no longer welcome in public. Sometimes, at a casual gesture from the Lord Chamberlain or Jonathan Knott, I would find my path impeded by a raised boot or descending halberd. Expulsions from the Library or the Great Hall were common occurrences, involving much impotent anger from me and embarrassed shrugging from the expelling agent. The older guards harboured few grudges against me – unlike the more recent recruits who, having been raised in the hamlets of the Weideland, were conditioned by public slander to despise me as the instigator of Felsengrunde's woes. With disheartening symmetry, the infamy of Thomas Grilli swelled in the popular imagination at the very time that Tommaso Grilli shrank to irrelevance in the Castle. Like a decrepit hound, I was tolerated in my former haunts; I snuffled at people's hips, subject to the occasional kick if I came too close but unlikely, just yet, to be dragged with my tail between my legs into a guttered yard and dispatched with a pigging hammer.

In this desultory condition, I was able to discover the cause of fearful lamentations.

A throng of courtiers, guards and citizens had assembled in the shadow of the gatehouse. A dozen or so peasants, remarkable less for the poverty of their clothes than for the roll and frenzy of their grief, formed the hub of this gathering. They wept and wailed like actors in a Passion. The men clasped their heads in anguish, the women pushed headscarves into their mouths. The cause of their sorrow was by now a familiar one. Armed men had emerged from the purlieus of the great forest. Hearing harsh voices and the rasp of weaponry, the peasants had abandoned their fields and fled to caves farther up the mountain. A day later they had returned to find their homes burned, their grain stolen and the livestock sunning its hoofs on the hillside. So much I understood at the crowd's perimeter. Worse, far worse than this assault on property (though it threatened all of them with cold and starvation), had been the peasants' discovery of one of their own, a father of three, death-rattling in the grass outside a cowshed.

The rebels had flayed him alive.

The body lay on a bier of pleached branches. Such a number of people grieving for one man: I doubted half so many would squeeze a tear above my corpse. The onlookers huddled together as a stained wool blanket was peeled from the bier. There were gasps from the townsfolk, several of whom turned away with their hands across their mouths. The peasants by contrast were numbed by the vision; they stood in silence beside their ghastly exhibit while the Duke (whose presence, revealed by a nauseated gap in the crowd, was almost as shocking to me as the body itself) took gulps of air through a silk handkerchief. The Duchess was also present, watching with her entourage.

I pressed my way through yielding bodies and came up against the flayed man. I thought my knowledge of the anatomical plates in *De humani corporis fabrica* would steel me; but those placid cadavers bore no resemblance to this grimacing mess on the birchwood bier. Where in this viscous horror, in all this fly-intoxicating pulp, did the divisions reside which were so clearly delineated in the woodcuts between derma and sinew, between sinew and wefted muscle? Granted, the perpetrators of this dissection had lacked the precision of Vesalius or a Jessenius of Prague; but could not Nature, even when so crudely exposed, have conformed a little more to aesthetic sensibilities? This wretch had had the life torn from him. Nothing could beautify the handiwork of those bloody tailors, not the shirring of the skin about the neck to create a livid ruff, nor the slashing of the forearms or warp of the torso. I stuffed my fingers into my mouth and vomited over the cobbles, drowning my shoes and staining irretrievably my last pair of lace cuffs. Wackenfels, Elisabetta's confessor, knelt beside the corpse and tried surreptitiously, without giving offence, to hide his nose behind his wrist as he sought words of consolation.

'Who did this to you?' the Duchess demanded of the widow. 'Was it Manheim? Did Manheim's soldiers commit this outrage?'

The widow's eyes were glassy, almost drugged with incomprehension.

'It is important that you understand. The soldiers. Who attacked your farm. Who killed your husband. Were they rebels?'

'Soldiers.'

'Were they Protestants?'

'*Soldiers.*'

Elisabetta stepped back, snarling as though vindicated.

'Beastly Manheim. Do you see now, your Grace, how just our policy has been?'

'*Our* policy?'

A silver coin was pressed by Wackenfels into the widow's hand. 'My husband makes you this promise,' said Elisabetta. 'Those devils will suffer for their crimes. The killing of your loved one shall not go unavenged.'

'Who will tend the fields for us?' an old man sobbed. 'Who will raise his children and put bread in their mouths?'

The Jesuit confessor traced a sign of the cross. '*Benedicite,*' he said. The peasants tried to silence the old man, calling him 'father' and leaning on his hands. A few remembered themselves sufficiently to bow as the noble factions pushed through the crowd.

Over the next fortnight, until the decisive skirmish, rumour and counter-rumour flourished in town and Castle. A massacre took place in Krantor when thirteen people were stuck like pigs in their fields, then restored to health by a countervailing story and finally deprived of life by a returning tax collector. In Spitzendorf, which the founding forebear of Albrecht had defended from the Swiss, a farmer and his wife were crucified for refusing to surrender their cow. The same happened, with variations, in Winkelbach (where a goat became the chattel in contention), in Kirchheim (three goats) and on the southern slopes of Berg Mössingen (a daughter). According to these apocryphal versions, the farmer and wife became a goatherd and his sister, then a family of tinkers, and at last reassumed their original identity. Other outrages were less digestible for being undisputed. On the High Plateau above the Augspitzer Wald, a shepherd's bowels were fed to his sheep; in Kirchheim the village priest was bludgeoned with a plaster Virgin and then hoisted by rope towards the weathervane. Women were raped in unguessable numbers and sometimes killed, left beneath their skirts on farmstead after farmstead throughout the Weideland. Only the capital and the few houses on the shore of the Obersee were spared these disasters, though nothing could dispel the gloom of a town besieged by unspeakable dread. The miseries of war that now afflict the wider Empire were rehearsed on the lush slopes and ripe valleys of Felsengrunde. Some days I would stand on the battlements, where the son of my friend Klaus hid me beneath his cloak, and try to make out the flow of battle. There was rarely much to see. One might hear a distant alarum or the plosion of musket fire; then the grace of late summer closed over the breach. The sun continued to shine on fields of climbing wheat, falcons hovered in the heights and on the shimmering rooftops of the town sparrows gaily chirruped. How out of place the violence seemed in this tranquil setting. Nature countered the affront by beautifying everything. The houses burned like festive candles; white smoke bloomed amid the ranks of dark pines, and fir trees on the slopes of the Augspitzer Wald pointed lost souls the way to Heaven.

Eventually, since all tragedy is endurable from a distance, I abandoned my vigils on the castle battlements and took refuge in my work. In the disorder of my cramped quarters, surrounded by objects and charcoal drawings, I gazed at a baby pickled in a jar. He was naked save for a string of black beads around his pale, almost translucent neck. In the dimpled fingers of his right hand he held a wilted pink flower which transpired, on closer inspection, to be an eye socket rescued from his mother's corpse. It was to be my last portrait. Other objects from the Duke's Arcana merited only brisk sketches, images for a doubtful posterity. With the baby, however, as for the duck-tailed dwarf, I felt I had a greater duty to discharge. A portraitist must distil in his picture some drop of the sitter's essence. But where had the soul fled from this floating infant? Though the eyes were open, I could not look into them. It occurred to me that this was a celebration of Death. Jakob Schneuber did not steal a march on the Reaper: he was one of its gibing minions, rubbing salt into the wound of our mortality.

I was shaken from these meditations by jubilant cries from the gatehouse. I rushed to my casement and flung it open.

'What's happening?'

Guardsmen on the battlements raised their muskets in celebration and did not hear me. Trumpets sounded, banners were hoisted, and up the canyon of Vergessenheit Street I could hear a rumbling like thunder. Standing on my work table, I looked down at the heads of servants as they dropped their chores and rushed to greet the cavalrymen.

Jörgen Manheim had been taken alive. After the final gouge of battle, when the last lung had flooded and no more smoke flowered on a musket's stem, the Bavarians had dredged him up from a Protestant swamp and carried him all the way to the dungeon tower. At this very instant, surgeons were patching him up for the gallows, like a lamb untangled from briars the better to ensure the sweetness of its meat. From a corridor window I could see victorious soldiers slumped in the courtyard between the chapel and the Banqueting Hall. They looked filthy and elated – their faces all used up. Some had built little pyres on the cobbles and were immolating them, as if to propitiate the god of battles. Others drank thirstily from buckets slung into the well, or washed their faces at the fountain, turning its spouts the colour of wine.

'Hell,' I told myself, 'infernal Hell.' Jakob Schneuber must have known that I would dread having to confront the soldiery. It was a jest for him to have recalled his pickled baby – leaving a note under my door so that I could not entrust the jar to a messenger but would have to return it in person. I had no choice but to obey; I existed in the Castle only to serve my enemy's pranks.

I descended the steps to Vergessenheit Street on quivering legs; hesitated at the corner beneath the Treasury windows; then launched myself into the open courtyard.

The tumult struck me like the blast from a furnace. I would have to cross this red sea to reach the Library, searing my nose with the tang of spent powder, spent terror. Moving through smoke and muttered oaths, seeing the heels of bloodied palms brooding on pommels and the butts of muskets upturned to serve as crutches, I was overwhelmed by the weight of the soldiery, by its animal stink and matter, as once in a field outside Nuremberg I had stumbled on a great herd of cattle and trembled in the loud brute music. Nobody taunted me, nobody jeered. All ears that were not clogged with mud or deafened by gunfire were trained on the desolate moaning, a dismal continuo from Weidmanner Platz where the wounded lay, waiting for the saw or the sacrament. It was almost a relief to hear, among the soldiers, some voices raised in argument – until I recognised Milanese insults and attempted to evade them.

'Christ on a stick! If it isn't old Zoppo!'

A mature soldier pointed at me from a group of bickering mercenaries. He was large chested, with a red-and-pepper beard and a nose that had been split in combat. I stared at the armour tanned with dried blood, at the clotted sparse hairs on his leathery scalp. Only the eyes shone familiarly through thirty years of smoke and powder.

'Do you not recognise me?'

Had he not called me 'Zoppo', I should never have connected this grizzled soldier with his boyish predecessor in a Milanese workshop. No doubt it was easier for him to identify me, my height and face having altered less over the years than his. I felt my bowels flutter and the skin of my nape pricking. Was this how it felt to encounter a ghost?

'Zoppo is unfair,' I replied, and took a few steps to prove it; for my walk had improved a little over the years.

The mercenary grinned. 'True. I always thought you walked like a goose.' Other soldiers – his comrades – let drop their argument and began to watch this unexpected encounter. 'Do you not remember my name?'

'Giovanni.'

'The very same. Son of a bitch, Tommaso, how can you be so old and living in this shit hole?'

Witless to think of an answer, I caught myself looking at his right hand, at the fingers that had been broken long ago by Gian Bonconvento. The mercenary – coarse father to the talented youth – interpreted my glance and held up a bearish paw to the failing light. 'All present and accounted for,' he said, bolting back his fingers. 'Though I must handle a sword with my left hand.'

'That makes us both sinister,' I replied.

Giovanni agreed with a grimace. He heard the murmuring of his comrades and followed their eyes to the pickled baby at my chest. He looked at the object as though seeing it for the first time; his face fell in dismay.

'This is not mine,' I said hastily. 'I don't mean in the sense of . . . The child is not *mine*. Nor the jar for that matter . . .'

I must have been a troubling apparition to those battle-hardened Milanese; several behind Giovanni crossed themselves.

'It *died* dead,' I continued. 'I mean it was born this way. Dead, that is. Not in a jar.' I saw the wisdom of moving on and ridding myself of the object. I assured Giovanni that I would come back later to find him, when reasons for *this* (the baby knocked gently against the glass) would be given to his satisfaction. Feeling oddly ashamed of myself, I hurried to the Library, all the while trying not to hear the moaning of injured men on Weidmanner Platz.

Jakob Schneuber had quite forgotten his request for the specimen's return, as I had anticipated he would. 'Put it down,' he said, neglecting to look up from the page of a book, 'over there.'

'Over where?'

'On the table.'

'Which table?'

Schneuber ignored me. I would not be angered by this puerile trick. I left the fetid Library and went in search of my childhood friend.

Giovanni was tearing a piece of salami with his teeth when I found him. He followed me, still nonchalantly chewing, all the way to my quarters – where I waited for him to explore with his eyes before inviting him to sit. Giovanni contemplated the chair as one might a dog, uncertain whether it bites. He squatted heavily, then shifted on his hams as though seeking the familiar roughness of a boulder or tree trunk. Framed by my window, with the Duke's mathematical instruments perched like metal birds on their stands on the table, Giovanni seemed out of place, as improbable as an ape in a lady's chamber. He tugged at the few gingery hairs on his scalp, puffed up his chest and released the air with a soft nasal sigh. I offered him a cup of wine and, seeing the avidity with which he drained it, felt ashamed to have forgotten his recent exertions. What had your narrator ever done so brave as to survive in battle? I felt his eyes stray across my courtier's clothes (the paned doublet of woven and worn silk, the stiffened collar of bleached linen, witnesses to my former wealth) and my restless, ink-brindled fingers. 'Are those yours?' He nodded across his cup at the gloves of cream leather, a gift from my

Duke in happier times, resting head to toe on the table beside my elbow. 'Yes,' I said, and nudged them out of sight.

'Especially made?'

'Tailored to fit.' I thought of Giovanni's coarse and bloodied fingers. 'Where will you be sleeping tonight?'

'Outside with my men.'

'You could sleep here. There's no bed but it is safe from the elements.'

Giovanni shook his head. It was in his experience unwise to sleep in the hours after battle. 'The pictures are too fresh in the mind. I mostly wait until drink knocks me out – or one of my comrades does.' He opened wide his graveyard mouth and emitted a gristled, hacking, mercenary laugh, with a condiment of rusty phlegm which he expectorated on to the floor; watching him draw it out with his boot into a slug's trail, I wanted suddenly for him to go away, to take his troubling mess and his vulgar Milanese and restore me to my drudgery.

'So,' said Giovanni. 'You speak first.'

I told him (not without hesitation, for the Milanese was furred and mouldy on my tongue) how my travels had brought me to Felsengrunde. I did not bother to conceal my recent fall from favour: what sense had vanity before such a man as this, an old sweat of a soldier rubbing blood off the back of his hands? He listened, heavily nodding, to my life story, and when I had finished made no guffaw nor began to lament his own lost chances. Had I not played a part in the act of rebellion that resulted in the smashing of his fingers? Could he not reprimand me for having survived intact and pursued my craft into maturity, when he had been forced to limp away, turning his back on his Muse? I braced myself for bitter words but none came.

'I have not fared so badly, Tommaso. I've been married twice and I still have a daughter in your part of the world. Her husband is outside.'

'Here?'

'Pardon?

'Your daughter lives in Felsengrunde?'

'No,' said Giovanni. 'She lives near Florence. Her husband's out in the courtyard. He's a mercenary like me.'

It was time for my guest to tell his story. I was about to learn the true fate of our former master, the man-elephant Gian Bonconvento. I had learned, you will remember, from my uncle's letter, received while in custody at Prague Castle, of the painter's death, which his grief-maddened mother had attributed to his ungracious pupils. 'We did more than pray for him to die,' said Giovanni. I felt a preposterous urge to open the door to my chamber and verify that no one was listening. I resisted and encouraged Giovanni to take up his story.

'After leaving the villa, I remember staggering into the city. My fingers were prodded and shrugged over by a student doctor at the Ca' Granda. He gave me a strip of leather to bite on while he bound them with a splint. What emerged from the bandages, he said, would never work as well nor feel so keenly as before.

'I wandered off and found a room near the Martesana canal. The mosquitoes got drunk on my blood, I wallowed in a filthy bed and tried to sleep through my pain. Just lying there somehow used up all my florins and within a month I was penniless. So I joined the lowlifes on the Porta Orientale, where I learned how to pinch a man's pocket and steer drunkards to the whores. Sometimes worse things were demanded of me. But enough of that. I could not think where else to go, you see, nor what to make of myself now that my vocation was gone.

'For nearly a year I scraped a living at the city gate, so close to our despised tyrant. I saw him once or twice, rolling lordly into Milan with Vittorio under his arm, but he didn't recognise me. Life with the lost souls of the Porta Orientale was brutish. I saw men fall asleep in doorways never to awake. I saw corpses on the roadside with their throats cut and ring fingers missing. Sometimes I hid myself in kitchen gardens outside the city, stealing cabbages and tomatoes or trying like a fox to catch a chicken for supper. In this way, without ever working out a plan as such, I found myself creeping back to Bonconvento's villa.

'Mosca and Piero were still there, cowering in the cowshed. Vittorio was indoors, warming the monster's bed. I looked for you from my hiding place in the bushes and was half glad, half wretched to guess that you'd escaped. Without the two of us to help absorb his wrath, Bonconvento was making life a hell for the boys. He would come out to the yard before breakfast and slap the brothers awake. Then Vittorio washed him from a bucket – you remember – and the Maestro raged at him for losing his boyish looks, for growing a beard and allowing his precious skin to break out in spots. I noticed that Bonconvento had started to cough, great explosions that forced themselves from his lungs and his bum and bent him over, hands on knees, his tongue sticking out and his face all boiling.

'Whatever it was that ailed him, it gave me an idea. All day long I sucked on it, that dream of vengeance. It was better than any pap for taking your mind off your hunger. I lay in the bushes, my stomach growling and my brain working. I watched the Maestro on his balcony eating his supper – disgusting green slop served by the cook. Bet you never guessed who *she* was? Maria, the old crone who pissed in our soup? I saw him mouth the word once. 'Mama'. Imagine that! Bonconvento kept his *own mother* in servitude. No wonder she hated us. In her eyes we must have seemed the cause of her son's perversity. After he'd eaten, I heard him yell for Vittorio. The light in his bedchamber went out. I crawled through the grass towards the shed where Mosca and Piero were sleeping. Mosca still snored like a trapped fly but Piero heard my scratching. We spoke through a gap in the wood and hatched our plan together. Mosca was frightened at first but Piero was the stronger and he thirsted for revenge as much as I did. Vittorio was a harder nut to crack. You could never guess how he was going to act. Mosca soiled his breeches expecting him to betray us and have us thrown into gaol. Were we not in gaol already? I countered. And what could be worse than this slow dying, this starving of the spirit? Eventually even Vittorio agreed to my plan.

'And soon the day came, a lovely summer's morning promising real heat. I gave the signal to the boys as Bonconvento came to release them – a tawny owl's cry. Mosca and Piero began, as soon as they were out of the shed, to beg their master for a swim at Lake San Marco. We never went there, did we, in your time? It's a secluded spot to the north of the city, more a pond than a lake, very popular with boys from the city. Gian Bonconvento grumbled, he had work to be getting on with. He became impatient with the brothers and threatened them with a beating. Only when Vittorio joined their appeal did the Maestro stow his anger and agree to the outing. Maria was charged with preparing some food. Vittorio fetched two bottles of wine from the painter's cellar. And so they set off for the lake – Mosca and Piero, Bonconvento and his bumboy – while I sneaked after them, keeping my distance.

'At Lake San Marco I hid for an hour in the bulrushes, shivering as fish rubbed against my legs, and watched the Maestro eat and drink in full view of his famished pupils. Piero and Mosca waded into the water first, naked as frogs and white as the dead. I could see them looking for me, maybe hoping that I had lost courage and run away. Vittorio also stripped off and lay on the bank, his pale body exposed to the sun. He squinted at his drunken master. Gripping a wooden staff, I crouched down and squatted in the water, my nose and eyes afloat, to watch Vittorio at work. He lured the old lecher towards him, then at the last moment leaped up and dashed into the water. There were bathers on another bank but they were screened off by alders and willow branches – so they could not have seen Gian Bonconvento stagger out of his clothes, exposing all that blubber, and crash like a walrus into the lake. They would not have seen three young men splashing and hollering with delight as they converged on the mighty bather.

'I dived and swam and opened my eyes on murky white legs swaying beneath me. Vittorio pressed up against the Maestro and took hold of his flabby arms. His belly was enormous, a pale moon in the green fog of the lake. I swam closer. I used my staff. Gian Bonconvento head-butted the water, bent double by the pain in his guts. I surfaced for a gulp of air and was kicked out of the way by Piero and Mosca. They leaped, as though in play, on the winded Maestro and hooted with laughter as they tried to leapfrog the top of his head. Bonconvento's arms flapped, working up great mountains of water. Twice he managed to snatch some air. His gasps sounded like merriment, and nobody passing by the lake would have questioned the scene – a father larking about with his adoring sons. I watched fascinated, not daring to go back for another strike. For a moment I thought Bonconvento might win, rescued by his unsinkable bulk. He dashed the brothers' heads together and they fell off him.

'For a terrible instant the drowning painter saw me in the water. His eyes, already huge as marbles, widened still further. Then Vittorio jumped on his shoulders. His passion for the Maestro's death was fiercer than anyone's. His prick was hard as he squeezed him under. Piero and Mosca, having recovered, clung on to Bonconvento's legs.

'I don't know how, somehow I *felt* the old man swallow water. His lungs filled up with marshy slime, with floating weeds and stickleback scales. He breathed in his death, while Vittorio rogered the back of his head. For a long time Vittorio stood proud of the water, until the bubbles ceased about his legs. Piero and Mosca eased him away from the Maestro. I could not believe that it was over. Then Bonconvento's belly surfaced, like a great cheese. The rest of him followed – the hairy limbs, the slug of his sex, his face that was both open and closed. He looked like a painter's dummy.

'The boys were shocked by what they'd done. I swam away as fast as I could, back to the bulrushes and the hidden shore. The boys began to weep and wail, calling out for help. "The Maestro! Help! The Maestro's drowned! Somebody help us!" What with all his fat, with all the wine in his belly and the wine-heavy bread, it would not be difficult to convince the world of an accident. How could such a sack of lard have stayed afloat? Only I could have imperilled our friends by my presence. If anyone, running towards the cries of alarm, had seen me in or near the water, suspicion would surely have fallen upon Piero and Mosca and Vittorio. I climbed through the rushes on to the wooded bank. I swept the water off my body and clambered back into my beggar's clothes. From all sides of San Marco I could hear cries of alarm and consternation. I did not hang around to see what would happen. What became of the orphaned apprentices I cannot tell you. I fled Milan that very day, and began my journey on foot to Tuscany. To your country, Tommaso. Where I started my life afresh . . .'

*   *   *

I saw Giovanni twice in the days that followed. With only the ghost of an enemy, and a murdered one at that, to unite us, it proved impossible to revive the old affection. Giovanni, after giving the account of his crime – which by the swiftness of its telling I judged to be well worn – could muster few words towards a conversation. Hating his silence, I asked about his late wives and his daughter. She lived with her parents-in-law in Settignano, he said, on a hillside facing Fiesole. Most gilded in his estimation, she was his life's achievement. But the tender, troubled love of a father for his daughter was unimaginable to me; I did not greatly care to hear about it.

Tents were erected in the Great Courtyard: they huddled for shelter alongside the Ducal House and spread out like dunes from the ramparts, so that a guard might almost have tumbled down the canvasing when his watch was over. I visited Giovanni in his tent which he shared with several mercenaries, including his son-in-law Paolo – a taciturn young man, lean and contemptuous, whose good looks were spoiled by a purple scar that crossed his cheek from earlobe to nostril. I ought to have relished my encounter with these men and revived the slang of my youth. Instead, the combination of familiarity and strangeness left us more divided than men who speak in different tongues. We felt that a bond ought to exist between us, and consequently were all the more aware of its absence. Meanwhile Paolo failed to disguise his suspicion of a Florentine dwarf who carried dead babies about the castle.

The following day I awoke to find that half the soldiery had left the castle. Giovanni was absent along with his comrades. They were being sent to the Wintertal, to finish once and for all with heresy. The purging of Predestiny, which in such a small valley would take only a few days, went against the Duke's wishes; it revoked the decades-old policy of toleration.

'We should not be surprised,' said Adolph Brenner. 'Between separate states divided on religion, a truce makes sense. But spiritual division *within* a state? That, for a ruler, is intolerable.'

The automaton-maker, seeming more frayed than ever, with the skin at his temples turning grey in place of hair, described the argument between the Duke and his court. 'It was the most open dispute yet. Albrecht ended up stamping his feet like a brat. You should have seen the grin on Winkelbach's face. I wanted to take a hatchet to it.'

Assailed by demands for action, Duke Albrecht had tried to hold out. His former namesake had dreamed of uniting the faiths in a single spiritual truth. So Albrecht (whom I doubt had considered the matter before) condemned both Manheim and the Catholic League that sought his destruction.

'You speak ill of those that saved your dukedom,' Elisabetta replied. 'Now they are willing to assist us in removing the cause of its troubles. There can be no half measures in religion.'

'Christian should not slaughter Christian.'

'Would you sleep while the world damns itself? To take no action, after they burned your lands and desecrated its churches, is to carry a firebrand yourself.'

'You will *not* interfere in the Wintertal!' cried the Duke, extending his authority on a feeble finger.

'Your subjects are in need of rescue. If they will not save their souls, we must do it for them.'

Adolph Brenner, as though orphaned by his son's departure, had lost all mirth and enthusiasm. His body seemed to be hollowing out, like a tree consumed by beetles, giving him a famished and fanatical look. I no longer reproached him for having sought an accommodation with Jonathan Knott: it allowed me to eavesdrop vicariously on disputes of state.

It was Brenner who, a few days later, reported the deciding of Manheim's fate.

To Elisabetta's dismay, the Grand Duke of Bavaria had been represented at the council meeting by his force's commander: a minor noble from Ratisbon who enforced his master's will as though dispensing largesse.

'The Grand Duke,' he had said, 'though his soldiers have captured the rebellious Manheim, prefers out of respect for your Grace to leave the man's execution to Felsengrunde.'

'*After* a trial,' said the Duke.

'In time of conflict, judicial process must sometimes be suspended. Besides—' said Winkelbach, '—Manheim has made a full confession.'

The signed document was passed from hand to hand. Nobody commented on the palsied scrawl of the signature; the debate moved on to the practicalities of the execution. The Duke pleaded for a beheading. The Bavarian commander, though supposedly impartial in the matter, recommended the stake to emphasise the heretical motives for the rebel's crimes. The brothers Winkelbach, outraged as much by the plundering of their estates as they claimed to be about Manheim's heresy, argued for a more severe punishment. 'Let him watch his entrails burn.' 'Let him lose his privy parts.' 'For God's sake, don't let us burn him as though he merely peddled *books*.'

'Of course,' said the Bavarian commander, 'the enforcement of the law in Felsengrunde is your responsibility, Lord Chamberlain. Manheim has disobeyed the Emperor's authority and that of his Holiness the Pope. He has proved to be wolfish, worse than a beast. But we must be merciful in conducting justice. Your Grace, it should be burning.'

The Duke, sweating profusely, looked to Jonathan Knott for rescue. The Englishman studied his folded forearms.

'Your Grace's judgement?' Elisabetta glowered at her husband until he thought up an objection.

'Felsengrunde,' he said, 'has no experience in the immolation of heretics.' The excuse, Albrecht knew, was a feeble one. Our friend the Sheriff imagined that it could not differ greatly from the burning of cats.

'If needs be,' said the Bavarian commander, 'my men will undertake the punishment. There are those with experience in the matter.'

Elisabetta's Jesuit agreed. In the ultimate battle to rescue a man's soul, it was needful for executioners to know their business.

A rough wooden fence had been erected around the pyre to keep the crowd from the flames. There were no tumblers this time, as there had been at the cat-burning so many years ago; but in other respects the scene was familiar. I saw apple-sellers and water boys, urchins shouting and upsetting their elders in the rush for a good view, fathers carrying children on their shoulders and feigning drunkenness or threatening to topple, and the vague mass of urban poor, hoping to stave off the intimate teeth of their hunger with the coming spectacle. Up on the dais where the worthies sat, Felsengrunde's banner rippled in the wind, mixed with the pennons of the Bavarian army. I was excluded from the company. Down on the pavement, the crowd surged forward to see the prisoner. A giant hand gripped me beneath the arm, pinching the tender flesh there. I squealed and tried to kick my assailant's shins.

'Easy, tiddler, *easy*.'

One of the Sheriff's men had been sent, on Albrecht's command, to rescue me from the commonage. 'Why? What have I done?'

'He wants you up with the lords.'

'On the dais?'

The brute raped my armpits with his fingers and lifted me into the air. People ducked to escape my swinging feet. On the dais my superiors laughed as I was hoisted towards them. 'If you kick me again,' muttered the brute into my ear, 'I'll break your fucking arms.'

I protested as other guards reached out to take me. 'No! I don't want to be carried. Let me down!'

'Grant him a favour,' observed Jonathan Knott to his neighbour, 'and all he does is complain. Dirty little ingrate.'

My humiliation complete, I tried to collect myself and bowed to the Duke and Duchess. Albrecht frowned as though surprised to see me – and I realised that he had given no order for my elevation. Knott and Schneuber, or perhaps the Winkelbachs, were up to their usual tricks.

'Sit down,' said the Lord Chamberlain. 'Or go and crouch in the corner. You're blocking our view.'

I knelt as low as I could, not daring to jump from the platform back into the crowd which, only moments before, I had longed to escape. Anyone looking towards the Duke might have taken me for his court jester – the licensed scourge of absolute rule.

Over at the northern end of the courtyard, upon the platform and its kindling, a small, stocky and very hairy man was being stripped and chained to the stake. As the soldiers lifted his wrists to clap them in manacles, I could see liverish yellow bruises about his ribs. The condemned man tried to scratch the side of his face; but he would never touch his own flesh again. The crowd, churning like the sea beneath the stake's promontory (but where was Perseus to save *this* Andromeda?), quieted its roar. Even so I could not hear Jörgen Manheim's prayers. He seemed to be panting, like a dog in shade. I was disgusted by that black hole of a mouth opening and closing inaudibly.

'Ordinarily,' said the Bavarian commander, 'we dispense with a pyre, trusting to the faggots piled about the heretic. When there are several to punish in one session, short cuts must be taken.'

Manheim, though still muttering, observed with what seemed a curious detachment the laying of birchwood against his legs and up to his navel. Some connection was made in my memory with my father, tucking me up carefully in my corner of the bed; it had happened only once, in Florence, after the Academicians had sniffed at my talent and Sandro Bondanella had spoken of a count waiting to see me. I remembered watching my father's hands, how they tucked my blanket beneath the mattress, as a traveller tugs on his precious bags to ensure that they are safely fastened. A similar kind of care, close to cosseting, was being taken by the half-dozen soldiers responsible for Manheim's consumption.

'I hope he appreciates,' said the Lord Chamberlain, 'the expense lavished on his execution.'

There was callous laughter on the dais. Elisabetta, I noticed, was resting her fingers on a psalter and moving her lips in whispered prayer. Now the crowd was losing patience; a few disrespectful boys hooted and whistled as the Bavarian chaplain stood on the ladder, with his Bible open, and offered Manheim a quick death in return for a recantation. When, gingerly, the chaplain descended and shook his head, the people cheered and stamped their feet.

'Savages,' said the Duchess.

All eyes in the Castle turned to the Duke. He shrank from the tyranny of his people's expectation, and feebly tugged at his Lord Chamberlain's sleeve. Moritz von Winkelbach stood up. Giving a signal to the executioners, he exclaimed:

'*Fiat justitia!*'

In the roar of acclamation that followed, several soldiers

lit their torches at a brazier. I was relieved not to see Giovanni or Paolo among them. Pitch had been added to the roots of the bonfire to save its builders the embarrassment of timid flames. Who was not surprised by the speed with which the fire took hold?

Jörgen Manheim began to scream. Was he still evil now that his death was upon him? Or do all creatures become innocent when they suffer? I could not see, in that piteous figure whose bowels betrayed him, the ogre for whose death the people bayed. I, that have been solitary most of my life, have never felt so alone as Jörgen Manheim must have felt when the flames began to bite. Was there not one face in the crowd with a look of sorrow or pity for him? Manheim's chest and groin smoked as the hairs evaporated. His skin was changing colour, like the flesh of an apple exposed to the air. How lonely had his victims felt, how broken in spirit, to scream for their own extinction? Perhaps it was necessary that Manheim suffer for those crimes to be expunged. But if every killing demands retribution, who would build the pyres for Manheim's executioners? Who would set light to Winkelbach and the Sheriff, or the soldiers for having stroked the kindling with their torches? I pictured a boundless scaffold, stretching right the way across the world, where every executioner died in atonement for the life he had taken. It was the consequence of Original Sin: a logic of reprisals by which humanity could exhaust itself.

A whoop of excitement greeted the vaporising of Manheim's beard and hair. As the eyebrows singed, I thought of Adolph Brenner. He was sitting at the far end of the dais, bent forward and staring at a fixed point on the ground, as though engaged in a phantom game of chess. Never had I seen him look so ill. I would ask him later what thoughts afflicted him and he would reply that a boundary had been crossed in Felsengrunde – a moral frontier beyond which anything, no matter how terrible, was permissible.

On the dais, I overheard Jonathan Knott explaining the execution in alchemical terms to the grimacing Duke. 'He is worthily killed, your Grace, if it saves him from eternal burning. As the beheading of the King signifies dissolution, the putrefaction of the body in the alembic, so the fire is the agent of transmutation. It is the element of Divine Love, purging Manheim of dross and exalting his spirit.'

For once the Duchess agreed with her rival. Through the roar of the crowd it was impossible to make out Manheim's cries. Some closer to the pyre swore that his last words were a curse on Felsengrunde; but the priests relayed news of his recantation. As the charcoal of Manheim's wrists snapped in the flames and his body crumpled into the pyre, Elisabetta touched the Lord Chamberlain's hand.

'God in His endless mercy has brought the sinner's body to death. We have rescued his soul.'

17

A Pickled Head

A ragged phoenix emerged from the ashes. It was less the golden bird of legend than a farmyard cockerel, with a malevolent eye as sharp as a pin and the evil temper one might expect of a scorched and partly baked fowl. The ashes (to pursue this dismal metaphor) were not those of Manheim's pyre. I refer to the charred timbers of peasant homes, to those black turves where, fleetingly, the forms of thatch or plastered wall or a clenched fist can be distinguished before the wind scatters them to dust. The phoenix was the people's rage. After the Manheim crisis and its costly resolution, after twenty years of misrule and plunder by the sequestered Duke, his subjects' patience was at an end. A tax collector, sniffing about the ruins of Krantor to see what could be rescued for his master's coffers, was soundly thrashed by the blacksmith's sons and sent groaning back to the castle. News of this defiance – this boot planted in the ducal rump – spread with the first flurries of winter snow. The freezing wind turned every stone to a cat's tongue; icicles formed in my bladder and scoured me when I tried to pass water; I was too preoccupied by my own pains to wonder what terrible flesh the peasants were eating, or how they managed to drink the snow without fatally freezing their innards. The situation began grievously to erode Albrecht's authority. With barely a roof over their heads, pinched by hunger and cold, the peasants of Felsengrunde had nothing to gain by meekness. Though they might die if they took up arms, at least the blood would run hotly down their faces. Yet there was hope that the Duke could be brought to his senses. Felsengrunde's real enemies were foreigners: an English conjuror, a Saxon ogre and that notorious dwarf with whom all troubles began. At Spitzendorf, where a starveling army gathered, the peasants demanded a meeting with Albrecht – a chance as respectful subjects to voice their grievances and request a share of the town's grain reserves. Albrecht was timorous. He distrusted the mob. A negotiator would have to be sent to Spitzendorf, a mild-mannered gentleman whose meek complexion and milky eyes would draw the poison from a rabble-rouser's tongue.

Martin Grünenfelder accepted his mission; he accepted also an escort from the Captain of the Guards to ensure his safety. Thanks to Maximilian von Winkelbach, the old man was saved from the mob. Not one angry word was spoken by its leaders; they accepted politely Grünenfelder's offer of a diminution in their rents, guaranteed him safe passage back to the Castle and showed great concern when his horse slipped on the ice, crushing its venerable rider and plunging – by freakish misfortune – his ornamental sword into his side.

The oration was delivered by the Lord Chamberlain. All the while I suffered memories of the late Duke's funeral, when my hopes had seemed boundless. The obsequies for Martin Grünenfelder were less enjoyable. The Duke wept openly, as he had not done for his father; the prayers dragged; I had to shake my feet for minutes afterwards to restore the stinging blood.

It was to be a winter of fatal accidents. Before the paper flowers had rotted on Grünenfelder's grave, Count Winkelbach returned to the altar to commemorate his beloved wife, whose neck had snapped on the ice-polished steps of the Duchess's Courtyard. Elisabetta grieved deeply for the Countess – although they had not been friends while the lady lived. Thereafter she devoted many hours to praying beside the Lord Chamberlain in the side chapel. Duke Albrecht railed at his wife for attending with so much fervour to the widower's loss. I know this last detail not through Brenner but from hearing it myself in the Duke's study.

It had been a great surprise to find his pageboy at my door. I had read the urgent, imploring letter. Now, listening to the Duke's grievances in his study, my heart sank back to its customary torpor.

'Their work to replace me has begun,' said Albrecht. 'Obstacles are being removed. First Grünenfelder, then Winkelbach's wife. You shall see that Moritz has ambitions. I should *never* have allowed him to do it.'

'Allowed him to do what, my lord?'

The Duke was stifled by outrage; his hands rummaged about the clutter of his desk – its papers and ink-pocked books, its curious objects – like fish gasping in the dregs of a pond. He found a glass phial similar to the one he wore about his neck and, pulling out the stopper with his black teeth, took several urgent sips.

'Is that the elixir?'

'*Aqua melissae*. The Carmelites make it in Prague to ease rheumatism. Oh!' The Duke grimaced and punched his haunches. When the spasm had passed, he tugged again at the unstoppered phial. 'Perhaps I am being poisoned.'

'Poisoned? By whom?'

'The unicorn horn from the Arcana . . . ground up and taken in boiled wine . . . offers protection against my wife's potions.'

I considered how best to respond to the Duke's distress. Was Knott aware of this present encounter? Could I speak freely? 'My lord, are you certain that your *remedies* are not poisonous?'

Albrecht gaped at my effrontery. 'How can they be, when

403

they keep the howling pains at bay? The red elixir softens the line between the world and my body. If I go too long without it – as sometimes when supply runs low – then it seems my head will burst and my stomach boils like Hell.'

'Perhaps that is how Knott keeps you in his power?'

Albrecht refused to accept this. 'You have never seen him when the spirits move him. You have not heard the voices as I have, nor learned their language. I suspect that Knott may be stealing from me. Things go missing. But those are small losses to bear when his spiritual gift is so great.'

This nonsense wearied me. 'Your Grace,' I demanded, 'why did you bring me here?'

Caught short by my question, Albrecht sat down. I could hear him breathing. There was a latch opening and closing in his throat. 'Tommaso . . . I cannot stop thinking about the Last Judgement. The Bonasone print. After Michelangelo.'

'What about it, my lord?'

'The despairing man pulling at his face. He comes to me in my dreams. He knows what the Calvinists know, whom I chased from the Wintertal. Our actions cannot rescue us when we are lost already. There was nothing my people could do to save their lives. So there is nothing *we* can do to save ourselves from torment.'

'Your Grace, that is Predestination. You must not believe it.'

'Must not? Or will not?'

'It is a false doctrine that cripples the will.'

'I know, Tommaso, that you believe we are masters of our fate. You of all my subjects have worked hardest to make it so.' I could not interpret my patron's face in the darkness. Its fatty accretions – the bulges about the neck and jaw, the jowls and furrows – deprived me of my former skill for judging his mood. 'Was it by your will that you found me in the tavern? Or that, years later, Jakob Schneuber exposed the truth about your time in Prague? And yet you persist in declaring yourself your own creation.'

I could find no answer to this philosophy and the Duke dismissed me. He seemed disappointed; had he hoped for words of reassurance, happier visions to eclipse his dark imaginings? Twice more I would be summoned to his study; twice more I would listen to accounts of his nightmares and fail to dispel them. Was he reaching, at this late hour, for the innocence of our first acquaintance? I was too old and empty of invention to satisfy him; so he remained the creature of my English rival.

But Jonathan Knott too was exhausting himself. Repeatedly, to distract the Duke from his failure to transmute more than a bunion's worth of base metal into gold, the alchemist had to think up new follies. (His ally, Jakob Schneuber, was abroad again in search of monsters.) Let him hang himself on his fabrications, I told myself. I should not have objected to his notion of finding treasure hoards in the earth, had he not elected Adolph Brenner to the task of inventing a divining rod.

There was of course no chance of the scheme working. Adolph Brenner was a maker of clockwork children: why should he be expected to find gold, a solution to Felsengrunde's financial worries, in so many leagues of soil? The Duke, however, was enthusiastic about his chances. An angel calling itself Abdiel had spoken promisingly through Jonathan Knott of riches on the eastern shore of the Obersee. Against such authority, I sensed a limp fatalism in my friend. I pleaded with him to rescue his dignity before it was too late. But Adolph Brenner waved aside my concerns. 'It seems fitting,' he said, 'that I should end my career chasing a chimera.'

The digging party set out in the orange squibs of a January morning. Soldiers accompanied the Duke and Jonathan

Knott; Knott's assistants and the diviner himself followed. They reached the water meadow of which Abdiel had spoken. Ice creaked underfoot. A prayer was sung by Knott's assistants while Brenner followed his flairing stick. The divining rod twitched and embedded itself in long grasses. Knott's assistants took four hours – with torches and boiling water, with finger-numbing picks and spades – to clear the mud from the auspicious spot. By nightfall, when the Duke was sweating with cold and impatience, the diggers conceded that no sign could be found of a treasure hoard.

The next day a smaller company searched the meadow, while Duke Albrecht drowned handkerchiefs and shook the pillars of his bed with coughing. Abdiel was scolded by Jonathan Knott and given up for a mischievous spirit; Adolph Brenner was retired from divining duty.

I was afraid for my friend. Ever since the flight of his son he had inhabited a desolate mental steppe, in that extreme solitude where no tree or shrub of hope can grow. The humiliating failure, forced upon him by Jonathan Knott, of his divining rod, compounded with other defeats and a shameful commission of which I was as yet ignorant, cast him deeper into the desert of himself. I tried to cheer him up in his workshop with a barrel of beer and a charcoal sketch, made from memory, of the lost Kaspar. There was a danger that I might pain him with this gift; but his own memory could rub more salt into that wound than any likeness and the gift was kindly meant, if not to console him for his misfortunes, then to reassure him of my unspoken concern. Adolph Brenner looked for a long time at the drawing. Had I expected a grateful embrace, a pat on the shoulder, or the fleeting intimacy of a handshake? He thanked me and pressed the drawing under a polished stone on his bench.

'Our stories are not yet written out,' I said. 'I for one am curious to know how mine will end.'

In recent months Brenner had spoken much of the Stoical philosophers, of Seneca, whose life was spent placating a tyrant and who chose, when the Emperor Nero lent his ear to malicious slander, to end that life in the high Roman fashion. I tried to rescue Adolph from dark waters of meditation with a salacious account of my years in Nuremberg. I chewed the loam stopper from the beer barrel and told him about the young Marquis of Felsengrunde, whom I had plucked by the beard of his disguise. Was it oafish to speak of Anna and Gretel and our patron's first night of love, when my friend's mind was fixed in the dismal soil or pined for a whirlpool in the Obersee? At last a change came over him. As though he had reached some private resolution, Adolph abandoned his slouch and straightened his posture. He turned to me with a settled countenance and accepted a cup of beer.

We sat together in the idle workshop, like statues in a garden that men no longer visit, and drank and reminisced for hours. I felt something akin to happiness as Brenner told me about his Tyrolean youth – about his parents' hopes of a son in the Church, which he had dashed with an impetuous flight to Venice. He described his apprenticeship to a maker of clockwork trinkets in the high stink of a workshop above the Pescaria, where he fell in love with an African serving-girl who bore him a son before dying of smallpox, quarantined in a condemned house before he could return from business on the mainland. The pain of her loss had never abated. He changed his name, as I had always suspected, to the more German-sounding Adolph Brenner; not in order to escape detection from his abandoned employer but rather in the poetical hope that bereavement would cling to the corpse of his name and leave its successor free of sorrow. Adolph Brenner's travels from court to court with the young Kaspar led them to Padua, where after a desperate year he had been forced to steal from Galileo's shop before seeking refuge in Felsengrunde. Not once in the flow of his tale did I wonder why my friend was telling it. There was a languid resignation to his gestures which I mistook for serenity, for an acceptance of his imperfect life. He told me about the year his hair fell out. We even laughed (oh, not long, not loud) at his descriptions of sneezing on his pillow, of waking up with shreds of beard on his tongue and rubbing his eyebrows to watch the hairs fall out like quills from a dying spruce. 'I felt ashamed when I went bald,' he said. 'Just the head would have been endurable but to lose one's eyebrows and lashes? No man should have to go so naked. I covered my head and painted my eyelids, like some pocky whore, until I saw how foolish it made me.'

'I knew a fellow once who was covered in hair from head to toe.'

'Lucky,' said Brenner.

'No, I mean *covered*. People took him for a werewolf.'

'Was he?'

'He was a man.' I told him about my former benefactor, Petrus Gonsalvus, about his steadfast wife and their spirited children. Adolph Brenner rolled his eyes in thought; he balanced his jaw on the subject.

'I wonder,' he said, 'would your friend have traded his affliction for mine?'

'Never. Though yours may seem less troubling.'

Brenner nodded mournfully. 'You never did paint *my* portrait, did you?' He slapped his thigh as though to dismiss the matter. Only when he had left my workshop, and I could hear his ponderous footsteps on the stairs, did it occur to me that he had never mentioned my own deformities.

Reader, you cannot tell, bound to the sequence of words on a page, how much time has passed since I wrote the last sentence. Perhaps if, hourly, at the striking of the campanile bells, I approached this desert of wood pulp and albumen and scratched an asterisk with my pen, then you would grasp the hiatus. But can you be relied upon to observe those hours, like notation in music, in order to read as I have written, with my own pauses and hesitations? I can feel your eyes straining to get past this diversion. Why do I corrupt the flow of my story in this manner? Why can I not bring myself to write what must be written?

I had not thought once of Adolph Brenner in the hours that followed our drinking. Only the news of an emergency session of the Court Council, called to discuss the threat of insurgency, prised me from *De Historia Stirpium*'s bruised daubs of watercolour and sent me back to the inventor's workshop.

The casement had been flung open, chilling the air inside and scattering like dead leaves the papers and designs that had gathered, over many years, on every surface. Being late afternoon it was dusk already; only the contrast between internal shadow and the cheerless, grey, nocturnal clouds at the window enabled me to distinguish the feet floating above my head. I do not know how long he had been there, like a strung ham, nudged by the prurient breeze. His face was a dark ink blue. A tendril of saliva had frozen on his chin. I tried to push him up by the feet, to absorb some of his fatal weight, but his knees buckled and I received a kick in the teeth. I righted the kicked-away stool (where Kaspar as a little boy used to sit, nursing a rag doll) and tried to hold Brenner up by his waist. I watched the taut rope emerging from his head – it never once slackened.

People must have heard my desperate sobs, my vain denials. After I had crashed to the floor, with the stool flipping over and striking my chin, I looked up to find myself surrounded by servants. A plump girl cupped my hand in hers, as though it were an injured bird, and seated me in a corner of the workshop while men cut down the body and, surprised by its weight, crumpled with it to the floor.

Adolph Brenner had left no message: neither Stoical paraphrase nor apology to the living. Someone presented me with a pinewood box with my name inscribed on the lid in black paint. Inside the box, I found the automaton Tertius blandly smiling. There was a rent in its thigh, sewn up with white twine, stark against the brown cloth. I probed the wound with a finger – and touched several coins. Gold ducats. Adolph Brenner's farewell gift. Taking his ghostly hint, I hurried from the workshop, averting my gaze from the lifeless effigy sprawled beneath a sackcloth. Nobody in that sinister darkness questioned my removing a sentimental keepsake: a smiling, mechanical boy.

Scandalised by the coroner's verdict, neither the chaplain nor the Duchess's confessor would perform the funeral rites. God in His goodness cannot forgive despair. Some of the money left to me in the automaton's thigh I spent on bribes, until four able-bodied servants – enough to dig a hole in the frozen ground – accompanied me to a designated spot of shame. We buried Adolph Brenner at a crossroads to the south of Felsengrunde town. I erected a cross of roughly knotted sticks above the anonymous grave but the chaplain, who had insisted on watching the body's disposal, ordered that it be taken down at once. I do not know if any pious Christian had cut out Brenner's heart, as some are reputed to do with suicides. Hoping that he was whole, I scratched my friend's alias in the ice. I never learned his real name.

A summons to meet with Albrecht, 13th Duke of Felsengrunde, awaited me even as I returned from Adolph Brenner's grave. I expected no commiseration for my loss: doubtless the Duke meant to bore me with his visions, recounting dreams as though they had befallen his waking person. In recent weeks the Englishman had seemed to withdraw from service, leaving him alone to brave the turmoil of his conscience. I was reluctant to fill the breach and did not bother to stamp the grave-mud from my boots as I presented myself in his study.

'Your Grace . . . ? Are you here?'

Four pale beans appeared on the stonework desk; these sprouted into fingers; a hand flattened itself on the surface and the Duke pulled himself up to a stoop. Though accustomed to his melancholy fits, I was shocked by my patron's swollen eyes, by the disorder of his beard and the deep furrows in his brow. 'Are you not well, my lord?'

The Duke clutched his throat in alarm. 'Do I look sick?'

'No, I assure you.'

Albrecht contemplated his cushioned chair and fell into it. 'Uh . . . did you drop something?'

'Why?'

'Because . . . your Grace, you were behind the desk . . .'

'And why should I not be behind the desk? No man demands explanations of a commoner for hiding behind furniture.'

'I did not mean—'

'Cannot a duke behave as he pleases? You *gods*, how they vex me!' Albrecht bent down clumsily and retrieved from the floor where he had been crouching a silver dagger. With sausage-fat fingers he beckoned me towards him. He was biting his lower lip; ambiguous shreds of food clung to his threadbare moustache. He ushered me closer still – he gasped with impatience at my slow progress and lunged at my collar. My chin struck the desktop. I dared not protest as Albrecht scrabbled for my arm, my wrist, then prised open my fingers. He pressed a monkey's claw into my palm. 'You must take this away,' he said. 'You must draw its attention from me. Make a wish if you will. I want *nothing* from it.'

'You are asking me to draw a curse upon myself.'

'Are you not my friend?'

I considered my answer. Did it suit me, in the present climate, to claim that privilege? 'My lord, this is a trinket. It has no power for good or evil – there is nothing to fear.'

The Duke blanched. 'I have seen hundreds like it, crawling like tawny spiders into my bed to strangle me.'

'Albrecht,' I said, 'you must burn the Arcana.'

The Duke's colour changed from wax to roast ham; he stared in horror at my offending mouth.

'You have spent too long in the presence of lifeless things. A man cannot live in a mausoleum.'

'It is *your* mausoleum. You built it for me and buried me inside.'

'Your Grace . . . please . . . you must calm down.'

'Take it *away*, I say.'

I nodded – forced a thistle down my throat – and pocketed the magical claw. I endeavoured to soothe the Duke with smiles but they must have appeared grins of terror. Should I call the physician for a calmative? 'Where . . . your Grace, where is the red elixir?'

'How should I know? The vial is empty. I call and call but Knott never answers. And the pains . . . I feel the pains returning . . .' Albrecht clawed and scratched at his breasts; he gripped his vast belly. 'If only I could deliver *stool*.'

'The other phial . . . The Carmelite water . . .'

'Gone,' the Duke whimpered, 'all gone.'

Confronted by the overthrow of the Duke's mind, I felt only pity for my own person. Perhaps Knott was hiding in the shadows, caressing the edge of a razor? Or else Schneuber had returned early from his travels, newly resolved to immortalise me as one of his exhibits?

'I shall try to find the alchemist for you,' I said.

Albrecht pushed himself around the desk and thundered

to his knees. His wet, slobbering lips pressed against mine; he sighed and pushed his cheek into my chest. 'Don't leave me, I beg you. I'm *afraid*. You are my only friend. We were companions once . . .'

No, it was impossible; my gorge rose at it; my soul drew back like a mouse from a baited trap.

'I will give you everything,' breathed the Duke into my throat. 'All that you had before Knott. And more. I will make you Lord Chamberlain. My *treasure* will be yours.'

I worked against his fingers, pulling them from my collar; I squirmed to free myself from his clammy grip. 'The offer is very kind. It is very tempting,' I said. 'I must beg time to think on it.'

'What is there to think about? I ask you to stay with me in my study. The claws portend no good to me – I will not sleep in my bedchamber.'

'You are entirely safe, my lord.'

'But the rebellion in the Weideland . . .'

'The Lord Chamberlain assures us there is no danger from that quarter.'

'It is not *that* quarter I fear.'

For several minutes that seemed a purgatorial age, I resisted the Duke's pleas. I did not behave generously. If I had done, would you be reading this document now, frowning with disapproval? I promised the Duke – yes, yes, with much pressing of hands and patting of his oily head – that I would return at a later time – tomorrow perhaps; very well, tonight – to keep vigil beside him, though of course his fear was unfounded. Reluctantly, threatening like a schoolboy to snivel and dampen his sleeve, Duke Albrecht relinquished his dwarf. He rocked gently on his knees as I genuflected and retreated. I could see him searching the frayed web of his mind for an apt word of farewell. But we parted without speaking, our eye-beams stretching until

– without a pang on my part – they snapped. The sorrow, the infernal loneliness on the Duke's face, has never left me in all the years since.

I must have believed it at the moment I said it. I *would* return to comfort him, though I needed comforting as much, if not more, for the loss of my friend and the uncertainty of my position in the castle. The Duke had appealed to the ancient bond between us. Yes, I assured myself as, exhausted by the day's emotions, aching in every limb from uncustomary exercise and the unrelenting cold, I clambered into my pillowed nest. I would have to keep Albrecht company, occasionally, when my work permitted; the assurance had been easy to give when it meant escaping his mawkish embrace.

Even as I drifted to sleep, I began to regret my promise.

*

Mutterings in my ear. Whisper of a moth's wings. My hand bounded up like a puppy and swept the moth away.

I woke up thinking intruders had entered my chamber. I listened, my heart still pounding from a too credible dream. Did I hear voices behind the door? No: they came from a deep, subterranean cavern. What were they saying? They were shouting; their tone was angry, violent, determined. I sat up and stared at the darkness, at the floating refulgent spots in my eyes, as though by staring I might improve my hearing.

The membrane of my dream snapped. There was indeed shouting outside: the clamour of men's voices. It came from the gatehouse.

I listened, sick with dread, to the assault on the gates. How had the peasants managed to bring down the drawbridge? And why had the alarm not sounded? Perhaps Maximilian von Winkelbach scorned the mob outside, mocking its rage and its power, considering it unnecessary to frighten the Duke over such a trifle. But the cries for justice and revenge, the pounding of an improvised ram against the studded oak gates, continued. These noises were joined by cries of alarm from the battlements as, unimaginably, the gates began to yield. The chapel bells rang out as the besiegers surged, a ferocious wave of humanity, into the Great Courtyard.

The Duke! I had to reach the Duke! Stumbling out of my cushions, I plunged my face into the washbasin.

When I came to, I plucked the shards of ice from my bleeding head and bandaged the wound with a stocking. Feeling queasy from my wound, I dressed with the clumsy thick gestures of a drunkard and shrugged on my heavy fur gown. I had to bully my cold-contracted boots for them to admit my toes, which at last they did, with a parody of my piteous whimpers, their frigid leather creaking. How long had I been unconscious? The sounds of anger had ceased outside. There were other shouts now: orders, appeals for aid, cries of alarm and entreaty.

I crept out into the corridor and down the deserted obscurity of the stairway. I sensed that the East Wing was empty, its human ballast missing, the people outside or else cowering for protection in the cellars. I took a long time to negotiate the slippery steps into the Duchess's Courtyard. The iron railing was furred with ice and sticky to the touch: I was loath to relinquish it and trust myself to the cobbles. Wooah – I slipped – weeh! The ground jumped up and spanked me on the rump. I struggled on all fours to right myself. Then it was off, squeaking and gulping at every step, down Vergessenheit Street until, with my wet gloves glued to the Chancery wall, I turned into the Great Courtyard. My view of the Library was blocked by the chapel. The tender pink glow in the eye of the weathervane confirmed my worst fears.

The Library was burning.

Servants were racing to collect buckets of water from the well. Men from the kitchens operated the winch. I gathered a slop bucket from somebody's hands and waddled with it to meet the disaster. Below the chapel – whose bells were now silent – a line of guards held the servants at bay. Some took charge of the delivered water, others exhorted returns to the well for more. I saw the Library's northern flank. The front door had been broken down and smoke emerged, occasionally disgorging from its orange throat a bucket-wielding guard. In this apocalyptic light I could distinguish bodies lying on the steps; what looked like water but was not water gleamed between the paving stones. I sidled towards the southern tower, carrying the slop bucket for passport. A maid slipped on the ice and struck her mouth on her gushing bucket. Several guards were moved by her distress and I was able to slip unnoticed through the blockade.

I tried not to look at the dead: so many dolls scattered, their eyes congested with vacancy. Hurrying up the front steps, I saw several guards also killed and recognised the older generation loyal to the Duke.

There were many more dead in the entrance hall. Most of the fires were under control; whoever had started them had not, perhaps, intended to destroy the Library, for there were drapes and chairs and uncertain heaps of broken matter burning, leaving the shell of the building intact. The partitions had been partly smashed between the reception hall and the Duke's Apartments. This reassured me to a degree, since my paintings were farther south, in the Kammergalerie and Long Corridor. As for the Duke, I knew that he had chosen to spend the night, not in his bedchamber where the mob would have sought him, but in the safety of the hidden study.

In the next rooms I was dismayed by the damage. The walls that divided the apartments had been partially or completed destroyed. The stage-set had fallen away, exposing the bones of the former stables. In a sense it seemed natural. Neither my Library, with its tricks and mirrors, nor Jonathan Knott's new seat of power had smelled of permanence; now their temporary structures had collapsed, yielding to the anger of a famished and misgoverned people. More shocking than this material damage was the number of dead piled in the Ritterstube. It looked as though the peasants – who were armed with pitchforks and staves – had walked into an ambush. Crossbow bolts were lodged in their flesh; musket shot had torn limbs and shattered skulls. Many had died attempting to escape, to regain the courtyard, only to be cut down in the ravaged doorway. Twice I threw myself to the floor when the Sheriff's brutes ran through the shambles. My hands were sticky with blood; I wiped them on dead men's garments and hurried on, hoping to reach a still undamaged secret panel and find the Duke unharmed.

In the Long Corridor, youthful guardsmen were carrying my paintings. I watched from behind a pedestal as they piled my life's work into a corner. Were they saving it from the risk of conflagration? Was the Duke safe, then, and issuing orders for his precious collection? My hopes were dashed when, profiting from a momentary lack of witnesses, I stole through the darkness towards the concealed panel, whose existence few people imagined – and found only empty space behind the tapestry.

I entered the ransacked study. The trapdoor that led to the Arcana Mysteria had been hacked and wrenched open. Blood trailed from its jagged lip. The Duke's books had been decorticated; prints and sketches lay scattered. Schneuber's gruesome exhibits were disordered in darkness. I snatched my foot from broken glass; there was a stink of preserving fluids. I had to find the Duke! Rummaging through his cabinets, I touched what I thought was a body but was in fact Adolph Brenner's automaton, formerly the girl Secundus, now adapted to a baser purpose. In faint light from the Long Corridor I could see its breasts, the grotesquely open mouth. I was filled with sadness for the Duke, that he should have needed such an aid, and for Brenner, who had made it on command. My own erotic sketches were piled in the cabinet, a lewd nest for the concubine doll.

Having almost forgotten my own peril, I was startled by voices rising up from the depths. For a distorted moment I thought I was hearing the Devil. Then I realised that the voices were coming from the tunnel that led to the Arcana. Breathless with fear, I jumped behind a felled partition which had come to rest against the side wall, leaving enough space for me to conceal myself.

The voices boomed as two young men emerged from the floorboards. I heard them chortle at their own audacity as they straddled the Duke's chairs in the ruins of his study. Emboldened by the obscurity, I peeped around the partition to make them out. One was dressed in a guardsman's uniform; no doubt he had just taken part in repelling the invasion. The second, to my astonishment, wore the coarse winter clothes of a peasant, with home-forged plates of armour strung about his arms and chest. I could scarcely believe the significance of the scene. Sitting together, talking like comrades in the ransacked study, were two mortal enemies. Screwing up my eyelids, as though by sheer force of concentration I might rip the mask of night from their faces, I grasped that they were conspirators: guards, like all the others to have survived the night, loyal to Winkelbach, now celebrating their participation in a bloody masquerade. I felt sick to hear their boasting of the night's work.

The gates of the Castle had, it seemed, yielded very quickly to the anger of about fifty peasants – the very men with whom Winkelbach had sealed a pact of amity. These peasants had made it as far as the Library of Arts, where they were met by guards loyal to the Duke. The night might have ended with arrests and a few broken pates; but the very human power which presided over the combatants' fate had decreed that none should survive to expose the conspiracy. If Moritz von Winkelbach's plan was to succeed, he needed his Duchess to believe the official version of her husband's death. Just in time to save face, though not fast enough to rescue the Duke, Winkelbach's men had defeated the mob. The danger had passed: the Duchess was safe. With the invited insurrectionists destroyed (and their victorious opponents also), a more proficient mob had set to work on the Duke and his creations.

Now the second man, as he shed his disguise and put on a guardsman's uniform, described for his comrade the hunt for Duke Albrecht. I knew that I was in mortal danger: to be caught with this knowledge would mean instant death.

'He must have known we were coming for him. God, it could've driven you mad ...' The Duke had exploited the labyrinth to try to foil the attempt on his life. Hearing shouts of battle outside, he had slipped through secret panels from chamber to chamber, like a fox confusing its spoor. Albrecht scattered breakable objects to cut his enemies' toes; he squeezed through trapdoors and snaked along under the floorboards. Why did I imagine my patron tittering as he listened to the men pursuing him? Did it lessen my suffering to diminish his own? The splashes of dried blood, the skid marks on the floor where they had dragged his body, persuaded me otherwise. He must have panted like a doomed animal, leaving bits of himself on the unstowed nails that jutted from the wooden staging in his frenzy to survive.

'We knew he was down there,' said the disguised conspirator. 'Like a grub in a log. There were rooms everywhere – little rooms with curtains and drapes. We pulled them down and burned the lot. But still we couldn't find him. Then Sergeant Heckler thought of the carpets. We pulled them back and looked for a trapdoor. We could hear him scrabbling under our feet.'

'Like a rat.'

'He kept bumping into things and cursing. He tried to hold still when he heard our boots.'

'You dug him out?'

'He was gasping like an old bitch. *Huh-huh-huh.*'

'Gave himself away.'

With the quarry located, a cry went up for axes to be brought from the armoury. A few enterprising youths produced ropes. They yoked themselves to the partitions and dragged down the panels of poplar and oak that I had decorated with my dead friend Ludolf Bresdin; they smashed the painted doors and pulverised the stairs; they hacked their way through the floorboards and prodded with staves into the joisted darkness, trying to prise out the cowering Duke.

They went in after him. I listened to the conspirator's account of the passageways. Somebody, charging head first like a bull, knocked himself out on a wooden beam. Another man touched Albrecht's shrinking heel with his fingertips and cried out in triumph and alarm. I imagined the guards almost afraid of their power, at what they were about to do, cornering my patron. I heard him wheezing and groaning as hands tugged at his clothes and pulled his gossamer-thin hair. In desperation, Albrecht lost his silver dagger in the arm of Sergeant Heckler. Oh, the blood spilling in darkness! The hot stinking breath of struggle! And my Albrecht, sterile Albrecht, old before his time and marooned in fat, making ten wavy lines with his fingers in the dust as they dragged him out. I was near the very spot where he had emerged, a ghost-coloured lord, from the hewn floorboards, and been delivered to his executioners. When had it happened? Half an hour ago? Not so much, even. Fifteen minutes? And yet I could do nothing to save him. He has died a thousand times since in my imagination – each time a little more quickly, a little less dreadfully, the horror abating with repetition. In setting these things down, I must kill him one more time.

'You know the orders,' said the assassin. 'We had to make it look real. Savage. Like a mob did it.'

Must you know? Must I tell you how they killed him?

The trail of blood from the Arcana tunnel belonged not to the Duke but to Sergeant Heckler. (He was rushed, fainting, to the infirmary – a genuine wound to lend credence to the lie.) Duke Albrecht was not yet irreparably broken. They pinned him to the floor, a man on each limb, while our present commentator smashed a jar where a pickled baby floated and forced him to drink the embalming fluid. Reader, they could not keep from laughing to see him splutter. They split their sides as he made spouts. He was a man fountain – a fantastical land fish – a beached Leviathan! I cannot tell whether he was drowned when they propped him up and hacked away his head. They stuffed Albrecht – at least the part that identified him – through the lubricated neck of one of Schneuber's empty jars and, smashing its counterpart with the double fetus, transferred the fluid into Albrecht's jar. They placed it on the display shelf next to the Dwarf Venus, which my patron while he lived had found so beautiful.

*

I never heard the Winkelbachs directly implicated. Who gave the orders for the coup, I cannot state with certainty. With conviction, yes. For the masterminds, more subtle than

Philip von Langenfels – lacking his actor's need for praise – concealed every trace of their crime.

While the hunt for the Duke had raged indoors, out in the courtyard Maximilian von Winkelbach had overseen the killing of the peasant conspirators. The older guards loyal to the Duke, all those beards that I had seen whiten over the years, had also perished, shot in the back as they fought their way into the Library. Meanwhile Moritz – the Lord Chamberlain and Elisabetta's unrequited lover – had stayed with the Duchess in her apartments, keeping her safe from the mob and ignorant of his part in her husband's murder.

These details of conspiracy I would surmise only later. For now I was horribly in danger, hidden behind a partition that could scarcely have kept the sigh of my foot from the conspirators' ears. With surprise and a little pride, I noticed how clear headed I felt. Panic and grief had evaporated like water on a hot slate. I heard the Sheriff calling his men to the Long Corridor. Feet shuffled; conspirators swore in whispers; their weapons sneezed and chimed in their hands. As though to conceal signs of their leisure, my unwitting informants knocked back their chairs and rushed out to join their colleagues. The Sheriff gave orders that the peasants' bodies, currently lying where they had fallen in the yard, be dragged to the study, to pin responsibility for the Duke's murder on those who could no longer deny it.

With lucidity and a kind of courage, I eased the panel away from the resting wall and opened the door that connected the Duke's study to the southern tower. Creeping would have taken too long, so I ran up the staircase of protesting oak. I tried the latch in breathless trepidation. It yielded – and I was back in a familiar space. This had been my studio, where I had stolen from my illustrious predecessors and bullied my assistants, some of whom now lay dead. I did not encounter Jonathan Knott. I would learn later that he had escaped the purge, fleeing several hours before nightfall with one assistant and two horses stolen from the Master of the Hunt. How much of the Duke's treasure he had taken with him none would be able to assess. All that he left, in place of a bloodstain, was a little heap of red powder: the fabled philosopher's stone, which is said to transfigure base metals into gold.

I did not escape, however. The main door of the tower was beaten down and Maximilian von Winkelbach thundered up the stairway, flush with his night's triumph. Having undergone the experience before (the scorching retreat of the scalp, the blood's sudden boiling), I ought not to have suffered my arrest so badly. The tiredness of a lifetime washed over me. I offered no resistance to my enemies, preferring a sword's thrust to a more lingering and inventive death. But the Captain of the Guard could not bring himself to run me through; it would have demeaned his honour to kill a midget. Besides, Felsengrunde had debts and I had one more public service to perform. So I was marched to the dungeon tower – a crow's flying shit away from my ransacked quarters – and clapped, as the saying goes, in irons. It was Dalibor all over again; with this difference, that I had no friend in the world to save me. But do not grieve, gentle reader. There was a kind of Providence in my misfortunes. Had Jonathan Knott remained in Bohemia, or Jakob Schneuber died at the Battle of White Mountain; had they never come to Felsengrunde and usurped my role as the epitome of all that Winkelbach and his Duchess abhorred, then I should have perished that night in the Library. As things stood, I faced a future no worse than rotting out my last years in a cell. It was exactly the fate from which Petrus Gonsalvus (the model of the man I might have become) had rescued me two decades earlier.

END OF BOOK TWO

III

Behold the Man

18

Gnomon's Shadow

In truth, it was not so wretched a cell as the latrine I had inhabited in Dalibor. There I had languished in Leviathan's belly, trapped in darkness and lucky to catch a shred of food that tumbled from its gullet. In the dungeon tower of Felsengrunde I enjoyed a window high up, which though it faced north and its glass clattered in the wind; though the glass was broken in places, admitting flurries of snow like dandruff brushed from a giant's shoulder; though I could not hope to reach it for the eye's fresh air of a tree or mountainside, yet it gave me, that aperture, enough light to keep my hope alive. In Bohemia I had been forced to sleep on hard damp rock; in Felsengrunde I was treated to a bed of rotten planks with a wooden bolster and a stained blanket – less yielding than the cushions in my confiscated lodgings but warmer and immeasurably more grand than a ditch filled with slime. To complement these luxuries, I was issued with a candle which my gaoler lit at dusk, granting me half an hour's light to read by. The order came from the widowed Duchess: the dwarf should not be abandoned to his damnable thoughts. I was presented with her very own copy of Boethius and, translated into German, St Augustine's *City of God*. Other books, chosen with less care by an unknown hand, were delivered by my gaoler with a grimace, as though they were made of excrement. These included the *Thesaurus hierogylphicorum*, which Jonathan Knott must have abandoned in his haste to leave Felsengrunde, Castiglione's *Courtier* and Lorenzo Ducci's *Arte Aulica*, that cynical antidote to Castiglione, which with my feeble

Latin I struggled to comprehend. All the courtier's service, writes Ducci, is to advance his own profit; he must be ready to do difficult and unpleasant things. This inclined me to suppose that the book had belonged to Jonathan Knott. But the lesson could equally have applied to Moritz von Winkelbach, whose engagement to marry the Duchess – once a suitable period of mourning had expired – was flung in my face one morning by our cuckolding friend the Sheriff.

Clever Winkelbach. His progress had been like the shadow of the gnomon, the sundial, 'invisible in his motion'. Now, at stroke of noon, he was ascending to power. His lieutenants were rewarded with high office; supposedly retributive sorties into the Weideland dealt with all the others. Did he silence the families of the peasant conspirators: those aged mothers who might have heard their sons' confessions, the intuitive wives, even the children lest they made sense, twenty years hence, of that anxious conversation by the dwindling fire? Pondering these things, I feared for my life. More strangely perhaps, I feared for my *death*, as though it were a beloved parent. I feared that I would be robbed of it in my own time, on my own terms. And I was in constant dread of torture, of the thumbscrew confession and midnight execution. There would be no knock on the cell door; keys would jangle, boots would punish the stone steps; a hand like a vice would seize my throat and Duke Moritz of Felsengrunde would pretend to wonder, in the company of his henchmen, whatever became of that Venetian dwarf whom his predecessor had so strangely affected. Night held the worst terrors. Not until the ghost of a February dawn – the grey wash of morning in March – an April's yellow haze, would I be able to snatch a fitful sleep. Even then bedbugs pricked me; my hand was the shuttle in a loom of itching sores; fuelled by stale bread and staler water, I was evacuating twigs and scalding snot. The dreadful anticipation might, over time, have eroded my wits, enabling my gaolers to kill me like a sick dog, in good conscience, as an act of mercy.

When at last they came, the gibbering terror I had so feared did not materialise. Having been deprived in my confinement even of the coldest company, I found myself in love with them – my fellow humans – and could not have expressed what joy they brought me by their presence.

'So,' I said, and a crust of phlegm broke in my throat, 'it is time.'

'Can you walk?'

'I don't know.' I extended my sore-pocked legs on the bed and tried to push them over the side. I almost wept to feel the touch of my gaolers' hands. I could smell pork and beer on their breaths. 'Thank you,' I said, 'thank you,' as they carried me like a sack of coal down the winding stair to the Sheriff's Chamber.

'*You?*' He was not the Sheriff I had expected. 'Shut up,' said Klaus, 'and wash this shit off.' I thought they meant to drown me in the water trough: I gasped before the shock but the gaolers did not hold me under. 'When you're rid of the filth, Sergeant Heckler will trim your beard. Then you must put these on.' Klaus stepped aside and revealed a chair whence an elegant dwarf had evaporated, leaving only his clothes: a new shirt and my old doublet with the worn patches mended. 'And be quick about it. The Duchess is waiting.'

Leaning on the rim of the water trough, I rubbed my face with aching fingers. I winced beneath the snickering butterfly of Heckler's shears – then sneezed as a perfume cloud dusted my body. When they unpeeled me from the floor, I could see the prints left by my buttocks in the powder.

The new Sheriff brusquely returned. 'Get him out of here,' he said. Grunting with effort, the stronger of my two gaolers hoisted me on to his shoulders. Thus I travelled by human dromedary through the dusky Courtyard into the Library. We passed swiftly through the ravaged hallway and down the Kammergalerie, where formerly the ducal portraits had been displayed. Stupid with hunger, I forgot to lower my head in the doorway. There was a smarting blow and I entered the Long Corridor with my brain swimming in soupy constellations.

A circle of strangers, seated about the Duchess in attitudes of strained formality, looked up from their paper catalogues. They checked their gazes on my mount's face and then raised them by the supplementary inches.

'Ah,' sighed the Duchess. She smiled through the dark mist of her veil. 'My husband's librarian, if you please.'

For a moment, addled by my encounter with the door frame, I fancied these were strolling players got up in costume. Never in my life had I encountered such foppishness. 'Perhaps,' said a wit, 'the gentleman might *dismount* before we address him?' His fellow popinjays laughed, insensitive to the Duchess's viduity, and prinked the lace at their throats.

The Duchess addressed me in explanation. By her tone it seemed I had just been summoned from a cosy study, rather than scraped off a dungeon floor. 'These gentlemen, Herr Grilli, have come from afar to sample our fine arts . . .' I attempted a reverence but lost track of myself somewhere in my descent and ended up seated on the floor. I heard someone whisper in Roman to his neighbour: 'Is this the court jester?'

'Gentlemen,' said the fretful Duchess, 'to business, if you please.'

The audience pushed back its chairs and flapped towards

me. 'Are,' my voice was cracked and nearly inaudible, 'are you gentlemen from the Academy?' In my confused state I thought I was required to give a demonstration; but the academicians surged past me towards tables where my forgeries and the Duke's print collection were displayed. With the alacrity of habit, they began to hum into their catalogues and twist their moustaches, peering every so often, like hungry wading birds, at the exhibits. I tugged on my gaoler's fingers.

'*Get off.*'

'Please, what am I supposed to do?'

'I don't know – it's your trash, you tell me.'

Of course I understood. These gentlemen belonged to no academy. They were not practitioners of art but profiteers from it – not artists but *agents*. No doubt I was supposed to assist the Duchess, to attribute drawings or reveal a painting's provenance. I saw her instruct, with a flick of her fan, the gaoler to drag me to one side. Evidently I was unfit to serve and had been kept alive in the dungeon to no purpose.

The agents inspected my forgeries. I watched their heads turn as they sought in one another confirmation of their suspicions. Reader, in my late anxiety to gratify the Duke I had cut too many corners. The afterlife of my forgeries had not concerned me sufficiently while their recipient lived. I had not thought the Duchess would try, in all innocence, to *sell* them.

'Look here,' said one of the agents, turning over the Dürer Nativity. 'No mark of guilds or fraternities of panel-makers.'

'And these woodworm holes,' said another.

'Drilled.'

'Or gouged with a needle.'

The agents wheezed and absorbed their guts in mounting derision. 'Imagine! No panel-maker's stamps!'

'And look at these laboured strokes.'

'This cross-hatching.'

The Duchess quivered on the edge of the company. She requested to know what on earth they were saying. 'Here,' said the Roman agent, shooting a brief and contemptuous glance at me, 'this is by Hans Burgkmair. *Lovers Surprised by Death.*'

'Do you not like it?'

'*Like* it, madam? It is a forgery.'

The Duchess blinked. Her mouth opened like a stuffed cupboard.

'The forger, my lady, bought a print and simply *painted over it*. Then he stiffened it with these boards.'

Ach! Pain mangled my forearm – the combined aches of twenty years' labour. Was my heart about to burst? Could God really be so merciful?

'This cartoon was made with a *pencil*. Not even the great Leonardo could have been so much ahead of his time.'

'Hm,' said another, smoothing his beard. 'It is altogether too skilful.'

'*Too* skilful?'

'You see, my lady, the drawing lacks freshness and character. Only a forger would be so meticulous, so halting in his strokes.'

I watched from my disgraceful corner as the agents compounded my humiliation. It was obvious that the Duchess had no part in the art's imposture, so they took delight in crushing her illusions. They were like children who at the same time want to impress their nurse and to devour her. I felt the bones of my pride cracking. The pain in my arm raged without issue, neither abating nor destroying me.

It was not all exposure and penury, however. Elisabetta, in her eagerness to assist the Treasury, had ordered the servants to gather everything, even the rejected scraps of her husband's collection. Thus my smudged abortions and three-headed monsters were presented to the visiting agents on the off-chance that one or two sketches of value might have found their way to unmerited ignominy. None of my drawings would be allowed to moulder in peace, nor a certain painting which, disliked by the Duke, had been entombed in a crate beneath the south tower's stairs. For this reason the agents were presented with the Librarian, my Arcimboldo forgery in which, had she taken the trouble to look, the Duchess might have discovered an allegory of her murdered husband.

I watched the agents converge on the canvas. They murmured and sucked the tips of their thumbs. A fat Bavarian expressed his own and his colleagues' opinion. 'This one at least appears to be genuine. Josepho Arcimboldus, whose trickeries used to be considered amusing.' At this unique vindication of my talent, the Duchess perked up. 'Did your husband show you the painting, my lady?'

'No. I mean *yes*. I think so.'

'And do you recall him telling you where it had been purchased?'

Elisabetta very nearly glanced at me for assistance. (What subtle gesture could have signified Milan?) 'He just said it was by Arcimboldus.'

The agents huddled together in conference. The Duchess sidled towards them. 'If it is genuine,' she said, 'will someone buy it?'

'Most honoured lady, it was executed not without skill.'

'Not with*out*— ?'

'It has a certain melancholy virtue. But nobody is interested in this kind of caprice. Who has heard of Arcimboldo today?'

So this one forgery, mistaken for an original, was sold

for a pittance, to the regret of the costive Duchess and the near-extinction of all my hopes.

My interrogation by Elisabetta in the Kammergalerie was mercifully short and free of violence – unless you consider a prodding finger to be an implement of coercion. By then the agents had gone, leaving their word of honour (a thing so light it was easily parted with) never to speak of the late Duke's 'mistake'. Elisabetta, by the constipation of her martyr's brow and her pallor of unstinting prayer, had managed to sway the coxcombs' hearts. Even I, in the pit of my humiliation, began to feel something like sorrow for her sorrows. It was her countenance which made me confess, though I was careful to implicate my patron's shade. This ensured that, upon her return to Winkelbach and his Treasurer, the Duchess would keep the forgeries a secret, ashamed of her late husband's conduct and her own innocence before it. Perhaps she also guessed what bloody punishment I – a feeble satyr weeping on the first fruits of scurvy – would suffer at Winkelbach's command if the extent of my duplicity were revealed to him. Could it have been pity rather than pride which silenced her? Whatever her reason, she lied to the unblinking lizard our promised Duke, explaining that Albrecht's collection, being too fusty and antique for present tastes, had failed to fetch a decent price. Perhaps she even felt compelled, through the intercession of a plump assistant, to smuggle some of her jewels out of the castle and present their revenue as a return on the sales? Her mercy went beyond mutism. Publicly she defended me from a return to the dungeon where I would surely have perished. At her command, I was fed and clothed and restored to health in a storeroom to the side of the servants' dormitory.

Did I entertain conjecture of a pardon in the long drift

of my convalescence? No: I was being nursed to facilitate my banishment, 'on pain of death' (so the *Hofdame* Maria told me on her mistress's behalf) 'if you so much as smell the air of the Duchy again'. My life was spared, then. But what of my forgeries, the unstamped paintings and laboured drawings? Elisabetta ordered them to be burned – all save those I could rescue from the flames.

So without ceremony, in the gelid hour before dawn when the mountains still slumbered beneath their caps of cloud and only the lowliest servant crept about his duties, I bade farewell to Felsengrunde Castle. One of the new Sheriff's men watched me, from beneath sleep-bruised eyelids, as I checked the packs of the two ancient donkeys given to me for my journey. 'Well then,' I said.

'Right.'

'That's everything.' I peered up at the sodden battlements. Unhappy guards were dozing in blankets, waiting for their relief. Within days, a few weeks at most, my existence in their world would be forgotten. I searched for a fitting and heroic farewell. 'Uh – enjoy the wedding.' The brute hugged himself against the cold. It was no good: no good at all. I tried again. 'I hope you prosper under the next duke . . .'

'Are you going to sod off or aren't you?'

Nodding in placation, I tucked a hazel stick under my arm and pulled at the front donkey's bridle. To my relief the creatures, being less obstinate than most of their kind, nodded into a gentle trot. We passed beneath the silent and vacant-eyed gatehouse, where the Sheriff's man caught up with me. 'I have a message for you,' he said, 'from the Lord Chamberlain.'

'Moritz?'

'His brother. If he catches you in Felsengrunde he will take out your eyes.' Having delivered his threat, the ruffian spoke with frank concern. 'Go quickly. Take the south road, through Winkelbach to the rapids. And *don't look back.*'

This sympathetic advice had the effect of making me doubt the strength of my bladder. I hastened my donkeys across the drawbridge into town, where I relieved myself shivering against a tree. Was someone following me, curling like a cat into every gutter when, in defiance of young Lot's instructions, I looked over my shoulder? On Milchstrasse I was relieved to find people already at work, although the sky remained a dark ink colour with only a smudge of brightness above the St Andreas ridge. A baker applauded his loaves in a cloud of flour; a blacksmith yodelled through a yawn and scratched the black nest of his armpit. They followed me with eyes free of malice or mockery, unawakened as yet to their worse selves. As was to be expected, given my reputation, I received unfriendly glances from a few visiting peasants; but their disapproval was as nothing compared to the dread of being followed, the sense that cold eyes were whetting themselves on the folds of my neck. I did not *see* any pursuer in Felsengrunde town (there were enough people abroad by the time I reached its outskirts for him to hide in their midst) but I *sensed* him – as a vole in its burrow must sense the hungry fox. Was he a thief, intent on stealing my donkeys and the forgeries they carried? There were other things of value in those sacks, including some books which might sell for food and the automaton Tertius Brenner which, though stalled at present, might at some point fill his foster-father's belly with a stuttering performance. In truth I knew not where I was going, nor how I would support myself. Perhaps my dwindling skills might still be of some use, though the number of agents likely to warn their clients of my duplicity would confine me to the backwaters of Europe. Setting my face to the dark slopes of the Felsengründische Schweiz and the Tyrolean peaks beyond, I set out on the puddled road to Winkelbach. When I glimpsed – with a frightful cramping of the heart – a hooded figure dart behind a thicket farther up the road, I stalled the donkeys. I considered my few options. To remain on the road in public view ought to have protected me; but I was travelling through the southern Weideland, where famine and the recent suppression of its discontents would not incline the peasants to help me. Could I expect to walk unharmed through the charred hamlets and burned fields which, according to their beliefs, I had done so much to ruin? 'My God,' I said to the donkeys. 'We must get off the road.'

South of the town on its granite rise, along the placid waters of the Tiefenwasser, the ravaged cornfields gave way to marshland and a forest of whispering reeds. I crossed the dwindled river on chattering stones and sought a path to the mountains. Instead of a track bristling with nettles, I found a swathe hacked by the Bavarian army on its way to the Wintertal the previous summer. If the Catholic soldiers (with Giovanni and his son-in-law among them) had attacked the Calvinists with half the ferocity they turned on the reeds, then the Wintertal would not see new growth again for a generation.

But I required no butchered stalks to remind me of my own peril. I scrambled, hopelessly exposed on the widened path, alongside the obscure river until, by midday, I reached the slopes of the Felsengründische Schweiz.

A journey which, along the open road, ought to have taken a day proceeded to take three. I barely slept in any of them, interrupting my advance only when the donkeys refused to continue, whereupon I would sit with my back to a boulder or nuzzle between the roots of a beech and, gripping my hazel stick for a weapon, watch the trees for signs of my foe. I began to hope that he had abandoned the pursuit, or even that I had imagined him. Yet branches snapped like traps under my feet, and the innocent blackbird turning over leaves in pursuit of springtails was magnified by my ears into a murderer's tread. On the second evening (so wretched was that season) snow fell on the forest: acid kisses on my cheeks, flakes settling like crumbs in my beard. I made painful progress on the rugged path, bearing west according to the setting sun and parallel with the southern road. On the third evening the donkeys chose their measly pasture, ignorant that by their intransigence and my fear of persecution we had prolonged our escape by at least two days and were about to outstay our welcome. Perhaps this was the hooded man's intention: to apprehend me in the Duchy a few hundred yards from my goal and lawfully to slaughter me for my disobedience? Winkelbach's shadow lay across the dial of my life. Even though dusk was falling, I had to press on to the Rapids Pass.

Exhausted by the sequence of climbs and descents, by negotiations with loose rocks and the long back-poisoning strides from step to mossy step, the donkeys consented to move only when I thrashed them. The poor weighted creatures: too much of their burden was in books and forgeries, my life's work with which, in spite of everything, I could not bear to part. The higher we climbed into a region of ghostly mist, the worse the donkeys fared. The mountainside unravelled beneath their hoofs. They were too old for this finicky effort. Far below, the rapids snored and I could just make out the road in the fading light. Perhaps we were already clear, for the Weeping Daughters, those peaks that seemed to lean together in sorrow, were visible on the northern side of the gorge. I patted the front donkey on its coarse cheek and tugged at the bridle. Fear made it hold fast. I pulled again more sharply. The donkey refused to move by so much as a pebble, digging in with its hoofs against my efforts. I shouted with fury at this obstinacy above the precipice and my fear was flung back at me by the mountains. There was a sniggering of falling stones. The rear donkey moaned and kicked a hind leg over the edge. Blocked by its companion, I could do nothing to unfasten the sacks before the body pitched into the void.

I heard the donkey scream as it tore on rocks but my eyes were bewitched by its cargo. Books tumbled from eviscerated sacks – they burst open and flapped like hens from a roost. Drawings floated, curled and dipped. Enchanted grooms and lecherous fawns, Leonardo visions of sea and storm and babies clenched in their mothers' wombs, all fluttered down the mountainside. They attached themselves to the boughs of trees, obscuring the spray of birch and chestnut, littering the stunted oaks and ash. I saw, and wept to see, the twitching corpse of Tertius Brenner, its clockwork revived by the shock of its fall. I tried, holding on to vegetation, to slip some way down the ravine and rescue my works. Far below, the donkey was dead, its vacant eye brimming with clouds. I stretched out my left hand to reach a damaged sack but the sapling bent in my right and shingle spilled beneath my heels. My heart and stomach lurched as I flung myself back on to the narrow ledge – where the remaining donkey trembled and appeared to be falling asleep. Once again Providence had worked for my survival. Of the original pair it was the animal carrying provisions – the food and blankets and water essential to life – which had survived.

Insanely, I would have wished it otherwise. 'Lost! My life's work lost! And nothing left me but *bread*!'

In my ungrateful rage I kicked the surviving donkey in the belly. It was my worst injury against God. The animal struggled on for two more days, suffering dumbly. On the fifth morning after our departure, when I crawled out from my shelter of dripping pines, it refused to move. Kneeling like a supplicant, it did not flinch at my exasperation. I pulled at the bridle and succeeded merely in dragging the donkey on to its side. It lay there with its legs crossed, its long-lashed eyes half open. Flies gathered about the head, they infested the placid nostrils. Unlike Balaam, I received no rebuke from the donkey's jaws. It struggled to breathe, depositing pellets of red shit. By midday it was dead. And still I had not learned my lesson.

I was sitting, numb with dismay, beside the corpse when the hooded man approached through the trees. He made no effort to conceal himself and at first I thought I was dreaming; or else he was a pilgrim leaning on his staff on the way to . . . where? It seemed inconceivable that my pursuer, whom I had come to dismiss as the figment of a fevered brain, should truly exist and that he sought me here, at two days' walk from the accursed Dukedom. If I was marked to die, it ought to have happened in Felsengrunde, or else in the gorge alongside my inventions. But then the Duchess might have learned of my death and blamed Winkelbach for ordering the deed. I had to be killed in *secret*, beyond Felsengrunde's border.

The hooded man saw me and nodded in ponderous greeting. What a surprise! I still wanted to live! I ran blindly through the forest, urging the slope to pull me along. The hooded man followed. He did not trouble himself to run but strode hugely through the brushwood. Like a pig on a rope, I could be toyed with – fed some slack and allowed the illusory distance. My enemy had only, when my legs tired and his amusement also, to pull on the rope and drag me in.

A merciful root, exposed by a boar or one of God's angels, captured my foot. I cried out in pain and horror, tumbled down a slope in the company of clods and pebbles, and slumped into a ditch filled with leaves.

There was a clearing in the forest. People sat in the clearing. They looked up from their campfire, astonished at my landing. A child ran for shelter behind her mother's skirt. Someone reached for a club at his side; another put out his hand to calm a snarling mongrel. 'Who are you?' a woman's voice demanded. I looked in a daze at the people's colourful rags and ribbons. A monster bounded towards me – a cretin to judge by the slobber on his lips. He suffered from the worst goitre I had ever seen. It flapped beneath his chin like a grotesque wattle, its third lobe so large that he had to sling it over his shoulder.

'Are you injured?'

The goitred cretin reached for my hands, gibbering to console me and lift me to my feet. I looked back up the slope and saw my assassin hesitate and draw back. 'That man – he's trying to kill me.'

'Is he a thief?'

'Please, you must protect me.'

'Vati, Ulrich,' said the woman's voice. Two men, one young and dark, the other older with a white beard and bandy legs, detached themselves from the group. When they had gone, I could breathe more easily and the cretin succeeded in pulling me clear of the ditch. His hands, which I feared would be clammy, were calloused and surprisingly dry.

'Konrad seems to like you,' said a stocky woman in a brown shawl, her face hidden behind a tangle of grey curls. 'We call him Cockerel Konrad on account of his neck. He's looking for a king to remove his lobes.'

'Cure,' shrieked the cretin, 'cure for Konrad.'

'Meantime he tags along. Children when they get used to him like to touch his neck for luck.'

'Like hunchbacks,' said a younger woman, behind whose legs a timid girl peeped. I tried to smile at the child but

441

something cracked in my face. I fell into massive tattooed arms, into a miasma of sweat and alcohol. I looked up and saw a bald and very red face – a nose with a ring through it – a row of carved teeth like arrowheads. '*Guten tag*,' said my rescuer. His stinking breath worked like sal volatile on my faint. 'I am Abraham.'

'How do you do?'

The grey woman crouched on a log and sought my attention. 'Who was that chasing after you? We don't want any trouble.'

'He was a . . . I don't know. A brigand I met in the forest. He offered to be my guide and then he tried to rob me.'

The woman's veiled gaze seemed to linger on the faded elegance of my clothes. I was not dressed for travel. After a time she nodded and sat back on her log. Abraham stopped squeezing my shoulders and righted me like an unsteady vase. Two young women in dirty white dresses offered me a mug of firewater. I drank and, like the Marquis in a Nuremberg tavern long ago, coughed and thumped my boiling sternum – feeling thereafter much revived. Who *were* these people? I noticed a pair of adolescents, brothers, I imagined, by their looks, sitting back on their heels and watching me, occasionally scrabbling for a pair of dice which they tossed between them. The young women who had brought me drink settled down beneath a stunted yew and busied themselves repairing a jester's cap. The little girl's mother conjured a baby from seeming nowhere and fastened it to her breast.

'You're not German,' said the grey-haired woman, who appeared to be their leader.

'No,' I replied. 'A long time ago . . .'

'What?'

'A long time ago I was a Florentine.'

Tawny owls hooted in the forest. Branches shook, bushes

crashed and my rescuers scrambled down the slope into the clearing. Between them they dragged the corpse of my donkey by its legs, which they had bound together with nettle twine. My supplies, such as they were, remained attached to the corpse: some bread and cheese, a flask of beer and a brick of seedcake which I had stolen from the servants' quarters. It was obvious to everyone as they gathered about my dishonoured victim that I had been its owner. 'And the robber?' the woman asked. The older man, Vati, shrugged. 'Fled.' The people looked at me; they looked at the bulging sacks. I knew that to win their favour I would have to share my supplies. Though they were clearly all hungry (the adults were bony and sunken eyed), there was no unseemly rush for the food. The grey woman, whom Vati and the others called Mutti, broke the cake into roughly equal portions and everyone received a share – starting with the little girl. Only the darkly complexioned young man, Ulrich, did not join the feast. I realised too late to protest that he had begun to skin the donkey. There was no question, in the cold and mizzle, of asking the owner's permission for this necessary act; nor was it performed with greed or malice, the young man working imperturbably, grunting occasionally and waving aside the curious Konrad. Now, with the bread and cake shared out, the company seemed to approve of me. Their faces, formerly grey with caution, took on the colours of gratitude; there was a quietly festive air at the prospect of fresh meat, of which I, the guilty party, would soon willingly partake.

Mutti and Vati took me aside and proceeded to question me. What were my skills? Could I leap? Jig? Tumble? 'I'm a painter,' I said. Mutti pulled back the hair from her face. I met with a handsome, square-jawed woman of about my age, whose mouth, though chapped by the cold, retained something sensual, the lips full and uncommonly dark. Her left eye was hazel, her right was blue with a band of fire about the pupil.

'A painter's no good to us,' she said.

Vati spoke with more sympathy. 'We are performers. We travel around villages. Never stay long. Don't want lords and bishops pressing us into service, getting fat on our labours. Where are you travelling?'

'I have been . . . My patron died and my services were no longer required. And to be straight with you, I do not know where to go or what to do.'

Seeing me weep, Mutti nodded and sniffed into her palm. 'He's frightened to be alone in these mountains. He's going to ask to join us.'

'But if he can do nothing?'

'Then we can't take him.'

Mutti was right: I begged for admittance to their company. 'Give me some paper,' I said, 'give me a pencil and I can prove my talent. Until two days ago I could have shown you my works. But I lost them all.'

Vati, who seemed more inclined than his wife to give me a chance, called out in some strange dialect to Johann and Jakob, the flexile brothers, who had abandoned their game of dice and were standing on their hands, practising a routine. As easily as one dismounts from a chair, they flipped back to their feet and brought us a sack from which they removed a familiar object.

'We found it on the road yesterday,' said Vati. 'Yours?'

'Mine.'

'We couldn't reach the rest of the luggage, I'm afraid.'

Blood rushed to my ears. 'You're not from Felsengrunde, are you?'

'We're from all parts,' said Mutti. 'We belong nowhere and wherever we please.'

444

I looked at the *Thesaurus hieroglyphicorum*. How persistently has this last and most useless item from the Library pursued me. Since none of the people could read, they did not guess that its ciphers and lists were meaningless to me also. Vati requested that I draw a likeness of Cockerel Konrad in a margin but I had no pens or charcoal. A burnt stick fetched from the fire broke into splinters and left barely a mark.

'Well,' said Vati. 'He *is* a dwarf. We haven't got one of those.'

'We have Konrad,' shouted Abraham.

'He's not a *dwarf*.'

Sensing a possible reprieve, I clasped Mutti's hand. 'Anything you ask of me, I can still learn new tricks. I have . . . I have entertained before, long ago, at great houses in Tuscany.'

Others in the company rallied to my aid: grinning Konrad, savage-seeming Abraham, the white-dressed sisters. Had I not brought them bread and cake and beer? Would they not have taut bellies for days to come and a donkey's pelt to shelter under, all thanks to this Florentine? 'He's fallen into our world like manna from Heaven,' said red-faced Abraham. I was startled and a little disgusted when Cockerel Konrad took my left hand and placed it on his head, as though seeking my blessing.

'Very well,' said Mutti. 'We'll take him with us. For a *trial* only.'

Konrad laughed and kicked his heels together for joy. Abraham drank to my health and, going to kiss an ember, exhaled a roaring flame. So on the basis of my deformity – in fulfilment of my childish humiliation in the Mugello, when a doe-eyed girl had made me quack like a duck – I, Tommaso Grilli, joined a group of wandering tumblers.

19

Tumblers

'Roll up, roll up, good people of Zug! Put down that barrow
– tether that pig – cast your catch back into the lake. For
you will feast your eyes on wonders, aye, and dine on the
tale till Doomsday. Come closer now, don't skulk away.
The great Sultan thinks himself a beggar for never having
seen us perform. Yes, madam, a *beggar*. And the Tsar of
Muscovy has a hundred knights chasing us for a repeat
performance. Now, ladies and gentlemen, before we begin,
are there any pickpockets in the audience today? You, sir?
Oh, you're just scratching your head. Nobody? That's just
as well, friends, because once we've started you won't feel
a thing. I've seen whole crowds robbed to their smallclothes
without even noticing. Let me tell you. Let me *tell* you . . .
(*'Isn't she laying it on a bit thick?'* 'Shh.' 'I mean – the
Tsar of Muscovy?' 'Quiet, Thomas. And go and fetch your
quiver.'*) Are there any gentlemen here with beards? Stand
well back, sirs, if you think you're tinder dry, for Abraham
breathes fire like your regular dragon. (*Abraham bounds out
from behind the dressing-canvas, causing a small girl on her
father's shoulders to weep inconsolably. Abraham falls to
one knee and spits a fireball into the sky; he extinguishes
the torch in his throat.*) But that's not all – no – just wait
till you see the magic tricks of the great De Burgo! (*A
sneezing flash, a pall of white smoke dripping with stars,
and Ulrich takes a bow to ragged applause.*) We've got
clowns and jugglers! Johann and Jakob the flying boys!
(*The brothers flip, as light as grasshoppers, through the
square into the audience – which parts with laughter and*

yelps of alarm.) Don't worry, ladies and gentlemen, they've never hit anyone yet. Just in case, though, we've Il Dottore on hand to bind your wounds. (*Vati strolls, cushion bellied, before the fountain and caresses his mask. Children laugh at his obscene nose. The sisters Steffi and Frieda buzz up behind and pinch his rump.*) These are zanies, my friends, and we've the Braggart and Columbine like your proper Italian comedies. And, prying over the lot, our little cherub here. What's that you say? Too *old* for a cherub? Why, good lady, look at his dimpled cheeks and ringlets. I grant you, he is a bit long in the tooth. He used to work for Dan Cupid – the little rogue of Love – binding young lovers. Now he mostly fixes dogs and cats, and a few older folk who ought to know better . . .'

And so behold your narrator, stripped to the waist with yellow stockings and a quiver on his hips, brandishing a bow and pretending to take aim at the crowd. A few people duck laughing; others are pushed to my attention. During the performance I will pop up several times to fire a dart at my well-padded comrades. I am, you see, a device in the comedy, an ingratiating imp who serves to advance a scene and then withdraws, panting with humiliation, to await his next appearance. At the end of our play, if my presence has been appreciated, I will appeal to the audience to empty its pockets. It is the only role the tumblers could find for me.

My first days in the company had not passed off well. Juggling, at which the sisters Steffi and Frieda excelled (keeping a dozen balls in the air, catching them in their mouths and exchanging them in flight), left me with a black eye and one of my own teeth for dinner. At tumbling I was likewise a failure. When others cartwheeled, I collapsed like a transpierced flan; when they rolled across their shoulders, so gracefully, I split my hose with a sonorous fart. And yet my fellow performers, with the exceptions of Abraham and

447

the grasshopper brothers, had been compelled to learn their skills in adulthood. What could excuse my ineptitude save a piteous plea of old age?

An alternative presented itself. Vati, who was a carpenter by trade, had built his commedia routine on scraps of memories of a Venetian troupe that had visited his home town when he was a boy. Since my Italian origins made me (briefly) an authority on the form, I was invited to join the cast. Alas, having squandered my life in performance, I had exhausted my reserves of artifice. I could not dissemble even in the innocence of play. Granted, Ulrich made a somewhat gloomy Braggart, reversing his magician's cloak for want of a second costume; but his wife Sarah more than compensated with her dainty Columbina. As for Steffi and Frieda, they so resented my earnest and hand-wringing zany, and assailed me with such furious looks from behind their masks, that I soon begged Vati to withdraw me from the routine. At last, in despair of finding a role, I recalled my Bohemian employment as a model putto for Bartholomeus Spranger. Mutti and Vati learned of the tawny skull, of the memento mori and my awkward pose between them. I saw my idea light up in their eyes; and so my palsied Eros was born.

And the audiences took to me; yes, for the year we travelled through the Appenzell and then west to Zurich, through Baden and the Albis Pass, the amorous midget provoked great merriment. I brandished my bow and, instead of love inflaming the people's hearts, spasms of laughter shook their bellies. For months I cringed at this humiliation. With my pursed nipples and flabby stomach exposed, I longed for a god to reveal himself in his splendour and burn away the people's eyes. Only with the end of winter did I learn to need my audience, to crave their enjoyment. As Abraham observed, whose brains flamed with a wit his savage looks belied, it was not Tommaso Grilli whom the Switzerlanders mocked but old Tom Cupid – the comic grotesque of juvenile senescence. So the people's silence became more hateful to me than its laughter; applause which for months I had resented as disparaging became a tonic for my weary blood. On chillier days even a guffaw at my antics (sowing Love's discord among the comedians, inviting the ribaldry of village drunks) would comfort and console me.

Then after the performance, when Vati brought everyone possets and, if the takings were good, warm flummery bought at the nearest inn, we would stand in our sweat and watch the audience dissolve: the heads bowed at labours restored, carts trundled and sheepdogs whistled at, the backs turning on us as though we had ceased to exist. Tomorrow there would have to be changes to our routine, and more the day after, if we were to keep our welcome; but for now, floating on pleasant lassitude, we could pack away our flags and ribbons and painted canvas backdrop. With Sarah and Ulrich's eldest daughter, Mitzi, I had the task of collecting props, the discarded wigs and zany masks about whose apertures I could feel the honeyed young sweat of the sisters. (Yes, I confess, Cupid was poisoned by his own dart. Frieda, however, was promised to Johann, while Steffi was too holy for such attention, with her fainting fits and terrible visions. 'Who wouldn't be holy,' Abraham quipped, 'with a face like that?' But I would have cherished her, madness and all, had I not been old and deformed.) Finally, when all our equipment was gathered, we would settle for the night wherever Mutti had found us shelter. Inns were mostly closed to us, unless we agreed to scrub the floors we slept on and smear the greasy dishes with rotten washing clouts. There were, however, plenty of stables where we could spread our aching bones, and barns filled with straw where we could sneeze and sleep in comfort.

I remember the warmth when nights swirled with snow and we slept in a heap, limb upon limb, sexless as children huddled against the cold. Sometimes rats as big as puppies would nuzzle against us in the straw. Mitzi and her baby sister feared their tails and twitching snouts – as did I – and since landlords sometimes offered breakfast in return for dead vermin, we would poke about the barn in the glow of Vati's lantern, Abraham skewering the rats and flipping them at a squealing, squeamish, fascinated Konrad. He was greatly intrigued by death, the young Cockerel, though I never saw him so much as swat a fly. The abrupt shift from motion and sense to a lifeless clod must have seemed to him as miraculous as the alchemical opus. I watched him attempting to plait the cold tails, or poking the mouths with a stick, nudging the rats as though he objected to their motionlessness.

Provoked by Konrad's scrutiny, which others thought cretinous, I fell one morning to the study of a juvenile rat and saw it more intensely than I had seen anything for years. It lay on its back, a puncture in its belly and the fur matted with a little blood. The pale white paws were rigid and I was surprised at the length of the hind feet, at the nails like grass seeds. I noticed the discreet button of the sex, the scaled and almost reptilian tail, the parted mouth with its yellow shards. A fly wandered already on the corpse. I turned it over with my toe and caught a reek of putrefaction. On its side the rat was mouselike, with ears that were fragile shells and eyes, half closed, like drops of ink. The rat, dismissed in common parlance as brown, was really beige in places, flecked with grey and turning to russet about the nape. Clogged up with death, it had less presence than the straw.

What did I make of Mutti and Vati, of Abraham and the

leaping brothers, with my replenished awareness of things? (Each of their stories could worthily have occupied these pages. What is humanity but a library of books unwritten, never to be read?) Freedom was the cause uniting them: freedom from the exigencies of temporal power, from sectarian passions and the cormorant war. They would not be pressed into service, would not passively live and passively die, like sheep maintained for the slaughter. They were in short what the Spaniards call *picaros* and we in Italy, less charitably, vagabonds, to be hounded from village to hamlet, from holt to forest, as though like vermin they carried diseases. Ousted from their homes, they had abandoned their trades and forced themselves to learn new skills, as I had tried and failed to do in north-western Tyrol. What choices are given to penniless rogues if they will live? Hawking in the wakes of armies is a profession adopted by many, together with prostitution, theft and a roadside tree for gallows. But Mutti and Vati declined to sully God's earth with their bloodied footprints. They chose instead the performing life, with all its hunger and uncertainty, exposed to the suspicions of worthy citizens and oppugnancy from every branch of religion.

But where had they come from? What drove them to these extremities?

Mutti, our leader, would never speak of her past. Abraham whispered that long ago she had been a whore in Augsburg ('Where else did she grow her quick and saucy tongue?') and that Vati, whose real name, never to be spoken, was Justus, had been one of her customers. Love had blossomed in the stews and then borne fruit in Mutti's womb; so the couple fled Augsburg, pursued by bawds and heartbroken customers, and settled in Chemnitz, where Vati resumed his carpenter's trade.

'And then what happened to them?'

'Four years ago they started drumming up recruits in Chemnitz to help in the glorious reconquest of Bohemia. Vati was too old to be pressed but they feared for Ulrich. He was due to marry Sarah, you see.' (A privilege never enjoyed, for want of means, by Justus and his Magdalene.) 'For two days they kept Ulrich hidden while they considered what to do. They had been fugitives before and would be so again. Now by chance we were travelling – the brothers and me – through Saxony when they made their escape. They begged to join us. Ulrich already had tricks up his sleeve, things to make girls laugh and other lads jealous. So we took them on, *I* took them on, thinking to be glad of the company. And ever since we've been growing in number – yourself the latest recruit.'

'So you trained them?'

'We trained them. How to leap, how to walk arsiversy on their hands. How to juggle and disport themselves on stage. Mutti took to it like a fly to crap. Her old doxy talents. She'd have made a powerful madam, between you and me.'

'What about Steffi and Frieda?'

They were the daughters of a glover of Dresden: a craftsman of such renown that he received a commission from the Lobkowicz family. In order to satisfy his noble patron, the glover moved with his wife and daughters to southern Bohemia; where one night after White Mountain a pack of escaping mercenaries, wolfish in their appetites, set fire to the cottage and to the glover and his wife while the sisters clutched one another and screamed in the yard. Abraham could not say – for they would not tell – what further sufferings the orphans had endured that night. They might have done better to chew off their fingers in grief than to give it voice and reveal their hiding-place. Ever since then, young Steffi had suffered visions and fainting fits. (One such, striking her in a comedy routine, had shaken the eaves of a village with mistaken laughter.) Headstrong Frieda, the elder girl, feared if they stayed in Bohemia or returned to Dresden that Steffi would be burned as a witch. So they wandered aimlessly, until Fate crossed their path with the tumblers and, in great hunger and trepidation, they passed Mutti's audition.

One summer evening above Lake Zurich, I was able to witness our Cassandra in a trance. Abraham had shaken me from a doze in a corner of the cowshed where we planned to brave the night. I discovered Steffi propped up like a rag doll against a bundle of straw, with Frieda in attendance and the brothers nursing her quaking hands. The girl's face was ashen. Pimples of sweat glistened above her lips. She had the look of one trapped in a fever. 'What drives the fire?' I heard her murmur. 'What is its fuel?' She spoke as though reading words ablaze in a fog. 'I saw great birds flying over cities. Their wings still and black. The sky was speckled with their flames. I saw Dresden burning ... a lion with its mane on fire ... people diving into boiling fountains.' Then she gasped, released from augury's fist, and subsided into a deep sleep.

'It's the dragon,' said Abraham as we took the air outside.

'What – you mean Mutti?'

'A *dragon*, man. In the hearts of men. It can sleep for centuries. Now it raises its head in Christendom.'

'You don't believe she's oracular?'

'Do *you* believe this – one day all this,' he gestured angrily at sublimity, 'will not turn to ashes?'

I would not have it so. I answered that things might change but the existence of things continues. At least so long as love remains to put out the flames. Abraham grimaced and tugged on his nose ring.

'I know about flames, Thomas. I know about fire.'

Yet love there was in the company. Mutti and Vati were adoptive parents to a family of fortune. 'Are we not brothers and sisters in Christ?' Vati would lead his children in prayer while I fidgeted, uncomfortable at their presumption of familiarity with a neighbourly God who might – after sufficient pleading – be persuaded to donate a warmer jerkin or salve a swollen gum. I concede the strangeness of my discomfort; for I had been no more observant of God than a pig in its sty, though possessed, according to priests, of an immortal soul. Burgeoning within me, like the flowering of a disease in the gut, was a desire for confession; but there were few opportunities to visit churches, whether of the miraculous or the metaphorical wafer. Too often we were on the road, or busy rehearsing and repairing our costumes. Nor was I familiar enough with Vati to broach my spiritual concerns with him. There was a consensus among the tumblers that discussion of theology should be avoided. Was it not the reason – for the peace that reformed and unreformed Christians alike avow – why the vagabonds had taken refuge in Switzerland? They sought peace of mind flowing from peace of the body. I alone, mistrusting my companions and doubting their affections, walked the precipice of despair.

We were performing in the town of Brunnen, on the eastern shore of the Vierwaldstättersee, when unwittingly I put my friends' loyalty to the test. Mutti's patter and Ulrich's magic had secured us a good audience and Abraham's fiery sneezes had thawed its congealed fancy. I was into my cherub routine, about to infect the Braggart with love for the pompous doctor, when a boatman in the crowd shouted an obscenity concerning what he termed my 'dugs'. (It was a cold day, I grant you.) To laughter from a clot of drunken louts, I sought the culprit – a burly, sandy-haired youth, pimpled about the fringe, with narrow insolent eyes and a stock of charcoal teeth. Without thinking, I tilted my bow and fired. The padded dart struck the boatman on the temple and he stumbled with a yelp into his comrade's arms.

'Socratic love, ladies and gentlemen. When a man's too ugly for women, he has to make do.' The audience, startled into laughter, backed away from the ruffian. 'It's love at first sight, look! Give him a kiss, Günter. Kissy-kissy.'

The boatman's mate helped him to his feet, then shrank away as from a source of infection. 'I'll get you, fairy boy,' my enemy croaked, impotent with fury – for in performance I was inviolable.

'Admire that countenance, ladies and gentlemen. Phew! It's a good thing Love is blind.'

Immediately the show was over and we had taken our bows, I met behind our dressing-canvas with jocular winks, a swig of wine and Mutti's disapproval. 'That was very foolish,' she said. 'You should not have done it.'

'He'll be laughing it off with his mates in a tavern.'

'Brunnen is his stamping ground. And you humiliated him.'

I too sensed, in the afterglow of revenge, what dangers I had engendered. I was like a lover released, contemplating the shambles of his passion; but my temper boiled at the reprimand. 'What gives you alone licence for mockery? You deride housewives and munching old ballards . . .'

'Housewives and ballards don't carry knives.'

It was Abraham, ever ready to counter Mutti, who came to my defence. 'Leave him be,' he said, squeezing my head playfully under his armpit, where I wept like a man peeling onions. 'He fired that dart for our company's honour. And raised a precious laugh in the bargain.'

'All the same, we shall have to stay on our guard so long as we play in Brunnen.'

After we had cleared the square we returned to our warehouse lodgings – under a timbered roof and surrounded by river freight – on the quay beside the lake. The boatman and his louts must have followed us there and waited, knocking back Ticino wine, until I detached myself from safety. Anger made them patient; it was not until one o'clock, with the moon melting like a soap in the lake of night, that I clambered over my snoring companions and went to relieve myself on the lime tree outside.

Suddenly they were upon me: the aggrieved boatman with his alleged sweetheart, a hulking Polypheme, and a greasy stripling unsteady from his cups.

'Remember me, fairy boy?'

I saw the boatman's member swollen in his codpiece and immediately wanted to be sick. I cannot have helped my situation by accidentally, in my terror, soaking the boatman's ankle. 'Help!' I mewed as I fell against the splashed lime, my ear smarting as it would burst. The stripling sniggered and a boot pressed into my ribcage. 'I'm going to give you such a fucking,' said my assailant, 'even the *fish* won't want to touch you. Grab him, Arnold.'

I realised with horror that my pee-flap was unfastened. 'Please – I'm an old man!' But they had no pity; I was gagged by a boiling hand, then flipped into Arnold's lap like a bosun over a barrel. 'No! No!'

Our voices must have travelled on the wind – for the ruffian never spent his fury on my flesh. There was a thud like a hollow branch falling, and a dull groan. Released from my assailants' grip, I scrabbled on to my back to see Abraham – naked from the waist up and red as Satan – pounding the boatman between the hammer of his fist and the anvil of his knee. Arnold rubbed his dead eye in amazement, recovered his finite wits and punched Abraham in the kidney; whereupon Ulrich pounced like a cat on to

Arnold's shoulders. Arnold staggered and tried to throw his rider but Ulrich clung on with two fingers hooked into the brute's nose. The stripling, our third opponent, fled the scene only to return moments later with a metal chain which he swung laughing, hur hur hur, striking Ulrich across the shoulder and his steed in the face. The chain whooped and writhed in the moonlight. Abraham left off stamping on the boatman's head and tried to catch it. The chain coiled itself greedily about his arm – he wrenched it out of the stripling's fingers and flung it far into the lake. Now the battle turned savage, the local men fired by drink and grievance, Abraham and Ulrich fighting for their lives. The bloodied leader, his eyes swollen like figs and his nose split, produced a dagger and swung blindly where the bodies tumbled. Abraham sank his dragon's teeth into the weaponed bicep and all of lakeland resounded to the screaming. I should have sought help but I confess that terror paralysed me. Only when Konrad joined the fray – bleating like a lamb with his wattles shaking – did I find the courage to volunteer. Sensing that battle was bound in our favour, I made good my derided stature by slashing the boatman halfway, so to speak, between wind and water.

The battle subsided. Victorious, Abraham and Ulrich allowed their adversaries to escape. It took all three of us to pull Konrad off the leader. 'Enough now,' said Ulrich, and Konrad, enribboned with spit, spun like a dancing-master on to the gravel. We crouched to watch the ruffian emerge from the carapace of his arms and copiously disgorge his supper. I felt very tired and almost sorry for him. So much *damage* to repair. Abraham sat on his heels and spoke with the boatman softly, as a general might address a wounded captive on the field; satisfied that his life was in no danger, he gathered us in his bleeding arms. 'Let's go,' he said. 'His friends will come back to collect him.'

Back at our shelter, the rest of the company had been woken by the screaming and was preparing a search party, while Mutti and the women packed our props ready for a swift departure. Sarah cried out at the sight of Ulrich's wounds; the others crowded about Abraham and myself while Konrad celebrated our exploits in dumbshow. Abraham turned storyteller for the occasion; outrage and a tribal sort of pride greeted his account of my ordeal and rescue. I was patted and applauded like a faithful dog – no, not a dog, a *comrade* – only to find Mutti scowling at the end of the approbatory tunnel.

'Are you satisfied?' she said.

'Pardon me?'

'Are you satisfied with this proof of friendship? When one of our number is threatened we'll fight to save him. Can you have doubted it?'

Abraham smelled injustice where there was none. 'He did not engineer this, woman. It would have been *stuprum*.'

'Who's to say the night watch won't come looking for revenge? He may have been a brute but he was local. To the authorities we are rogues and vagabonds. Now we must leave Brunnen – this very night.'

'I'm sorry, Mutti. Forgive me.'

'There's nothing to forgive,' said Abraham angrily.

Confrontation dissolved as each assumed his fardels – the poles and banners, placards and provisions, babies and goitres. I took charge of props, including my offending quiver, and our scant supply of bread and small beer. One last hand settled in benison on my head before brushing away. I looked and could not doubt, by her rigid feigning otherwise, that it belonged to Mutti.

The clouding of our fortunes took my scalp for harbinger. Though it was fresh-leafed June in Switzerland a kind of autumn soured my blood, causing black wires to sprout from my toes while the curls on my head, of which I was justly proud, fell out in clumps. I could not keep from caressing and patting my scalp, fascinated by the abomination. None of the tumblers passed comment on my baldness save Abraham, who advised me to pocket the curls for kindling. A stout Narcissus, I sought my reflection in mountain pools and piteously sighed, endeavouring to press the dying hairs in place. Within a month the lot had gone, leaving a trail of nesting birds scarcely able to believe their luck. 'Let it be by way of tribute,' I told my watery image, 'to a much lamented friend.'

I was bald as a pebble – and playing host to a lousy Cupid wig – by the time we reached Andermatt in the heart of the St Gotthard Massif. We had spent our longest period so far living off the land and Mutti appeared, like my vanity, to have suffered from our privations. Reluctantly she showed us the rashes on her throat, which by exposing once she hoped to denigrate for ever. Her temper worsened: the slightest twitch or cough from Vati earned an exasperated reprimand, while Abraham, who could never ignore Mutti's provocations, quarrelled with her daily. It emerged from little Mitzi that she had been receiving her grandmother's rations of cheese and bread and bilberries and the rare sliver of rabbit. These sacrifices, which Mutti angrily denied, were understandable, even laudable; for our little girl, the company's mascot and collector of coins, had grown wan and brittle-seeming in the last months and had often to be carried on Ulrich's back when her blotched legs would not support her. So the focus of worry (and we were always worrying: about food and shelter, about indifferent crowds and suspicious magistrates) shifted to our leader – the grand matriarch, as Abraham called her.

The town of Andermatt was not welcoming; Mutti's

health could not improve on its paltry revenues. Eyed suspiciously by enforcers of the law, we pined for the mountain passes, for the flowering meadows and ambered forests where, like monarchs, we could take our food and shelter without answering to any human power. Mutti was as keen as anyone to leave our majestic slough; so, keeping to southern slopes, we ambled for days without purpose or direction, enjoying a spell of clement weather which baked the skin and engorged with juice the gaudy alpine flowers – the dandelions and cornflowers, buttercups and lilies, sagely nodding poppies and starlike columbines. I found a kind of solace in the cleanly etched peaks, in the murmuring forests of dark spruce mottled with paler larch at whose borders the stolid cattle lay, like amputees, in the grass and flicked each other's noses in mutual devotion. Necessity offered me very little time for brooding, as we attended to the making of shelters and the search for food, to the straining of water from streams and the stripping of limes for cordage. Abraham offered further proof of his talents when, tired of hearing me complain about my corpsed boots, he measured my feet and manufactured a pair of lime-bark shoes. The pain of chafing duly lessened, though with only rough wool for padding I felt more keenly than before the cold nights and the morning dew. 'Don't complain,' said Abraham. He unwrapped his stockings and showed me his feet, both of which lacked their smallest toes. 'Frostbite. Burns worse than fire. I was only twelve.'

Physical courage was not their only attribute. The longer I lived among these fugitives, the more I wondered at their invention. Adolph Brenner would surely have praised the snares laid by the brothers, with their savage alliance of weights and levers. A cutpurse might have cheered to see Abraham poised in an eddy pool, stooping in the water to tickle our supper. His flesh would turn blue with cold but he persisted until, with a gasp of release, he hoisted the flipping trout into the air. I myself learned to use a bramble's thorns for fish hooks, how to fillet a fish and then strop my knife on a bracket fungus. Having long believed myself a travelled creature, I learned only now to read in Nature's book: casting a thread of imagined filigree between the stars, finding south from a tree's branches or discovering, in the wet turves of a stream, the partly plucked sunflower of an otter's print.

Stealth and stillness opened worlds to me. Lying on my belly in a bed of violets, I spied on a family of pine martens as they frolicked between roots and boulders, darting and twisting, with the speed and gloss of eels, for what seemed like joy. Another time I sat motionless beside a rustling thicket until a wood mouse, lured by cob nuts, came snuffling to my fingers' ends. My instructor in all these things was Abraham; for he and the brothers were real Gypsies – bereft by smallpox of their families when they were children yet bequeathed their talents and a trade of sorts.

'Romany?' I exclaimed when he told me. 'That was the language Vati used when he addressed Johann and Jakob.'

'He has learned a few words,' Abraham conceded with a shrug of the mouth. 'The brothers are still young. They are like children, they will forget our parents' tongue. And you – how is your Italian?'

'I think I've dreamed in German for thirty years.'

'When you return to your country you will get your language back.'

Once again Abraham had thrown me by his comments. I was staggered by the obvious: why had I never formulated the thought? My longing for confession, for the fainting Steffi and her buck-toothed sister, was the sublimated yearning of the exile for home.

*   *   *

461

I had almost reached my destination, if such it was, when Mutti's condition worsened and we came to a halt in the Italian-speaking region north of Locarno. Grim visaged, we put up our shelters in a forest clearing, about a campfire whose solace Abraham sweated to keep alive. I was anchoring with branches my thatch of dead leaves and moss when Mutti cried out in agony. For several weeks she had been complaining of her mouth's soreness, of nausea and diarrhoea that scoured and ravaged her innards. Now the life force seemed to clot in her throat, along with her reason, leaving only gross invective and delusions of unwashable sin. Cringing into our shoulders, we heard her shriek in condemnation of her whorish past. A mob of crows fled cracking from the forest, black rags shaken in alarm. Two hours later, she suffered the first of her paralyses.

And so I learned Mutti's real name, which Vati surrendered as he pressed her masculine hand to his cheek. 'Anna – Anna don't leave us now. Stay awake, my petal. Stay with me.'

Initially the company was roused to action by disaster. We devoted ourselves to hunting and foraging, leaving Vati to clutch his petal's hands and implore the distracted heavens. Steffi and Frieda made soups of nettle and marrow and diced burdock roots for our rabbit stews. Mitzi with her mother and toddler sister wandered in search of bilberries, or made infusions of coltsfoot which they attempted to smuggle past Mutti's lips. Oh, we hated to hear her refusing to eat and the violence of her retching afterwards. When the devil inside her granted a reprieve from paralysis and she attempted to hang herself, Abraham confided in me his fearful diagnosis. 'I have seen this before. In my family we called it the Rose. Because of the redness about the neck. Your physicians, I think, call it rough skin. There is a black whirlpool in her chest that will not cease until it has drowned her.'

Steadily a profound gloom settled on the company. Though we continued to forage we abandoned our rehearsals; for who would attend our performances without Mutti's grand introductions? Mitzi and her sister cried perpetually, sensing the group's unhappiness as we waited, without admitting it, for Mutti to die. Several times, unable to endure this atmosphere, I braved my dread of wolves and bears and that more fearful creature, Man, to explore the mountains beyond our foraging. When I found a tumbledown village scattered on a barren hillside, I was able to persuade Ulrich to leave his vigil for a few hours and come on a bartering expedition.

With trifles carved by the brothers in wood (spoons with handles shaped like owls, heronish forks and a pair of raucous flutes), we set off from the encampment at midday. Ulrich's posture eased as we walked, dread's incubus dropping from his chest to gambol a while in the flowering verges. 'It's like walking out of a fog,' he said, and I saluted the precise metaphor.

In the village three hours later, an old farmer mashing his gums took pity on us and exchanged six eggs for Jakob's spoons. Others villagers were less generous in their dealings, yet we managed to acquire some cheese and bread and a medlar tart piping hot whose baker, a corpulent woman at her window who leaned into shadow to wipe a baby's mouth, pushed the tray towards us as though she feared I might infect her brat with dwarfism. 'If all else fails,' said Ulrich in his innocence, 'you could always turn to extortion for a living.'

Returning in the evening, with birds singing their orisons and dark pines set against a drowning sky, I felt as it were in my bowels the gathering of the boughs, the whole forest seeming to crouch at the sound of our approach. A fox darted across a meadow, green sparks of eyes catching the moonlight. 'This place is cruel to us,' Ulrich said. I barely heeded him, distracted by the crab apples and beech nuts that crackled underfoot and trying to avoid the glistening slugs, like itinerant turds, strewn across our track.

I knew it before we arrived by the silence. In the shelter of leaf and moss her body lay, illumined by candles of cat's-tail seed dipped in tallow. From a distance the glowing tent looked like a shrine and more lovely than a church on Christmas Day. Ulrich ran sobbing but I held back, breathless with admiration. It was the antithesis of a Nativity: the over-sized crib whose occupant had no future but decay, Vati as inconsolable Joseph leaning on his staff, the others reverently dumb and kneeling like cattle. Or else it was a kind of Assumption – yes – the clouts damp with deathsweat, the friends and disciples praying beside the body and the wide air, such as Dürer granted his kitchen Madonna, provided for Mutti by the heavens themselves, with no bricks or rafters to obstruct her parting ghost.

Later that night, when all save Vati had abandoned their vigil and Konrad lay beside me whimpering, I was summoned from my kennel by a most malevolent colic. The stars were extinguished; clouds rumbled like the guts of heaven; I had to grope my way to our latrine beneath the trees. No sooner had I begun to strain than I was caught in a violent downpour. I cursed and struggled to dress. Then, negotiating a small slope back to the encampment, my feet slipped and I tumbled into wet grasses.

The shock of Mutti's death flooded my senses. I saw clearly, profoundly, what depths of sorrow my life had plumbed, and how much sorrow I had caused others in the living of it. I felt years of pain compacted, mound heaped on mound, pressing me down until the juice burst from my eyes. Misery's fruit, I wept without restraint, my tears washing with the neutral rain. I wept not for my present self – not for that muddied wretch whom I barely recognised – but for all my dead selves, for all the Grillis sloughed off in Time. I wept for the infant born too ugly to console its dying mother, for my adolescent ghost and the ghost of my father writing dead letters to his son. I felt again Adolph Brenner's dead weight in my arms. I saw mad Albrecht hacked and lopped, his head in the pickle jar most clearly imagined because never seen; and then the suffering eyes of the donkey I had killed and whose greasy flesh, so sinned against, I had willingly devoured.

Troubled by my absence, Cockerel Konrad braved the chilling deluge and crept behind a bush to watch me. Seeing me plumped in the gathering mud and pressing the heels of my palms to my eyes, he must have thought I was performing a task of ablution; for he made no attempt to retrieve or console me and crawled off, believing himself unnoticed, to chatter his teeth in the kennel.

As for me, I stayed out a while longer, trying to purge myself of corruption and asking the long-forbidden questions.

Had I brought about Albrecht's murder? Were my actions the seed from which all suffering had grown – the rape and plunder of Felsengrunde? Had not I, a middle devil of appetite, tried to gorge myself on the Dukedom, had I left the Marquis to assume his doubtful powers and preside, as his ancestors before him, over an ignored and ignorable parcel of rock, might Felsengrunde be fertile still and gentle to its children? And yet was I to blame for *everything*? For crippling debts, for Manheim and the Bavarians and the Duke's fatal melancholy? Or was this *mea culpa* which I wailed against the drumming rain a manifestation of spiritual pride, of grotesque self-importance? Bring punishment upon my head, O Lord! Though I am tiny in body and negligible as an artist, yet have I exceeded my limitations in sin. Truly I am the greatest sinner, God. Look at *me*.

20

Nunzio

Abraham had created the future in predicting it.

South of the great and fatal St Gotthard Massif, on the balmy shore of Lake Lugano, there was a tang of Mediterranean pine and clover. On the same breeze wafted a kind of Italian, chewed in the mouths of shepherds as they drove their flocks to autumn pasture. This rustic chatter – the precipitous slopes silvered with olive trees – the insistent cicada and plunging swift, all conspired to one purpose. Acquainted with my heart's desire, I resolved to leave the tumblers.

I have read that some creatures, when they feel their end approaching, seek out the places of their birth to die. Thus, in the lofty elephant and the lugubrious eel, a desire for symmetry runs, a need in the face of extinction to trace a circle with their lives and so to give them meaning. Do not assume, because you have these words of a premature cadaver, that I was brooding *yet* on my demise. Perhaps – I grant you the possibility – as I trudged behind the bier all those tedious miles to the churchyard where Mutti's flesh was to melt between paupers' bones, I may have contemplated my own mortality. Certainly, as Abraham and Ulrich lowered her body into the pit where already a corpse lay, wrapped in cerecloth like a fly in spider's silk, I determined not to rot in a foreign grave with a bribed priest yawning through my obsequies and caring nothing for my unshriven soul. But I had no wish yet to emulate the spawning salmon or circumferent whale. Quite the contrary: eighteen months' absence from Felsengrunde had allowed a tremulous spray of illusions to sprout from a hacked and mouldy trunk. I began to envisage a renewed career in Milan or Verona, when so many deaths and disasters, the eclipse of my creations, ought to have caulked that dream for ever.

And so you find me in Lugano, squatting at a remove from my fractious and, alas, disunited tumblers, staring across the lake – our Italian Ceresio – upon whose eastern shore Lombardy and my future lay. You might assume, from my posture and the sullen mutism of my companions, that I felt unhappy, beleaguered like a toad in a retreating swamp. Though Vati, six weeks into his desolation, was attempting without success to revive our stale routines; though Abraham, after a suitable period of mourning, had resumed his grievances against those who refused his leadership ('How should we follow a *ghost*, Justus?'); though everybody could sense the cracking of our fellowship, yet I felt strangely exalted. I was dreaming of commissions, no matter how humble, to paint a scholar's study or immortalise, in so far as fire and woodworm allow, the fidgeting offspring of a Spanish court official.

Only yesterday we were performing in Lugano's main piazza (myself, as sole Italian speaker, limping where previously Mutti had soared, compelled to apologise for our comedy that fell like wet dough on the audience's faces) when I glimpsed the engine of my escape. I did not know the gentleman; he paid us little attention, busy remonstrating with a fat Lugano merchant and showing him, with eloquent emphasis, the amplitude of his fist. As we took our sheepish bow, I noticed him again, seated in a linden's shade and fondling the merchant's purse as though testing its ripeness. He was a minor colossus, bearded like Cosimo, with a ginger crop of hair. He raised one eye, hound-fashion, with the eyebrow leading, to note our reception and then resumed his contemplation of the sand between his toes.

467

By chance our paths crossed minutes later. I was scampering with my colleagues from the scene of our disgrace when the stranger emerged, gripping his sword's pommel, with sweat in his beard, from a doorway and called out in surprise, 'Eh! *Compaesano!* What's become of your hair?'

Already puffing behind my companions, I fell back farther still.

'It dropped out,' I said, 'for shame.'

'You were lucky they didn't lynch you. But this is Switzerland. Where do you come from, Signor Cupid?'

'There's no easy answer to that question.'

'Ah – a man of mystery. I am from Brera. I was born with the stink of the canal in my nostrils and the shouts of bargees in my ears.'

'Brera? It's a long time since I heard that name.'

'So you *are* Milanese,' he said in gentle triumph. If he was to follow me, I wished he might volunteer to carry my bundle.

'Do you live in Lugano, signore?'

'I have a boat on the Ceresio. I'm a ferryman and a man of trade.'

'What sort of freight do you carry?'

'That depends on the customer.'

Conscious that I was sweating, I assured myself that my comrades were out of reach of hearing. 'How much to ferry a small countryman to Lombardy?'

'Is the small countryman on the run?'

'He is not. He . . . well, I wish to get home. Take me across the lake, signor, and I will make my own way.'

The boatman shrugged and named a price. When I failed to conceal my disappointment, he appraised me with an expression that I had seen him fix on the merchant's purse. He smiled and clutched his giant hips. 'I am to cross tomorrow. My cargo is already loaded – I'll take you free of charge. It's no great distance and you don't look a sinking weight.' I was perhaps too effusive in my thanks; he rescued his scurfed knuckles from my lips. 'Very well, very *well*. I can hardly allow you to continue inflicting yourself on these people. They are my debtors, after all.'

And so you find me – as I say – remote from my companions, who rescued me in the mountains and taught me how to live with nothing, who fought for me as for one of their own and whom now I must abandon. I was gripped in the belly with hope and despair: hope to see the land of my youth again, despair never more to see those familiar faces. I groped in the mind's pocket for words of farewell but extracted only false pieties to justify my betrayal. *Was* it betrayal, when staying would have obliged me to take a side, to choose between the meek father and my fire-breathing cousin? Better to flee, never more to sully my conscience with scheming.

Vati lay asleep, slumped against his travelling sack, his head jutting at a right angle almost from his body, as though he were trying from a recumbent position to look along his shirt front. Next to him, his son Ulrich twined little Mitzi's pigtails, while Sarah sang gently and fed chewed apple to her toddler. Farther up the meadow, Abraham and Jakob whittled tools from strips of ash. Abraham grimaced every time his knife emerged, with a lurch of liberation, from the shaving's curl. Could I tell him perhaps? Would he comprehend, with his Gypsy blood, the sadness of an exile? Yes, Abraham alone would understand and justify my actions to the others.

Before I could press my limbs into service I heard, we *all* heard, a great commotion from the olive grove higher up the hill. We turned in alarm at the wailing: a cry barely to be endured, full of past and present suffering. Frieda tore from the olive grove, her face sleek with tears. The company rose to catch her but she marched through our midst. Only when she passed me did I see the angry weal on her right cheek and the bleeding demilune an inch below the eye. Next Steffi ploughed through our shadows and caught Frieda by the arm. Together the sisters continued, despite all entreaties, to stride towards Lugano.

'Steffi! Frieda, dear!'

Vati was awake and haggard. He clutched his son in bewilderment. Farther up the hillside, the author of this scene appeared. Johann, Frieda's long-time suitor, sought out his brother and Abraham. In shame and fury he complained, he complained and explained – I heard the words 'whore' and 'slut' and variations on the theme. Johann looked unseeing across the lake and slapped, unknowing, the knuckles of his offending hand with its unstained twin.

Vati and Ulrich ran up the meadow to demand an explanation. In all this shock and disorder, where could I find a sympathetic ear? My arm sank towards my old saddlebag; it took the weight of my worldly goods, of the battered *Thesaurus*.

'She has not betrayed you,' I heard Ulrich cry. 'You have done the worst possible thing! The most unforgivable!'

Johann cowered behind Abraham, who gripped in one hand the peeling wand of ash and in the other his carving knife. Fissures were splitting open, cleaving the company. Vati and Abraham leaned brow to brow, like bucks sizing up for a clash.

'Was she bleeding?' Sarah asked me. I shrugged the saddlebag on to my shoulder and reluctantly nodded. 'They're going to destroy everything,' she said in despair.

Now Vati and Ulrich were pacing downhill to join us. (Johann had fallen to his knees and begun to sob, his brother and Abraham crouching to console him.) Ulrich took charge of his frightened daughters while Vati clasped Sarah by the hand and pulled her to her feet. 'I'll explain,' he said. 'She will not lie with him and he has beaten her.'

Vati and Sarah set out in the girls' pursuit. 'I'll come with you,' I said.

'No,' said Vati.

'I might be able to help.'

'Don't follow us.'

Ignoring this ban, I ran up the slope and kissed little Mitzi on the cheek. She brushed me indignantly away. 'Goodbye, Ulrich.' Ulrich nodded without listening, absorbed in watching his wife and father. I waved farewell (a pebble lodged in my gullet) to Abraham, my frightful tutor, and to the obscure brothers with whom in sixteen months I had exchanged barely a pleasantry.

'I must go,' I shouted. 'God be with you!'

Abraham, thinking I meant to play the conciliator, gestured at me to shog off.

Now I was shuddering down the hillside – my breasts nodding and aching, the wind roaring in my ears and causing my eyes to liquefy. Was it pollen which made the air so abrasive, which caused me to cough and splutter and wipe my cheeks to ease their stinging? The cathedral clock was tolling the appointed hour when I reached our meeting place. The colossal boatman was nowhere to be seen but his mate recognised a short-winded dwarf and signalled to me. I waved back in recognition . . . and failed to advance for the restraining hands on my shoulder.

'Konrad!'

He was panting and wild eyed, his greasy hair stirred to a nimbus and his tongue lolling in foam. 'Don't go,' he said. 'Don't *go*.'

'Konrad, I must.'

'Uh, no! No!'

'I have a calling. You understand that word? I have a

calling, like you for your . . . I must go home.' Konrad shook
his head. He pointed north to our fragmenting company;
he mimed a bow and arrow and mimicked my banter.
'Abraham has a gift for words,' I said, trying to acknowledge
the waiting ferryman. 'You don't need me.'

'Who, who,' hooted Konrad, '*who* speaks in Talian?'

I had not considered this problem and hated the cretin
for minding me of it. 'You could head back north where
they speak German.'

'*Winter*!' Konrad protested, and he stamped his foot with
a sense of injustice he could not express.

'My speeches were no good,' I pleaded with him. 'Not
like Mutti's. You'll be happier without me.'

Konrad's face contracted horribly. A long cry – half low,
half mew – squeezed from his monstrous wattles. To my
alarm, he gripped my ears and pressed me into his belly.
'Coo, coo,' he seemed to say. 'Coo for conman.'

'I cannot help you find a cure,' I said when he released
me. 'I cannot help you, Konrad. My dear friend, I do not
know any kings, and then I doubt very much . . .' I silenced
myself before I could compound my offence. 'Stick with Vati
and Sarah and Ulrich. They are a family. They will never let
you down.'

'You do,' said Konrad, '*you* let me down.'

He backed away. On his slackening face I read our
estrangement and almost implored him to come back. 'Tell
the others!' I yelled after him. 'Tell the others I am sorry!'
Konrad staggered into the dribbling runnel, then righted
himself and leaned against the slanting street. The ferryman,
too, was turning his back on me, his patience consumed, and
I was grateful for having to catch up with him: it enabled me
to run out on my friends.

On Corsia dei Servi my neck threatened to crumble,

consigning my dolorous head to the dust. The pain had travelled from my legs. Why it had begun down there, when the wooden tray stuffed with pamphlets was strung from my shoulders, I cannot imagine. But there it began all the same: the muscles of my buttocks in spasm shooting poison in both directions, down to my feet and up to my lumbar and thence my spine, whereupon it gathered in the seat of my troubles, that is to say my shoulders, and began like rats gnawing at rope to devour the tendons of my neck. My whole body, I tell you, was one violent insurrection of maltreated limbs, the regions in revolt against my will – which was not my will at all but that, expressed by proxy, of Rocca Mengone: printer of verses and sententious prose, whoremonger, spy for the Spaniards and unknowing master to your aged narrator.

For six months it had been my task to carry this tray from the Piazza del Duomo (where my self's ancestor had met the gentle Arcimboldo) up the haggling pother of the Corsia dei Servi and then back again until, hoping that none of Rocca Mengone's spies would see me, I took my rest in the shadow of the cathedral. In this strange Milan, with its unfamiliar clothes and customs, its hordes of impostors, a hawker of pamphlets was of little interest. I had to call out my six allotted words until my voice warped and I was hoarse as a lizard; only my uncommon stature, and the improbable width of my tray, attracted a little scoffing custom. I was not averse to such mockery. Supplementary to my pitiful income, I had the lightening of my load for incentive. Every morning I would begin afresh with crisp new papers (their number counted beforehand lest I be tempted to discard a few during the day) and resume my painful drudgery, like some adjunct of Sisyphus.

How, you are wondering, had I found myself in this state of servitude, when my escape to Lombardy, despite the unprincipled manner of it, had begun with benevolence?

The colossal ferryman spoke to me, on the buffeted lake, of his youth spent plying barges on the Martesano canal. He had a cousin still working there, a certain Agostino, whose tenement address he wrote into my *Thesaurus*, tearing a page from the same (despite my reluctance to damage my only investment) and writing a letter for him, which he sealed with wax against my prying. I left the ferry on the Lombard shore, jubilant to be treading familiar soil, with a contact already made in Milan. This Agostino would doubtless be a rude sort, coarse and pungent; but he would put me up for the time it took to establish myself in the city. My hope in the goodness of strangers, which the tumblers had rekindled, flamed brighter than ever when the skipper gave me a small purse to assist me on my travels.

Two days later, I was helped down from the warm marrow of a silk-thread merchant's cart on the Corsa Orientale, in front of San Babila and a few yards only from Gian Bonconvento's villa. I dawdled a while beneath the pillared Lamb, hearing the poignant seminary bell and debating with myself whether or not I dared to venture farther. I decided against it – mindful of Heraclitus on rivers – and wandered into a city that recognised me not.

My hand cannot take much more of this.

The ferryman's cousin received me with suspicion until I handed him the letter and he recognised the seal. Then he embraced me as a brother, shared with me his thin gruel and his fetid bed and in the morning introduced me to my employer's factotum. Rocca Mengone (this unctuous scoundrel said) was a philanthropic Croesus, a benevolent father to the people of the Brera district. Lord, he chuckled, I was a *very* short fellow. How easy it would be for me to hide in a crowd, disguised as a child perhaps, that most innocent of human creatures whom Our Saviour so valued. What regions of a man's apparel might not these dextrous fingers explore, while the wearer gawked – let us imagine – at a procession in the street, or praised the Virgin floating on a tide of devotees? Reader, I felt violated by these propositions. Was I to work as a *pickpocket*? Agostino sat a short way off against a pillar, looking out for rivals and chewing the stem of his smokeless pipe. I mused bitterly on my duping. So many avenues of adventure or misadventure down which, even at my great age, I could still wander, straying as it were into whole chapters, encountering new galleries of rogues and simpletons, dupes and conspirators. I would not, however, repeat a second time the squalid errors of my youth. Though I had lived for the most part without honour, yet I would not dishonourably die. So I was forced to disoblige Signor Mengone and his agent; Agostino, shaking a face sloppy with terror, could not dissuade me.

What did I expect to achieve, alone and friendless in Milan? Despite the factotum's angry threats, I do not believe that he (let alone his nebulous, almost Olympian employer) expended energy on frustrating my efforts. The truth is that the city had no need of me. Regardless of his memorious tomb in S. Pietro della Vigna (where I shed an effortful tear), my blessed teacher Arcimboldo was forgotten. His house, which I found with much retracing of my steps, had been usurped by an official of the Habsburg government. The silently screaming guardian that so haunted my imagination had been wrenched from the door, and perhaps I was unique in the world to discern the faint oval stain from which it used to stare. There could be no help from the dead. Milan was under the afflatus of a new dispensation whose priests were unfamiliar to me: the late and infamous Caravaggio, Lombards whose names (Cerano? Morazone?) would not adhere to my memory, a Roman Fleming much admired by the name of Rubens. To the splendid tastes of Counter-Reformation, my dour northern Masters could never have pleased. Like my father before me, I found myself excluded from commissions by the new and seemingly omnipotent Accademia del Disegno. I met some of its luminaries but they scoffed at me. Was their founder, Cardinal Borromeo, unaware that my works were on display for all the world to see in his palazzo? The academicians laughed. Had I left a turd in the courtyard? 'The *Mary Magdalene*!' I piped indignantly. 'Bought by His Eminence Federico Borromeo. Or the *Last Judgement* at San Sepulcro in – uh – Bergamo, I think.'

'You *think*?'

'Go and see if you don't believe me! Only let me be admitted and I'll show you how I painted them.'

'The Cardinal will not have frauds in his presence,' said one of the masters. 'And I know you lie, for the *Mary Magdalene* – though a very minor work – was painted by Gian Bonconvento.'

'Yes! I was his . . .' (Thirty years on, was Bonconvento's death still a subject of contention?) 'I was his friend and admirer. I worked with him on some of his paintings.'

'I do not believe it. You are a scoundrel.'

When, after receiving this judgement, I was smuggled by curious students into a tavern and asked to draw something, I found no discipline in my fingers. The charcoal trembled on the page; my ill-remembered Magdalene came to resemble a eunuch in a wig, with pouches of fat instead of breasts, whose pious invocation suggested nothing more exalted than vulgar relief after shifting wind. 'I can do better, I *can*,' I said. 'But I am out of practice.' The students of the Academy laughed without mirth and awarded me a drizzle of small coin.

The next day – having stolen a man's cap that I might come with it in hand – I returned to Agostino and begged for a second chance. Rocca Mengone's agent duly arrived, and Agostino smiled to see me sink beneath my burden.

And so you find me doubly dwarfed by this tray, with my head a sullen moon above its lengthening plain, struggling up the Corsia dei Servi. In my torment I was reminded of the failed mountebank who accosted me once in Prague's Old Town. Geronimo Scotta (whose body must be entertaining worms in the Bohemian slime) was exhumed by my delirium. Clutched by the damp rags of his flamboyance, he met me as a kinsman, his tray of placebos to mine of unreadable prose. 'Brother charlatan – you who lost a carriage and two score plumed horses, whom in mockery the soldiers frisked on Bridge Street – are these pains in my neck and shoulders, these fetors of rancid cheese that rise from my body, the just deserts of a fraudster?' Often, while I suffered my daily penance, the pain made me delirious. I wandered from my prescribed route and went looking for the boyhood I had abandoned. It was as though I expected to see my double, another Tommaso Grilli, out flaunting his wealth, selecting a print from one of my rivals or directing a servant to buy that pheasant, those gaping trout. Milan was populated by impostors; and were those real or imagined ghosts who startled me at every turn? Was it Piero in that doorway caressing the rump of an ecstatic cat? Or Mosca nursing his gainful stump and begging in the gutter? Once, after a triple hanging on the Piazza della Vetra, I found myself in pursuit of a handsome blackamoor as he wove through the crowd. On Largo Carrobbio he was embraced by a plump gentleman who, walking beside him, rested a nervous hand on his thigh. I followed the men as far as the Duomo and satisfied myself that Kaspar Brenner lived elsewhere, if he lived at all, for he bore no resemblance to this smiling catamite.

In the end, Rocca Mengone's henchmen discovered me

away from my pitch. I was cheerfully punished and spent the night in great discomfort, chewing my finger not to vex my neighbour with my groans, and ruminating on my condition. At cockcrow a solution revealed itself. Of course – Giovanni! My erstwhile companion, who had settled and married near Florence. My journey home was incomplete. The streets of which I dreamed, and the hills I walked in memory, were farther south. Before daybreak I set out in hope of Tuscan sanctuary.

'She lives with Paolo's parents in Settignano, on a hillside facing Fiesole . . .'

I was guided by Giovanni's words like a magus by his star. Approaching from the north on the Bolognese road, I skirted along the edge of my native city, chastened from entering it by my wretched afterlife in Milan. Having emerged from that infernal state with only dented shoulders, could I hope for a gentler purgatory in these hills? At Lapo I begged a lift of a vintner in his cart and was jogged, sticky with wine, up to Fiesole (where I had to wait two hours, stinking like the village drunk, for burly lads to lighten the load) and then east along the Vincigliatta road to Montebeni and my destination. Guessing that my appearance, together with the tart breath from my drunken clothes, would rouse passions of horror in local residents, I couched beneath a parasol pine and swiftly fell asleep.

Rising on the morrow quilled like the porcupine, I went in search of directions. The first people I met had little chance of smelling me. A fishmonger and his wife, glittering with scales, frowned at my rambling enquiries. I knew only the girl's Christian name and that of her young husband; her father, who was not of the village, meant nothing to them. Did I not mean the widow Scarbi and her daughter – was she not her daughter? – anyway, the girl who was expecting, and with the father gone to war? A mask of gratitude, I bowed and thanked the fishmongers for their goodness (hoping to earn a tuft of smoked cod) and followed, empty bellied, their directions until I reached the edge of the village.

It was – it is – a single-storey cottage, a hut almost, that has seen more prosperous days, with a cork oak so close to its southern wall that it seems an outgrowth from the stone, with myrtle and juniper and a canopy of honeysuckle above the door. There is a terraced garden patched with beans and cabbage and aromatic herbs and demarcated by ancient olive trees, very crooked and gnarled, like Bacchantes transformed in their frenzy with arms still plunged in their hair. A bearded goat leaned on her forelegs against one of the trees and attempted to strip its leaves. Alerted to my presence by the chelping of hens, the dwellers in the cottage opened the door before I could knock.

Even as I write this episode, on the same spot where it took place, I cannot believe the kindness that followed. The widow Scarbi was inclined to chase this ragged crow from her property but her daughter-in-law came to my rescue. I saw a pretty, girlish face spared the common scars, of a pale complexion, with a spray of freckles along the cheekbones, inherited doubtless from her father, which combined most pleasingly with her black hair loosely worn. I admired all this, to my relief, without a pang of desire.

When I had given my name, Teresa fixed me with amazed eyes. 'You are Tommaso Grilli? My father's childhood friend?'

'The same, madam.'

It required, as you can imagine, no effort to convince her of my claim. Teresa asked me at once whether I had news of her husband and father. It may have helped my cause to embroider my account of our two-year-old meeting. But there was something in her countenance that neutralised my guile and I frankly confessed that I had no news. Though I came to their door as a mendicant and not a messenger, I was welcomed – and that most warmly – into their home.

It is a cramped dwelling, with a combined hall and kitchen where the women sleep beside the hearth, amid the materials of domestic life, the pots and dishes and knives, the hanging hams and sprigs of thyme. On the southern side of the cottage lies Paolo's chamber, which he used to share with his brothers, and to which I was sent against my modest protestations. Teresa was determined to be hospitable to the friend of her father.

'He spoke often about you, Signor Grilli. He thought most highly of your courage and fortitude, and on his last visit . . . on his last visit six months ago he described his joy at meeting you in, uh . . .'

'Felsengrunde.'

'So I feel as though I have always known you.'

'Or at least – signora – my younger shadow.'

I learned that Giovanni and Paolo, after a brief visit to the cottage, had returned to the German wars. When the widow sang her son's praises, I watched Teresa's hand settle on her swollen belly as though she stowed her husband there; which in a sense she did. Now, pressed by my hostesses, I gave my account of our meeting in Felsengrunde – continuing thence to recount my life (with some omissions) for the penultimate time. I dared not suggest what bloody work their son or husband performed. The ardour in the old woman's eyes and the pale attention of Teresa conduced me to euphemism and vague assurances. 'They serve with the finest and most noble army in Europe,' I lied. 'I am sure they are a credit to the True Church.'

This seemed to work little relief on the women, and to escape my lies I enquired about the family's history.

Signora Scarbi told me how, along with Paolo and her

other sons (God rest their souls), her late husband had worked the quarries of Vincigliatta. When Teresa's father, newly arrived from Milan, had settled in the Borgo di Corbignano, he had taken up the same arduous employment.

'My husband and Giovanni became close friends. I like to think that Paolo and Teresa were born to unite our families.'

But life in Settignano soon became difficult. There is so little building taking place today in Florence; her glories are frozen, her patrons defunct or indigent. Although he was beyond fighting age, Teresa's father was still hale and fearless. It was he who made the decision to seek fighting work and – after Signor Scarbi's death – took Paolo with him to Milan to fight for True Religion. Of course the women lamented the men's absence; but if life on the hillside was endurable, it was thanks entirely to their mercenaries' pay.

And so it proved. Modesty in Settignano was not a mask for want. Mint, tarragon and chives grew along the cottage wall, and I ate capers and olives and cuts of gross meat for my supper, succulent snout and chitterlings bought at the market. An ample meal to Grilli the Courtier was a king's feast to Grilli the Vagabond, and for weeks thereafter I was to be fattened on soups and goat's cheese and sweet bread and even, on my birthday, a jar of spiced wine or hippocras.

'My father and my husband are generous to a fault.' Teresa smiled.

How much of their generosity has been funded by Felsen-grunde, I dare not wonder; for I have enjoyed this relative plenty, until these last weeks, when the very odour of meat appals me.

Melting on Paolo's mattress that second night in Settignano, I thanked God for so much kindness. 'You must stay here with us,' Teresa had said, 'as my father would wish it.' Later, when their diminutive guest was tucked away in presumed sleep, I heard the young woman pleading my case. The widow was reluctant to have a strange man under her roof. Visceral devils pronged me in the belly (Oh, I would be sent away!) until Teresa in a whisper impugned my manhood and I became innocuous; whereupon the Signora relented and I tipped over into dreamless sleep.

The valley of the Mensola resounds to the industry of stone. In the quarries of Maiano the land has been trimmed of its blue-grey flesh, the *pietra serena*, like a giant ham being slowly consumed by ants. It is here, and as far north as Vincigliatta, that our ancestors quarried much of Florence. If a giant fist descended from Heaven and crushed the city, it might fill the gaps in these hills with the rubble and the world would be returned to its lonely innocence. Closer to home, in this village, I recall from my Vasari that Michelangelo was entrusted to a wetnurse – his very own Smeraldina – and must have been lulled to sleep by the faint tutting of the quarriers' picks. It was in Settignano that the young Master first heard the cries of statues imprisoned in the rock, and dedicated his life to their liberation. Here venerable names of artists and sculptors seem linked to every lane and cypress tree: Desiderio da Settignano, Antonio and Bernardo Rossellino and my half-rhyming forebear, Bartolomeo Bimbi.

But I was no longer of that world. Now, to earn my keep, I helped out in the vegetable plot, tending baskets for Signora Scarbi, tilling the dry earth and refreshing it with water from the rain barrel. Sometimes, concerned at her heaviness, I accompanied Teresa to the fountain in the village square, where I was greeted and mocked in equal measure and spoken of as 'Signor Grilli – the *artist*'. At the wash house (so far from the Martesano canal of blushing memory) I was the only male to slap and pummel wet clouts, while Teresa gasped and held her back, cultivating a pink bloom on her cheeks, and the widow rocking beside me chid me for my slowness.

To these public outings I preferred the task of feeding the animals: forking blue chicory to the goat or scattering feed for the voluble chickens. And there were occasions to admire wilder creatures – a green lizard tilting its head to devour a cricket, moths that hovered and darted from nectar-throated flowers, swifts that sewed up the patchwork fields and kites in reels above the city, for which, without Teresa's kindness, I might long ago have made a meal. Yet I could not call this existence 'peace'. There remained a duty and a penance to perform.

One July morning of unwonted heat, a scream that was cousin to grief wrenched me from my slumber. I rushed from my cot and found Teresa lying in sweat on the women's pallet, with the widow crouched over her. 'Get out!' she cried. 'Run and fetch the midwife. And don't come in here till it's finished!'

My mission in the village accomplished, I spent the rest of the day chasing the shade of the olive trees, fending off the amorous muzzle of the goat and imploring God, dear God Almighty, for the child's survival. My soul would bleed at the shrieks of pain coming from the cottage. I ran several times with our bucket to the fountain and deposited the water outside the door, with a knock to announce my offices. It proved to be a cruelly prolonged labour. When seven of the clock sounded, the midwife flung open the door and called me over.

'Go and summon the priest,' she said. 'We may need a baptism.'

All the way to Santa Maria, and then back with the roused and surpliced priest, I promised my devotion to

God in return for His mercy. The priest entered the cottage without knocking and I remained outside, in dust and in dread, steeling myself for the keening voices. Instead I heard a cat's miaul. For an absurd instant I feared for the chickens, and my precocious right foot regarded the coop as though my body would follow it there. That was no cat. My ears prickled as though I had brushed against a gorse bush. Bless my soul! The priest emerged with his colour restored and, forgetting the improbability – nay, the impropriety – of it, shook my hand as though *I* were the father.

'You may go in now. She is asking for you.'

Of the three women it was Teresa, bloodied and soaked with perspiration, her face blotched red and curd white, who spoke first. I beheld the swollen bundle, the pugilist's face and its miniature fists.

'His name is Nunzio,' she said.

A child is born incomplete; its mother, having nourished it with her blood during gestation, must nurse it with her milk. I myself had been forced to consume the bleached blood of strangers; but Nunzio was clamped to the maternal breast and drank heartily, to roll about afterwards in his mother's hand until his prodigious belch. (Applause, my son, will never come so easily again.) I could not resent the midnight mewling or the creamy fetor of used swaddling clothes. The kitchen was always disordered; my toil and the widow's became an industry to keep mother and child happy. Yet I admired the infant from a respectful distance. Signora Scarbi was reluctant to place him in my arms and I dared not press my claim.

My concern that the family, such as it was, would close ranks about the puking prune – that cherished germ of manhood – was allayed when I stood with the widow and Teresa at the baptism ceremony. Nunzio, an impossible sage for his few days, endured his regeneration in silence, peering at the benevolent smudge of the priest's face and then squinnying at the anointing thumb. After the priest had departed, the widow told Teresa to roll the child on the altar – 'to strengthen his muscles and save him from lameness'. Nunzio's godparents bashfully kissed outside the church to protect him from muteness, and the children of Settignano followed our procession clanging kettles and pots to make sure the baby would not grow deaf.

Now that Teresa was fully occupied, I was given to understand that I might stay and work the smallholding – at least until, or unless, Paolo Scarbi returned from the wars. I knew how much he had disliked my popinjay double in Felsengrunde, and so languished in contrariety: hoping never to see the man for whose safe return I daily prayed.

Perhaps because I felt old age approaching, or else my sins were blackest bile within me and in need of purging, my life when I was not working veered towards observance. I began to say the morning prayers I had never practised with my father. I recited my Pater, Ave and Credo and, while crouching on the dung heap, considered my Commandments and Christ's Beatitudes. The widow Scarbi was my model in faith; I attended confession with her, bleeding my poisoned self in small doses every week. While others – the quarriers especially – vaunted their distrust of our 'leaky' priest, I found great comfort in my unburdening, and in the solicited words, never quite believed, *ego te absolvo*.

For a year I managed to put off the writing of this Life. There was so much domestic work to do, and I took such delight in watching Nunzio grow. His embryonic haze of russet hair thickened and darkened to his grandfather's red; his face lost its bruised concentration and broadened; the eyes of an indefinite colour (Paolo's own, the widow insisted) tightened their grip on the world, and the soul, hidden at first like a kernel in a fruit, began to shine through. Even as he had grown from milky automaton to sentient child, little Nunzio learned to animate things, nudging his wooden toys (gifts from the more attentive quarriers) and delighting, like a petty god, in knocking them over. At nine months Nunzio learned to crawl – clumsy leg over leg, crabwise – and to butt against me in hope of being dandled. Perhaps I appealed for not towering over him so? For what giants he lived with otherwise, whose knees he could scarcely moisten with his hungry mouth.

My affection for the boy grew, as it did for his mother, and the widow dropped her objections to my playing with him. When Nunzio took his first faltering steps, she insisted that we bring him to the churchyard – where Teresa set him down to walk between the gravestones. 'A child must always walk among his ancestors,' she said. 'Let the dead see how they live on, their dry bones continued in his.'

There are those, in view of the Reaper's love for children, who consider it unseemly to form as strong an attachment to a child as to a grown person. I hold it not so. Nunzio is precious to me as a son, or a grandson. His playful grace delights my eyes (he is no boisterous brute like some of his playmates); his gentleness moves me to solicitude when he grips my ruined hands like bars to walk with. In this child, Philosophy lies latent. Newly delivered on this earthly plain, he seems yet to trail some of Eternity's dust; as when, observing me at my writing, he believed that I was scratching an overlay from the parchment to release the words beneath. Thus Nunzio the Platonist! In his imagination I discern a strange benevolence, as he invests objects with inner life: babbling for his dolls, or making his pinewood horses canter. Where is the malice that must inhabit his father's arm? Where the disregard for the world's pain in this boy who weeps when his grandmother kills a chicken? Pray Heaven he be spared.

On the morning after my coughing fit (when for half an hour I hawked up gaily bubbled blood), I sent a boy from the village to my forbidden past, into Florence, to buy quills and ink and a commonplace book if he could find one. I spent my last coins on this purchase and on the boy's fee, and heartily congratulated him when in the twilight he returned. The volume which now you hold had only three pages soiled by its original owner. Whatever life was preserved in those fragments I carefully excised to make room for my own – and the memory of all those I have known who are gone.

But my task was Herculean; the book sat expectantly, nay, accusingly atop the *Thesaurus hieroglyphicorum*. No recrudescence of my coughing diminished my sense of urgency. I returned to my labours and slow ageing until, one night in August of my fiftieth year, I was entrusted with Nunzio while the women attended to a sickly neighbour. I had torn a single sheet from the tattered *Thesaurus* and, misusing the ink intended for this confession, was drawing a dodo for the boy's amusement. So engrossed was I in the fat bird's beak that Nunzio wandered off unnoticed.

I seemed to feel the scream before I heard it, and flung my last work into the air as I dashed into the hall – where I found Nunzio backing away from a puddle of fire. He had spilled the oil lamp which I could not remember lighting. My hands fastened on to the widow's shawl and I advanced in great slowness and lucidity to smother the fire. When Nunzio screeched in terror I saw the flames biting at his shirt. I snatched up the boy in my arms and put out the fire with my hands.

For a day, by Teresa's reckoning, I teetered close to death. Even in the deepest abyss of my faint, some part of Tommaso Grilli – why not call it my immortal soul? – observed my body's turmoil. That quintessence was insensible to the agony of burned fingers, to the blisters already seeping where my nails used to grow. Teresa, on the mortal side of that spiritual curtain, must have summoned the priest, with his holy tools, in case Death gave birth to me. And I wonder – having been granted a stay, as it were, of dissolution – can there really be a *prima materia*, an original self over which, in a lifetime, imperfections like excrescences grow? Or is the world the alembic in which the Soul is created? I feel that my soul is no more myself than my breath is when, escaping, it mists in the cold evening air. It is clean and bland and impersonal as water – a divine tincture contained, for the heartbeat of an incarnation, in this earthly vessel.

That most perilous phase of my sickness, when body and spirit threatened to disband, was however a paradise compared to the recovery that followed. I swam up from the depths to the shallows of a swoon, and a million crabs of pain fastened on to my cohering senses. The self's anguish, deeply rooted in molar and marrow and far older than those clapperclaws, seized hold of my quaking brain. Even in my faint I knew that I was injured, for my dreams took a pedantic and obsessional turn. I dreamed that I had a field to plough. I was both on that field, standing behind the plough, and far above the field, looking down on its unbroken soil as upon a blank page. It was the first expression of this book's desire to be born. I knew that I would never rest until that square of earth bore fruit.

The fever abated. I resurfaced from tumultuous currents to find myself crippled, my hands devoured by fire.

Nunzio was carried to my bed on his mother's hip. At her soft instruction he kissed me wetly on the cheek and then pinched my nose with soggy fingers.

He was unhurt. I had saved his life.

I will not now – lest I rouse these agonies in their remembrance – recount my convalescence. Its only pleasure lay in my heroic status within the family. Teresa attended with unguents to my trembling paws, while Signora Scarbi gave me licence to use her Christian name (it is Eleonora) and baked me sweetmeats of fig and orange rind and popping currants, which she placed inside my slobbering mouth without a hint of displeasure. Once the swelling in my hands had ceased and the pain diminished to an endurable throb, I realised that I had lost my art. My fingers now are clumsy and insensitive. Writing is painful enough but the sensuous flow one needs to draw is shattered; the sweep of a line or curve, the feel of a paper's grain, have all vanished from me.

Often, in contemplation of my martyred hands, I have wanted to put an end to my life. And yet I could not do it. Not simply for fear of divine retribution (though God, if He is good, will not torment Adolph Brenner) or a reluctance to lumber Teresa with my dangling corpse. I have survived in order to pacify the dead. What would they say to me, in their dark grove, if I tossed away what they most dearly would have kept? Peace, now, to those sunken ghosts.

Outside my chamber, swifts wheel and whistle and cicadas wind their watches. Teresa comes to my door bringing goat's milk and the soft of a buckwheat loaf. So we have come full circle, to conclude at the moment before this confession begins. I sit on the edge of my mattress and look at the *Thesaurus hieroglyphicorum*. Will my written life make more sense than its recondite symbols? I take down, with some difficulty, the *Thesaurus* to serve as my writing board and jotter. In my pockets for days my goose quills and knife, my bottle of ink and a leather strap to bind my fingers, have waited. Under my other arm I carry the unpopulous wastes of the commonplace book. I can hear Nunzio playing and Teresa singing at her work, as I step through the cluttered hall and open the door to the day.

Now . . .

Note

Many of the characters encountered by Tommaso Grilli actually existed, while history, in a number of places, kindly arranged itself to suit his itinerary. Petrus Gonsalvus, however, has had his life miraculously prolonged for the purposes of fiction and transported to a Prague that he most likely never visited. Nor did he work as a teacher, of mathematics or any other subject. We do know that he lived for many years in Parma, and that along with his children (all of whom inherited *hypertrichosis universalis congenita*) he earned a living as an itinerant curiosity. You can indeed find him with his Dutch wife on the frontispiece of Hoefnagel's book, as well as with his children in Aldrovandi's *History of Monsters* and in several paintings. Gonsalvus's daughter Tognina (Antonietta) was painted in the 1580s by Lavinia Fontana; Caterina is her later, fictional twin and Carlo her fictional brother.

This book was written with the help of a Writer's Award from the Arts Council of England.